DEEP BLUE

By the same author

LOYALTIES

DEEP BLUE

Gavin Esler

HarperCollins*Publishers*

HarperCollins*Publishers*
77–85 Fulham Palace Road
Hammersmith, London W6 8JB

Published by HarperCollins*Publishers* 1992

1 3 5 7 9 10 8 6 4 2

Lyrics from 'All My Ex's Live in Texas' by S. D. Shafer
and L. J. Shafer: Acuff-Rose-Opryland Music Ltd;
'Desde la Oscuridad' by Gloria Estefan: EMI Songs Ltd

The author asserts the moral right to be
identified as the author of this work

A catalogue record for this book is
available from the British Library

ISBN 0 00 224039 4

Set in Sabon by
Rowland Phototypesetting Ltd
Bury St Edmunds, Suffolk

Printed in Great Britain by
HarperCollinsManufacturing Glasgow

For my mother and father

'Extremism in the defence of liberty is no vice.'

Senator Barry Goldwater, Presidential Candidate 1964

'The United States has no intention of striving for a Pax Americana . . . we seek a Pax Universalis, built upon shared responsibilities and aspirations.'

George Bush, Presidential Candidate 1992

1

Miami, Florida

If he had known that within two hours he would try to commit suicide, Phil Lewis would have dressed differently. No one who was prepared to suffer, purely for reasons of style, the additional heat of a black limousine in Florida at mid-day in late June would have been content to die in a brightly coloured Hawaiian shirt, now staining with sweat down the back, white shorts and socks and Reebok trainers. All this had been fine for brunch with the Cubans, and perfect for the afternoon sport Lewis had in mind, but it would not have done much for the fat Englishman's image as his body was strapped down and hauled past the cameras on the evening news like an overweight out-of-town tourist dragged from a back alley after a mugging.

On the Miami streets the air stuck like hot vaseline, slackening the skin, the sky hazy blue, the buildings white and pastel above the palms. Downtown near the Federal courthouse a vagrant threw a fist in hot air, a crack cocaine deranged punch at nothing and no one. He muttered, yelled, staggered through the heat. In a shabby Hispanic barrio a plain man shot his neighbour twice in the stomach with a .38 Smith and Wesson, then once in the head as he lay bleeding on the sidewalk, the blood sticking to the concrete, a deepening red. The gunman stood vaguely unconcerned, the .38 resting gently on his hip, the barrel hot through his trouser leg. Sirens in the distance. In Liberty City two patrol cars blocked the street as Latino police and young black men flexed their muscles.

'Dissin' me,' one of the young blacks yelled. His tee-shirt pictured the snarling faces of a Miami rap group, '2 Live Crew', and the slogan 'Nasty as they Wanna Be'.

9

'Motherfuckers disrespectin' me, goddamn mothers . . .', he shouted, until the quarrel faded and they disappeared into the back streets of somewhere no one wants to go.

Phil Lewis's large and highly polished black automobile sped across Rickenbacker Causeway from Key Biscayne, along the oceanside drive where the palm trees have lost their colour in the beating from the sun. No shade. Hot as a grill. Nothing on the water at Coconut Grove but a dirt-coloured pelican bobbing on a waveless sea. Lewis turned up the car's air-conditioning. It blasted full force on the tinted windscreen, not yet completely cool but half drowning the sound of the music on the radio. Lewis leaned back into the deep grey leather seat of the Lincoln Town Car, enjoying the automobile's glide. He had parked the car for more than two hours in the unshaded sun while he ate brunch by the poolside at one of the large Cuban-owned sea front houses on Key Biscayne. When he climbed back inside a few minutes after noon the steering wheel was so hot he could barely grasp it.

The leather seat stuck to the sweat on the back of his legs, and the stale air inside was a wet handshake. Black was the wrong colour for a limousine in southern Florida. Lewis knew that. Everyone knew that. But highly polished black was the right colour if you happened to be Phil Lewis, and he knew that too. The dark tinted windows and the whitewall tyres were right, his tan leather briefcase was right, the way he finely parted his hair was right. They were simple matters of taste which Lewis was proud he had acquired over the years; an Englishman abroad.

He belched slowly. The belch tasted of *mojitos*, the rum, lime and mint drink he had swilled down with the Cuban exiles, backslapping and talking Spanish, drinking from the pitcher brought by one of the servants to the poolside. Nice people. Good times, even if he could never get used to the way they mangled the elegance of the Spanish language he had learned in Granada and Malaga, and which on Cuban lips sounded like a machine gun with epilepsy. Lewis licked his own lips and turned up the volume on the radio. It was tuned to a Country and Western station.

'Talk to me Texas,' the radio sang. 'Let me hear that drawl . . .'

10

Lewis belched again, thinking that belches were like a reminder of how the good things in life one day got back at you.

'One long distance call . . .

Won't you talk to me Texas . . .'

'Salsa,' Lewis muttered.

He had been living in the United States for so long he had begun to speak with an American accent, to think and especially to eat like one, resulting in the new model Lewis belly which ballooned in the flowered Hawaiian shirt.

'Gone native,' he said aloud. 'Eating salsa. And those goddamn spicy beans with the rice. For brunch. Jeez. Why can't' – belch – 'they eat like the rest of us? Goddamn Cuban food.'

Lewis smiled. The truth was, he liked the Cubans, their food, and their politics – all except some of the crazier inter-community vendettas which nobody except a Cubano could ever understand. He was sure the various factions of exiles hated each other more than they hated Fidel Castro, which was saying something.

Still, they were true exotics bringing life and colour to an America which Lewis was beginning to think would soon be turned into one huge homogenised shopping mall from New England to Los Angeles. The Cubans would resist. They knew how to make it in America – came to Miami, most of them, with whatever they managed to salvage before Castro took over. Now they were running half the state of Florida. Lewis liked that. Big on the American Dream.

'Goddamn,' he thought. 'Some operators. Have to hand it to them.'

Another belch.

'Jesus!' he said, pronouncing it the Spanish way.

Lewis took the freeway north towards Miami Beach, turned right towards the ocean again, then into the driveway of the Miami Beach Sheraton. He liked the Lincoln. It had everything he wanted, everything America was good at. Big. Powerful. The perfect car for someone who really does not like to drive. Lewis smiled to himself. He wondered what he might be driving if he had stayed in England: a British family saloon that leaked oil on the driveway, powered by a lawnmower engine and made out of compressed Coke cans.

'Jeez,' he muttered, through clenched teeth, as he remembered only shabbiness in the England he left behind. That England swirled in his mildly drunk mind like a memory of an old sickness which scared him in case it returned.

'Afte'noo', Mr Louie,' the Nicaraguan kid who did the valet parking called to him, taking the car keys. 'How's it goin' wit' you today?'

Lewis nodded.

'*Bueno, eh. Que tal?*' Lewis asked, not waiting for an answer.

The heat hit him like a rock on the skull. The heat and the *mojitos*, a double punch throbbed the blood in his temples. He stood for a moment by the flower beds filled with oleander, hibiscus and impatiens, their leaves dripping with water from an automatic sprayer. Lewis was dripping too. He had to have a shower – a long cold shower that might last an hour, and long cold beers that could last even longer – just to get himself straight. Lewis smiled. He bounced in to the hotel on the thick soles of the Reeboks, scanning the lobby, holding his smart leather attaché case with its gold buckles in one hand and wiping the sweat from his face with the back of the other. He pressed the Hawaiian shirt to his chest and the wet stain spread sideways.

He smiled at the check-in girl, who glanced up then turned back to complete a computer entry before giving Lewis her full attention. Lindy Bishop had been working the desk long enough to be able to sense which clients were having affairs with other men's wives, which of the Hispanic girls in the tight miniskirts were on the make – all of them, she reckoned – which clients looked like theirs was drug money, and which did not look like money at all.

'I'm a people person,' she would say to new acquaintances. 'I got the right people-to-people skills. I know people.'

That was what made her uneasy with Lewis. The fat Englishman always arrived at the check-in desk around the same time – shortly after noon on a Friday – always looking bloated, always slightly drunk and, to Lindy Bishop's taste at least, always vaguely disgusting. But she knew he was real money, and none of her alarm buttons had ever been pushed before.

Now, as she looked at him, there were bells being set off inside her head, and fireworks and fire-alarms and all kind of things that a people person would know were wrong. Maybe it was the heat, Lindy Bishop thought. Maybe the heat had somehow upset Lewis.

12

She looked at him for a second and a word came to mind. Nervous. No, not quite. Fear? Well, maybe. Right idea, wrong word. It seemed too strong for the way Lewis shifted from toe to toe, playing with the gold buckles on his thousand dollar attaché case. Lindy ran through her ideas like fingers in a thesaurus of pop psychology. Stress? Anxiety? Angst? Apprehension? Whatever.

She started to complete the check-in formalities, content to think only that Lewis was different today from all previous Fridays when he stayed a few hours, had his fun with whichever girl in a tight miniskirt was on order, then left. She tried not to imagine the demented blubber trying to perform and gazed vaguely over the shoulder of Lewis's Hawaiian shirt. A shop-boy from one of the hotel's concession stores was lugging a case of freshly squeezed orange juice towards the elevators, and behind him there was a handsome Latino man, maybe early twenties, in a dark suit and white shirt talking to some big bear of a companion half hidden by one of the giant ferns at the back of the lobby.

Lewis continued to play with the tan attaché case, jabbing his fat fingers at the gold buckles, twisting them nervously as if something inside worried him. Money, Lindy Bishop wondered absently. Wasn't it always money. Or drugs. Money. Drugs. Drugs, money. She sighed. Same thing. Same story.

She handed Lewis the registration card to sign. He pulled a large Mont Blanc fountain pen from the breast pocket of the Hawaiian shirt and scratched his name with a flourish in loud turquoise ink. She began to cut Lewis's computerised key card. She knew Lewis's face from the newspapers. The *Miami Herald* always carried his social dealings, the parties he hosted on some big yacht he owned full of Arabs and Latin American politicians and oil men from Venezuela, the charities he was backing, that kind of thing. She knew he was a high roller, big in property down on the Keys, or investment, or somesuch. People said he bought and sold islands. Then out of nowhere in the past year he was always there, regular, checking into the hotel on Fridays, checking out a few hours later like it was some kind of office card-punching clock-in, clock-out routine. Lewis, the heavy hitter in Miami, mixing with the celebrities at the race track or the yacht harbour or down at city hall, the petty details of his life

13

chronicled in the society pages like this was royalty. He had received so much publicity she even recalled the name of his yacht – the 'New World'. Sleeps twenty in comfort, all guest quarters with hot tubs, *People* magazine had said. Lindy Bishop sighed. She knew the name of his yacht and he did not even know her name though it was pinned on a plastic label on her left goddamn tit.

'Sure I was curious,' she told the police afterwards. 'When money like Lewis was using the facilities, you'd have to be curious. Specially for just an hour or two. Kinda interesting, know what I mean?'

The way she saw it, Lewis was married with a couple of teenage kids, screwed around, but no big deal. Just a bit of play on Friday afternoons to put him in a good mood for the weekend. She knew the type, had him figured for newly rich in search of the best good time his money could buy before he was too old to enjoy it.

Nothing wrong with that, only she wished he might be a little more friendly about it. It was, she theorised to a tired lieutenant, as if Lewis was living two or three lives all at once, all at high speed, and Lindy Bishop sensed that all these lives were going to catch up with him. Today. Right now. The high society life, the business life, the partying with the hookers – three lives in one lardball of a body, colliding disastrously under the Hawaiian shirt. The computer bleeped hard three times. It had finished cutting the new key card.

'There you are Mr Lewis,' Lindy said, offering again her best receptionist smile. No eye contact. Lewis stared at the buckles of his case. She wasn't that attractive. 'You're all set. Room 1345, with the full ocean view. Would you care to order food and beverages now?'

There was a perverse social dance in all this between the receptionist and the 45-year-old Englishman. For all his money Lewis was strictly hamburgers, barbecue sauce, french fries, cokes, Molson beers. And he would insist that the beers had to be cold – as if in Miami they would deliberately warm them up just to spite him, or because they knew he was British and wanted him to feel right at home. And it had to be Molson. Then he would go to his room and make a telephone call. Within twenty minutes, or at least before the food arrived, as all the room service boys could testify, the girl would appear. There seemed to be three or four on the current list. One, a particular favourite, was olive skinned, Latin, might have been early

14

thirties, but could have been ten years younger. Depended how hard you thought she had been working.

Full lips and a big bust, tight cotton skirts, heavy eye make-up and low cut blouses. Not exactly Polo Club or yacht harbour. The other two, Lindy Bishop remembered when the police asked, were younger, also Hispanic, maybe Puerto Ricans. Long black hair, painted fingernails, good legs, the works. Anyway, whatever was on order, some four hours later Lewis would leave with a smile on his face. As for the hotel bill, he would put it on his corporate American Express card – 'WHBL & L Enterprises', some fancy investment corporation. Lindy was sure the whole thing would be claimed later as a legitimate tax deductible business expense, hookers included. American Express? Sure. Never get laid without it.

That was the thing about people like Lewis. The petty rip-offs. People like her, they paid taxes, were polite. People like him, well, everything was deductible, every goddamn thing. And the Nicaraguan kid at the Valet Park said Lewis would stride out, mumble a few words in Spanish, hand him five dollars and expect to pick up the black Lincoln Town Car immediately. Not in two minutes. Right now. No patience. No waiting.

'No LPT,' Lewis once yelled at the kid so he never forgot it. 'No Latin People's Time. This is America, you get it?'

And he snapped his fingers like some aristocrat ordering around the servants.

'You know the type,' Lindy told the reporter from the *Miami Herald* after the police had gone. 'One of those hyper guys who says he wants to relax. And he wants to relax RIGHT NOW!'

Lindy Bishop giggled, and the reporter laughed and wrote it all down.

'Burger would be fine,' Lewis said, after an effort of decision, wiping the sweat from his eyes with a handkerchief. 'With everything.'

'For two?' Mischievous.

'One. Barbecue sauce. Fries. And make sure the Molsons are cold. Can't stand warm beer.'

Lindy watched as Lewis padded towards the elevators, bouncing on the Reeboks. He took the elevator to the thirteenth floor, opened the door to his room and threw his attaché case on the bed. He turned to the mini-bar and raked around in the beers, impatiently pulling the bottled wine coolers out on the carpet. He knew that for some reason they never put Molson in the mini-bars. Some kind of perverse patriotism, to keep out the Canadian brews. No, not patriotism. It was just that they never listened to what their guests really wanted.

'Out of touch with the goddamn customer,' he grunted in irritation. 'Going the same goddamn way Britain did before I got out and the Japs took over. Falling apart while congratulating themselves how wonderful they are. Shit.'

Lewis was desperate. The *mojitos* had died in him, the rum and the heat left a terrible thirst. Any beer was now acceptable. He grabbed a Heineken, swigging it down from the bottle in one deep gulp until it was half gone, another gulp draining it, then picking up a second. For Lewis, fast-food would never be fast enough. Never. His doctor told him that was the main reason he had put on so much weight, throwing food down his throat like a wild dog determined to finish whatever was available before someone else from the pack could steal it.

Now in the hotel room Lewis switched on the television set and turned to CNN. Perhaps something was happening in the world. Something was always happening in the world, wasn't that the beauty of it? The trouble was, it was all at such a pace that Lewis could not hope to keep up with it, what with the presidential election campaign and the debates, and the shake-out in the Democratic party, and all that stuff. CNN was saying there would be more news on the riots in eastern Europe and the trouble in Moscow. As he watched the Marxist dinosaurs teeter into extinction over the past few years, Lewis had grown happy beyond all expectations.

'Game over for communism,' he was fond of saying.

Even the localised gangsters like Saddam Hussein learned that the US was like a monkey in a cage. Okay, so you play with the monkey, but God help you if you pull its tail. Lewis smiled. He was pleased to be part of the team that won the Cold War, even if peace breaking out was bad for business. Very bad. He belched again and took another swig of beer. So what the fuck. So we kick a few tinpot dictators, a couple of Saddam Husseins every few years, and the Marxists go have a nervous breakdown. Was that an excuse to get soft? What was it one of the Cubans — Jorge Lopez, the ugly turtle-faced bastard — had said at lunch?

'Believe me, Phil, lookin' at this presidential election campaign, by the year two thousand there will be only two socialist parties left in the whole world. Britain's Labour Party and America's Democrats.'

They all had a good laugh.

'Jesus,' Phil Lewis said aloud, this time with the English pronunciation, distracted. Now there was something wrong with the Sheraton's goddamn air-conditioning. He walked across to the window and turned the dial to Maximum Cool and High Fan. Then he racked up the television volume to cope with the new noise, pushing a pudgy hand round the back of his neck to feel the sweat at the bottom of his hairline. Lewis decided to take a shower. He let his wet shirt fall to the floor and took off his shorts, rubbing his belly in the mirror. There was a lot he did not like. The belly, mostly. One way or another it had to go, or he was going to look like this for the rest of his life. And the rolls of midriff fat that were hanging like pleats over his buttocks. Them too. The Reebok trainers had been part of an attempt to get into jogging, but after a couple of outings Lewis decided Miami was too hot. They were fine for driving the Town Car. Looked sporty enough, and that was part of it. Look right, feel good. Slogans for his continuing new life in the New World, built over twenty years. And no one was going to take it away. No matter what they were trying now. Lewis took off his underpants and stood naked, still staring at his body, knowing he had let go too much, and regretting it. Just like the country, he thought. Flabby and soft from success.

'Real USDA prime cut,' he said with a grin, slapping his belly. 'Me and Uncle Sam getting nice and comfortable together.'

Should toughen up. Cut lunching with the Cubans. All that Salvadoran and Nicaraguan and Panamanian food, the deep fried yucca and pupusas and the salsa, all that shit. Lewis sighed, running his hands over his still-glistening body, feeling the cool of the air-conditioning now reaching him.

'Born again,' he said to himself. 'I could be born again like those

17

bullshitting preachers on TV. Forget the religious crap, just be born again the way I want. I did it once getting out of England. Why not turn the same trick one more time?'

He caught sight of the attaché case sitting on the chair at the far side of the room. It caused him to straighten up, like a cold spray on his face. The attaché case made him suddenly think of the thing which really might change his life. He remembered something that in the heat and *mojitos* he had half forgotten, remembered why he was in the hotel room, the papers and files he had pulled from his office and stuffed in his attaché case and two plastic supermarket bags. He would need them if the fight got dirty. He was sure it would. He had taken the supermarket bags with about a thousand sheets of company files into the Korean photocopiers on 25th Street. He'd pick them up later. It ought to be enough. That and the stuff in the attaché case. Enough to make them think twice about messing with him.

'Bastards,' Phil Lewis said aloud, staring intently at his face and snarling his lip back in a wolfish grimace. When he was angry he did not sound English at all. The American accent which had grown over twenty years in the United States swept upon him in his sudden fury. He tensed his shoulders as if about to throw a punch at the reflection in the mirror. 'Think they can make me piss away everything in a few days, when it's taken years to get this far. Maybe they think people like me aren't needed any more. Fuck'em. Gonna blow those suckers outta the water.'

Just as suddenly as he angered, Lewis relaxed. He smiled at his words and walked calmly into the bathroom to run the shower.

Outside in the thirteenth floor corridor a thin and handsome Latino in a dark suit straightened his bow tie and pulled down the base of his jacket. He walked from the elevator and turned, closely followed by another, far larger Latino, a bear of a man with a touch of black blood, carrying a silver tray like a toy cradled in his bear's paw.

The Bear balanced the tray effortlessly on his left hand, then raised his right fist revealing fingers so fattened they bulged round his wedding ring, the knuckles sunken like dimples. The dimples knocked hard on the door of room 1345.

'Room service,' the Bear yelled at the door. A slightly Hispanic accent. 'Room service.'

Lewis pulled a towel round his middle.

'Whaddyawant?'

'Room service,' the thick-set Latino repeated, smoothing his bow tie again with his fingers.

Lewis shook his head in irritation, opened the door then turned into the bathroom to check the shower. He called out sharply over his shoulder that the tray was to be put down on the table next to the television. If he had been watching or even thinking of anything other than his thirst and the increasingly unpleasant size of his own body, Lewis might have wondered why it took two men – the Bear plus the thin and handsome one now appearing from somewhere down the corridor and walking lightly on training shoes – to carry one tray. Lewis had other things on his mind.

'Goddamn beers better be cold.'

The big one put the tray down by the television as ordered. The handsome one smiled, showing a set of perfect teeth beneath his well-clipped moustache. He shut the door.

'Sign please sir,' the Bear called into the bathroom, now full of shower steam.

Lewis shook his head in irritation again, but emerged with the second bottle of Heineken in his mouth, trying to drain the dregs. At least there were Molsons on the table, he noticed, as the round mestizo face of the Bear came into view, handing him the check with his left hand. As Lewis went to take it, the big man's fist quickly pulled back and caught him full in the belly. Lewis's eyes widened white.

He spat beer, coughed, choked, crashed backwards into the bathroom in a stagger of bare flesh. The towel round his midriff fell to the floor as the Bear hit him again with a kick to the face, cracking open Lewis's nose before he had time to fall.

'Not the face,' the handsome Latino yelled, dancing around in his training shoes. 'For Chrissake not the face.'

Lewis's back hit the toilet cistern and he bounced on to the seat. The big man grabbed his hair and threw him on the tiled floor, then fell upon him with his full weight. The other pulled Lewis's left arm

19

across the floor, holding it down with a towel. He drew a flick knife from the pocket of his trousers, snapped it open and slashed hard and deep across Lewis's wrist, rolling the towel tightly across the wound.

'Hold it, Kiki,' he said to the big man, Enrique 'Kiki the Bear' Mendoza, who altered position on Lewis's chest to grab the towel.

The handsome guy, Jorge Luis 'Lula' Martinez, picked up another towel from the rack then grabbed Lewis's right arm, cutting again until the wound gaped. When he had successfully slipped the towel over the slashed wrist, Lula told the Bear to move. Together, one bleeding arm each, they pushed the half-conscious Phil Lewis head-first into the bath. Lula threw the knife and bloody towels on top of him. Then Kiki the Bear made to go.

'Check,' Lula ordered. 'Check me.'

Big Kiki stopped and looked Lula up and down for blood, from the top of his fragrantly greased black hair to the bottom of the white rubber soles on his $100 training shoes.

'Turn round Lula,' Big Kiki demanded. Lula turned. 'Only on your left arm and hands. Check me.'

'On the jacket,' Lula said, pointing at a small gobbet of blood. It was not much considering the remains they had left in the bath. 'Left side. The rest's just water from the shower. No big deal.'

Big Kiki took off his jacket and threw it down beside the sink for a moment while he washed his hands in the shower's spray. Then he dried them quickly and rolled up the jacket with the bloodstains on the inside. Lula rinsed his hands and arms in the sink.

'Enough,' Lula said, signalling that they should go.

They each took a last quick look at Lewis, slumped with his face into the bath, his blood swirling down the drain under the force of the warm shower water. Big Kiki grunted.

'Looks like we got ourselves one dead hog.'

They moved back towards the main elevators, the big man ponderously, with his jacket rolled up under his arm, the other bouncing on his rubbery soles, smiling behind his moustache so the teeth showed white in a tanned face. As the doors began to close Big Kiki held out a stubby finger to hit the button for the basement. He noticed that somehow in the middle of it all blood had stuck to his cuff, and would have to be removed. He shrugged at Lula.

Behind them, and despite their best efforts, in his blood spattered bath, with the shower of room 1345 beating on his back, the hog stirred.

2

The president of the United States had never looked more unattractive. It was not that Alex Newman had ever been a fan. You can't follow the most mean-spirited presidential election campaign in recorded history without thinking the correct answer to the question 'Which candidate would you choose to become the most powerful democratically elected human being on earth?' has to be 'None of the Above'. It was like deciding between chocolate cake and chocolate pudding if, like Newman, you did not have a sweet tooth.

'An America that cares', one of the candidates had drooled. Newman could not remember which one. 'And shares its great wealth with those less fortunate among us. An America not afraid to share and care, care-and-share.'

Or was it bears and hares? Buckets of pears and foxes' lairs. Did they even know how much crap they talked? The entire election campaign debate on the New World after the Cold War world was reduced to eight seconds on the evening news, what a friend at Cable News Network told Newman was a 'sound bite' – a little clip of the candidate which everyone would remember. Like a bumper sticker. Or the motto in a fortune cookie. You know the thing: 'Don't Mess With Texas', or 'The Best Man for the Job is a Woman', or 'America: Love It or Leave It', as if half a dozen words settled the matter.

Newman tried to imagine sound bites from Disraeli or Metternich or Napoleon until his brain ached. The best he could come up with was Julius Caesar: 'Veni, Vidi, Vici.'

He scratched his head from boredom and frustration. America trying to elect a president made him more pleased than ever to be

British. He was an angular forty-two-year-old, with the kind of blond curly hair that would never show grey or recede. Now he had finally arrived as a newspaper foreign correspondent in the United States he was constantly surprised that a previous life dominated by American movies and television had failed to communicate how foreign this posting really was. He hit the remote control mute button to silence the president. It was always the same. All these men in suits from the big American television networks would stand in pleasant locations from sea to shining sea and dictate who was up, who was down, and who wasn't doing so good on the cares and shares issue.

Adverbs, Newman thought. That was the other thing. Two hundred and fifty million Americans and they did not have an adverb between them. To his surprise it angered the hell out of him that the only time they used adverbs was when they split infinitives with them. The president always wanted 'to quickly achieve' or 'to boldly begin'. Complete gibberish. And they were always coming up to Newman – total strangers, waitresses, flight attendants – saying how much they liked his accent when it was absolutely obvious he had no accent. They had accents.

Newman looked back at the dumb show on television. Maybe, he thought, gazing at the sincere presidential face staring at the autoscript, maybe Americans were blessed with the one real benefit of a mature democracy. They did not have to spend too much time worrying about who their next leader was going to be or what he or she was up to.

If the leader proved too despotic or incompetent then someone else would yell loudly about it. That was what made the United States the land of opportunity. Everyone got their eight seconds. It was no longer fifteen minutes of fame as Andy Warhol had assumed. Things had speeded up since the 1960s.

In the meantime – and, thankfully, there was a lot of meantime – they could work, eat, drink, make love and attempt the pursuit of happiness, whatever that might be. He guessed they would all know it when they found it, though to have it constitutionally enshrined made Newman feel good. He hit the button on his television remote control to switch back the sound, heard a few words about fiscal restraint. It was now eight fifteen P.M. and the president had been addressing the nation for fully fifteen minutes. His lips were moving and sounds which could have been mistaken for words were coming out, but he was not saying anything. Newman cranked up the sound.

'The rule of law continues to be the sole way in which we can judge civilised conduct,' the president said, reading the autoscript as if it were written in a language he knew how to pronounce but did not fully understand. 'Those countries where the rule of man was the sole arbiter of human relations, the many Communist regimes around the world that decayed into the dictatorship of one man, those are now lands where freedom's bell rings out . . . while other dictatorships even in our own hemisphere . . . Fidel Castro's Cuba . . . where now opportunity, prudently exploited . . . where the day of the dictator will be over . . .'

Opportunity. Prudence. Freedom's bell. My ding-a-ling. God, Newman sighed. It was so much more fun when all they had to do was climb on top of a chair and yell Kill a Commie for Mommy. Or even in the Middle East when you could go for a video war in which the good guys could win on prime time television night after night without so much as breaking sweat. He never thought he would be nostalgic for the hot little conflicts of the Cold War, but at least then you got some attention. He put down his pen and checked that the video recorder was switched on in case by an extraordinary feat of hitherto unpredicted oratorical power the president ever got round to saying something interesting.

Newman sighed and walked into the kitchen. The refrigerator was full of bottles of water – Ramlosa, Perrier, Malvern, Saratoga Springs, Quibell, Evian, plain Seltzer. All manner of good things. Newman stared vacantly. The designer water corner in the refriger-ator was a result of his first and only resolution on getting the Wash-ington job for the *London Tribune*. Well there had actually been two resolutions, to give up alcohol and to go vegetarian, but two great changes plus the upheaval of moving to the United States made it unlikely he would manage either. As things currently stood he boasted he was comfortably eating dead animals but found giving up alcohol had been easier than he feared. Americans were great givers-up. Newman detected in many of them the uncomplicated desires of faddists who liked to believe they could change their lives

24

any number of times, by taking up running or giving up salt, or whatever the fad of the month was, which would make them effortlessly and perfectly perfect.

He poured a glass of chilled Ramlosa over ice with a twist of lime. The designer water had become an innocent passion, allowing him to divine the differences between brands as if savouring the relative bouquets of fine burgundies. He had to drink something; not alcohol, not Coke, which to his certain knowledge no European past puberty had ever consumed, and not fruit juice because it made his gums ache. At least having a choice between all these European and American waters encouraged Newman to believe he was drinking something interesting rather than tastelessness with bubbles.

'Like the bloody president,' he muttered, sipping the drink. 'Tastelessness with bubbles. Dammit.'

What was so disappointing was that he had finally made it to what was supposed to be the *London Tribune*'s top foreign assignment as the election gathered momentum, only to find himself cheated by the fact that the beat was not really worth covering. The story was just not that interesting. It was like a Moslem getting to Mecca and finding he could not pray.

Newman carried his glass and the rest of the Ramlosa bottle back into the main room of his apartment, and glared at the face of the president, still droning on to the American people. Outside, the night was hot and he could hear the lonely wail of an ambulance snaking through the Georgetown traffic towards Wisconsin Avenue. His fifth floor two-bedroom apartment was ideal for all manner of Washington evening entertainment, including observing the low life, the crime and the police patrols. Newman looked at his watch. Eight thirty. He thought about going out for a meal and walked to the window to touch the glass. It was hot. Another sticky night in the swamp. It made no sense to go anywhere.

On television the president was plonking on, being prudent or cautious, either about the same thing or something else. Bears and hares, maybe. It was hard to tell. Newman looked at the clock on his video recorder. Eight thirty-two. He knew he could make the final deadline in London. It was only just after one thirty in the morning, London time, but there was nothing for him to say. No story.

'Prudent,' Newman said out loud. 'Cautious. Boring.'

He put the glass of water to his forehead and felt it cool the skin, then he took an ice cube in his mouth and crunched it until his teeth began to hurt with the cold. The president had to be desperate for re-election publicity, making a major speech on network television just before Independence Day. Anyone with any wit cared more about the beach than politics. He began composing the opening line to his piece with something about the American Century growing weary and beginning to snore, the sound of Washington a long low whine emanating from the Oval Office and . . .

The telephone rang. It was one of those transparent models that revealed its guts and the ringing caused the handset to light up. Newman kept watching the television screen like a doctor waiting for some sign of life from a comatose patient as he slid his hand to the right to pick up the phone.

'Hello,' Newman said wearily, assuming it was his foreign desk desperate for some – any – news to fill empty pages at what was the beginning of the summer silly season.

'Hi, Alex?'

Newman recognised the American woman's voice but could not remember why.

'Speaking.'

'Oh, I always love that,' she giggled. 'The way you British always say "Speaking" instead of "This is he." Especially since I know you are "speaking", because you just spoke.' Peals of laughter, and then Newman remembered. No one else made quite that tinkling sound. Helen DeVos, the one with the Manhattan bounce that cheered him up.

'Hiya, Helen. How're y'all doin' today? That American enough for you? What can I do for you anyway? Don't you know I'm busy listening to the leader of the free world, or do we say the whole world now, talking to us about the fate of democracy hanging in the balance?'

Helen DeVos giggled again.

'You watch that kind of stuff, Alex? Jeez, we're talking hardcore here. We're talking weird. Guess it's up to you what goes on in the privacy of your own home.'

26

Newman had gone through this bizarre foreplay with Helen DeVos a hundred times before and knew she would get to the point eventually. He liked her and supposed she was attractive. Possibly very attractive, but not, well, not his type. Too much trouble. It would be like starting a relationship with a whole bag of Manhattan neuroses.

'You still going to Florida?' she asked. 'On vacation?'

'Yes. As soon as they send the relief reporter across to cover for me, I'm out of here. There's a gap in the election campaign before the party conventions so it's my one chance before November. And heat I like on the beach in any amount. Just not here in Washington.'

'I know. It's the same swamp in New York too. Listen, I called because I have a story for you. A good one. Want it?'

Helen always did things like this, and more than anything it irritated the hell out of Newman. And he always replied as he replied now, with an exasperated edge.

'I do not know, Helen.' He enunciated the words extra clearly so that she might sense his annoyance. 'Until you tell me what it is about, clairvoyance not being one of my big subjects. You'll get the usual fee if we run it.'

Helen DeVos freelanced as a television researcher for the American networks, mainly long term investigative stories, usually about intelligence or defence. She used the freelance fees, which were generous, since she was reckoned to be good, to subsidise a bi-monthly magazine on the workings of American intelligence called *Combat*. She ran it with a left-wing Bostonian, Chuck Lowell. Lowell might have been one of the reasons Newman did not think DeVos was quite his type. She lived with him, to Newman's surprise. He had greying black hair tied in a pony tail. Newman thought he looked like a faded, ageing refugee from the seventies: leather jacket, blue jeans. He was part of a big wealthy Boston family. Lowell had run off to California in the early seventies, as he put it, 'to discover himself'. He dropped out of Berkeley and returned to the east coast, working as a freelance news video cameraman on the graveyard shift, selling pictures of overnight murders to local stations round New York city. Like a vampire, Chuck came out at night and slept by day with his wings across his face – at least when he wasn't editing, or helping Helen DeVos edit *Combat*. Despite the gung-ho title the magazine was about as irritating to the CIA, National Security Agency, Defense Intelligence Agency and all the other bits and pieces of American intelligence as it was possible for DeVos, Lowell and their friends on the Nicaraguan Support Committee and suchlike to make it. The magazine was a shoestring operation, available mainly by mail-order and from a few left-wing book stores in the big cities. In the past it had scored what Chuck Lowell called 'a series of Cold War triumphs'.

Combat had printed names of active CIA agents in Central America, lists of intelligence officers in Greece and Italy, in Zaire, Argentina and Chile; the story of the intelligence war in the Middle East; the collapse of the Nugan Hand bank in Australia, with all its CIA associations, and of intelligence links with the Bank of Credit and Commerce International. There was a short decline followed by a boom in the late 1980s when *Combat* published edition after edition on the Iran Contra affair and Colonel Oliver North's shadow CIA run under the cover of the National Security Council in the back rooms of the White House.

'Ollie sells,' Lowell used to say, shaking his pony tail with amusement. 'He was *Combat*'s Playmate of the Month three editions running. A record.'

Newman grinned, but he considered Lowell the last refugee from Woodstock. DeVos, on the other hand was irrepressible and friendly in a way he believed was typically and wonderfully American.

Talking to her was like hearing a good joke: it cheered him up. Beyond her Lowell-inspired tendency to see the world as a series of conspiracies manipulated by the CIA, DeVos did always seem to know which nuclear power stations were having the worst problems, which defence projects were the most over-budget, and which Congressmen were most in the pay of the big defence contractors. She was worth keeping sweet.

'What's the story, Helen?' Newman said at last.

There was a short pause and an intake of breath on the other end of the line.

'I'm speaking from a friend's phone and think I can speak freely,' Helen said. Terrific, Newman thought. Now my mind's at rest. Then speak freely, for Christ's sake. 'It's a story about the Agency out of

Miami,' she continued. 'And an operation called Deep Blue.'

There was another pause, and Newman thought he was supposed to respond, but could not think of anything to say except 'So?', and that would seem rude.

'Deep Blue,' he repeated, slowly. 'Deep Blue. Means nothing to me. Which Agency are we talking about, anyway?'

There was another pause and a longer intake of breath as if Helen DeVos had decided she had telephoned an imbecile.

'The Central Intelligence Agency, Alex,' she said softly. 'Yes. The CIA. And one of their people. Name of Phil Lewis. That mean anything to you?'

Newman could not place it. Two hundred and fifty million Americans. One of them called Phil Lewis.

'No,' he replied. 'Never heard of him. Some relation to Huey Lewis?'

'No relation,' DeVos snapped.

She realised if she really wanted to sell Newman the story she would have to come to Washington, there was too much to explain by telephone, especially if he was going to be obtuse. For his part, Newman didn't think it was worth her flying to Washington. What did he care about CIA spooks in Miami or, more to the point, what did his readers in Britain care? Still, he had his own bumper sticker slogan: you could never tell if something was worth looking into until you had looked into it.

'Lewis is English,' DeVos added, as if that would clinch it. 'And what he's been doing will interest your newspaper – promise.'

Reluctantly, but with a show of good grace because he liked the idea of seeing her again, Newman agreed that Helen could meet him in Washington, but only if she was coming down anyway. No special trips. The *London Tribune* was not in the travel agency business.

'When can you make it?'

'Thursday. I have work to do for *Combat* on Capitol Hill. Profile of the new members of the intelligence oversight committees. You know, the dogs that can't bark because they don't know how.'

They made arrangements to have dinner, and Newman clicked the telephone back on its cradle.

He took a pull at his drink. It was revolting. There was no bottled

29

water left in the glass. The ice cubes had melted, making it taste of Potomac chlorine. He looked back at the television screen. The president was finishing with the American people for the night, and so it might soon be safe to watch television again.

He was quoting one of his predecessors, changing the context, saying something about trusting in the nation's new manifest destiny during these times of uncertainty as the world seemed ready to re-invent itself in the name of democracy and America picked up the torch and continued to do the hard work of freedom. A metaphor too far, Newman thought.

'Manifest destiny,' he repeated scornfully, putting aside his glass of water. 'Manifest bullshit.'

3

As he drove past the old Executive Office Building next to the White House, Warren Cabot felt that, on such a moonlit night, the structure simply did not fit into the centre of Washington. With its lights shining into the street from the deep-recessed grey granite façade, the EOB, as everyone who worked there called it, looked like some misplaced refugee from the Austro-Hungarian Empire awkwardly transposed into the New World.

Cabot drove slowly, searching for a parking space. The EOB had, he thought, a kind of heavy grandeur. It was a temple of unbending imperial power that was not right for the heart of an American revolutionary republic devoted to freedom. For that reason, and perhaps because he had too many bad memories of long nights working there in the 1970s, it was Cabot's least favourite building in Washington.

Cabot had swept along the Whitehurst freeway, watching the full moon shine over the Kennedy Center as the lights from the Rosslyn skyscrapers danced on the Potomac. The river coiled out towards the Tidal Basin, sluggishly pushing its warm summer waters through to the Chesapeake Bay. Cabot smiled. However long he lived in the nation's capital he still delighted in the way the moon rose over the Washington Monument, its image mirrored in the reflecting pool or playing silver on the white dome of the Jefferson Memorial and the United States Capitol.

These were the parts of the city which meant something to him, the marble embodiment of the ideas of the patriotic heroes of the revolution, not the rather more grubby business of day-to-day government that he had been part of inside the EOB, and which –

he noticed from the lights – still ground on after eight o'clock on this sticky summer night.

As he drove, Cabot had listened to the president's address on the radio, irritated that he could not watch the whole thing at home on television. The country's economic crisis was unlikely to bring about the president's defeat in November's election, but it could lead to the unravelling of the administration in a difficult second term. That worried Cabot a great deal. He saw the second presidential term as the first Cabot administration at the head of a new CIA and revitalised American intelligence community. Despite – or maybe because of – all the successes of the past decade there was a mood for urgent reform. The Democrats in their dumb way had even begun asking whether America needed a CIA any more. Plain stupid. Cabot had a simple ambition: promotion to a job he had coveted for years; to set the whole intelligence community on a new track in a way even the Democrats could not quarrel with. And a more complicated plan: how to achieve it. Success depended upon a peculiar combination of circumstances which Cabot felt were at last coming together, where being an outsider during the intelligence struggles of the Cold War might actually be to his advantage. At fifty-two years old, after a lifetime in and out of public service, he was currently special legal counsel to the Director of Central Intelligence, Bill Richardson. As the CIA's leading lawyer, no one would expect him to make it to Director of Central Intelligence.

But this was the year in which every political battle proved that the Outsider was In. That was why the president was in such re-election trouble. No one trusted Washington politics any more. Cabot, however, knew he had two strong cards to get what he wanted: one, a long standing, if not always intimate, friendship stretching back to university days with the president himself, and two, the mess that was bubbling in Miami. What had happened to Phil Lewis – whatever it was, and Cabot was not entirely sure – was indicative of all the things that Cabot wanted to change.

'It ain't broke, Warren, so why're you trying to fix it?' was the usual response from Richard Boone, the Deputy National Security Adviser, and the man Cabot was about to meet. But the Lewis affair in Miami was sufficiently dangerous it might persuade the White

32

House that they had to fix some of the remaining garbage from the Cold War, and in that category Cabot enthusiastically included Boone himself. The president had appointed Cabot 'Mr Clean' – his own words – a professional lawyer with an intelligence background, who would advise the current CIA Director Bill Richardson and his staff on the legality of difficult cases. It was billed as a touchstone of the new ethics of the administration, making sure that the only remaining superpower combined moral with political and military leadership. Cabot grinned at the thought of being in charge of the Ten Commandments for Spies, but his ambition to make it to Director of Central Intelligence had turned into insufferable hunger when Richardson announced that he wanted to leave the CIA after the election, to go back into the private sector and make some money for his old age.

He would not be missed, certainly not by Cabot, who considered him just another cheerful political time server who had helped the president win California in the last election, was rewarded accordingly, and yet was now way beyond his sell-by date. Preoccupied by thoughts of how to manage his own rise, Cabot looked around him as he searched for a parking space. It suddenly struck him how Washington tonight was the splendid city L'Enfant had planned, not the other city it sometimes appeared to be. You could forget that this was the capital on the mud flats of the lower Potomac. With the radio on and the president talking firmly in his loud, sonorous cadences, you could ignore the gunfire down in South East or in Anacostia where dope dealers were killing each other over a few yards of turf.

Cabot despaired at the thought of street drug wars as the sharp end of triumphant American capitalism, preferring instead to believe in the republic of George Washington or Jefferson. He parked carefully a few hundred yards from the White House at the back of LaFayette Park, stepping into the hot night air, smelling the power of Washington like some exotic spice which made this company town (where the company just happened to be the US government) into a great city, fresh and alive. As he walked, Cabot brushed his grey suit with the palms of his hands. Dog hairs. His wife Robyn's labradors were like golden hair machines, shedding

33

all the time, jumping around in the Volvo and leaving bits of themselves behind.

He brushed harder to remove most of the mess, wanting to look his best for what he thought could be an unpleasant confrontation with the Deputy National Security Adviser. Cabot had dressed carefully, 'power dressing' the dumb newspaper social critics would have called it. His grey light wool suit had been made by Gieves and Hawkes in Savile Row, presumably for the London weather. It was almost unbearable in this heat. Tonight nothing was cool enough except being somewhere else, like Robyn's family ranch in the mountains of Montana, where he longed to spend his summer vacation as soon as the grubby Miami business was settled.

Cabot crossed the park towards the lights of the White House. This was the part which really made his heart pump even though he had been in or near here for the past twenty years. The White House. The president. Like the Flag or the Pledge of Allegiance there was always going to be a lump in the throat or you could not be a real American. Clearly lit by the full moon, there were a few street people camped out in LaFayette Square. The down-and-outs and homeless, the disturbed and drug-befuddled were in little knots, some holding up placards, others adding cardboard to supermarket trolleys and plastic sheeting to blankets to carve a home for themselves. A home, ironically, less than four hundred yards from where the president of the United States was talking to the nation – this part excepted – live on television.

A hopeless drunk in worn-down shoes and dirty jeans yelled across to another lying on the grass to pass the Thunderbird wine.

A black man, his hair in dirty tangled knots, pulled a blanket round his head. He wore four or five sets of clothes, one on top of the other despite the heat, shelter from the storm. Cabot quickly crossed to the White House perimeter and gazed inside. Near the north-west entrance there were extra pools of brightness, lights from television crews setting up outside the press room and the West Wing. As soon as the president finished his address, Cabot knew the journalists would spill out, connect up and be ready to deliver their pronouncements on the presidential performance, judging his words with their own commentaries.

'Journalistic fast food,' Cabot muttered, shaking his head as he strode briskly past the metal fence, watching the technicians test their sound levels while moths fluttered round their ears in the strong light.

He could feel the sweat as the light wool of his trousers stuck ever so slightly to skin. There was a wail of a siren in the distance.

Somewhere up Pennsylvania Avenue towards Georgetown, ambulances were speeding through the streets. Cabot turned the corner by the Executive Office Building and stepped in to the entrance, happy to feel the air-conditioning as he spun through the revolving doors. He brushed a stray grey hair behind his ear and settled his gold-rimmed glasses on his nose.

'Warren Cabot,' he informed the guards at the desk. 'For Richard Boone in the National Security Council.'

'I.D.,' one of the guards replied, matter-of-fact, bored.

Cabot reached for his wallet, looking at the vacant stares of the guards and the electronic security paraphernalia surrounding the entrance.

He remembered a time when a white man dressed as he was dressed, with his kind of patrician bearing, could just about walk in to the White House itself without the guards saying much except, politely, 'Have a nice evening'. Now there were lumps of concrete outside the White House so that Arab terrorists and suicide bombers could not crash through. There were surface-to-air missile batteries hidden on the roof, bullet-proof cars, and a president who travelled among the people who elected him in a heavily armed convoy as if he were the despotic dictator of a Third World tyranny, not the leader of a country which was synonymous with freedom and had just won the Cold War. It had come to this. In fact, it had come to this in less than thirty years. Eventually Cabot was allowed inside. He was shown through a high-ceilinged ante-room into the office proper, where Richard Boone sat behind a dark cherrywood desk nursing a glass of Chivas Regal, rolling it slowly around in ice. His feet were on the desk top, and he kept them there as Cabot walked in, saying nothing, motioning Cabot to sit down. The president was still speaking on television, winding up his address to the nation. Cabot stood and watched.

'It is still morning in America,' the president was saying, sounding unconvinced and looking relieved as he galloped towards the finish line. 'We are still, as a nation, the last best hope of mankind for a better future as dictatorships crumble and fall. But we must ensure our leadership is unfettered by budget deficits, dragged into an economic black hole which our children and their children will have to pay for. This nation, the richest and strongest ever seen on this earth, rich in spirit as well as strong in material wealth, must face our rendezvous with the future knowing we can pay our way. We can do it, we must do it, and with your help we will do it. Thank you, goodnight, and God Bless America.'

Rendezvous with the future, Cabot thought. That wasn't bad. Tomorrow's headline. One of the speech writers in the EOB, one of the rising stars, had done well. He turned to see Richard Boone take a swig of whisky, set his glass down on the papers on his desk and fire the remote control at the television to switch it off. Cabot stood and stared at him. They had yet to exchange words.

'Siddown, Warr'n,' Boone said, reminding Cabot of his lazy habit of swallowing words.

Cabot sat down, staring across at the bull of a man, his feet still on the desk, his short-cropped hair leading down to well-muscled shoulders. They knew each other vaguely, cocktail party acquaintances, a veneer of friendship over ten thousand Washington canapés. Mercifully, Boone did not often mix with Cabot's Georgetown friends, preferring to hang out with the defence and intelligence types over in Arlington or McLean, on the Virginia side of the river. Cabot's only real insight into Boone's character came from party small talk and a bizarre article in the *Washingtonian Magazine*. In the glossy pages the Boone style – 'One to Watch in Washington' – was laid bare. Boone, the magazine informed its readers, was one of the most powerful men in government, a political heavyweight. It was meant to be a joke, accompanied by a photograph of Richard Boone wearing a tee-shirt and sweat pants holding a hundred pound weight with one hand above his head. His arm muscles bulged with effort, a wide grin across his heavy-set face like a gash in a melon. The Deputy National Security Adviser, *Washingtonian* said, arrived at his office every morning by 6 A.M., worked weights for precisely

36

forty-five minutes, showered and thumped his bulk down at his desk by seven.

He never left the office before seven o'clock in the evening. A tough workaholic, typifying the new 'Can-Do' spirit of the presidency and the nation, the spirit of the new millennium. Oh, yeah? Well, it was now way beyond eight o'clock in the evening and Boone was still at his desk, his black and shiny wing-tip shoes pointing towards Cabot's face showing their leather soles, and behind him, neatly framed and mounted, a copy of *Washingtonian* with his picture on the cover. So he loves himself, Cabot thought. Hardly an offence in this town, otherwise the government would have to close down.

But *Washingtonian* had not mentioned the Chivas Regal, which even at first glance Cabot could see was being drunk to excess. Drinking hard liquor had gone out of fashion just as taking exercise had come in. Boone, no doubt, neglected to mention it to the magazine, sticking to what he knew would be the best for self-promotion. He leaned heavily in his chair, pushing back from the desk.

'Well,' he said, slurring the words from habit rather than from the drink. 'Whaddya think, Mr Lawyer? How'd the Man do?'

Cabot perched on a leather chesterfield next to the television. He pulled back the long grey hair which kept straying from behind his ear and shrugged.

'That's about as good as we're going to get,' he said. 'Demagoguery is not the president's strong suit, and when he comes out with all these Peggy Noonan purple phrases about destiny and the American dream . . . well, he doesn't make it, even though he really means it. Isn't it ironic that some of the ones who sounded better were the real phonies?'

Boone laughed until his bull neck went red.

'You're right,' he said. 'At least Ronald Reagan could deliver the lines, even if he didn't understand what the hell they meant. This president's trouble is that he understands too well.'

Warren Cabot crossed his legs. He felt good in the Savile Row suit, though Boone was not likely to notice it. You go to do business, Cabot's father had always told him, you dress like you mean business.

'Drink?' Boone asked. Cabot was confident he knew the type:

wanted to look tough so he pulled on the weights; wanted to sound tough so he cursed a bit. Then the business with the tie, which Boone had loosened a few inches at the neck, a studied casualness. One of the many Washington acts.

'Whisky and soda,' Cabot said. 'A weak one. I have to drive.'

Boone grunted something and shifted his bulk over to a tray of drinks. He filled a glass with ice, splashed in some Chivas Regal and topped it up with Club Soda.

'You kill goddamn good malt whisky doing that,' he said to Cabot. 'You should drink Chivas on the rocks.'

Cabot nodded. Like all men who knew very little, he thought, Boone was determined to share what he had persuaded himself he did know. What the hell. Cabot did not do remedial social education. If Boone did not know the difference between a good malt scotch and an over-rated blend, Cabot was not going to play Miss Manners to the White House pet goon. He took the glass from Boone's fist and rattled the ice once or twice to mix it.

Boone was making conversation again.

'Unh-unh,' Cabot muttered, non-committal, friendly. He took a sip of his drink. He knew it would be too strong. It was. 'I'm glad you could see me,' he said, setting the whisky to one side. 'Even at short notice and at this late hour, it seemed to me there were a number of things we should run through if I am to go down to Miami.'

'No problem, Warr'n,' Boone replied expansively. 'Anything I can do to help, pal.'

No one had called Warren Cabot 'pal' ever in his whole life. No one, not even New York taxi drivers. If it was an attempt to annoy him, Cabot ignored it. He knew enough of Boone to recognise a man probing for weaknesses, like a dentist searching for cavities. Once he found them he would twist metal in the raw nerve.

This son-of-a-bitch, Boone was thinking now, coldly eyeing Cabot's smart grey suit and teal-coloured tie, looks like he stepped out of television central casting: the senior doctor in one of the day-time soap operas, the fifty-year-old multi-millionaire with a heart of gold, the businessman Lothario – except that his glasses made Cabot look too intelligent, too bookish for stardom. He reminded

Boone of those old-time WASP sports coaches who thought it did not matter whether you won or lost the game so long as you played fair. Boone wondered how to convince assholes like this that the truth was if you won the game you could sort out the details later.

He could see Cabot positioning himself for a run to succeed Richardson as Director of Central Intelligence, but that meant the lawyer was suffering from a bad case of delusions of competence. No one wanted him in the job. No one. If it came to a fight, Boone was sure the current Deputy Director Vince Terrelli would have to win. And even if there was some problem with Terrelli, the Agency's senior officers would prefer just about anyone – including Boone himself – to this goddamn Boy Scout. Putting an asshole like Cabot in the CIA Director's office at Langley would be like making Mother Teresa Commandant of the Marine Corps.

Cabot came to the point. 'I need information. As much as you can give me about your role in the Miami finance and investment corporation that has just gone belly up. I need to know what you know about Winston, Hamilton, Bellingham, Lewis and Lopez, and especially about Philip Lewis and the potential he might have to embarrass us.'

Boone took a long, slow pull at his Chivas Regal.

'What's the problem? You can see all that in the files out at Langley.'

'I've read the files,' Cabot shot back. 'Or as many of them as Vincent Terrelli will make available to me. Apparently he thinks I'm not cleared for everything the Directorate of Operations is up to. The files I have seen show that as CIA liaison officer here at the White House you helped set up and run the Lewis operation. I want to know before this thing leaks into the news media what the problems might be.'

Cabot looked at the bullet head in front of him. He could see the blood beating in a heavy pulse on Boone's neck, the menace beneath the short-cropped hair. It was difficult not to think of him childishly as Ba-Boone, a kind of strong, not quite human beast who thought with his glands not his brains.

'What can I tell ya,' Boone shrugged. 'I got involved with Phil Lewis when we set up Deep Blue in the early eighties. I was working out at Langley then, in the Op'rations Directorate. So Congress was giving us the usual hell over covert op'rations, and we were trying to get Deep Blue started. Then I got transferred to the White House staff because that made it easier to keep everything away from Congress's prying goddamn eyes. Executive privilege, Warr'n. You ever hear of it?'

Warren Cabot was not interested in civics or legal lessons from Ba-Boone. Every president since Jimmy Carter had used the White House National Security Council staff to run secret operations to avoid Congressional oversight, but not every one of those operations had gone bankrupt owing millions of dollars to American citizens.

'So what went wrong with the investment company?'

'I guess Phil Lewis screwed up on the legit side of the business,' Boone replied. 'It was real complicated the way he ran the money.'

Cabot could have worked that out himself.

'I'm concerned that this could tarnish the reputation of the administration,' Cabot said, taking off his glasses with a worried air, and polishing them on his tie. 'In the run up to the election we need to be beyond suspicion. I thought operations like this were being run down. I want to know why Deep Blue was kept going.'

Oh, do you, you mealy mouthed son-of-a-bitch, Boone thought. I bet you do, so you can dump on me and Vince Terrelli. Well, screw you. This is no turkey waiting for Thanksgiving.

'Listen up, Cabot,' Boone said heatedly. 'Before we go on with this, I just want you to know a couple of things about me. When I came out of the Marines and into government service it was through the Pentagon then into the Company. They used to say to me then, right in the Ford pres'dency, that with a little polish Richard Boone could be a rough diamond. Some joke, eh? Well, you know what, I like that joke. All my goddamn life there have been people underes'mating me or trying to get to me, but I love this country, and I work for its president and I am proud of what I do. Part of all that was to work with Phil Lewis, and even when it's gone wrong, I'm still proud of what we achieved. You got me?'

Cabot was not sure where the monologue was leading. He nodded anyway, thinking Ba-Boone had taken one whisky too many.

'I've got you.'

'What I'm trying to get you to un'erstand,' Boone said, 'is that there's things that we do for the good of the country and because the president wants them done. The test is whether they work. That's what makes them right. So I'll answer your questions, but you gotta see that Deep Blue was part of its time in the Cold War, that's all. Maybe we kept it going too long, but don't judge it by what we would do now. Judge it by what we needed then. You followin' this, lawyer?'

Warren Cabot finished polishing his glasses and put them back on, nodding gently. Boone spent the next hour and three whiskies talking about Phil Lewis.

He explained that under his own general direction Lewis had used his investment company, Winston, Hamilton, Bellingham, Lewis and Lopez to channel funds to intelligence personnel in Latin America, the Caribbean and the Pacific rim as part of the whole series of operations known as 'Deep Blue'. They were the covert side of what the Reagan administration had called publicly the 'New Maritime Strategy' – building up the US Navy, securing the Atlantic and Pacific oceans as American lakes. Any threat in the western hemisphere – Grenada, Nicaragua, Cuba, Panama – had to be controlled and subverted. Lewis's company was used to pay the bills. Boone walked over from his desk to the bookshelves behind Cabot and produced a leather-bound volume. He looked at the index, rifled through the pages, then continued speaking.

'G'way back,' Boone said, with a slur, 'to the fifties. The CIA had a gen'ral counsel then called Lawrence Houston. A lawyer, kinda like you, but not so important, know what I mean, Warr'n?'

Warren knew what he meant.

'Anyway this Houston guy was talkin' about how you set up operations and how you need money you can't trace. This is what Houston said: "Provisions of unvouchered funds and the inviolab . . . inviob . . . invi-bility of such funds from outside inspection is the heart and soul of covert operations." That's what he said.' Cabot put down the book and went back to his desk. 'Got that, Warr'n? Heart and soul. The boy Houston knew his stuff. That's what Phil Lewis did for us. Heart and soul of our operation.'

Cabot tried not to show his disgust. He wanted to know why

Boone thought the company, heart and soul, had collapsed. Boone laughed, picked up his drink and took a swig.

'Ask Phil Lewis,' he said. 'The son-of-a-bitch pissed it away, prob'ly. He was set up for life down there and got greedy, started skimming a little here, a little there until the roof fell in. That's my guess, Warr'n. Then somebody got angry and tried to flush the fat English lardball away in the tub.'

'Who?'

Boone laughed again.

'You are some Boy Scout,' he said, his heavy shoulders heaving with amusement. 'How should I know who'd want to kill Lewis? Maybe they were lining up three deep. It was not the United States government, Warr'n. Not any part of it that I know or that you're responsible for anyway. We might be getting stiffed by the bastard, but we don't go 'round cutting wrists. Cut his balls off, maybe. Not wrists, Warr'n. Too goddamn tacky.'

Warren Cabot looked at the whisky-and-laughter-reddened face of Ba-Boone heaving in front of him, and felt a wave of optimism. He was now sure he understood the game correctly. There was a big poker hand to play, but he knew he could play it. All he had to do was work out how to inflict the maximum bureaucratic damage on yesterday's men, Boone and Terrelli. The difficult part was that he had to minimise any public damage to the administration. Vincent Terrelli had himself opened the door by demanding that Cabot go to Miami to ensure the courts sealed the Lewis files containing references to CIA operations and the payments for Deep Blue.

'You've got to get down there, Warren,' Terrelli demanded in words which echoed in Cabot's head. 'Prevent an accident turning into a crisis.'

As Cabot watched the imbecilic Ba-Boone treat him with such contempt, he saw things a little differently. In an administration which prided itself on prudent handling of all policy matters, two key officials, Terrelli and Boone, supervised precisely the kind of clandestine operation that the president wanted to avoid: an embarrassing one. In Cabot's honest opinion that meant his two principal rivals were unfit to hold their present jobs, never mind be promoted to DCI. An accident. The words kept turning in Cabot's mind, over and over like some mantra or prayer, as he half listened to Boone's drunken narrative. A crisis in Miami.

Warren Cabot suddenly recalled something he had learned years before when he worked on China policy for the Nixon administration. Someone had told him the mandarin Chinese written characters for 'crisis' were a combination of two other characters: those for 'danger' and 'opportunity'. A crisis in Miami. What remained was to ensure the danger pointed one way, towards Terrelli and Boone. Then the opportunity was his to exploit.

'Thank you, Richard,' Cabot said decisively, standing up to leave and cutting off Boone in mid sentence. 'You have been very helpful.'

4

Havana, Cuba

The noise from the drums and the cymbals carried well past the Riviera Hotel into the sidestreets. There were about three hundred students wearing red and black headbands left over from the previous year's anniversary of the storming of the Moncada barracks. Their tee-shirts read '100% Cubano', though the blue dye was beginning to fade after only a few washes. They were warming up with songs and dancing for what was supposed to be a massive show of strength in the evening with a huge torchlight rally to be addressed by Fidel.

Ah, Fidel.

Fidel who was on television talking for four hours in one of his grand theatrical speeches, or greeting the visiting delegation from Moscow to discuss the continuing economic 'readjustments' demanded by the collapse of the Soviet Union. Fidel who had been to the inauguration of one of the presidents recently elected in Brazil or Peru or Argentina – it did not much matter which, because it was Fidel who (as ever) had been the star, not some here today gone tomorrow product of Yanqui ideas of democracy. It was Fidel that all the television cameras had featured; Fidel to whom the interviewers had wished to talk; Fidel whom they had all come to see, magnificent, resplendent, the only leader in military uniform, triumphant, unbowed, *el lider maximo . . .*

Fidel! Fidel!

Cuba, Si! Cuba, Si!

Fidel! Fidel!

General Oscar Padilla Sanchez stood in civilian clothes in the shade on the north side of the street, listening to the students rehearse

44

their chants, watching the demonstration pass before he could cross. Thirty years of practice, and they were good at it.

Venceremos! Venceremos!

Padilla was slim, wiry, with a shock of thick steel-grey hair. He liked to think he was still fit, swam every day when time permitted, smoked too much but supposed one day he would cut down. He looked at three eighteen-year-old girls swaying past, hips tight in their *milicia* uniforms, their pelvises thrusting from side to side with the beat.

Socialismo o muerte! Socialismo o muerte!

At least we made socialism sexy, Padilla thought, pulling a cigarette from the packet and tapping it hard to keep the tobacco inside. One of the major successes of the revolution. Padilla looked despairingly at the packet in his hands and the flakes of dried tobacco that had fallen out.

'Unlike the cigarettes,' he muttered.

It was the hottest time of the day, three in the afternoon, and no one with any sense or any choice was on the streets, except the students. They were members of *Juventud Rebelde,* the youth movement, which meant they were part of the earliest and sweatiest stages of what would eventually become the night time rally. In the humidity, people were moving around slowly in the shopping streets near the Capitolio, where, his wife Eva had assured Padilla earlier in the day, new shipments of North Korean underwear and women's dresses had arrived.

Padilla lit the cigarette and drew heavily. The students had moved on, the last of the wiggling *milicia* girls smiling and giggling, turning the corner as the music and chanting dimmed in the distance.

Padilla knew it would be a long time before the demonstration reached the Plaza de la Revolucion, a thirsty walk which he himself had danced many sorefoot times before, high on rum and patriotism, fuelled by Fidel and Havana Club. Too many times to count. But not today. And not ever again.

He crossed the road, turned a couple of blocks and walked towards his office. The military guard stood in the shade of the sentry box and saluted even though General Oscar Padilla Sanchez was not in uniform.

Padilla ignored him, striding into his office and closing the door. There was an old thick nail behind it which served as a coathook, and he took a pair of light civilian trousers from a hanger and a spare summer shirt and folded them carelessly. He picked up his tennis shoes from a corner where they lay with his files, and put them with the clothes into a string bag. His general's uniform lay roughly folded on a chair in the corner. He put it properly on a hanger, shutting it in the wall-closet. Then Padilla picked up the telephone to call his secretary.

'Luisa,' Padilla said. 'It's too hot. Too hot for business. I'm leaving.'

Luisa agreed. She had been one of Padilla's girlfriends for a year or two, tight and firm in her own *milicia* uniform until she began to put on weight and droop here and there. Padilla had dropped her gently. He liked her, liked her laugh and her sense of humour, but not the widening girth. The nights were never that cold in Cuba. All things must pass, Luisa, *mi amor*, he told her, though Luisa took less comfort from his attempts at philosophy than the fact he had offered her, as a kind of consolation, a job away from the Ministry of Defence proper, and in his own new project, the Revolutionary Coordination Unit.

'Too hot for business,' Luisa assumed, was Padilla's latest code for spending time on the beach, or with one of his girlfriends or, most likely, both. She didn't care.

'Get my uniform cleaned and pressed,' Padilla instructed her on the way out. 'It's in the closet. And I'll need my dress uniform for tomorrow's parade. Make sure they send it back in time.'

It was another dreary anniversary. This time it was something to do with the Socialist International. Then it was Carnival, which used to be fun, but not any longer. Padilla kept comparing it to the great carnivals of the sixties, when it was truly fun to be alive and wonderful to be a Cuban; when they had faced down the United States, and led the non-aligned countries; when tens of thousands of foreigners came to see the revolution for themselves.

From Europe and Latin America they had come to worship the revolution and to learn its secrets, speaking bad Spanish and asking their questions about the Cuban system and Fidel into the tropical

46

night. And then? And then like Luisa the revolution had become flabby round the edges – but far worse than Luisa's gentle ageing. She had preserved her good humour at least. The revolution? Padilla now believed that the revolution had lost its youthful vigour without finding contentment in maturity. It had become a sour old maid, menopausal and charmless. He wanted to preach the heresy aloud, but knew it would be futile. Those guilty of such conduct – like two recently arrested air force officers from Oriente province – could expect no mercy. Padilla thought it likely they would be shot. Their stupidity – if not their treachery – deserved as much, and it would head off the rumbling discontent within the Cuban armed forces. Like Fidel himself, the revolution had become older and greyer and more boring. Beneath the skin Padilla could still detect the bold outline of the young and handsome beast that had made them want to sacrifice their lives for an ideal, but not now. He felt disgusted, as if he had fought for years for Helen of Troy and in his victory ended with a decrepit old hag. Padilla smiled. Whatever else he might long for, whatever else he might miss it would not be the parades, the endless rallies and constant marching up and down chanting the latest slogans.

'*Socialismo o muerte,*' was fairly new. He heard them chanting it two or three years before for the first time, like the chorus of a dreary pop song that everyone would be expected to sing before long. 'Socialism or death.'

It was not much of a choice, he thought, running his hand round the sweat on the back of his neck.

Socialismo o muerte.

It was not as if the slogans meant anything any more. Or the policies. In the past few months they had been forced to suffer bread rationing for the first time Padilla could remember since 1960. Bread rationing after more than thirty years of the revolution. The latest excuse was that there had to be 'rectification' of the economy. Padilla laughed. It was like 'rectifying' his father, God bless him, who had been dead for twelve years. The only thing that was not in short supply were the excuses and the slogans themselves. The pity was you could not eat them. And the rallies, like tonight. There were no shortages of those either. The country had anniversaries the way some people had mice.

'Certainly.' Luisa broke into his thoughts. 'Clean and press one uniform. Get the dress uniform back from the cleaners quickly. Of course.'

Even after he dumped her, Luisa knew more than Padilla's wife did of his affairs, covering for him, keeping it all discreet.

'No, the General is at a meeting of the Revolutionary Coordination Unit staff,' she would say when he took off for his beach house.

'No,' she would tell the RCU staff in the same breath. 'The General is at a meeting at MINREX with the deputy foreign minister to discuss foreign trade matters.'

'No,' she would tell MINREX, the Ministry of the Exterior. 'The General is in a national security meeting in the Defence Department.'

And so it went, and Padilla would do whatever work he found necessary, travelling around the island and to Panama or Mexico, and when he did not feel like working too much, Lucia would cover. He had even taken to confiding in her about his affairs, saying that there could never be more than two or three women at any one time on his list of new conquests. It was too complicated.

'I'm getting old,' he said, with that little boy grin men hide behind when they think they are being clever with women. Lucia smiled as Padilla left the office. He smiled back thinly and she could see the general was not quite himself. He had been much preoccupied lately, and she could not work out why. She assumed it was something to do with the Revolutionary Coordination Unit which was a peculiar – and to Luisa a largely unintelligible – enterprise. She knew it shipped cargo out of Varadero. It earned hard currency, mostly US dollars. She carried out some basic administration, and typed accounts. Whatever it was, judging by the way in which members of the Political Bureau and others paid court to Padilla, the RCU seemed to be both important and successful, 'a cornerstone of the revolution', she had once heard the Deputy Defence Minister call it.

At the main reception desk General Padilla ordered the soldier to call for his driver to bring the car to the front door. When the Lada arrived Padilla dismissed the driver. He threw the bag with his spare clothes onto the rear seat, climbed in and turned the car through the side streets past Havana University, then down to the Malecon at Maceo Park. As he drove he began to feel nervous for the first time in years. His decision had finally been made: somehow, sometime soon, he would leave Cuba forever, abandon the revolution which had already abandoned him. His new nervousness was like one of his earliest tastes of combat on the edge of the Sierra Maestra more than thirty years before. In early 1957, twenty of them – two small columns of ten each – had slipped down towards the police station at Guama. They had lain in the long grass for hours watching the sun set and the police inside cook and eat dinner until, bloated and tired from the meal and rum, they had leaped into their hammocks. The twenty guerrillas crept forward from two directions, hit the sleeping guard by the front door, then fired from two windows and through the door, leaving blood spilling on the floor, dripping from the hammocks. For a teenager, as Padilla then was, it was the most exciting thing in his life, more exciting than the hour he had taken with a whore in Santiago de Cuba a few months before; more exciting than what was to follow, marching into Havana in 1959 on New Year's Day in a new country at the head of a new revolution. That day in Guama Padilla had stood and looked around at the blood on the floor and the dead in their hammocks; looked closely at their surprised and loutish faces as the others picked up food or boots from around the warm corpses of the police. The guerrillas had moved through the police station stripping Batista's men of ammunition and weapons which were to be used to win the revolution against Batista himself. Standing in the flickering lights of oil lamps as the others carried out their looting, Padilla learned the most important fact about his character: within him was a formidable iciness, as if at the moments of greatest danger he was most assured and composed. He had felt in his bowels the nervousness all normal men taste before combat, a nervousness which was replaced in the attack by the sudden rush and relief of action after hours of marching through the mountains and waiting for dark to come. But in all this Padilla became more calm and lucid as the danger and confusion increased. He was able to give orders without emotion to men twice his age because even as a teenager he refused to become intoxicated by the joys or terrors of one moment. The others saw that coldness

49

in him in Guama and obeyed him and called it 'leadership'. '*El Tempano*', he had been christened in Guama and the name stuck. 'The iceberg'.

It set Padilla on a track for promotion and favours even at a time when the main purpose of the revolutionaries was not to win but to survive. Now, as he drove through the heart of a city he loved and a revolution which had come to disgust him, all this seemed so long ago.

'*El Tempano,*' Padilla muttered to himself, glancing at his face, impassive in the car mirror. There was a grimness about the eyes which he did not like. Beneath the strict calm of the suntanned and handsome mouth and the heavy lines on the forehead, there were flutters in his belly which he hoped he could control. Padilla threw his cigarette butt out the open window and turned right at the junction with the Malecon, the long wide sweep of road that skirted Havana on the oceanside.

He felt a stiff breeze blowing from the sea, heavy with salt and catching the sleeve of his shirt as he turned. It refreshed him to be near the sea and hear it crash on the shore. He felt the breeze dry the sweat on his forehead, changed into top gear and accelerated eastwards. He had always prided himself on frugal habits, the lessons learned three decades ago in the mountains, which now seemed like a mystical time of innocence, a revolutionary Eden before this dreadful fall back into the real world of waiting for North Korean ships to bring in women's underwear, bread rationing and dreary political rallies. It was not that he particularly cared for material things. He knew he could survive on very little, rice and beans, a pair of boots, clean water. It was just that he did not know why it was still necessary to do so.

The traffic was light and he was nearing Old Havana. The breeze from the Caribbean was pushing waves over the barrier wall running along the Malecon, the road moist from the ocean spray. It was, he thought, glancing to his left, the greatest sea-front in the world, sweeping along the bay from the Riviera Hotel towards the old Spanish castle, El Castillo de San Salvador de la Punta, the harbour with its colonial fortifications and rusted cannons. Padilla could see half a dozen freighters steaming towards the harbour and a coast-

50

guard fast patrol boat bursting through the waves, tossing in the spray as it headed towards the Playas del Este.

'Underwear,' he said absently. 'To support the revolution.'

It was, he supposed, Africa that made him decide that the revolution was fatally sick. He had been posted there from 1975 onwards, mainly in front line command posts in Ethiopia and Angola.

Everyone assured Padilla, and he readily believed, he was merely helping the Africans. Now the arrogance of such a mission struck him as truly dreadful, rather like the first Christian missionaries who brought the 'Truth' to Latin America and stayed to witness the slaughter of native Indians and the destruction of their culture. Padilla had shared the hardships of his soldiers in a way that no one else – not the Angolan officers and certainly not the Soviet advisers – had done, and that endeared him to the men while making him a public figure back home. Newly promoted when he arrived for his first tour of duty, Padilla was proud he had been responsible for the biggest counter-punch against the UNITA troops, sending them reeling three hundred miles into the bush and capturing a stack of South African artillery, troop carriers, machine guns and small arms. What followed was Cuban superstar status, numerous articles in the Havana newspapers.

The newspapers loved the way he lived with his troops, acting as if he were the most junior recruit rather than the most senior officer, a sense of moral leadership when it was known that his brother officers of a certain rank did otherwise. When there was nothing else, Padilla ate monkey with the ordinary soldiers. That fact was not reported in any of the papers only because it was considered bad for morale to think of an army marching on a stomach filled with monkey meat. But Padilla genuinely believed that this new generation of young Cuban fighting men could learn from the hardships of the times as he had from the Sierra Maestra, to share the little they had and the suffering.

But in Angola, instead of sharing men stole each other's boots. Even worse for morale than physical hardships were the night-time conversations between officers, Cuban and Soviet, about politics and the future.

'Demonstrations in Prague,' a Soviet Colonel said. 'Workers' protests against the state in Poland. Newspaper stories of corruption in Moscow and other things such as you would not believe.'

They had found a case of Bucanero rum and were drinking it warm and neat.

'Such as?' Padilla asked.

There were six of them, very drunk by this time.

'Such as calling for all Soviet aid to be cut from Cuba,' the Colonel said calmly. Padilla remembered his flushed red face, his inability to hold his drink, swaying with the words. Padilla, *El Tempano*, said nothing. So they were considering cutting Cuba adrift, alone in the sea of capitalism to sink or swim by itself. He took another swig of Bucanero and threw his head back, staring at the stars in the African sky. What it really meant, this peculiar piece of political gossip between a Russian and a Cuban in Africa, did not hit Padilla properly until he returned home to a welcome fit for heroes. There was a hug on the airport tarmac from Fidel, a medal and talk of Padilla being given command of the western military district, the area round Havana. That would have made him the most important military commander after Fidel and Raul Castro. Padilla wanted that job, wanted it above everything, but there was also jealousy from some, and his own peculiar sense of disappointment, returning to a revolution which had changed so little in all the time he had served it, fighting in the trenches in the dirty little wars of the world. Eating monkey was easier on his stomach than coming home.

'Tired,' Padilla thought to himself, now as he drove eastwards past the harbour entrance. 'Tired of this.'

The nearest ship had turned hard to starboard and set course directly for the mouth of the channel. It was flying the Chinese flag and Padilla wondered how much longer such ships would steam halfway across the world just to keep the Cuban revolution afloat.

'Cuba,' he despairingly told one of the few senior colleagues he trusted, General Juan Antonio Fernandez. 'Cuba is like a hospital patient whose existence depends upon life support machines operated from ten thousand miles away. Sometimes I think it is better that they are turning the switches off.'

'Oscar,' Fernandez had replied. 'It is dangerous for someone in your position to think like that, never mind say it. If we do not keep

52

faith with the revolution, then all our adult lives have been wasted.'

Padilla was unrepentant. Despite Fernandez' words, Padilla tapped a deep vein of military disgust at the state of the country after so much sacrifice. That was the real waste. Failing to recognise it merely compounded the error. He cursed softly, then took a long breath and began to feel the tension pass. He was now on the road sweeping east round the coast from Havana. Driving past Cojimar, he saw that the beaches were full of life.

Anyone with any sense or any influence had left work early. There were volleyball games, girls in bikinis with ice creams, white-fleshed tourists from Europe and Canada sitting in the shade of the palm trees. Padilla thought how fine and cool the water looked. He slowed to let a bus drive away from the stop, then changed down a gear and overtook. He checked his Bulova watch. It was now 12.45. There was no time for a swim. He had to keep going to make the rendez-vous. Padilla pulled out again, this time to overtake a sugar cane truck, belching fumes and struggling with its load. Spare parts for the Hungarian bus engines were already becoming scarce, and so were those for some of the East German and Czech trucks, now that East Germany no longer existed and Czechoslovakia was far from friendly. The ingenuity of Cuban mechanics in keeping vehicles on the road while the societies which had produced them collapsed, astonished Padilla. In parts of Havana they had returned to using horse-drawn carts. The revolution was boldly propelling itself into the nineteenth century. He smiled grimly, recalling one of the slogans he had heard a few years before in Nicaragua when the Sandinistas had vainly tried to win a free election.

'*Todo Sera Mejor,*' the Sandinistas had yelled at every opportunity. 'Everything will be better.'

Padilla looked in his mirror. There was an official-looking Lada behind him with four men inside and Ministry of the Interior plates. He slowed down slightly to let the MININT men pass, but they slowed down too, making him feel a twist of nervousness. *El tempano,* he said to himself. Calm. He took a sharp right hand bend and saw the ocean before him, a stretch of palm trees sweeping along the shore.

They turned too. He cornered again and realised they were

53

probably going to Matanzas, nothing more. He took a deep breath and looked at his watch. Just past one o'clock. He would be in Varadero for lunch, in plenty of time to inspect the hangars and talk to the ground staff. He turned again to his mirror. The Interior Ministry car had gone, thankfully, turning off as he had predicted where the road for the centre of Matanzas split away. He breathed deeply again. Guilt. For nothing, except bad thoughts. Treason enough.

The airfield was about thirty kilometres further on, near the beaches at Varadero. Padilla pulled up to the guard post and one of the sentries came out, holding his AK47 with bayonet fixed towards the Lada. When he saw who was driving the car, the sentry came to attention and saluted.

'Easy, *companero*,' Padilla smiled. 'Without my uniform I am no more a general than you are.'

The sentry grinned back nervously, raising the barrier to let Padilla drive in. At the far end of the airfield there was a small tarmac ramp for private planes and an old hangar, behind two stacks of razor wire. A small group of Revolutionary Coordination Unit personnel were sitting in the shade under the open door of the hangar, eating out of mess tins. One of them recognised the Lada as it followed the track round the airport perimeter, and they quickly tidied themselves, ready to greet Padilla. Outside the hangar he could see a twin-engined Piper Navajo with Colombian registration, being re-fuelled ready for take off. Padilla parked the car at the gate of the hangar. The sentries snapped to attention then let him pass. He walked through proudly, the general at the centre of his command, until he came to the hangar's warehouse area.

The pilot of the Piper Navajo was sitting drinking coffee with the RCU major, Rico Herrera. Both stood up. Behind them Padilla could see a military van being loaded with the cargo from the plane, small bales, wrapped tightly in black plastic. Padilla counted them quickly. Twenty large parcels in all, each sub-divided into ten smaller packets. That meant the shipment contained exactly two hundred kilogrammes of cocaine.

'*Todo sera mejor*,' Padilla thought, smiling as he walked towards Major Herrera. 'Everything will be better.'

5

When Phil Lewis woke, he looked straight up at the ceiling and saw it was exactly as he had feared: white plaster. There had been no dream. This was real life. As real as the dirt-grey windows with the bars and the heavy metal locked door of his room in the hospital secure wing, which was either to keep him in or others out. He could not remember. It was as real as the pain which split through him like the beatings from a meat cleaver, bludgeoning him so that every nerve in his body ached. It had been like this for days, pain that began somewhere between his shoulders, stiffened up his neck before exploding over the top of his head into his eyes. He pulled back the rough green blanket that lay across his bed and grabbed the bottle of Extra Strength Tylenol. That had been his first victory. They had been persuaded to leave a few mild painkillers in the room after he convinced them he had not tried to commit suicide. He counted four capsules in the bottle. They were still taking no chances. As he stared at the Tylenol a doctor and an orderly arrived. They said nothing, no good morning, no social foreplay. The daily examination was conducted with a few obligatory grunted questions, until Lewis was told, yet again, that there was nothing wrong with him.

'Nothing physical anyway, beyond the cuts, and the fact you could do with losing about fifty pounds in weight.'

'Thanks,' Lewis muttered, thinking: you Georgia scumbag.

The doctor was almost completely bald on top and had tried to hide it by combing his brown hair across his head from the side. It looked like a dead squirrel that had been hit by a truck and glued in place.

'Thanks,' Lewis repeated, eyeing the dead squirrel, 'for the advice.'

When the doctor left he returned to the Tylenol, put three in his mouth and tried to swallow, but his tongue was too dry. Quickly he poured a glass of water from the pitcher by the side of the bed, gulping it down, feeling each of the three slide into his stomach. He looked at his watch. It was ten minutes before nine in the morning.

'Soon as Tom Holgate arrives,' he thought, anxious for the meeting with his lawyer to begin, 'I'm gonna get some real painkillers. Then get myself out of here.' He heard a movement in the corridor and another rustle of keys. He catapulted to his feet to greet Holgate, but the effort made his head swim and he sat down with a thump on the bed.

'Jeez,' he muttered, rubbing his eyes hard with the tips of his fingers. 'Can't sleep, can't think. Can't even shit in this place.'

The door opened and the lawyer was ushered in. Tom Holgate had a hearty manner which made him look fitter and younger than his years – late forties. But the ever ready Holgate smile was too cheerful to greet this client, slumped on the bed, a heavyweight depression. Lewis looked up at the tanned face and knew Holgate had been in the sun at the weekend. Probably on his boat, having a good time, sailing off the Keys. Damn him. No matter that it was more than a hundred degrees outside, Holgate always wore a grey pinstriped three piece suit with a gold watch chain.

'Hi, Phil,' he said, patting Lewis on the shoulder. 'How's it going?'

In their first meeting after the attack in the hotel, Holgate had come to his bedside and begun to talk Lewis through what had happened. The room service boy had found him in the bath, the shower water pounding on his back and his blood pumping down the drains. The two Latinos who had sliced him had otherwise left the room intact, trying to make it look like suicide. They did not even disturb his attaché case. Inside it, along with a few of Lewis's most important company files, neatly bound and held with bulldog clips, was $30,000 in cash, bright new one hundred dollar bills. Some of the newspapers and all the local television stations had reported the suicide theory on day one, but they had mostly changed their stories, or at least raised doubts. The room service boy was becoming a celebrity, appearing on the local evening news.

56

'Lucky,' Holgate said. 'You're goddamn lucky he only dropped his tray of food and beers and didn't faint altogether. Then you'd have really gone down the tubes. You were minutes away from dying, Phil. Minutes.'

Lewis looked down at his wrists and arms, felt the pounding inside his head and thought that he was draining away in the hospital's secure unit anyway.

'This place's just like prison,' he muttered. 'Only with enemas.'

Holgate and Lewis had known each other for five years. They had fished for marlin together off the Keys, for albacore off the Baja de California, gone hunting in Louisiana and Mexico, shared a few business deals, partied on 'The New World'. The mainstay of Holgate's practice was what they called in Miami 'the white powder bar' – cocaine dealers, money launderers, low life mostly, but low life with money, which made a difference. They might seem like grifters and misfits but they could afford to pay Holgate's fees.

'The best justice money can buy,' he used to say with a wink and a grin – which in the case of wise guys with $1500 hand-stitched suits and $600,000 power boats, was plenty of justice. Besides, Tom Holgate merely defended them. He was not obliged to like them, nor was he compelled to like Phil Lewis. But he did. The fat Brit was okay, Holgate thought. Full of the right stuff. Sure, Holgate knew about Lewis's Friday afternoons with the girls at the Sheraton, did not care for it particularly, but made a kind of joke about it with his wife.

'That's the way it is with Europeans,' he would say to her. 'Even if he's half Americanised, talks a bit like us. Still got different standards.'

'Like they don't wash so much,' his wife responded.

'Yeah,' Tom Holgate replied. 'Guess you could say that.'

The suicide story had run for the first two days unabated. You had one hysterical Latino kid could hardly speak English, the financial disaster in Lewis's company, plus the helpful police chief and the director of Dade County Hospital trying to get in on the act – two men who never saw a television camera they did not like.

'Did he try to commit suicide?' one of the reporters had yelled at the hospital director. Holgate remembered watching it on the news,

stunned. The police chief and hospital director jostled for the microphone. Police brutality won.

'I can't comment on that,' the police chief had said, puffing out
the chest of his uniform. 'All I can say is that the hospital tells me
the patient has sustained deep wounds on either wrist consistent with
slashings from a knife.'

'Exactly right,' the hospital director interrupted, speaking up and
edging in from the right. 'Deep slashings consistent with knife
wounds.'

'And a knife was recovered from the scene?'

'Sure was,' the chief said. 'At the scene.'

So that was a 'no comment', Holgate thought, watching the indig-
nity of the proceedings, as they repeated the clip showing the fat man
naked under a hospital blanket. He never believed the suicide idea.
The Phil Lewis Holgate knew was one of those stubborn Brits, a
fighter, not a quitter. Dunkirk spirit. Foul mouthed and pig headed,
but not the type to run at the first sound of enemy fire. And that's
what he was under now. Enemy fire. Two days before the scenes
in the Sheraton, local television news had videoed Lewis dodging
reporters, slipping in and out of the Winston, Hamilton, Bellingham,
Lewis and Lopez offices like a sneak thief caught with his hand in
the till. Some crazy story from the Channel Six Eyewitness News
'Investigation Team' tried to say there were serious financial irregu-
larities at WHBL&L. Holgate thought the story stupid beyond belief.
It was obvious to hear the reporter speak that far from being able to
uncover a financial fraud he would have trouble counting to ten
without adult assistance or the use of both hands.

The way it went was: a would-be investor had complained to the
television station that Lewis refused to take his money and offer
him the same high interest that other investors were supposed to be
receiving. So he contacted the local television station, because that's
how you get things done now, and the television journalist had investigated, and was unable to find anyone called Winston or Hamilton
or Bellingham connected with the company. So what? Holgate could
not work out why the fact that Phil Lewis did not to take someone's
money suggested he was crooked.

'I always thought it was the other way round, Phil,' Holgate joked.

'You know, that ripping people off was about taking their money, not refusing it. Call me old fashioned.' But Holgate also told Lewis his first mistake was handling the whispers of bad publicity so miserably. 'Jeez, Phil, some low grade company munchkin would appear to assure investors their money was safe, saying the chief executive officer was unavailable for interviews. Then the cameras would catch you skulking out the back door, or driving off in the black Lincoln Town Car like a cast-off from the Godfather. Boy, that was smart.'

Lewis snorted, but took it.

'If you'd wanted to look like a sleaze,' Holgate continued, 'you couldn't have gone about it any better. If you'd had a PR man then, you might not need a lawyer now.'

Lewis shrugged and looked down at his bandaged wrists.

'The goddamn alligators were out to get me,' he grunted. 'And you say I should've made it easy for them? No way, Tom. You want to know what I think?'

Holgate did not in the ordinary course of events ever want to know what his clients thought. It was a waste of time. But he felt sorry for Lewis and figured that maybe once in a while, listening to opinions when what he really wanted were facts might not be so terrible.

'So what do you think, Phil?'

'Screw the bastards,' Lewis said, sitting up. 'Fuck them all.'

'A Channel Six Investigation,' was how the first television report had been by-lined. 'By the award winning Mike Alpert.'

'Goddamn butthead,' was all Lewis could say about him for days, and he repeated it now without even mentioning Alpert's name. Holgate did not have to ask who Lewis was talking about. It made Holgate feel surprisingly comfortable that his English multi-millionaire friend handled adversity in the same way as the worst of the Colombian narco-traffickers. Lewis had watched the original stories from Alpert with astonishment then increasing alarm.

'Scott Lehtinen wants to know,' Alpert had intoned, referring to the man who was unable to invest in Lewis's company, 'why Miami's classiest investment corporation Winston, Hamilton, Bellingham, Lewis and Lopez are refusing his investment of $40,000. What's wrong with his money? And why does this man,' – they cut to

59

newspaper *Style* section pictures of Lewis sipping cocktails on the stern of his yacht – 'why does this man, British born playboy' – playboy! – 'financier Philip Lewis refuse to return Channel Six phone calls? And who is fooling who when this highly secretive Miami-based investment consultancy boasts two former three-star generals, a four-star general and a former commander of the Pacific fleet on its advisory board?'

Lewis recalled he almost kicked in the front of the television set in anger. Some bozo who did not know his whos from his whoms and his is from his are was calling him a goddamn playboy.

'As usual with this company,' Alpert continued, staring at the camera like a blow-dried Moses delivering the Ten Commandments. 'As usual, questions are plenty, answers few. Mike Alpert, Channel Six Eyewitness News Investigation Team.'

That was it. A string of almost meaningless innuendoes, a few disconnected pictures and a voiceover that managed to be both portentous and empty had brought him to this room, with this pain, and this smiling suntanned lawyer opening his attaché case in front of him. Holgate took out a notebook and pen and looked across at Lewis, as he sat on the side of his bed, head aching, legs dangling.

'What'll it be today, Tom?' Lewis asked, with resignation. 'And when can I get out of here?'

'We're working on it. They've got no charges yet, but they will have. Fraud. Grand larceny. They really want to nail you, Phil. Which means you've got to tell me about it first. I mean, all of it. Not the Alpert version. The real version. The whole nine yards.'

Lewis rubbed the front of his belly, felt the bandages on his wrists, looked straight at Holgate and smiled.

'Tom, we've been friends a while, but you gotta realise there are big stakes here. Big enough for someone to want to kill me. Details don't matter.'

'They matter to me,' Holgate said. 'Because they will matter to the prosecution. And the judge. And the jury. I need the whole picture or else I can do nothing for you. This isn't your lawyer speaking. It's your friend. And while I'll still be your friend, I won't be your lawyer much longer unless you start talking. You're in the secure unit in the hospital partly because they want to keep out the guys who sliced

60

you up, but mainly because they want to show they're as tough on white collar crime as on some crackhead mugging a grandmother on the street. We can beat 'em. And when we do we could sue Alpert from here to Alaska if he screwed up and caused material damage to your business and good name. You want revenge, don't you?'

Lewis nodded. Revenge was good.

'What do you think?'

'I think that if we are playing on the same team, then you're going to have to trust me,' Holgate said.

Then he explained how it was, or just as important, how it was now seen in Miami: that there was something wrong with WHBL&L even if no one could quite put a finger on it. Generous – too generous, given market conditions and overheads – rates of interest guaranteed for those who were on the inside, cold shoulders for some of those trying to invest. Strange. And folk who saw others making good money did not exactly appreciate being outside looking in on the feast.

'Look at me, Tom,' Lewis replied. 'If I'm conning people out of their money, would I turn down investors? Would I?'

'Never mind,' Holgate shot back, 'about what you know to be true. Just think what outsiders believe. Something stinks about this. Nothing certain, but a bad smell. A company where some of the big names don't exist, full of military people, for some reason. A company where the chief executive is a playboy Brit.'

'For Christ's sake, Tom,' Lewis tried to interrupt, but Holgate was unstoppable.

'. . . The chief executive is a playboy Brit who won't even talk to the local media. At best he's a stuck up son-of-a-bitch. More likely crooked. You liking it so far?'

Friend or not, there was only one kind of client Holgate wanted, and that was one who did as he was told and answered goddamn questions.

'You getting the picture?' he repeated. Lewis must have nodded. 'So then the investors get spooked. Driven off by this big row and so-o-o-o public. They start asking for their money back, and turning up at the offices where they meet closed doors and a few camera crews on stake-out. So they start talking to the media. "Yeah, I want

61

my money, and I want it now" or "I'm real pissed; what's going on?"
That kind of thing. You heard it yourself.'

'Yeah, Tom. I heard it.'

Holgate took a pause for breath and looked at Lewis. His eyes
were downcast, the width of his jowls making him look more
depressed than any man the lawyer had ever seen, including those
on death row. Holgate kept going.

'So anyway, Phil, they all start looking after themselves, you know
what I mean. Asking for their money back, making waves. And you
are running away trying to drive over the camera crews in your
big black limo. Everybody thinks you're left-over garbage from the
greed-is-good 1980s ripping them off. They think, Ivan Boesky,
Michael Milken. So they decide to nail your ass.' Lewis moved his
head and looked straight at his lawyer. Holgate met the gaze calmly.
'So by now, and we're talking day three, the Friday you and your
friends got together in the Sheraton shower, by now there's a major
run on the company funds. You got a liquidity problem. You got a
public relations problem. You got World War Three going on right
in front of your company offices, only you don't care to do anything
about it, except issue statements telling all passengers to keep calm,
the *Titanic*'s gonna miss the iceberg, believe me, no problem.'

Lewis lay back full length on the bed, staring at the white plaster
ceiling. He heard Holgate rustle through a sheaf of papers and begin
reading. 'Winston, Hamilton, Bellingham, Lewis and Lopez seeks to
re-assure investors that recent media allegations about the running
of the company have proved unfounded. Volume of business means
some transactions involving investors seeking to withdraw funds will
be delayed. We ask investors to be patient while this temporary
situation is rectified, and thank our clients for their patience until
normal service is resumed.'

Lewis kept his eyes on the ceiling.

'You write this?' Holgate asked derisively. Lewis stared in silence.
'So,' Holgate continued. 'I'm this little old lady down in Fort Lauderdale with my life savings with you, and I hear this trash on television,
and I think: well, that's all right then. This foreigner with the bimbos
on his yacht, this guy who has shut up his offices and won't talk to
anyone, says not to worry. He's got my money under his mattress

62

only he needs a few days to get it out. And I think . . . what do I think, Phil? Look at me, Phil. What do I think?'

Lewis's voice was hoarse and broken. He continued staring at the ceiling and spoke softly.

'Think what you goddamn like, Tom. Just leave me here to sleep.'

Now it was Holgate's turn for anger.

'Listen, you sorrowful son-of-a-bitch. We've got to get something straight. If you want me to stand in front of a federal court trying to keep your ass out of jail, then the least you can do is realise they don't take kindly to foreign swindlers in south Florida. Homeboys are bad enough.'

'Foreign?' Lewis said. His voice regained some of its strength and he turned to look at Holgate. 'Foreign? After all the investment money I've brought to Miami they still consider me foreign? After all I've done for this city and this country! Jeez!'

'Yes, foreign,' Holgate interrupted. 'Even if you've married an American and you speak half like one and you've been here nearly twenty years, you screw up and you're still a Brit, a foreigner and a playboy. And while some of us might like the wet little patch of bogland in the middle of the Atlantic that you call England, a lot of the jurors won't think of Winston Churchill when they see you in the witness box. They'll think Cornwallis or the war of 1812, they'll think foreign enemy trying to rip off good old red-blooded Americans.'

There was a pause while Holgate collected his thoughts. He started speaking again in a flat voice.

'I just want you to understand that so far this does not look good. There's a paper chase in this company of yours somewhere, and I've got to get to the end of it otherwise we're in big trouble in court. And when I say "we", Phil, I mean of course you.'

Holgate decided to go quiet, let it sink in. The fat man rolled himself upright on the bed. Holgate thought he looked more like a corpse revived than a live man half-killed.

'Four million dollars' worth, Mike Alpert said on the evening news,' Lewis muttered, talking of the value placed on his personal wealth. 'The true figure – sorry to disappoint you, Tom – is nearer two million. That's what I've got to show for twenty years' hard work. Then Alpert says there's at least one power boat, a yacht tied up in the Cayman Islands, a limo, a Porsche and that's just for starters. Well, those things were tools of the trade. Like a blacksmith needs a forge or an anvil, I needed the yacht and the limo. I worked with those kind of things. Then he said investors want to know why Phil Lewis should lead the good life while their savings go down the tube. You think this is the good life? Look around you. Jee-sus.'

'No,' Holgate said. 'I don't think this is much of a life, and if we can prove Alpert brought you to it we can clean out Channel Six News. But we have to handle this real careful, begin to change public opinion way before the case comes to trial, show you acted in good faith in the interests of the community. But' – Holgate paused, knowing Lewis had ducked the question once, and had to answer it sooner or later. 'But all this could be saved if you have the money to pay off all your creditors. Do you have the money, Phil?'

Phil Lewis took a deep breath.

'No,' he said quietly. 'Not after the collapse. A lot of our investments were long, turned a good enough profit when they matured, but impossible to get at in the short term. We were paying interest to everyone, no problem. But now it's different. Can't do it. Confidence gone, whole house of cards collapsed.'

Near to tears now, Holgate thought. Fat Man almost crying.

'Dumb fuck,' Lewis yelled. 'Goddamn dumb fuck.'

During their first two or three meetings in the secure ward Holgate had felt more like a court appointed social worker than a lawyer. And now the Fat Man looked as if he was about to have a relapse, his face ashen.

'Look,' Lewis was saying tearfully, jabbing a pudgy finger at Holgate, and all the while the lawyer could not take his eyes off the wrist bandages as the finger hung in the air. 'Look,' Lewis repeated, 'I can explain it all, and I guess once I do, Tom, you'll either think this is the most extraordinary con in the history of Florida, or just a straight business deal by someone who loves this country and what it stands for and has been helping its government. It's gotta be one thing or the other.'

Holgate was still transfixed by the bandages hovering in the air.

'The money is there,' Lewis was saying. 'To pay off all of them.

Every single friggin' one. But not all at once. Not today. Not tomorrow. Not when they wanted it because of that dumb fuck's television report.'

Lewis snorted loudly thinking of a painful death for Alpert. 'The money is definitely in there somewhere,' he snarled. 'Because the investments were good. Backed up by the best analysis in the world today. Investment analysis that people would pay millions for, that Wall Street could only dream of. And we had it. On our team.'

Lewis was becoming so angry Holgate thought he might pop his stitches.

'You know what interest we were offering?' Lewis yelled at Holgate accusingly.

'Do you goddamn know? Fifteen per cent. *Fifteen!* Shit. With the prime at seven and dropping we were able to guarantee twice that much. Some of these dumb fuckers don't seem to realise you can't do that by sticking it in a goddamn chequing account with Chase Manhattan.'

Lewis was sweating hard, despite the air-conditioning. Holgate decided to push on with the obvious question.

'What's the secret? How do you guarantee fifteen per cent, Phil?' Turn it into a joke. 'And how come you didn't cut me in on the action?'

Lewis smiled, a creepy smile.

'And have you beating on my door like the others screaming how I'd robbed you of your life savings?' he joked, chuckling grimly until the fat on his jowls shook and he heaved under his shirt.

'Look,' Lewis continued. 'You want to know how our business works? We talk to the high rollers, the big names. We had our consultants operating out of Miami across the Caribbean and through Latin America. We had a second team in the Pacific Basin – everywhere from Korea and Singapore. Thailand, the Philippines. Even Red China. Guangzhou. Asian Tigers, you got it?'

Holgate nodded. The Fat Man was on a roll. Somehow he had come back to life.

'We pulled in the big names to sail off the Keys or go fishing for marlin. Maybe play polo. Whatever. You were in on it, Tom, only you goddamn lawyers must've thought it was all pleasure. For you maybe. For me it was business. Strictly business. Always business. All those social facilities helped us get at the real expertise – not just the big industrialists but the finance ministers, the senior government bureaucrats and the national bank chiefs all over Latin America and Asia. They had their fun with us, we provided certain currency services for them, and they gave us information on what was hot in their area. And it worked, until some goddamn asshole called Alpert started pretending I was a playboy, whatever that is.'

Lewis held open his hands as if it was as simple as that, the full explanation. Holgate's ears prickled at the words 'currency services'. He had figured Lewis for a money launderer all along – a high-class one, but a cleaner of dirty dollars nevertheless. A hooker is a hooker is a hooker. The most difficult part with all money laundering was getting cash dollars into the banking system, any banking system. A high rent investment house like WHBL&L would be a good place to start.

'Run that by me one more time, Phil,' Holgate asked. 'How it all adds up to fifteen per cent guaranteed.'

Lewis looked surprised, but then decided to repeat it in words of one syllable.

'Piece of cake,' he replied, smacking his lips. His mouth was feeling dry, and he grabbed a glass of water, swigging it down. 'The information we got was the best you could imagine, which meant we rarely got burned. I mean, when you're handling personal finances for a government minister in Venezuela, or the head of the Philippines national bank, he knows it's best to keep you on side, keep you sweet. So it was like a club with everyone playing a part, having fun, making money. If you were in, it worked smoothly. If you were outside, like that Lehtinen, then maybe it looked like there was something suspicious, like it was a Masonic society or something.'

Holgate was still puzzled.

'Look,' Lewis explained. 'Secrets always seem such a big deal to those not in on them. We are handling sensitive transactions for people who worry that their jobs may not be secure. How many coup attempts were there last week in Manila? Anyway, our clients owe us. We did the usual spread of risk, but because of that expertise, we ended up backing sure things. Had a few dogs, but mostly we

66

came out all right. Fifteen per cent was no problem. We could've made it more. The only problem was the total package had to be long term. When you're talking about hundreds of millions invested in projects from Hong Kong to Buenos Aires, you need a little patience. Alpert screwed us all. You don't have to be a rocket scientist to figure it out. All he did was broadcast a scare story, so there's a run on the consultancy. He's the one should be in jail awaiting trial. He lost the money. We could not service that volume of withdrawals. Once confidence started to go, because of his reports, everybody wanted out. Once everybody wanted out, none of our big name clients would have anything to do with us. If you were preaching austerity to the people of Argentina as part of your political programme, you'd hardly want it known you were part of what everybody thinks is some scam with the playboys in Miami. Alpert sneezes and everybody gets hit by the avalanche.'

Holgate smiled. He was surprised because when he started to look over the documents Lewis had shown him, the investors seemed a pretty weird group. Or groups. Holgate concluded Lewis was laundering pure and simple, and, looking at his client list, probably not drug money. More likely hot money, trying to avoid exchange control regulations or taxes. Maybe he would turn a million in hot money into $800,000 in legitimate investments, tell the customers it was two to one, and skim off the extra $300,000 profit. That would allow him to pay legitimate investors a healthy margin to cover for the laundering deals. There were a million ways once the money was in the system. Holgate rattled off the mental arithmetic with ease. He had seen it all before. But there was something which staggered him – unlike any money laundering operation he had ever seen. According to Lewis's client list, which was probably incomplete, ninety per cent of the investors in WHBL&L were retired American military or State Department officials, all sorted and coded according to rank and affiliation. Maybe there was another secret list of foreign customers – the high rollers Lewis was boasting about, but even if that were true, there was certainly $500 million of homegrown American dollars, mostly from military types, of which maybe $200 million had disappeared. That meant that if Phil Lewis was a swindler he had caused more humiliations to the US military than anyone since Ho Chi Minh. Holgate still could not understand what the hell was going on, and he was suspicious and curious in equal measure.

Holgate had talked to a friend in the Miami District Attorney's office for a steer on where this was going.

'Can't help,' he'd been told.

'You owe me.'

'Can't help because the Feds are looking it over. Don't know where it's going. Ponzi scheme, they're saying. That's it, Tom.'

'Thanks.'

A Ponzi scheme was a pyramid investment racket in which as long as Lewis sucked in new investors at the bottom he could pay the ludicrous interest rates he had promised to the original investors at the top. It was enough to tell Holgate the case against Lewis was getting nowhere. Ponzi schemes like all pyramid cons had two parts – aggressive selling, plus no real investment, because the only source of 'income' was finding new suckers to pay off the old ones. Yet as Lewis pointed out, his downfall came because he was turning away potential investors, and the overheads seemed to go entirely into foreign travel or expenses for hundreds of names who were drawing investment consultancy fees. Holgate could not add it up.

'We made mistakes,' Lewis was saying. 'Real bad mistakes. But not the ones they think we made. We never ripped anybody off. Never failed in seven years to pay the interest we promised, when we promised it.'

'So what were the mistakes?'

Lewis sighed. Holgate looked at him carefully. It was difficult to tell with the Fat Man when he put on his poker face. Angry, Holgate could understand. The big surly look was something else. Maybe the fat boy had worked out a new scam that none of them had ever heard of. Holgate was not pleased. He did not like poker. Or surprises.

'The mistakes,' Lewis answered slowly. 'Or rather the mistake. One big mistake.' He stood up and shifted his bulk uncertainly from foot to foot, then leaned against the wall. 'The one and only mother of all mistakes: we got too big and spread too far outside our true client base. We took on some uneducated investors who panicked, bringing the whole goddamn thing crashing down.'

'What do you mean, outside your true client base?'

'The military,' Lewis shot back, exasperated that Holgate did not grasp the point. 'Our domestic investors were nearly all military. I thought you'd looked at our client list, Tom. Think, for Chrissake, about who we've got on the board.'

'General Seitz,' Holgate said, trying to remember the other names. 'Admiral Cresswood.'

'That's just the start,' Lewis said. 'General Elliott Bradley, former commander of the 82nd Airborne. Former Marine Corps Commandant General Norman Johnson. The ex-CIA chief of station in Chile, Walter Creschi. People like that. Nobody's goddamn fools, and all advisers to my company. All bringing in top level foreign contacts, and all goddamn investors too. You think I could con people like that into parting with their last nickel? This was no widows and orphans fund. These guys were sophisticates playing in a sophisticated market. And it may not have escaped your attention that none of them is squealing that I robbed them. Unlike this Alpert guy that I never heard of and that Scott Lehtinen whose money I would not take.'

Lewis paused for a moment to let it sink in. For a moment the aching in his head had subsided.

'The mistake was to start letting in friends and relatives, then friends of friends and relatives of relatives of the first military people we signed up. All greedy for a bit of the action. Would have offered it to you, Tom, if I'd thought you fitted in. Didn't do it, because I did not want us to spread so wide. But I should've stopped the others from insisting on it. Those were the people who panicked at the first sound of gunfire. Greedy enough to take the risks; too chicken shit scared to hold on for a day or two. Goddamn investment virgins.'

Holgate looked at the fat man in front of him, wobbling with anger. It might just be that Lewis was telling the truth, but not the whole truth. Holgate could smell rotting fish.

'How was it,' he asked, looking straight at Lewis's reddened face, trying to work it out, 'that one news report, which proved to be inaccurate, on a less than popular television show, could bring the whole thing down? How was it, unless your business was shaky anyway?'

Lewis looked at him, perplexed. The headache came in waves, and now there was a sudden return and a thump over his forehead. He grabbed the Tylenol and swallowed the last one.

'Look,' he answered. 'We can follow the entire paper chase if you want, real easy. The DA's office and the Feds will have a dozen accountants going through the files right now. Trying to work out what I'm guilty of. But they'll never be able to follow it. We channelled the money through Panama and the Cayman Islands, Aruba and Curacao, through Hong Kong and wherever else it was necessary to go to ensure anonymity for our clients.

'The company has a liquidity problem, nothing more. Start working on the figures and you'll see how difficult it is to unpick what we've done. But allow some of our own investment consultants to talk you through it and you'll see that I'm telling the truth, Tom. No bullshit. This was a neat idea. A real neat idea.'

Maybe. But what worried Holgate was the speed with which all Lewis's bank accounts had been frozen after a flood of law suits from those he had labelled the investment virgins. It was true that none of the generals or former military officers had panicked, but they had not spoken up in Lewis's defence either. They all seemed to have disappeared. Holgate decided to finish for the day, and called the orderly to let him out, thinking that however dreadful the reporter Alpert had been, he was right in one of his clichés. There were more questions than answers, whispers that the files might be sealed on the grounds of national security, rumours of a CIA connection, something he had been hoping his client might volunteer.

'Tell me something, Phil,' Holgate said, almost as an afterthought. 'There's this talk about a national security angle. CIA maybe. About the Feds planning to get heavy on some of the paperwork. Anything you can help me with?'

Lewis said nothing until he heard the orderly open the door. He looked at Holgate, started to shake hands.

'Easy, Tom. On my wrist. Don't want to loosen the stitches.'

They smiled at each other.

'Nothing I can help you with on that right now, Tom. Let's wait and see what happens with this supposed investigation. They come up with something that looks like it's gonna put me in jail, well maybe I will have to answer all your questions.'

70

Holgate nodded.

'Sure Phil. Have it your way. We'll see how it goes.'

Holgate padded out of the room and down the corridor which smelled vaguely of cabbage. As soon as he left, Lewis began to pace the length of his cell. Four full paces and maybe a half. He turned and paced back. Four full paces and a little more. He turned again. The secure wing was beginning to sound noisy, as if tranquillisers were wearing off the lunatics around him. One loudmouth a few cells down the hall had begun to wail as he did for hours each day. That set off some of the others, and the cacophony began.

'Shut yo' ass, motherfuck ... Yo, yo. Shut fucking up ... Hey ...'

It could not be long now, Lewis thought, before he would be fit enough to leave. A day or two. The investigation of his files might take months, months of questions from accountants and police and FBI agents and journalists and from the Agency itself, months of trying to re-build the house of cards. His head ached again in the stale air. The thought of what was to come made him feel ill. Suddenly he wished he had not been discovered in the bath under the shower, wished the room service boy had been delayed just long enough to let another pint of blood drain away, wished he could sleep forever without waking up to this nightmare of pain and humiliation and betrayal. At that moment Phil Lewis closed his eyes and prayed that he might die.

6

The heavyweight Cuban opened the door of the red Camaro and rolled out into the Florida heat. He walked to the side of the gate and punched a stubby forefinger like a stiff sausage at the key pad beside the gate bell, hitting four numbers which played an electronic tune on the speaker.

Bing – bong – bing – beep.

Kiki the Bear Mendoza pulled a white cotton handkerchief from the pocket of his oversize Levi dockers and wiped the sweat from his forehead. Hate this shit, he thought. Standing here. Always having to wait while Lopez's cameras looked you over like you was some kind of freak show. Jesus. The Bear turned to his right and gave the eye to the staring lens of the nearest of the closed circuit cameras. He was six foot six, 240 pounds, with a mean look that made people back off unless they were armed or feeling especially lucky or tired of life. Kiki stared again at the closed circuit television camera. One of these days. Tear the goddamn thing off the wall, drive the hell out of here. Screw Lopez, screw everybody. One of these days. Not today.

Kiki the Bear could see the iris widen and hear it whirr as it turned in the socket, looking beyond him to the Camaro where Lula Martinez was sitting inside listening to salsa music on the car's compact disc player, blasting it out so loudly the Camaro shook and throbbed with the beat of the bass. Lula Martinez bobbed his carefully combed head to the rhythm. The closed circuit camera made another humming noise and re-focused. Eventually the large metal gates began to roll open.

'Welcome to Paranoid Palace,' the Bear muttered. He stuffed the

72

handkerchief back into his pocket and made his way to the car.

He felt the stickiness of the sweat through the shirt that ballooned round him as if he were pregnant. He clambered inside puffing, put the Camaro in drive, spun the wheels on the gravel and drove through the gates towards the house. Then his fat finger moved to the CD deck and popped Lula's disc out of the machine.

'Eh,' Lula grunted. 'Whad the fuck you doin', *Oso*, eh?'

Lula was chewing hard on gum and pulled his Ray Ban sunglasses down so they rested on his chest, secured by a hot pink cord round his neck. Lula had slicked back his hair so he looked particularly mellow, he hoped, for the meeting with Lopez, cool enough in his new Banana Republic khaki pants and a white and black diamond pattern cotton shirt that he'd just bought in the Coral Gables Mall. He was feeling content with himself, until the Bear started messing with his music. He blinked angrily.

'Yo,' he yelled, trying to gain Mendoza's attention. 'Y'gone fucking crazy, *Oso*, or what?'

'I gotta think,' the Bear said, still sweating hard. 'And this stuff gives me a headache.'

'Whadthefuck,' Lula Martinez shrugged from the passenger seat. 'So Lopez's pissed at us. Whadthefuck. He can go do his own fuckin' dirty work next time, goddamn fucking twinkie, fucking *maricon*, fucking *hijo de . . .*'

Kiki was in no mood for bad tempered Cuban macho. Rule One, you don't mess with Lopez. The man nurses his grudges. Rule Two, if you screwed up, you had to make amends. That way honour was served all round.

Lula, he just did not get it. Thinking with his *cojones* as usual.

'Just keep talking, Lula,' the Bear growled. 'Do what you're good at. Only don't start speaking Spanglish. You know Lopez hates that shit.'

Lula Martinez sniffed huffily. They drove in silence along the gravel flanked by bushes which helped guarantee Lopez's privacy, screening the house front from the road which rose beyond the high surrounding walls. Jorge Lopez Ibarruri had never married, not, Kiki guessed, because there was any truth in the rumour that he was homosexual, but because at the age of forty-seven his ill-tempered septuagenarian mother, Dona Maria, was more than enough woman in his life. Lopez never seemed to be much interested. Neuter. Which meant he had plenty of energy for other things. Worse, Kiki Mendoza thought, as he dreaded the confrontation ahead, was the possibility that Dona Maria herself would be there, make a scene. Lopez might bear grudges, but Dona Maria had a shrill tongue that bored into you like an electric drill. This dry husk of an old woman was as terrifying as anything he had ever encountered. He anticipated her rising voice scrape through the air.

'*Jor-ge*,' she would shriek in Spanish. '*Jor-ge!* A simple task. That was all you asked. Simple. And they failed. Look at them, Jorge. Look at them! Idiots. Why does a clever boy like you have to surround himself with idiots?'

If Dona Maria were there Kiki would have to force Lula to adopt an even more servile air of politeness and civility. The way Kiki knew it would be: they would grovel judiciously and she would treat them like servants, him particularly just because he happened to be part black, not one of the whites she perversely believed were still in the majority in Cuba.

But the point was that Don Jorge had asked them to do something for him, something simple, and they had failed. Big Kiki knew that Jorge Lopez was one of those who really believed in the trickle down theory of human affairs. You make the man at the top happy, everybody's happy. You fuck up, and you eat your share of misery. Which was what they were now going to do. The trouble was, it was far from their fault. It was Don Jorge's, though neither of them would dare tell him. Jorge Lopez was the one who had insisted they try doing a piece of work on Phil Lewis but make it look like suicide instead of keeping it simple, making it work. It was like one of those James Bond films Kiki Mendoza used to watch when he was a kid. You know the type. People were always trying to throw Bond from aircraft or fry him with electricity wires, or hang him upside down from cable cars in Rio de Janeiro, or have him pulled apart by alligators. None of them kept it simple and just shot the fucker. The Bear could not understand it. The thing was, they had known the best place was the hotel, before the hooker arrived, but the windows wouldn't open on the floor Lewis always chose, so they gave up the

74

idea of making him fly 150 feet straight down to the car park without a parachute, and started thinking complicated.

'We shoulda blown the motherfucker away,' Kiki said for possibly the five thousandth time as he drove up to Jorge Lopez's house. 'Only way to do it. Take something big, say a .45 and bang, bang, you're dead. None of this fancy suicide shit.'

'Sure,' Lula agreed, running his fingers back through his hair. 'We'll know that next time. Save us getting all messed up.'

Kiki Mendoza parked the Camaro on the gravel in front of the large sweep of Jorge Lopez's house. It was a bizarre sight.

The house looked like a replica of the White House transported down from Washington DC to the Florida coast. The reason it looked that way was simple. It was the White House. Really. It had the same bow-windowed colonnade looking out to lawns and neo-classical facade, the same kind of proportions though smaller in size.

'Same goddamn security too,' Lula had said to Kiki Mendoza as soon as Lopez had moved in and began his thing with the cameras. 'Like *La Tortuga* needed it.'

'*La Tortuga*,' the Turtle, was the nickname Lopez had been given from his earliest school days at the Jesuit Mission in Havana. As a child he had developed a rough and reddened skin, a kind of eczema which meant his eyes were always hooded and his neck even in childhood had an old man's look, heavy folds and rough jowls. The skin condition kept Lopez insecure and unhappy, and though he had grown into the kind of rich and powerful adult for whom childish names never seem right, the eczema remained untreatable. If no one had dared use the Turtle nickname to his reddened face for years, no one in the Miami Cuban American community forgot it either.

Jorge Lopez Ibarruri's father left Cuba in August 1958 with as much as he could carry. He had run a chain of sugar mills in Oriente province and near Matanzas, and had interests in one of the island's rum distilleries before the revolution. Seeing the way things were going, Ricardo Lopez had put enough money into the United States to ensure that when the fight to save the Batista regime became hopeless, his entire family could move to Florida in the first wave of refugees. The second wave of Cuban exiles came from those who initially had welcomed the revolution then became disillusioned with Fidel Castro and the failure of his regime.

Then the third wave came with the Marielitos, those who left in the Mariel boat lift in the late seventies when conditions became intolerable. It was even worse now, and there were wavelets of refugees all the time, which Jorge Lopez believed might in the end present him with an opportunity to abandon his re-creation of the White House in southern Florida for a real position in the government of a Free Cuba that would rise again once Castro was overthrown. Next year, in Havana. Lopez had increased his father's fortune a hundredfold by property speculation in the 1970s. Behind the Turtle's skin there was a keen businessman, an advertisement for what he saw as the American Way, which by a remarkable coincidence was also his own way.

'I have built condominiums from St Augustine to Key West,' he told *Florida Business World*, when the magazine interviewed him for a feature on immigrants-made-good. 'And made money from Clearwater and Tallahassee to Daytona Beach and Fort Lauderdale. The skill is to know when to take the risks to make the profits. This is still the country of opportunity. And,' he said, straightening his back and proudly raising his reddened neck, 'to that extent I am proof: the American Dream still exists.'

Phil Lewis had put it differently when the two men first met. The expatriate Englishman found in this strange-looking Cuban a degree of fellow feeling about America and its opportunities. He joked with Lopez that the two of them knew the real truth. The American Dream owed less to the rhetoric of Thomas Jefferson than the desires of the Conquistadores or pioneers to make it in the New World.

'Know when to hold them, know when to fold them,' Phil Lewis said, quoting one of his favourite Country and Western singers.

'That's what's great about this country, Phil,' Jorge Lopez agreed, recognising a companion of the soul. 'You take the risks and take the profits, win or lose it all. Hopes, dreams, hard work.'

Lewis nodded enthusiastically. There had been much backslapping and mutual congratulations as the Cuban American exile and the Briton came closer together, combining political interests with personal profit, the pursuit of freedom with the pursuit of happiness.

76

'You know what they say,' Lewis told Lopez when the Reagan administration began gearing up for the Contra war against the Sandinista government in Nicaragua. 'What they say in Washington, what the Anglos say, is that their forefathers came to this New World for political and religious freedoms. And that your forefathers, meaning those who came from Spain, came to the New World only for gold and conquest. It's time people of Latin descent in this hemisphere began to disprove all that and establish their own commitment to democracy.'

Lopez had been more impressed by that comment from Lewis than anything he had heard for years. It was like a charge of electricity, a revelation which put into context all his past life and everything which was to come. The Turtle quickly became involved in Winston, Hamilton, Bellingham, Lewis and Lopez once the special nature of the investment house was explained to him. He also decided to spend some of his windfall profits from the 1970s in celebrating American democracy. That meant five million dollars having his new home designed and built on Key Biscayne, a home that would look like the White House, a home that would show that Latin people had a commitment to democracy too.

'Country's been good to me,' Lopez declared, stiffening his jaw and running his hand back across his thick black and grey hair. He was just over six feet tall, and as fit as any man who swam a mile a day in his own private pool, even though the best dermatologists said prolonged exposure to chlorinated water would make his skin condition worse. 'This country's been good to me,' he repeated, almost to himself, though the target was an architect to whom he had been introduced by Phil Lewis. 'And Ronald Reagan is good for this country. I want you to build me a place like the White House. Casa Blanca for Jorge Lopez Ibarruri, just like the one for Ronald Reagan, two small town boys who didn't do so bad. Get it?'

Lopez made a strangled kind of laugh, and the architect had laughed along. When it came to drawing up the final plans the architect had compromised more than a little, especially when he realised that his client mistook the rear of the Washington White House for the front. But he supposed Lopez knew what he wanted, and he had the money, so back to front, sideways or upside down was what he got. Everybody happy?

Kiki Mendoza parked the Camaro at what was now the front door of Jorge Lopez's re-created mansion, though it was the backside of the symbol of American democracy. Lula Martinez pulled his Ray Bans up from his chest, placed them carefully on his nose, and picked up an Armani cotton jacket from the back seat as Kiki Mendoza's big bear's paw stretched towards the doorbell.

As they waited for the maid to come they looked to the lawns at the side of the house where twenty or so workmen were erecting a large marquee and lining up red, white and blue bunting.

Jorge Lopez was planning to hold a five hundred dollars a plate dinner in aid of two Republican candidates – one for the Senate, and one local South Florida Congressman. It looked to the Bear as if Lopez was hedging his bets: despite all the talk about returning to a free Cuba, Kiki guessed what Lopez really wanted was a safe Republican seat in Congress representing a strongly Latino district. The way he was spending his money backing the right people, it couldn't be far away.

'Remember,' the Bear said to Lula Martinez, doing the thinking for both of them. 'Let me talk. You nod and apologise. You got it? Okay?'

Lula ignored him in silence. There was a stiff little Salvadoran maid, no more than twenty years old, pretty, with a lot of Indian blood, dressed in a white linen uniform who showed them inside. Kiki wondered for a second if his bear's paw might eventually find its way . . . but before he could get around to saying anything Lula was into his *'Como estas, chiquita?'* routine, all teeth and suntanned smiles.

'Como te llamas, eh?' He tried again. *'Que linda.'*

The maid was as happy as a wet weekend, silent and unsmiling as she opened the double wooden doors into a sombre drawing room which in turn opened out through patio doors into a conservatory full of ferns and vines.

'Friendly,' Lula said in English. Still no response. 'Maybe you think English is the lovin' tongue? Eh, *chiquita*? Or you speak Spanglish

78

like me and *mi companero*? *No se habla* nothing, eh, babe, dumbstruck by Lula's awesome charm?'

Lula winked and grinned and the maid backed into the corridor still without a smile, closing the door and leaving them together. Lula was about to say something obscene to Kiki when the big man gently tapped him on the shoulder and nodded towards the conservatory.

A ceiling fan was whirring over a swirl of smoke which coiled out from behind the ferns. Beneath the smoke, sitting in a leather armchair, wearing shorts and a tee-shirt, reading *El Diario de las Americas* with a fat cigar in his mouth sat Jorge Lopez Ibarruri. His face looked particularly red today, the folds on the neck rough and scaly. The Bear could smell Aramis cologne which Lopez used to disguise the creosote aroma from some of the creams he needed to cool the eczema. One blessing: no sign of the Turtle's mother, Dona Maria. Lula strode forward until he was sure Lopez could hear above the noise of the ceiling fan, and then coughed. The Turtle looked up from the newspaper over the top of his reading glasses. He folded the paper and put it to one side. Then he took the glasses off the bridge of his nose, stood and walked towards them.

'You fucked up,' Lopez said matter-of-factly as if wishing them a good day. He walked into the drawing-room and sat on a dark leather sofa. Kiki did not know whether to stand or sit. He looked across at Lula, shuffling his tan loafers on the persian rug.

'Don Jorge,' Kiki said, but was cut off with a wave from Lopez.

'I don't need to hear excuses,' Lopez said, jabbing the cigar end towards the Bear as if it were some kind of weapon. 'You tell me you have done the piece of work for me like I ask you. Then I switch on the television news, and it says something different. It says Miami financier in failed suicide bid. That's what it says. Failed suicide bid. Did anybody ask you for a failed suicide bid? I don't recall anybody here asking anybody for a failed suicide bid.'

Lopez stuck the wet cigar butt back in his mouth and chewed on it, the folds on his neck showing red through the smoke.

Lula Martinez wanted to say something, to explain, but decided it might be better to say nothing. Leave it to the Bear. Do like he was told. He straightened the collar of his new cotton Banana

Republic shirt which cost him fifty dollars and folded the Armani jacket, which had cost him five hundred, carefully over his left arm. Big Kiki was wet with sweat, wringing his fists like there was something inside he wanted to crush or mould into a ball. Lopez took the cigar out of his mouth again.

'I want Phil Lewis to be history,' he said. His grey eyes remained cool. He might have been ordering new wallpaper for the library or a replacement for his Mercedes sports car. 'I want nothing fancy. Nothing com-pli-cat-ed this time. Just Phil Lewis dead.'

The words came out syllable by syllable like a series of daggers aimed at the other two.

'Sure, Don Jorge,' Kiki said. 'That's right. But . . .'

Lula Martinez could not hold it in.

'But *you* was wanting it complicated. Kiki and me'd just want to blow him away. You know, dead is dead, doesn't matter how he got there. You was the one said suicide, but we thought . . .'

Jorge Lopez Ibarruri gave an indulgent presidential wave and spoke coolly, silencing Lula Martinez and making Kiki Mendoza wish he had neither been born nor conceived.

'No buts,' the Turtle said, his face reddening. There was silence then a kind of smile as he thought of a joke. 'Butthead.'

No one laughed, though Kiki Mendoza reckoned: good sign he's in good humour. Maybe he realises it was him who made us screw up. Maybe he won't get pissed at us. Lopez was still talking.

'I want him dead. Within the week. And to make it easy, I don't care this time whether it looks like suicide or not. I even decided to take on a little more help. I got Tony Montoya and Miguel Morales to come in for the job.'

Kiki Mendoza stole a glance at Lula Martinez who sighed loudly at the names. He thought Miguelito Morales was a Puerto Rican sleazeball, a psycho who worked with a Colombian crew and liked the work so much he was supposed to video-tape beatings he gave out. Antonio Montoya was a dim-witted cokehead who hung out with Morales and who Lula thought was about as hard as a cinder block and half as smart. Jorge Lopez was still talking.

'Now the whole goddamn show's come crashing down everybody wants Lewis stiffed. Like it's a society event or something. I could sell tickets to it as easy as to tonight's Republican fundraiser. Just do it, and do it right. Now get out. I've got a dinner to organise.'

There was little point arguing with Jorge Lopez in this kind of mood, and if the Turtle wanted them out of the house before his dragon of a mother appeared that was just fine with Kiki Mendoza. But it was not enough for Lula.

'Look,' he said, making a chewing motion with his jaw like there was gum in there somewhere. 'Look, boss. Me an' Kiki are real sore we didn't do right, okay. So we fucked up, and so we're sorry, okay. But don't make us work with those two scumbags Miguelito Morales and Tony Montoya. I mean, we're talking shit here. It's like, if I got to work with that psycho and that cokehead, well, you know, I guess I don't need that kind of work any more. That's it. I'd rather flip hamburgers or somethin'.'

Jorge Lopez Ibarruri stared at Lula in silence, puffing his cigar until the smoke formed a screen between them. He had already told them to leave once and was not of a mind to repeat it. They stood glaring at each other for a full two minutes until Lula Martinez began to get angry.

'Yo,' he said, raising his voice, as the Bear put a heavy arm on his shoulder, strongly suggesting it was time to go. Lula tapped the side of his head with his index finger, glaring at Lopez and beginning to shout. 'Yo, Jorge. You got some kinda problem here, eh? Maybe you're not hearing too good. I said I'm not working with the psycho, no fucking way. No fucking way. *Entiendes, Tortuga?*'

Kiki the Bear dropped his restraining arm from Lula's shoulders, astonished that he used the nickname, but the Turtle just stood and stared, impassive.

'I mean,' Lula was yelling, 'me an' Kiki bust fucking ass for you day in day out, lookin' after your interests. We don't need Montoya and Morales to make this work. You can count me out. You gettin' this?'

Whatever the Turtle was getting, it was not immediately obvious from his steady eyes and the gentle puffing of his cigar. Jorge Lopez realised there were suddenly two problems in his life, Phil Lewis and now Lula Martinez, where once there had been only one. Still he said nothing, until big Kiki Mendoza's tugging at the sleeve of Lula's Armani jacket became irresistible.

'Okay, okay, *Oso*,' Lula said, calming down and moving towards the door. 'So it's no big deal, okay. But I only work with the people I work with. And I don't work with scumbags like Montoya and Morales, okay. Everybody getting this? Okay.'

As soon as Lula Martinez left, Kiki Mendoza tried to settle his own breathing. The Bear turned to Jorge Lopez and saw obsidian eyes behind the smoke and hooded lids.

'*Lo siento, jefe*,' Kiki said, his jowls heavy with genuine sadness. 'I am sorry. Very sorry. *Lo siento, Don Jorge*.'

Jorge Lopez stiffened from the neck and acknowledged the profound apology with a slight nod.

7

Washington overnight lay like a fruit from which all the juice had been squeezed. Now the liquid was pumping back, re-invigorating and swelling the city. The first of the government workers moved in snaking commuter convoys across Memorial and Chain Bridges. There was an early morning mist over the Potomac, wisps of clouds lingering on the water before the rising sun drove them away. The river was at its summer lowest, slowly pushing through the rocks, down past the wooded banks at the Chesapeake and Ohio canal to where it widened at Georgetown. The night had been stiflingly humid. Without air-conditioning the bed sheets stuck and hung on bare skin; with air-conditioning the shock of the morning humidity hit like a wave of dampness. Rumbling across the tarmac towards the north-south runway at Washington's National Airport, Alex Newman, wearing an open-necked shirt and light cotton trousers, his blond curls moist with sweat, tightened his seat belt, sat back and waited for take-off. He was impatient to get moving, breathing with a sigh of exasperation as the superannuated Boeing 727 lumbered to the end of the runway.

The morning had begun badly as he struggled to put his carry-on luggage in the back of a taxi cab, only to find the driver refusing to turn on the air-conditioning.

'Eats the goddamn fuel, man,' he said when Newman complained. 'Just eats it.'

Newman suffered in cranky silence, his bad mood with the heat and taxi driver nothing compared to his irritation at the thought that he had allowed the only possible holiday he could take before the November election to be hijacked by Helen DeVos.

She might be delightful in some ways, but she was also exceptionally demanding and he was desperate to rest in Miami, to lie like a slug by some pool in a hotel where telephones were unknown and cold drinks came with a snap of the fingers. If he could not escape DeVos and her crazy ideas about CIA conspiracies, Newman could see his annual vacation as nothing more than an extension of the work sausage machine followed by the relentless swathe of Democratic and Republican conventions, campaign tours, the election and the inauguration. He resented seeing his future spread out like a bad horoscope. The aircraft engines changed pitch and Helen DeVos offered him a boiled sweet.

'For your ears,' she said.

'I stick it in my ears?' Newman muttered childishly.

He was unsure how to cope with the presence of the terrorist in chief in charge of the holiday hijack. He did not want to be directly rude, since somehow he had been persuaded to let her come along. Reluctantly, he supposed she was attractive. He admitted to himself he liked her, yet could not find it in himself to be polite and make conversation. Taxi driver. Aircraft. DeVos. Trinity of demons.

'I thought you jet-setting Brit journalists knew that when you suck candy it equalises the pressure in your ears,' she replied in the didactic tone that made Newman want to jump on top of his seat and yell at the top of his voice for her to shut up and give him peace. It had been lecture after lecture, self-improvement tutorial followed by American politics seminar for a week now, and it made him want to throw up. He controlled himself and smiled. DeVos smiled back, indulgently. She found this Englishman mildly eccentric, which seemed a national characteristic. And interesting.

Though for the moment she suspended judgement on whether it was interesting/good or interesting/awful. Newman looked to her to be younger and fitter than his age, early forties. He was slim, peculiarly boyish, almost immature. With his curly blond hair and skin which looked soft enough not to need to be shaved in the morning, she thought him vaguely cherubic. His eyelashes were long and fair and his blue-green eyes, which constantly displayed irritation and an impatience bordering on rudeness, also had a kind of life and vibrancy that she liked. The enigma was that he seemed deliberately to

84

ignore the fact that she was attractive, as if he had stubbornly set himself against finding her sexy or funny. Since Helen DeVos often found men who flirted with her more than tiresome, she was surprised to regard his sober lack of interest as a challenge.

'I do stories,' she remembered Newman telling her when she first formally tried to interest him in 'Deep Blue' over dinner in a Washington Chinese restaurant, 'for three reasons. Because I think they will be fun, because they might advance my career, or because my editor tells me I should do them. This "Deep Blue" Miami nonsense fails all three tests.'

Only an Englishman, DeVos thought, could say something quite so stupidly reductive, yet she knew he was interested in the story and he took little persuading to call his foreign editor who said he thought it might be worth looking into. But what depressed her was the thought that even if the cynicism was part of a show, she was now travelling with someone who probably made the same kind of inert statements about everything in his life.

'I like women,' DeVos could hear him intone, 'for three reasons. For fun, for decoration, and for sex.'

And she realised she was again failing all three tests. But she would be polite and bear it because Newman, or at least his newspaper, was paying the bills on a story which *Combat* magazine could not afford to pursue any other way. They sat side by side guardedly as the aircraft taxied to the end of the runway and waited for clearance to take off. She stole a rapid glance at Newman's fallen cherub face, then pulled out her magazine and began reading.

Newman decided his best defence was silence. There were so many subjects which Helen DeVos knew so much about and was just bursting to let him have it, that if he said nothing at all, she might not dare open up a conversation. He had compiled a list of real taboos: nutrition, exercise and health were the worst. He discovered DeVos was not only a militant vegetarian, but actually part of the evangelical wing of the crisp green salad movement. No fish or eggs, but she did eat ordinary cheese and for some reason, seafood, or at least prawns and scallops and crab, but not fish, which Newman thought peculiar.

'I don't really think of them as animals,' he recalled her announcing, perplexingly. 'You have to draw the line somewhere. My rule is, if it's got a face on it I don't eat it.'

Sitting beside her, staring blankly out of the aircraft window, Newman shook his head in disbelief at the idea that advanced and consequently non-edible life began somewhere in that wide biological spectrum between the shrimp and the flounder. And she could lecture endlessly on sugar in the American diet, its effect on dental caries and a million and one other important issues from cholesterol-free potato chips, to packaging on food products. That was what put him off.

She was nice, but like all Americans took everything so seriously she was incapable of having fun any more.

'Remember fun?' he wanted to yell in her ear. 'F-U-N. Fun?'

She ate what was good for her, read what was good for her, exercised because it was good for her, and had cleared away fun like some unwanted and unplanned undergrowth that cluttered up her otherwise moral behaviour. After her first mysterious telephone call from New York about the collapse of Phil Lewis's investment company, DeVos had turned up at the *Tribune*'s office in Washington to discuss 'the project' as she insisted on calling it. The project, Newman realised, was attempting to persuade him that the story had such strong British and CIA connections it was worth paying for her to travel to Miami to research it. Newman was unimpressed, beset by difficulties in writing a story which tried to explain a Congressional row about the budget deficit and its implications for the election campaign.

'Maybe that budget mess is big news in England,' DeVos said, with an edge to her voice. 'But don't you want to do something original that you don't find on the wires? Don't you want to report on the real America outside Washington?'

Now that was irritating. There was nothing Newman liked less than being told he was merely re-writing AP or Reuters news wire stories when he was working fourteen hours a day trying to make something of a job he had wanted for years.

'Thanks, Helen,' he said. 'Something original. I'll remember that.'

He also remembered that DeVos had worn an extremely short skirt.

Despite all the routine feminist drivel she occasionally spouted, she had attractively long legs, even though they were hidden, bizarrely in Washington's summer heat, behind knitted woollen tights. That figured. DeVos was always going to be a few sandwiches short of a picnic. He supposed it was part of the new feminism: she feels guilty about the fact that men like looking at her, so she starts covering up with woollen leggings her grandmother might have worn.

Shit, Newman thought, shaking his head as the 727 rumbled down the runway, picking up speed. I'm getting more and more eccentric as this stupidity progresses. Right now, as he looked sideways at DeVos he saw her figure was hidden behind a loose cotton shirt, bagging like a sail. Her brown hair was tied back and disciplined which was a disappointment since he liked it long across her shoulders. Her face – no make up, of course, or none that he could detect – was always animated, always interested; high, firm cheekbones and liquid brown eyes full of energy. But the tongue. The pink perpetual motion machine with the slight New York accent that could cut through the traffic noise of Mid Town Manhattan. Aaah!

The 727 accelerated hard and Newman closed his eyes.

'Deliver us, Lord,' he said silently to himself, and meant it.

To his surprise, Newman had begun saying such things. This Lord stuff had become something more than finger crossing. To his great alarm Newman had started to believe there might be a God. Worse, he had even started to talk to him, as if lack of alcohol or impending old age had turned his mind, twisting it through the banality of a midlife crisis by searching for the meaning of life.

'Well, that's easy,' he thought. 'I'll just ask Helen. She's bound to know the meaning of life. Knows every other damn thing.'

The God business had begun in January, during the presidential election primaries when they were trying to land in Manchester, New Hampshire in a blizzard. Newman had said 'Deliver us, Lord,' to himself, just because the words came to him, not addressing anyone in particular, and then somehow the pilot had managed to put the plane down, bumping through the snowstorm, skidding across the frozen runway. Newman suddenly believed that his prayer, three words, had saved them all from crashing and dying. It was stupid.

The pilot had landed the plane. Alex Newman had said secretly and silently 'Deliver us, Lord.' There was no connection between these events.

None.

The plane would have landed anyway.

No connection.

Deliver Us Lord.

The engines whined. Suddenly the nose of the Boeing 727 edged upwards and a few seconds later Newman could see the waters of the Potomac, 14th Street Bridge and the traffic pushing in nose to tail from Virginia. The pilot turned hard left. Before the wing rose to block his view, Newman caught a glimpse of the Capitol, stark against the blue sky, the green sward of the White House lawn, the Ellipse, the Mall, all the splendid colours of a fine hot day in Washington.

The jet turned a half circle heading southwards over the Pentagon following its coastal flight path for Miami. Newman took a can of La Croix mineral water (no sodium, no calories) from the flight attendant and insisted on no ice either. Then he produced a tourist guide to Florida from his carry-on luggage and read it ostentatiously. He looked over at DeVos, reading her copy of *Time* magazine, catching her eye then turning away. The thing he truly could not understand was her most peculiar relationship with Chuck Lowell. She not only produced *Combat* with Lowell, but also chose to live with him – which, like living in Manhattan, seemed to Newman a pretty strange choice. Newman met Lowell during his first month for the *Tribune* in America, while spending a night with the New York police. The plan had been to write an article for the *Trib*'s colour supplement about crime: bright lights, big city, the idea someone has once a year on any British newspaper.

'Did you know,' the *Tribune* foreign editor Mike Holroyd said to Newman in the apologetic and lugubrious Lancastrian tones he used when organising his foreign correspondents. 'Did you know – and I'm sorry to tell you this if you do, Alex, but did you know that if you are young, male and black in New York City the likeliest cause of death is murder.'

Newman admitted he did not know that, but silently vowed that

88

if ever during a visit to New York he started becoming younger or blacker he would leave immediately.

'Or,' Holroyd continued, 'that the life expectancy of a black man in Harlem is about the same as that for a Bengali in Bangladesh. So much for a kinder, gentler, America.'

The result of this conversation was that Newman was travelling in a police squad car in the Bronx. He had arranged with New York Police Department public affairs to be driven to the scene of every murder in the city that night, to write a short profile of each: 'Last night another brutal slaying . . .' was the headline, taken from the local television news. Newman was with a *Trib* photographer sent over from London. At the first scene there was a smear of red on the sidewalk and a crumpled body with what remained of its head in the gutter. The body had once been a twenty-five-year-old Puerto Rican shot dead as he stood on a street corner. Two things Newman would never forget. The man had been chewing gum, and as he lay on the sidewalk a pink ribbon which Newman at first thought was his tongue, dribbled out from his lips. Second thing: the corpse wore a light blue muscle vest. Tattooed on his right shoulder was a line from a 2-Live Crew rap song.

'Me So Horny,' it said.

What made the whole thing so eerie was that hovering above the splatter on the sidewalk was a tall, skinny cameraman with his hair in a pony tail and a straggly beard. Chuck Lowell, a Sony betacam on his right shoulder and a battery light pointing full blast at the human debris in the gutter, was filming the corpse.

'Vulture Video,' the New York Irish hardnose from police public affairs had said to Newman.

'Stiff Patrol. That's his job. Howdja like that for a living?'

Newman and his photographer climbed out of the squad car and when Lowell switched his battery light off, Newman introduced himself.

'Alex Newman from the *London Tribune*.'

'Hey, Chuck Lowell, what's happenin'.'

Lowell explained he was a freelance cameraman who worked nights mainly on the police beat, filming the drug murders and other big crimes, selling pictures of the mayhem after dark to whomever wanted them. While the *Trib* photographer did what he could to take a few shots, Newman kept Lowell talking. He was intrigued by the idea of someone earning a living filming dead bodies on the streets of New York night after night. It would make a better feature than the routine idea of following police patrols under NYPD escort. 'The New Yorker for Whom Crime Does Pay,' Newman thought. 'Cashing in on Crime in the Big Apple.' That sort of thing. He arranged to spend the following night with Lowell, writing a profile of the video artist at work. Lowell said that sounded like a neat idea, then demanded a fee of $200. They settled on $100, plus dinner before they set out. Newman was not sure how big a dinner he would want before looking at the rare meat on the city's sidewalks.

'It's easy when you get used to it, man,' Lowell said, pointing at the array of radio receivers inside his van, all switched on at full volume. He tidied up a stack of Eric Clapton cassettes to allow Newman to sit down.

'See,' Lowell said, pausing as if his tongue worked only slowly. 'See, the way it is. None of the local television stations wants to tie up their people on this work. There's no percentage in it for them. No profit in it, you know what I'm saying? How many times they use this kinda stuff? Drug killings, every day, every night. It's like a war zone. Beirut or something. People get tired of it. I do the business and turn over the pictures to whoever wants it at $200 a pop. A good night I can make a grand. One good murder. Five customers.'

'Well,' Newman asked, 'tell me about a good night.'

Lowell signalled to him to shut up for a moment while one of the radios crackled with urgency. Then he laughed.

'New York's finest are just arranging to meet at an all night DoNut shop on the Upper West Side. No shit. That's why our cops are really New York's fattest. Mr Pig's always got his goddamn nose in the trough. Somebody's trough, anyway.

'No,' he said, turning serious again. 'A good night has nothing to do with the quantity of what's going on, you know what I'm saying. Quality is what sells. Like any business. Always quality.'

Newman was now truly puzzled. Lowell, Helen DeVos later told him, came from a well-connected Boston family, had gone to university on the West Coast and dropped out after spending a lot of time either blowing white powder up his nose or trying to stop doing so. He was clean now, otherwise DeVos would have had nothing to do with him, but the parental money had run out.

'Quality,' Lowell said, sensing Newman's confusion, 'means rich people gunned down in their homes: a preppy woman mugged and murdered on her own doorstep, mainly the rich and white facing up to the shit that happens to the poor and black. If it's poor and black drug killings in this city I can't sell it. You wanna get on television, go murder someone rich. See, there's even a class war when it comes to crime and publicity. Whole goddamn thing sucks.'

Newman wrote it all down.

'Even death has its price in New York City,' he wrote. Holroyd would like it. Newman spent the night with Vulture Video listening to Lowell's assessment of the class struggle in America and watching the man at work. At the end of his shift at nine in the morning he was taken for coffee and danish with what Lowell had mysteriously called 'the love of his life'. Newman was led to a dingy office with an apartment attached off East 30th. Inside there was a very attractive brown-haired and younger woman – Helen DeVos. Newman assumed she was the love Lowell had been referring to. Not quite.

'Welcome to *Combat* magazine's international headquarters,' Lowell announced proudly, dumping his battery belt among the papers and dirty coffee mugs on the table. 'This goddamn magazine sure is what makes it all worthwhile.' Newman did not like to say he had never heard of it, never seen a copy. Lowell gestured round the room.

'*Combat*,' he said. 'Best investigative magazine in this country. Exposes what the bastards are up to and They Don't Like It.'

Newman heard how *Combat* investigated CIA covert operations and US foreign policy, particularly in Latin America. Politely he asked for a few copies and while Lowell put on the coffee, he skimmed through them. The magazine was surprisingly slick, reasonably well written, though too detailed. Newman was going to tell Lowell as much but abruptly the cameraman said he was tired and wanted to go to bed. Newman rose to leave. Lowell told him to finish his coffee.

'Just leave the hundred with Helen,' he called over his shoulder,

91

and went to bed. Newman munched through his danish, sipped the coffee and began making conversation with DeVos. He soon discovered she was responsible for much of the writing in *Combat*. She had graduated with a Masters in Journalism, met Lowell while researching for ABC television on a crime documentary series. Lowell had wandered in to the ABC offices one morning with pictures of the overnight murders.

'Oh,' said Newman, thinking this was not quite Romeo and Juliet. 'Oh, I see. And now you're in a crusade against the CIA.'

DeVos shook her head.

'I don't go for all this secret government-shadow government conspiracy stuff,' she explained, as if Lowell were to blame for the worst of the 'CIA as Anti-Christ' tone of *Combat*. 'Conspiracy theories and crusades I'm not interested in. Real conspiracies, maybe I am interested in, just skip the theories. We try to publish the facts about US covert action, because if the press does not scrutinise it, who does? And if that has a political spin-off, it's not my problem. These people should be held accountable for what they do in America's name.'

Newman tried to figure out what this bright woman saw in Chuck Lowell, who seemed like a piece of Fleetwood Mac that had been cryogenically preserved since 1972, loon pants still intact. He arranged to keep in touch with DeVos, ignoring Lowell as soon as he wrote out the cheque for $100, but subscribing to *Combat* anyway. Soon afterwards she began supplying occasional tip offs. Newman followed them up and mostly he liked what she found and what he made of it. In all of this he had repressed his vague feelings that she might be attractive, assuming that one quick grope of her knee would blow their whole professional relationship forever. Now in the aircraft over southern Virginia, as if reading his mind, she pushed her magazine to one side and smiled.

'I'm looking forward to this,' she said, nudging his arm. 'Haven't been in Florida for a couple of years.'

'I've never been.'

'You'll like it. Maybe you should go see Epcot and Disneyland.'

The aircraft levelled out at its cruising altitude as it moved down the barrier islands on the Carolina coast. The day was clear and Newman could see the chain of sandy beaches and shallow lagoons.

Disneyland, Newman thought. Well, every time she explained the Phil Lewis story to him he thought it part of Disneyland anyway.

'You've got to do the story, Alex,' Helen had said at the dinner in the Washington restaurant. 'You're going to Florida anyway, which would make it easy for you to look into it. Why not persuade your office to let you have a few extra days to research it? Maybe extend your time in Florida. A longer vacation.'

Newman took a swig of iced water, remaining unconvinced.

'Stories about CIA skulduggery in far away places are not going to run in Britain. Anyway, if it's such a big story why is none of the American papers or TV networks interested? You must have tried them.'

Helen smiled.

'The American networks,' she had said, swallowing rice, 'do not take risks. They have bureaux in Miami which tell them this story is just a financial scandal, $200 million maybe, complicated to explain. No pictures. Some of them did offer a piece, only it was knocked out because the anchors don't much care for it. And there's the election, the budget mess, the Middle East. No room. Anyway, CIA stories are not really on the American agenda any more. They think that all passed with the Cold War.' She put the scallops in her mouth daintily, dabbing at the corners of her lips with her napkin. 'So the networks hear from Miami that there is doubt about the CIA connection, and they play safe. Newspapers are the same, leaving it to the *Miami Herald*, though I hear the *Wall Street Journal* is interested. But they'll do the wrong story, a profile of Phil Lewis "The Brit Who Conned Miami" or something like it. It's not a bad story, but it's not *the* story either.'

'Okay, Helen,' Newman said, exasperated at her inability to get to the point. 'You tell me what the story is that I should be so keen to waste my holiday on. In a sentence, what's the scoop in Miami?'

'I don't know,' she had said, picking at the plate of shrimps. 'Truly. It is not clear to me, except that I have an instinct for these things and I know there is a story there. Have I ever failed you before?'

'Probably,' Newman had replied. 'Anyway, I'm not going to tell my foreign editor it must be a story because a radical troublemaker from New York has an instinct it might be.'

93

Helen laughed.

'I told you. I'm a journalist, not a radical. Chuck is the radical. I'm just interested in the stories. The facts, dear Alex, let's start with the facts.' Newman sipped his bottled water while she recounted what she knew about Lewis and his investment corporation.

'So?' Newman had asked when she finished.

'So, like I say, Lewis and Lopez are big names down in Miami, but Winston, Hamilton and Bellingham aren't in the team photograph. They don't exist. Never did, as far as I can see. They were just added to the notepaper to make it look good.'

'Is that a crime?'

'Not that I know of,' DeVos said. 'But unless it's some English tradition, it certainly didn't arrive on the Mayflower. Let me finish.'

She meant it would be quicker if Newman were to shut up. He shut up. She concluded with the story of the disgruntled former investor, and the local television investigation, then she paused, picked up her beer and drank a little. Newman noticed there was just a hint of lipstick on the glass. Cherry coloured. Some radical. There was a concluding moral to the story.

'You can write the script yourself. There's a run on the company because thousands of investors start thinking, Jesus, it's another Bank of Credit and Commerce International scandal. We've been ripped off and there's no safety net. Everybody wants their money back, and they want it yesterday. Lewis files Chapter Eleven. Twenty-four hours later he tries to kill himself, because he's been disgraced. Or more likely, somebody tries to kill him because they've been ripped off. Like it so far?'

Newman shrugged. Helen sat back as if in triumph, waiting for a proper response.

'So?' Newman asked again, meaning, so why should I be interested?

'So,' Helen replied acidly. 'We have at the very least one hell of a con-man story. Lewis was a Brit who had been in the States for twenty years. He ran Miami polo club. He lived in a two million dollar house off the back of Coral Gables and he mixed with the celebrity set of the Caribbean, the East Coast, Palm Beach, you name it. The Sultan of Brunei played at the club. Marcos's banker socialised there. Hong Kong businessmen, tired Japanese carmakers, Australian mining magnates came to paradise to be looked after by the guy who is now facing one-to-twenty as a swindler of widows and orphans.'

'So,' Newman repeated irritably. 'So, so, so, so, so what?'

Helen DeVos looked at him as though he were a hopeless case. She pushed back a stray brown hair with her left hand and leaned forward towards him across the table, looking at him with those very liquid brown eyes. Newman knew then he could get to like her if she wasn't so damn prickly about everything.

'As I tried to explain on the telephone, Lewis is now claiming that his whole investment company was a CIA front. He told the *Miami Herald* it was a CIA proprietary, though he refuses to spell out what it was supposed to be doing, and the *Herald* is trying to figure out whether he's telling the truth or now trying to con them as well.'

'Tell me again, what's a proprietary?'

'The CIA owns it but it's run through front men, carrying out legitimate business. In other words, we have at least a con man story with a strong British angle, a high society con, and the Brit in charge of it says he did it all for the boys in grey suits out at Langley. Good, huh?'

'Why would they want a proprietary company based in a finance house in Miami?' Newman asked.

'Don't know. That's for us to find out when we get there. But the Agency needs to pay agents with untraceable money. It doesn't help your cover to get a monthly cheque stamped CIA, does it?'

'Okay, but why shouldn't Phil Lewis, if he's such a great con man, come up with the CIA story as well? Claim he did it for his country, or his adopted country, or whatever, just a different kind of con.'

'You mean national security as the last refuge of a scoundrel,' Helen laughed. 'Well, we have some evidence already I suppose. The company board – even if Winston, Hamilton and Bellingham do not exist, those who do are an interesting bunch.'

'Such as?'

'Lopez for one,' Helen whispered. She had looked round the Chinese restaurant as if suddenly it was full of FBI agents. All Newman could see was a black family group and what looked like half a dozen businessmen sipping martinis. DeVos was paranoid again.

'His father Ricardo was one of the heroes, if that's what we're supposed to call them, of the Bay of Pigs. He was captured by the Cubans and was held until they were all exchanged by Castro for baby food. He was supposed to have been CIA. Nobody can say the same for sure about the son, though he took over from the father's small time export business and built it up.'

'That doesn't make him CIA. It's not a genetic defect,' Newman argued.

'No, but it's a start. Even if Lopez can prove he was a non-executive director he's still part of the mess. Then there's Sonny Hunter. He's a three star US air force general – well, retired general – now living in Fort Lauderdale. He was part of the supply team for the hill tribes in Laos during the sixties. He's not CIA directly maybe, but he's got a long intelligence background. There's General Seitz, who was also in on it, and Walter Creschi, who retired two years ago as CIA chief of station in Santiago, Chile. Interested yet?'

DeVos finished her scallops and turned to the stir fried vegetables, not waiting for an answer.

'Then there's Vice-Admiral Cresswood, formerly commander in chief Pacific Fleet based at Pearl Harbor until he retired ten months ago and moved out to southern Florida, where he also found his way on to the board of this cosy little company. And most intriguing of all, Charles Atwood. He was an earlier CIA head of station in Chile, way back in 1973 when Allende was overthrown. In 1989 he was in Panama right up to the invasion, and had been in Argentina at the time of the Falklands War in 1982. Now he's retired and he winds up with a seat on the board. And those are just the ones I've tracked down. There are others too, I'm sure. But even you must be starting to get interested, Alex.'

Newman was interested, and amused.

'So you're telling me this con has been perpetrated on the good investors of Miami by some blow-in from England, aided and abetted by all the military commanders in US forces between San Diego and Guam, plus the CIA?'

'Maybe,' she laughed. 'Or maybe not. I mean, do we believe all these guys are crooks? If so, quite a story. Or do we believe that Phil Lewis duped them like he fooled the widows and orphans who

96

invested with him? Could be. Another good story. Or do we think the Agency was really in this after all, and all these old buzzards were making their pensions stretch by doing a little freelance work for Langley while enjoying the sun of Miami? That's what I'm betting on.'

Newman began to laugh. He did like this woman. Mostly.

'You know, you're a really fucked-up person, Ms DeVos, if I may say so.' He was pleased she seemed startled. 'I mean, here we are in the capital of the world's greatest democracy, where America's leadership is being decided by the most excellent electoral process man can devise, eating decent Chesapeake bay shrimp and scallops, and all you can tell me is that US intelligence is conducting a stinking conspiracy to rip off American investors.' He paused for breath. 'I like it. Sounds terrific. When do we go?'

Newman spent the next three weeks regretting those last four words, or at least his use of 'we' when 'I' would have been sufficient. He realised he had invited her to ruin his holiday.

Now sitting together on the aircraft he turned the conversation over and over again. They were in clear blue skies over the Georgia coast and would soon be in Miami. Something came to him, something so obvious and yet missing from Helen's original story that he nudged her gently.

'Hey, Helen,' he whispered. 'You never explained to me why you said all this was connected to "Deep Blue". What's this "Deep Blue"?'

DeVos pushed her magazine away and smiled. It was another lecture. Newman could see it coming like a gathering cloud, and he had asked for it. Then she looked rather coy.

'Just a hunch,' she whispered back so softly he had to lean towards her until he could smell the sweetness of her light perfume. 'Not facts.'

'A hunch about what.'

'Well . . .' She began to explain that in the early 1980s after the Reagan administration had adopted the New Maritime Strategy to increase the US Navy to 600 active warships, there were constant internal disputes.

Some in the White House argued that the 'Six Hundred Ship Navy'

97

was a slogan not a strategy, a pointless show of firepower which would never be used. The real threat came everywhere from Afghanistan to Lebanon and Angola to Iran, when hostile regimes defied the United States and Washington looked impotent.

'So some of them at CIA – especially the Director, Bill Casey – wanted to get Reagan's attention about rolling back communism, not just containing it. They wanted to get the president to fix clearly on the problem.'

'What'd they do,' Newman scoffed. 'Make a movie? Draw him a cartoon?'

'Almost. They drew him a picture.'

Newman frowned. He was not very good with riddles. DeVos smiled again.

'Out at the Naval College in Annapolis, the first class they teach you in strategic studies is real simple. The idea is to demonstrate the importance of shipping lanes. They give you a map and you are told to colour the coastline of countries allied to or friendly with the United States blue. Then the bad guys, you colour their coastlines red. And the neutrals get a yellow.'

DeVos paused as if she had already delivered the punchline. Newman frowned again. The captain of the 727 announced they were making their descent into Miami. They fastened their seatbelts then drew close together.

'Well,' she continued. 'The story goes that in the early eighties when they were working out the New Maritime Strategy some of the boys at the CIA produced just such a map for Reagan. They wanted to offer him an achievable way of rolling back communism. So they drew the map of the Western Hemisphere, and presented it at one of the morning intelligence briefings. It was as simple as anything from grade school. It showed Cuba a big mass of red all across the Caribbean, and Grenada, and Nicaragua red on the Atlantic and the Pacific side, and the threat to the Panama Canal. El Salvador, Honduras, Guatemala and Colombia were coloured pink to let him know just how the subversion was spreading. So they said to Reagan, hey, look at this, Mr President, you see the problem. We got to do something. Red everywhere. Red tide coming up to Texas.'

98

Newman drew back for a moment and looked into DeVos's intent eyes. The 727 was bumping towards the tarmac.

'And?'

'And what Reagan is supposed to have said was authorisation enough in that where-the-hell-am-I way of his for any kind of covert operations they could dream up to roll back the red tide and anybody else who got in the way. It led to the fight against the Sandinistas and the FMLN in Salvador, and the invasion of Grenada, and I guess, indirectly, to the overthrow of Noriega in Panama as well.'

Newman perked up.

'So what did Reagan say?'

'Well,' DeVos replied. 'The story goes, Reagan picked up their map of the Americas, with its red coastlines and pink parts, the threats to the sealanes, the Panama Canal and the worries about communist expansion, and Reagan goes: Deep Blue, guys. Next time I see this, I want it coloured Deep Blue. All of it. Deep Blue.'

The aircraft hit the tarmac with a thump, braking hard as the pilot reversed thrust. When they slowed down to taxi speed Newman looked at DeVos, their faces a few inches apart, scenting her perfume.

'Jesus, Helen,' Newman said, shaking his head and breathing hard. 'Jesus.'

He turned to look at the terminal building a few hundred yards away with the sign 'Welcome to Miami' emblazoned across the airport roof.

'Deep Blue,' he muttered. 'Deliver us, Lord.'

8

There was a shower moving across Key Biscayne, warm moist air and raindrops puckering the surface of the sea and turning the sky from blue to grey. As the rain cleared in the early evening a rainbow began on the seashore and ended behind the palms further down the beach, their leaves rustling on the tail of the breeze. Phil Lewis watched the shower's progress anxiously. Thinking he heard a noise he suddenly stood up from the sun lounger in the covered patio at the back of his house, accidentally kicking over an open bottle of Molson. He swore violently as it emptied on the grass.

'Shit. Is there nothing around here which is capable of going right? Shit. Shit. *Shit.*'

Lewis kicked the beer bottle so hard it skidded across the grass and into the water by the dockside. He waddled inside and checked the security system. Nothing. He looked at his watch. Fifteen minutes to go. There was still time. He had rehearsed his big scene so often he was like a star footballer tense until the game begins. The house was low and long, one of a dozen different styles clustered round a man-made lagoon just south of Coconut Grove, each with its own dock where power boats or yachts could tie up. The house cost Lewis two million dollars seven years before, and was worth at least twice as much now. Yet like everything with Phil Lewis's name on it, the court had seized it as a material asset which could be used to pay off those he had allegedly defrauded. Lewis and his family had been told they could live in the house until the criminal case and subsequent civil actions were settled, but Lewis's wife, Nancy, had already left.

'I need you now,' Lewis had pleaded. 'Help me.' But the marriage had been functionally dead for so long his appeal made his wife laugh wildly.

'Help you!' she shouted. 'Why don't you get some of the girls you used to spend Fridays with to help you? Or some of your big name friends who were always at the parties on your yacht, parties, in case you've forgotten, that I never got invited to.'

'That was business,' he replied lamely. 'Government business.'

Lewis paced up and down at the back of the now largely empty house bare chested, wearing shorts. He rubbed his fat belly with the palm of his right hand and began moving round the garden, rehearsing his speech for the dozenth time. On bail, he had become a kind of transient, living in tourist hotels in the Art Deco district of south Miami Beach, working on his case by day in a corner of Tom Holgate's office, returning to his own house infrequently to sit for a few hours and think. And for special occasions, like today. It was too dangerous to move in again permanently. Next time they would use something more accurate than knives. Lewis rubbed his bare belly and sighed. He thought of the years when he first realised he had made it in America. A success. Rich, witty, slim and good company, and no one ever turned down an invitation to play tennis at the house or to a party on board the 'New World'. That was the real greatness of this country. The way people could pick up their lives, change, start again, begin a new business or hobby and be the best they could be – then drop it and start again. America was the land of eternal beginnings. Everything was possible and nobody cared what you were but what you are. And what Lewis was now, as he suddenly realised, was nothing.

Suddenly all the women who could not get enough of him were out of town, permanently washing their hair or otherwise unavailable. He had spoken to more answering machines in the last two weeks than in twenty years. Lewis picked up another beer, walked into the main room, lay on the sofa and nervously switched on the television. He kept thinking how he would have to play his few remaining cards, like a desperate gambler looking for one big win to reverse a string of bad luck. He knew that was precisely the kind of gambler who usually lost. He could not settle, flicking between channels aimlessly on the automatic control, finding nothing he liked, but leaving the pictures on anyway. Then the fat man pulled out his collection of Country and Western tapes, slipped one into the deck and racked the stereo up loud.

'*Allison's*

In Galveston . . .'

He sucked at the top of the beer bottle, deep in thought.

'*All my ex's*

Live in Texas . . .'

It was difficult to think clearly. Difficult to see how anyone could win with the cards he had been dealt. There was only one hope. That was to persuade them his desperation was so great it presented a danger to them all, that if he lost this last big hand he would destroy the whole game, turn over the table, bring everything and everyone down.

'*That's why*

I hang my hat

In Tennessee . . .'

If the Agency was prepared to play hardball, sealing the files and denying all knowledge of his affairs, then he would have to show them he could go even further. There was no middle course. He would nuke the bastards. Mutually Assured Destruction. The old Cold War deterrent. Lewis closed his eyes and sighed deeply, trying to relax, trying to discount the inevitable dangers of pushing them too far. Then he heard the gate bell ring in the hallway and he stood up and pulled a short-sleeved shirt over his shoulders. He switched off the music and padded on bare feet towards the closed circuit television cameras at the security station. He saw a tall, distinguished man in a dark suit standing by a car at the front gate.

'Who is it?' Lewis barked, looking at his watch. Six o'clock. He was punctual, at least.

'Warren Cabot.'

Lewis checked Cabot was alone and opened the gates. The lawyer slid back inside his car and drove through, parking at the front door of the house.

'Nice place,' he said. 'I like the Spanish style.'

'Huh,' Lewis grunted, reluctantly shaking the proffered hand. 'C'mon in.' From the moment the two men looked each other up and down there was a distance between them. Cabot saw the

102

unbuttoned shirt and fat belly spilling over ridiculous shorts. He heard Lewis's English accent corrupted by American inflexions, and wondered where all that he admired in the British was hidden in the fat sweating body before him. For his part Lewis saw an overdressed dummy with an Ivy League manner which grated on him. He recognised immediately in Cabot the habit of condescension which repelled him so much in upper-class Englishmen, and which he had hoped he'd escaped in the United States.

'Glad to see you left your hit men at home this time, Mr Cabot,' Lewis said, leading Cabot to the covered patio by the pool. 'I don't need another shower right now.'

Cabot began protesting that the hit men had nothing to do with Langley.

'Wasn't us,' he said firmly, sitting in one of the wicker chairs as Lewis heaved himself back on to the sun lounger. 'You must believe that, Mr Lewis. It had absolutely nothing to do with us.'

Lewis sucked his Molson bottle like a wet-nurse's teat.

'Well,' he snorted. 'I guess you would say that, wouldn't you.'

'Absolutely wasn't us,' Cabot repeated irritably, shining his spectacles on the end of his tie and staring myopically in Lewis's direction. 'Whoever else you have defrauded and tricked in this sordid mess, we do not settle grievances with renegades that way. I should have thought you had been around long enough to know that.'

'Huh,' Lewis snarled. 'If Vince Terrelli's as pissed off with me as you said on the telephone, then how come he hasn't tried having me stiffed? Not the sort of guy to have ethical problems on a little matter like that, is he? Or Boone. He's a real moralist, wouldn't you say?'

Cabot silently agreed. In the heat of the patio the lawyer was feeling uncomfortable in his grey suit, button down shirt and blue-and-teal-coloured tie. He pulled a handkerchief from his pocket and began wiping his spectacles again, clearing away the small beads of sweat from his eyebrows.

'For God's sake take your jacket and tie off,' Lewis bawled. 'You look like you're going to blow a fuse.'

Cabot did as he was told, unbuttoning the shirt and rolling up his sodden sleeves. He had asked for the meeting, insisted on it, and he wanted to get down to business, but as he prepared to begin Lewis waggled a fat finger threateningly under Cabot's nose.

'Before you say your piece I want you to know one thing. You take me to court, Cabot, and I'll blow apart every operation I was ever involved in. Every goddamn thing. Maybe you're not too familiar with them, now the Company only does social work, or whatever they call it – analysis.' He spat out the word like an oath. 'Analysis, yeah. But Boone and Terrelli and me, we go way back to when we sometimes had to get our hands dirty, and Langley knows I know where the bodies are buried and who buried them. Go ask them if they want to keep pushing me until I tell everything in court, or to the media or in Congress. Ask them if that's what they want.'

The finger stopped waggling and Lewis slumped back on the lounger.

'And while you're at it, remind the miserable sons of bitches that I have a stack of company documents – part of my unwritten memoirs, you could say. If anything were to happen to me, like another accident in the shower, my lawyer and the *Miami Herald* would receive enough information in the mail to embarrass Boone, Terrelli and the Agency right through to the next millennium. That's supposing the Agency can survive that long, bearing in mind the effect all this might have on the election campaign. You getting the picture?'

'Is that a threat, Mr Lewis?' Cabot asked brusquely, using the word 'mister' like a knife.

'Fuck me, no, Mr Cabot,' Lewis responded in mock surprise. 'It's goddamn blackmail. Just make sure you recognise that.'

Cabot raised his eyebrows and watched the sweat trickling down the side of the fat man's face. Lewis took a pull on his beer, and calmed down. This was mean poker, but he was on top. He offered Cabot a Molson, but the lawyer refused.

'How about a soda?'

'No thanks. Maybe a little iced tea.'

Iced tea? What was this idiot trying to pull with his iced tea and his doctor-telling-a-patient-he's-about-to-die-of-cancer manner?

'Sorry,' Lewis said cheerfully. 'We're fresh out.'

'Listen,' Cabot said, leaning forward towards the fat man. 'After what you've already done, and particularly in view of what you're now threatening to do – disclosures which might embarrass current intelligence operations – there will be plenty of people at Langley who will wish that whoever tried to eliminate you in the shower had succeeded. But nobody in the Company was behind it. Nobody. You have my word on it, and I have the word of the Deputy Director, Vincent Terrelli. It was not one of ours, Mr Lewis.'

'What exactly do you want, Cabot?' Lewis interrupted, the bad temper returning. 'You insist on coming all the way to Miami as a messenger boy. So what's the message? If it's to tell me the Agency didn't try to have me stiffed, you could have saved your airfare.'

Cabot sat back in his chair and rubbed the sweat from his eyebrows with the palm of his hand. Despite the hostility in Lewis's manner, he could sense that Lewis was on the run.

'We have a deal for you,' Cabot said flatly. 'And even before I spell out a single word of it, I must advise you to take it. If you refuse or start quibbling, the offer will be withdrawn. If you act on the threats you have just outlined you will go to jail for national security crimes as well as fraud. There are many who want to see you suffer each ring of purgatory, and are only prepared to contemplate a deal now because you have kept your indiscretions within bounds.'

'So far,' Lewis interrupted again, childishly taunting him. The more he listened, the more he found in Warren Cabot everything he detested about the English class system but with an American accent. Cabot had a thin and handsome face with a hint of a suntan from what Lewis suspected was yachting off Cape Cod. But he also had a get-in-your-place-peasant manner like some anal retentive upper-class Brit coming to tell the poor grammar school boy what was good for him. Well, Lewis thought. Screw you and your patronising bullshit.

'You have to go to jail,' Cabot was saying. 'There's no way out of it. Terrelli wants you inside for ninety years and thinks he can get you held in solitary if necessary, maybe in Terminal Island or Texas or Marion, Illinois. The way he sees it, you should spend the rest of your life where your family will find it difficult to visit, because you betrayed the Agency's trust and are embarrassing and threatening something very dear to him.' Cabot paused. 'His career,' he concluded with a grim smile. He was not sure how far to push with this. He decided to try a little more. 'You probably know Terrelli wants to succeed Richardson as DCI and hopes he might make it after the election. You, and the potential scandal you represent with its echoes of the bad old days, appear to be one of the few things standing in his way. I suppose you know that.'

Cabot paused again to let Lewis picture his next ninety years in Marion federal penitentiary. When he thought it had begun to sink in even to Lewis's Molson-befuddled brain, he twisted the knife again.

'Where is your family, by the way?' he asked with a pleasant smile.

'Why don't *you* tell me where my family is,' Lewis shot back, resenting the crude manipulation. 'And how they're doing. You must have tabs on them. If you know everything about me down to the last detail so that you are certain I'm going to accept a deal which involves me going to jail for no crime, then I guess you know it all. Where do you think my family is? Playing tennis out by the pool?'

Cabot stared unblinkingly at the fat man, who was reddening in his temper.

'Wherever they are,' the lawyer said calmly, 'you had best be advised that if you fail to cooperate, Terrelli will ensure that your jail sentence will be served to cause maximum inconvenience to all of you for the greatest possible length of time. Don't forget that.'

'Scottsdale,' Lewis interrupted icily. 'My wife is in Scottsdale, Arizona, since you were polite enough to ask. Existing on family charity and whatever she can scrape together since you froze all my funds, seized the house and shredded my credit cards. But I am sure that punishing the family of someone who has yet to stand trial is all part of the new American way, all done in the great cause of national security and the new world order. It's what we won the Cold War for, isn't it?'

'You used to be rather keen on national security yourself, sometimes,' Cabot replied. 'For example, when the Internal Revenue Service tried to enter the Winston, Hamilton offices to conduct an inquiry. If I remember correctly, the files show you demanded not just that the CIA issue a written instruction telling the tax investigators to look elsewhere, but you also said the White House should become involved. Boone tells me you tried to force the National Security Council to call off the IRS as well.'

'You know nothing about the operational side of this business, Cabot, or about my relations with Richard Boone. I simply informed the CIA and the White House of the potential for trouble – for them, not for me – if the IRS were allowed to look at our accounts. That was a legitimate security concern. So don't sit in my house and tell me I tried to pull something dirty. You have no idea what is at stake here, and it seems to me you have no idea of the sacrifices people had to make for their country or what they believed in.'

There was a prolonged silence, during which Cabot stared at the pool and the boat dock beyond. It was true he did not know much about operational matters, but he wanted no lectures on patriotism or morality from an alien criminal. He let the silent depression hang in the air between them for a few more minutes, studying Lewis's porcine face. Lewis gazed back, determined to show no emotion. Cabot cleared his throat and began again.

'The alternative, if you co-operate, is that even though you go to jail, you'll be out in a year. Two at the most. We'll make sure you're transferred to a minimum security prison near Scottsdale or wherever is most convenient. We will also ensure that your family receive an ex gratia stipend for the period of your incarceration.'

Lewis snorted.

'What do you mean by co-operate?'

'Plead guilty.'

'On all indictments?'

'Yes.'

'No.'

Silence again. Lewis was on the edge, but had no choice. To plead guilty to a series of fraud indictments meant everything would collapse. He would go to jail. Yes, fine. He would lose the house, the money, the polo club, the yacht, Miami, everything he had built up and had tried to create over twenty years serving – he was sure – the best interests of the United States during the worst times of the Cold War. Then he would be out of jail in two years time, a broken down ex-con, no future and because of his work, no past either, wife and family long gone. A failed Englishman in a corner of a foreign field that was forever . . . merely foreign. He could not do it. Cabot broke the silence again.

'I repeat. While you are in jail your wife and family will collect a service pension from the Agency – half what you would have earned if you had retired honourably, but considerably more than they will have to live on if you go to jail without this deal. And if you want my opinion, much more than you deserve.'

Lewis wanted Cabot to shove his opinion, but he also wanted the lawyer to realise something.

'It may come as a surprise to you, Cabot,' he spat out, 'but the reason I have so little interest in your schemes is because I believe I have done nothing wrong, broken no law, stolen no money, and acted in no way which was contrary to the interests of this country or the oath I took when I began working for the Agency. All I did,' Lewis continued, rubbing his fat cheeks with the palm of his hand, 'at worst, was to set up the most effective money laundering operation anywhere in the United States for the exclusive use of American government officials carrying out business in support of the foreign policy of this country. If that is illegal, then I plead guilty. If these were crimes then they were crimes of patriots.'

Cabot was repelled by the self-satisfied nasal whine in which Lewis tried to justify his actions. It was the familiar bleat that patriotic ends were so wonderful that any criminal means were permissible, especially in Lewis's case, ends which happened to enrich him by three million dollars a year, according to the preliminary FBI report. Cabot was incensed to think that Boone and Terrelli could have recruited and used the fat slimy creature before him, and allowed Lewis to build up a crooked empire for personal profit as well as a dubious public service. It showed precisely what was bankrupt about the Agency's leadership. And who was this Englishman to appeal to American patriotism?

Cabot was so disgusted that he was determined to sniff out the whole trail which would inexorably lead back to failed judgements from Terrelli and Boone. In the meantime it would be pointless to argue with Lewis, who appeared to have calmed down, asking only what would happen after he was released from prison if he accepted Cabot's deal.

'Would the family pension continue?'

'Yes,' Cabot said. 'But remember, if you create waves of any sort all bets are off.'

Lewis snorted in disgust.

'Look, Mr Lewis,' Cabot said energetically, twisting the 'mister' again. 'I get the impression you still do not realise how angry you have made some people. You start taking unauthorised investments from people you are not supposed to deal with, outside the circle of those with specific Company or military clearance. Then you start playing games with currency exchange and money laundering. You skim off the profits, such as they are, and mismanage the rest so it's like a juvenile accountant's idea of a game. You might think all these are the crimes of patriots, but up in Langley we think you are a dangerous loose cannon that has to be thrown overboard or else the whole ship might get blown up. Am I getting through to you now?'

There was no response from the fat man.

'I've read a lot of your paperwork,' Cabot continued heatedly. 'How you ingratiated yourself by spying on the anti-Vietnam war radicals. A few lucky breaks and then you somehow convince the Company you're an asset on international investment. A street pimp would be better qualified. You seem to assume that because the essence of the operation was to falsify accounts and commingle funds, you could introduce your own bank account into the process. Well, you were wrong. Dead wrong.'

Cabot stopped for a moment to hide his exasperation, then began again in more moderate tones.

'Either you take the deal and protect the Agency and all it stands for, or you attempt your smear and suffer the consequences. The choice is yours. Think about it.'

Lewis liked the flush of anger on Cabot's cheek. For an Ivy League asshole it made him seem almost like a human being.

'Let me think about all this,' Lewis said coolly. He was sure he still had a manageable hand to play, and he knew most of all that the Boy Scout in front of him did not have a clue about the true nature of Deep Blue and what he was dealing with. Fat Phil Lewis decided that now was a good time to raise the stakes.

'Yeah, let me think about it,' he repeated. 'Consult a few people. Talk to Tom Holgate, my lawyer. But you say you looked into my background file: are you sure you saw my complete file?'

Cabot shrugged. What was a complete file? When was anything complete? He had seen enough to indicate that for twenty years the

CIA had promoted this foreign mediocrity to a position of great influence and allowed him to act dishonestly on a grand scale.

'I saw what I needed to see,' Cabot replied.

Lewis laughed, a full-bellied laugh like Falstaff before Prince Hal. 'Let me tell you a little something about myself,' he said, his eyes alive with passion. 'Why do you think I came to this country? Eh? Well I'll tell you. I defected from Britain. That's right. I escaped over the wall, or over the Atlantic – it's much the same thing – because I had a certain vision of the country I wanted to be part of, and Britain in the seventies was not it. This was the land of hope, this was the place I could re-invent myself. And it was convenient for your government agencies to have someone with a British passport yet an American wife and a commitment to the American way of life, running things in Latin America. I was the one who could travel to Cuba with no problems. I was the one who, when Deep Blue started, was the obvious choice on the financial side. Not any of the grey suits from Langley, but some poor goddamn Brit who really believed there was an Evil Empire of communist subversion that had to be confronted not just contained. I'm one of the genuine believers, and there used to be a time when people valued that.'

Lewis stopped for a moment, cooling down. He looked at the impassive face in front of him. He began to think that maybe the dull lawyer might be right for the new times and that he, Philip Andrew Lewis, warrior of the Cold War, had had his day. Maybe.

'I asked you whether you had seen my complete file,' Lewis continued. 'And you were unable to answer. That is because you most certainly did not see it. No one would give someone like you the right to assess my contribution to the national security of this country, because you are not trusted enough, Cabot. You get that? You are not *trusted* to know what I know. And if you think that makes me feel superior to you, damn right it does. Damned superior.'

Warren Cabot blinked behind his spectacles. He wondered whether the fat man was about to explode as he puffed out with self importance.

'Question Two,' Phil Lewis continued. 'You ever hear of something at the heart of Deep Blue called Columbus?'

Cabot stared back blankly. He did not need to answer.

'Terrelli never mention Columbus?'

Blank.

'Boone?'

Blank.

'That's what I thought. Well, I want you to make sure they realise what's at stake here. Tell them the word in Cuba is that Columbus is unhappy. He wants out. What with the publicity this is getting here I shouldn't be surprised if the Cubans don't track him down and shoot him. You tell Terrelli. Tell Boone. Think you can remember it? Want to write it down? THE CUBANS MIGHT SHOOT COLUMBUS IF YOU KEEP JERKING PHIL LEWIS AROUND. Got it?'

Cabot had, he supposed, got it. He would also tell Terrelli and Boone that their man in Miami was disintegrating mentally.

The meeting was over. Phil Lewis was giggling to himself after his little speech, laughing at some unseen and unintelligible joke, presumably about Columbus. Whoever that was. Cabot stood up and Lewis, still chuckling, stood with him and together they walked to the hallway. The two men did not shake hands, nor exchange another word. Warren Cabot opened his car door, started the engine and spun the wheels on the driveway gravel, accelerating through the open gateway without looking back.

As Cabot left, Lewis closed the electronic outer doors. The beer bottle in his hand was empty. He stretched his arms above his head and yawned. Then he ran his hand down his face to wipe away the sweat, thinking he had done enough for now to persuade Cabot and the others he had the weapons of deterrence at his disposal too. He pulled a beer from the refrigerator and popped its top, pouring half the contents into his mouth and swallowing quickly.

'Shit,' he belched, suddenly thinking of the dangers Columbus faced, and feeling sorry for him. 'Maybe the way this is going Columbus really is gonna get smoked in Havana. But if I don't keep up the pressure, the bastards are going to put me away for ever in a stinking jail in the middle of nowhere. Jesus. What a choice.'

He belched again, then held the beer bottle in the air for an imaginary toast.

'Columbus, old son,' Lewis said aloud, waving the bottle in front of him. 'It was me or you. An' it looks like you lost.'

9

Before the bedside alarm clock could ring in his home in Arlington, Virginia, Vincent Terrelli silenced it. He looked at the time, shortly before six in the morning, slipped from bed and glanced at his dozing wife. It had been an uneasy night, hot and full of bad dreams, the terror of pursuit by faceless men along dark passageways. Terrelli woke repeatedly, sweating hard, turning up the air-conditioning and the ceiling fan. Normally he slept well: like a baby during the Gulf crisis; blissfully when the Soviet Union was falling apart or the invasion of Panama was contemplated; but not now. The telephone call he had received late the previous night from Warren Cabot lay in his stomach like a bad meal.

'Columbus,' Cabot said. 'Lewis keeps talking about Columbus and Deep Blue. Says Columbus is in danger. That he could be exposed. I don't know what to make of it. Thought I should raise it with you, Vince.'

'Don't worry about it, Warren,' Terrelli replied coolly. 'Leave it to me.'

'But Columbus . . .'

Terrelli repeated, 'Leave it to me, Warren,' again in a tone that meant the conversation was over, and Cabot rang off, perplexed but somehow cheered by the reaction. Now, in the early morning light, Terrelli pulled on shorts, Nike running shoes and an old tee-shirt. He opened his front door, threw the newspapers inside and began to jog in a loping stride down the long driveway towards Chain Bridge and the C and O Canal tow path. When he was appointed Deputy Director of Central Intelligence it was suggested that Terrelli might need personal protection for his early morning runs.

112

He insisted otherwise, with a stubbornness and hostility to opposing views that had carved out his long intelligence career in the Air Force, the National Reconnaissance Office and at the CIA. Despite his education and high technology background, Terrelli liked to play up to the image that when you think Italian American, you think tough. Once when his staff jokingly called him 'Don Vincent' after a Mafia Godfather, Terrelli liked the idea so much he signed a few general office memos with the nickname.

'The worst failing,' he repeatedly told his staff, 'is not to make a decision. I'd rather you decide wrong than that you don't decide at all. In this building we should stand up or sit down but never wobble. That's the biggest failing in our analysis. We never get off the goddamn fence. When I'm briefing him, the president gets nothing that wobbles. Everybody understand this?'

Terrelli settled into his running stride on the footpath across Chain Bridge. He felt better in the open air. Cabot's report of his conversation with Phil Lewis made Terrelli recognise that he was facing tougher decisions than at any time in his career. A month ago Terrelli would have said – barring accidents like the voters going weird on election day or the president's sudden need to reward someone for political favours – that he was sure Vince Terrelli would become the next Director of Central Intelligence, the first Italian American ever to hold the post, setting the tone for the year 2000. Another immigrant would have arrived in America. He could not imagine anyone standing in his way.

'At the top level, the Agency is still a gentleman's club,' Terrelli once joked with Richard Boone. 'And you're no gentleman.'

'Guess that's true,' the Deputy National Security Adviser replied. 'And I guess the moment Don Vincent takes over, Congress will realise they've been made an offer they cannot refuse.'

Under the Bill Richardson regime Terrelli already carried many of the responsibilities of the Director anyway. Richardson insisted that Terrelli, the intelligence professional, deliver the morning briefings to the president, thus granting him unprecedented access to the White House. It also left Richardson free to do what he was best at – stroke egos on Capitol Hill, bring together all the other disparate bits and pieces of the intelligence bureaucracy, and stop the turf wars between the CIA and DIA and NSA and NRO and the rest. Now Cabot was beginning to emerge as a pain-in-the-ass candidate for Director, on the margins but impossible to ignore, and the business with Lewis suddenly made Terrelli recognise the increasing seriousness of the challenge. Above all, the CIA did not need to be led into the new world of the twenty-first century by some Boy Scout intelligence virgin with five university degrees and no common sense.

Terrelli jogged towards the steps that led to the Potomac river and took them slowly, at a walk, until he reached the sand-covered towpath beside the C and O Canal, one of his favourite jogging trails. He began running again, his breath coming in easy, regular bursts, as he felt his stride settle. The truth was that the Cold War had been good to Vince Terrelli. And maybe now it was all over, it might be all over for him too. Instead of emerging as the leader of American intelligence in the new order, he might be nailed by Warren Cabot as the definitive Yesterday's Man.

'Huh,' Terrelli grunted. 'Not without a goddamn fight.'

A few months back Terrelli had contributed an article to the magazine *Foreign Affairs* which he called 'Reflections of a Cold Warrior'.

'For four decades,' he wrote, in what he thought was his most trenchant passage, 'the Cold War motivated every major US initiative from foreign aid and the creation of the Peace Corps to the Bay of Pigs and the Vietnam War. It led us into dubious alliances with ungrateful allies and sometimes blatant enemies of freedom, yet when the profit and loss columns are added up by historians, the fact that we were prepared to bear any burden, support any friend, oppose any foe so that liberty might triumph, will make the forty-year struggle one of the most significant in the history of this nation. And,' he added as a final justification, 'do not forget who won the Cold War. We did.'

Terrelli smiled as he jogged and silently recited the words to himself. Extracts from the article had been reprinted in *Time* magazine under the headline 'The CIA and the Next Forty Years – Langley's Intelligence Intellectual Speaks Out'. There had been some ribbing among the foreign policy hands he socialised with at the Cosmos club, jokes at his expense about the word 'intellectual', which normally came with uncomplimentary epithet 'liberal', but in this case

114

'intelligence intellectual' sounded fine. There had even been comments at the White House during the regular morning national security meeting about Terrelli's attempt to 'set the agenda' for the 'new CIA in the New World Order'. Whatever that meant. The point was, they liked it. He had built up credit at the bank. He might need it. Terrelli checked his watch and at the end of twenty minutes turned for home. He climbed slowly up the steps back to Chain Bridge, re-crossed the Potomac as the earliest commuter traffic began heading towards Washington.

He ran up his long driveway and stood on the porch at the rear of the house overlooking the river, pulling an old warm-up top over his sweat shirt, letting the panting of his breath and pounding of his heart subside as he thought again of his conversation with Cabot.

'Columbus,' he gasped in disbelief. 'Jesus. Lewis is actually talking about Columbus.'

It was clear to Terrelli that Phil Lewis knew precisely what was at stake. This election would be a turning point. If the president lost, Terrelli was sure the new administration would dismantle the effective heart of the US military, cutting the guts out and then scrapping the most expensive parts of the intelligence community. Didn't these bozos realise there were plenty more where Saddam Hussein came from? Did no one learn anything from history any more?

'It is like giving away your overcoat,' Terrelli had written in his Foreign Affairs article, 'just because it's the first sunny day of Spring.' The trouble was, more than enough members of Congress seemed willing to risk the cold, and he knew Warren Cabot would be happy to sit in the chill, buck naked, if that was what they wanted. Terrelli rubbed the sweat from his eyes. The simple fact was that if Cabot found out the full story of Columbus – from Lewis or anyone else – he could use it to ensure Terrelli would never become DCI. And there was an even more awful scenario. If Lewis did as he threatened and told everyone the full story, the whole thing would come crashing down: Columbus, Terrelli, Boone, maybe even the Agency. Surely the fat Englishman could not be quite that crazy? The maid brought freshly squeezed orange juice, coffee and wholemeal toast. Terrelli could see the Potomac valley and the trees sweeping towards Washington to his right.

115

He took a sip of the juice, which made him feel better, then he thumbed routinely through the *Washington Post*. There was a story leaked by a 'senior administration official' who he assumed, reading the Washington code, was the Secretary of State. It smelled like one of his. This 'senior administration official' claimed that the Cuban economy was on the verge of collapse and had been weakening steadily since Moscow cut its aid to concentrate on its internal upheavals. Nothing new. Terrelli had said as much himself in public testimony on Capitol Hill two months before. He checked the story byline. It was from their State Department correspondent, which meant it really was just the Secretary of State sucking up to the *Washington Post* and preaching the latest accepted wisdom. Nothing new in that either.

He picked up the *New York Times*. There were more reports of chaos in Moscow and unrest in the Balkans. Zero on Cuba, and more importantly zero – not even on the financial pages – about Phil Lewis and the mess in Miami. Nothing, thank God, about Columbus. According to the press digest of major newspapers FAXed to him at home every morning, there had been nothing on the story beyond the Miami or Florida papers and one short and turgid article with no CIA dimension, in the *Wall Street Journal*. Terrelli sighed. Ever since he had become Deputy Director he had shared a sense of foreboding that one day his job of predicting the unpredictable would come unstuck because, bizarrely, those who supported the CIA and those who were most hostile suffered the same delusion: that the Agency had extraordinary powers, Good or Evil. The right wing zealots always criticised the CIA when foreign policy went awry, as if the Agency was either incompetent or lacked the political will to pursue America's interests. Terrelli thought it was like a clergyman criticising God for allowing Evil to exist. Even worse, in Terrelli's view, were the left wing screwballs with their stupid magazines and paranoid politics, and their own version of the omniscient omnipotent agency. To them Vincent Terrelli was not God but the Anti-Christ, one of those in charge of the forces of evil across the globe, manipulating the world in Satanic American neo-imperialist interests.

'I'm trying,' Terrelli thought. 'Doing the best I can.'

He smiled and drew apple butter across his toast, pouring a mug of coffee. Terrelli's own view was that ever since the CIA had been created there had been divisions between the Cowboys and the Analysts. The Cowboys were the men in dirty overcoats who handled covert operations. They wanted to change the world, and Vincent Terrelli was for a time their boss in the Directorate of Operations. The Analysts thought it was difficult enough to understand the world never mind change it. They thought the CIA's main function was to provide the president with information. Now, as the key briefer to the president, Terrelli was their boss, and the president had made it clear which side he was on. He wanted better analysis, and the Cowboys had had their day. Just after the last election, but before his first inauguration, the president-elect travelled out to the CIA headquarters at Langley, Virginia to see Terrelli. They sat together for two hours, drinking coffee, planning the new intelligence gathering apparatus for the new century. The president-elect said he found the CIA building disappointing, unable to live up to its own mystique. It seemed like the headquarters of a third rate, provincial manufacturing company. Two things stood out: the fifty or so small stars carved in stone in the entrance hall, each star standing for a CIA agent killed in the execution of his duty; and the quotation from St John which formed the CIA credo and was the lobby's centrepiece.

'And ye shall know the Truth, and the Truth shall make you free.'

'There will have to be changes,' the president-elect had said, staring round Terrelli's office. He was puzzled, because for an Italian American Terrelli had peculiar taste, decorating the room with a series of paintings and objets d'art reflecting life on the frontier and the American West.

'I'm going to put a career politician in as Director of Central Intelligence. Bill Richardson,' the president-elect said. 'His job will be to kiss butt on the Hill. Keep Congress out of the intelligence business, but make them feel good. Your job, Vince, will be to clean up any of our past mistakes. Bury the bodies. I'm also going to put a lawyer in here – old friend, name of Warren Cabot – to be, if you like, the moral guardian. Keep it all clean. And Boone can stay as CIA liaison at the White House.'

The president-elect paused, his attention momentarily distracted by a brightly painted Navajo war shield. 'Look,' he continued. 'I want no sleaze. We just don't need it. The tide's turning irrevocably in our favour. Think every day on your way to your office that I want no more stars carved on the wall of CIA operatives killed. I want more of St John and less of the stars. No surprises. Clear?'

Yeah, Terrelli thought. No surprises. Clear. The conversation, as he was sure the president knew, haunted him daily as he strode through the lobby, caught between St John and the carved stars. Immediately he began an internal audit of the kind of operations that might run into trouble, and scaled down the remnants of Deep Blue.

He never thought it necessary to mention to the president the existence of Columbus or his role as the most valuable asset-in-place at the top of the Cuban military. Besides, the compromises they had to make to keep Columbus were ... tolerable, Terrelli thought. Tolerable, but best not discussed with the moral guardian.

Terrelli drained the last of his coffee and rubbed the stubble on his chin. As he shaved moments later, he wondered whether he should now begin to explain everything before the White House found out some other way – from Cabot, Lewis, or worst of all, from the newspapers. Terrelli nicked his face with the razor and watched the blood spread through the foam. He pulled out toilet tissue and stuck it down to seal the cut, washing the remains of the shaving foam away. Then he stood looking at his face again in the mirror, the pink toilet paper sitting absurdly on the nick on his cheek, reddening slowly. Damn it, he thought. It was like Pearl Harbor. The whole Lewis mess could have been prevented, and yet it might turn into a complete catastrophe.

'Pearl Harbor,' he spat out, thinking of it as a massive strike against him and everything he was trying to achieve. He rubbed his face with a towel and stepped into the shower. The water pounded on his face and hair, shaking him fully awake. He dried himself briskly. The truth was simple. Sometime, a long time ago, in a different world, under different pressures to attack every weak point of communism, they had done things he was really proud of, and a few things he was not proud of any more. Columbus was a bit of both.

'I guess we sold our souls for Deep Blue,' he had once said mournfully to Richard Boone when the Lewis affair first broke.

'I guess,' Boone replied. 'But we got the map to change colour,

118

didn't we? Not just in this hemisphere. Most of the goddamn world. All except Cuba. And with Columbus and the others, it's just one more heave.'

Terrelli splashed after shave on his face, wincing when the alcohol hit his open cut. He dressed with care – dark blue suit, starched white shirt and red and white striped tie – then he walked into the bedroom where his wife, Elizabeth, was awake listening to National Public Radio news. He kissed her gently on the forehead, mumbled a goodbye, then walked outside to his black limousine. Once in the back seat, the driver handed him a small package with a summary of the overnight cables and intercepts. He skimmed it briefly – nothing much to add to what had already been prepared late the previous night – political gossip from Moscow, naval intelligence about the Russian Far East submarine fleet, movements out of Petropavlovsk. Rumblings in Syria. As the limousine moved gently down the drive, Terrelli pushed the button to slide up what was called, he assumed with forgivable hyperbole, the Total Security Screen between him and the Agency driver. He selected a secure channel and called a direct line to the old Executive Office building. Richard Boone had just reached his desk after his morning workout. He ran his hands backwards across the stubble on his head and felt the strength in his neck muscles.

'Fit for anything,' Boone thought, remembering the old motto from Laos. He wondered how long he could keep at it. Right through his fifties, he was sure. But at sixty? Seventy? When did even those who don't quit have to quit?

'Boone,' he said, answering the secure line.

Terrelli's voice sounded slow and grave, as if there'd been a death in the family. Boone sucked in his breath.

'Rich,' Terrelli said with strained bonhomie. 'How are you?'

'Fine, Vince,' Boone replied, with little interest in the social chatter. 'Just fine. How about you?'

'Great. You had a good workout?'

'You know the way it is. Not as good as it used to be. Like everything else.'

Terrelli quickly dropped the Washington foreplay.

'Warren Cabot has seen Lewis,' he said grimly. Boone waited for the punchline. 'He called me last night. Lewis says he'll think about our proposition, but Cabot thinks he's flaky, that it'll be no deal. It looks as though he's going to try to make a fight of it, the crazy bastard. He doesn't realise who he's messing with.'

'That's too bad, Vince. Too bad for all of us.'

'Yes,' Terrelli said. 'And he asked Cabot to pass on a message.'

'Oh, yeah.'

'That Columbus was in danger.'

There was an ominous pause on the line. Boone took a deep breath, flexed his muscles and set his jaw.

'Jesus,' he said. 'The son-of-a-bitch.'

'Yeah, Rich.'

'Did Lewis say anything else?'

'I don't think so. Not about Havana anyway. All he did was threaten to expose everything to the newspapers or Congress unless we make a better deal.'

Boone rubbed his forehead with the palm of his hand, then swept the fingers back over the stubble on his head.

'Pity the fat bastard didn't get it in the shower,' Boone said. 'Real pity.'

'We've got to talk about handling this.'

'I know.'

'There's a lot at stake.'

'You think I don't know that?' Boone spat out angrily. Then, coolly, 'Why don't you come round here after the briefing?'

'Yeah.'

Terrelli put down the telephone. His limousine was running along the C and O Canal towards Georgetown, speeding in light traffic. He could see an aircraft taking off from National Airport making a sharp turn for the west towards Virginia. Absently he watched the joggers running on the canal towpath. A few minutes later the limousine turned into the south west gate of the White House. The sun was playing on the White House walls, long shadows in the early morning light.

Terrelli climbed out into the heat and humidity. It was already beginning to feel uncomfortable. He walked past the Marine Guard thinking that if all this went wrong he might still go down in history.

Instead of being the first DCI of the new order he might simply be dismissed as the last dinosaur, made extinct by Warren Cabot. There had to be a way out of checkmate, and he would find it. Somehow he would ensure that Lewis did not talk. Somehow he would protect Columbus from the Cubans, and from Cabot. Somehow he would explain to the president the problem that lay before them all. A cover up was unpalatable but necessary. Prudent. As he walked towards the Oval Office, Terrelli felt his knees tremble the way they did when a teacher spoke sharply to him in fourth grade. How sympathetic would the president be to the surprise that Deep Blue had been run from the White House by Boone and the National Security Council, to avoid oversight by Congress of CIA covert activity? Terrelli was becoming seriously agitated.

He sat in the small ante-room nearest the Oval Office and smiled at the secretary who offered coffee.

'No, I'm fine thanks, Melissa.'

He was early, as always. Richardson had not yet arrived. The president was calling Europe. The National Security Adviser was with him. Terrelli should check the cable summary one more time. He pulled the presidential briefing papers from the case and sorted them on his knee, looking for the summaries. Stony faced, he pushed them aside. Instead he drew out another brown manila file from behind the rest, put it on top of his case and studied the cover intently.

'Columbus,' the file said in capital letters. Terrelli breathed hard as he opened it and hoped for inspiration.

10

The grey parrot at the pool of the Miami Blue Lagoon Hilton croaked once and turned its head to the right. Alex Newman padded down through the hotel lobby in his new floral print swimming shorts, his Ray Bans perched on his nose, carrying a plastic bag with towel and sun screen and the combined bulk of the *Miami Herald*, *New York Times* and *International Herald Tribune*. Newman exchanged pleasantries with DeVos and forced himself to chew gracelessly her recommended Hilton Health breakfast which seemed to consist of various types of animal feed, bran, oats, nuts, twigs and leaves mixed with fresh fruit and No-Fat Ultra-Lite non dairy creamer, all washed down with decaffeinated coffee. It made Newman feel ill, expanding in his stomach like the contents of a horse's nose bag.

The alternative – blueberry pancakes and syrup or two eggs over easy, fried bacon, hash browns, toast and jelly was too disgusting to contemplate on an empty stomach. Besides, he could not face having to sit through an entire breakfast with Helen DeVos looking at his fried bacon and telling him meat was murder. She went to her room to make a few calls while Newman returned to happy thoughts of possibly enjoying his Florida vacation after all. Standing at the side of the hotel pool he stretched in the warm sunshine and turned to find a lounger. He was perversely cheered by the lack of success DeVos was having in trying to contact Phil Lewis. Lewis's lawyer, some overpaid stuffed shirt called Tom Holgate, had refused to take the calls. That meant as far as Newman was concerned the work of the trip was falling apart. He would give it twenty-four hours, then rent a car to go down to Key Largo, maybe try scuba diving for a few days on the Keys and return via the Everglades and Alligator Alley.

The prospect put him in such a good mood he thought wildly that he might even invite DeVos to join him. When she skipped the lectures about politics, the CIA, and the future of the world, to his surprise Newman found her good company. Extremely good company. He grinned. All in all, Phil Lewis's lack of interest in giving them an interview was very encouraging.

'Mr Holgate is busy with another case right now,' the secretary stated repeatedly. 'But he sure will call when he gets the chance. All righty, thank you and have a nice day.'

All the nicer for talking to you, Newman thought. He took a lounger facing due east into the rising sun. It was already strong as he rubbed the suntan cream on his forehead and cheeks. Across the lagoon he could see the first of the morning's skiers trying mono-ski deep water starts and falling off as the tow rope skimmed the water behind the circling motor boat. Newman had always found holidays difficult. Once, almost ten years before, he had travelled to the Grenadines at a moment of crisis – a marital crisis provoked by the ultimatum from his former wife that their relationship had a slender chance of surviving unless he was prepared to come away and talk things through with her without interruption. No newspapers, Newman promised, were available at their hotel on a quiet beach in St Vincent.

'No television, and no radio. Promise. Just you and me.'

She had been unconvinced.

'You mean you won't take your shortwave,' she asked suspiciously.

'No radio, I said. No BBC World Service. Nothing. Just the two of us.'

On day three of that holiday Ronald Reagan had ordered the 82nd Airborne Division and US Marines to invade the nearby island of Grenada. On day four, Newman found himself trying to rent a boat in St Vincent that was prepared to risk sailing through the US Navy to land on Grenada too. Newman's soon-to-be-ex-wife was unable to understand why, as she put it, a military action with fewer casualties than a British first division soccer game could force him to walk out of their marriage and into a leaky sailboat bound for Grenada. Newman did not much care. He promised himself two things: that he would never marry again because there was too much emotional capital locked up in such an arrangement; and two, of more practical use, he would never, ever, allow himself to be without a shortwave radio. He stretched across from the sun lounger to the table, picked up the *New York Times* and scanned the front page.

'*Economy in Jeopardy*,' the paper said. '*White House seeks reversal of Fed tight money strategy. Democrats scent Campaign Issue.*'

Always the ones for the snappy headline. Newman looked round the pool to see half a dozen other sunbathers reading books or newspapers. He felt his back stick on the plastic stripes of the lounger. He was beginning to relax properly when out of the corner of one eye he caught movement from the hotel. Walking past the palm trees towards the pool was a striking woman with long brown hair and a well-fitting yellow bathing suit which showed off her figure.

'Ah,' Helen DeVos said, as Newman stared at her body hoping the Ray-Bans hid the precise direction of his gaze. 'I thought I'd find you here. Well, we have time for a quick swim. We have to meet Phil Lewis in an hour.'

Newman walked across the hotel car park feeling the sun reflect off the concrete like heat from a grill. He quickly opened the doors of the Chevy Beretta and felt the sticky air inside hit him in the face. He'd decided he should wear a suit, shirt and tie for the visit to Holgate's office and the hundred metre walk from the hotel lobby to the car meant he was already sweating right through the shirt, feeling it stick at the neck, cuffs and on the back. He started the car and turned the air-conditioning on full, then opened the door for Helen DeVos who looked cool and happy.

'You do most of the talking,' she instructed, as usual organising his life, though he was beginning to accept it in good spirit. Enjoy it, even. 'Lewis might take to you as one Brit to another. And anyway, the lawyer will be impressed with your accent. They always are. Sort of guy who thinks if you say "simply mah-vellous tom-ahto", you are part of the aristocracy.'

124

'Maybe I am,' Newman laughed, turning on to the freeway.

The raised section pulled left, showing the full Miami skyline. Newman steered the Beretta towards Crowne Plaza business section in Coconut Grove, parking in the underground car park. A large glass and steel sign revealed the obvious: Holgate was on the top floor, a penthouse suite which straddled the entire roof area, including a small garden and patio.

'Mr Holgate will see you now,' the secretary said, pointing towards a large oak panelled door.

Inside, the office was enormous, enough for a score of workers to sit comfortably without overcrowding. Newman supposed that space was power, and like male hippos spreading dung around their territory to keep out rivals, in corporate America, ownership was marked out by ferns and bookshelves and square feet and oak panels. There was a peculiar clash of styles, a mix of high technology and the great outdoors. The massive plate glass windows were tinted against the sun. The first ten metres or so of the office were taken up with a black wood, steel and glass conference table surrounded by about twenty leather chairs. One metre further, and the ultra-modern gave way to the décor of a nineteenth-century English gentlemen's club. There was a rich brown carpet leading up a few steps to a platform around which were arranged two leather chesterfields, two easy chairs and a large deep brown cherry desk. In this part of the room were shelves carrying thick leather law books, and between each shelf section there was a large stuffed animal, as if the contents of some old-fashioned British museum had been distributed in the headquarters of a computer company.

This was having it all, Newman thought, amazed. Standing at one of the chesterfields was a porcine man in a loose fitting pair of grey slacks with a short-sleeved open-necked shirt spilling over his belly. Behind the desk, and between what Newman thought was a dead sheep and a stuffed goat, stood a tall and good-looking middle-aged man in a three piece grey suit with a watch chain, hand outstretched. The word 'LAWYER' was branded on his forehead.

'Tom Holgate,' the grey suit said, shaking Newman's hand warmly, then turning to Helen DeVos and doing the same. 'And this is my client, Philip Lewis.'

125

The fat man now offered a hand. Newman shook it and noticed pink bandages on his wrists.

'Please sit down,' Holgate said, smiling.

'Before we begin properly I want to establish a few ground rules. My client will talk to you today on the record and for publication. He has not spoken to any of the American news media, largely because they have attempted to portray him inaccurately and unfairly as a foreign swindler. His wife is American, his roots are here, but he believes that in talking to a reputable London newspaper he will be given a truly fair hearing.'

Holgate paused, and Newman noticed Phil Lewis nodding in agreement with a smirk across his face. The fat man was trying to imagine how the volcanic-tempered Vincent Terrelli would react when informed by the CIA chief of station in London of the contents of the *Tribune* article that would soon hit the British streets. Then we'd see who was bluffing and who had the balls to play to win.

'This should get the bastard's attention,' Lewis thought.

Holgate was still talking. 'Mr Lewis has nothing to hide from you or the American, or British, public. But there will be times when he simply cannot answer your questions or when to do so would place his freedom and even his life in jeopardy.'

Newman slid his notebook out of his jacket pocket, propped it on his knee, clicked his pen and began taking down Holgate's words. The lawyer was smooth, turning on the charm so oozingly that Newman could imagine him before any jury. Trust me, the suntanned smile said. Do I look like the kind of man who would defend a real criminal? Yes, Mr Holgate. You certainly do.

'So I do not wish you to regard any refusal to answer on Mr Lewis's part as an attempt to be unhelpful. On the contrary. But in order that he might not cause legal problems or expose himself to more danger he may not be able to say very much to you today.'

'Or for reasons of national security,' Lewis interrupted, his first and not quite successful attempt at a sentence since the interview began.

'What do you mean,' Newman asked gently, anxious to begin the interview proper. 'National security? Whose national security?'

'That of the United States of America,' Lewis responded flatly.

'And of its allies. Of the free world. The West. However you want to characterise it.'

Newman looked at the fat man closely. His accent still sounded half English, but there were definite American cadences, a kind of rise in tone at the end of a sentence. His hair was well combed and clean but slightly long in the fashion of the early 1970s, not the 1990s. For someone who lived and worked in the sun of southern Florida, Lewis was deathly pale, his face puffy and beige with a darkness around the eyes. He looked worn out.

'Thank you for agreeing to talk to us today,' Newman said with a smile. 'I can understand the kind of stress you must be suffering. And thank you' – this to Holgate – 'for arranging the meeting. We are very grateful to you.'

Nodding and clucking.

'Could I begin by asking you, Mr Lewis,' Newman said, 'to describe a little of your personal background. How you came to the United States, what your involvement was in this company of yours and so on.'

Lewis stared at the carpet for inspiration. Newman followed his gaze.

Eventually, Lewis began talking in a low monotone, as if recounting the most significant milestones in his life was of no real interest to him.

'I first came to the United States on a student exchange programme in the late 1960s,' he said. 'To Columbia University. It was an exciting time, not just because academically it was interesting or because New York was a wonderful city. It was also the beginning of the Vietnam protests, the Students for a Democratic Society, campus sit-ins, all that kind of thing.' Lewis's voice started to go hoarse, and Holgate called for his secretary to bring a pitcher of iced water. 'Through various friends and contacts I decided I would stay in the United States. My Spanish was already pretty good,' – he pronounced it priddy – 'because my father had been in the British diplomatic service and I'd picked up French and Spanish at school. I came to the conclusion there was no hope in England any more – or no hope for me in England any more – and I thought I fitted in better here.'

'In what way?'

Lewis smiled.

'Maybe you don't remember what England was like in the early seventies. Miners on strike. Inflation. Trade Unions were running the goddamn country because the government certainly was not. Jeez, what a mess. Anyway, by that time I'd already kinda got involved with the Agency at a peripheral level, through friends of my father, and . . .'

'The Agency?'

'Yes. The CIA. They were looking for information on the anti-war activists and protest movements and I guess I proved fairly helpful. Nothing much. Names, dates, places. After a while they asked me to join the anti-war movement just to keep an eye on things. Didn't really fit in, but the anti-war people thought I was a harmless eccentric Brit, and let me take part anyway. Crazy time, almost as bad as things were in England only the government here did not just sit back and take it. That's always been the difference. Nobody in England was trying any more, you follow? Here, there was energy and optimism that you could change things. In England it was nothing but the habit of failure. Managing decline. Anyway, I got a few dollars for expenses, told them what I saw or heard. No big deal.'

The secretary came in with a tray and four heavy crystal glasses. She poured the iced water and handed it around. Newman looked at DeVos sitting demurely with her notebook on her right thigh, impassive, reading her notes in the interruption. Lewis began a long and rambling discourse about his various financial ventures in Central America and how he made a little money, lost it again, but managed to establish a series of important contacts. He travelled to Cuba, he said, in search of possible business opportunities, but returned disappointed. Newman realised the fat man was now staring directly at him, as if to give his words extra significance or credibility.

'Cuba's an economic basket case,' Lewis said. 'Run by communist gangsters. Even the Mafia were better. Now it's an island paradise occupied by devils. A shambles. Nothing for me there.'

Newman wanted to move off the routine right wing rant, and tried to turn Lewis towards to his financial dealings in Miami, asking how he became involved in Winston, Hamilton, Bellingham, Lewis and Lopez. There was another smirk from the fat man. He picked up his water and took a swallow. This was the tricky part. He knew he had to ensure he gave them a story big enough to make a splash and irritate the hell out of Vince Terrelli, without causing any real damage – just a hint of what he could do, if they did not help him out. It was like exploding an underground nuclear test so the other side knew you had the technology.

'Well, I kinda kept in touch with the Agency all this time and it came as an idea from the chief of station in Miami. This was no domestic operation, obviously. But Miami is a convenient and safe place for the Agency to do a number of things.'

Lewis stopped abruptly waiting for Newman's prompt. It came.

'Like what?'

'Like everything from paying agents to coordinating programmes across Latin America. Ever since the Reagan years they were trying to improve their collection of information on drugs. That was co-ordinated out of' – he said oudda – 'Miami, along with the DEA and the prosecutors' offices. That kinda thing. Well, there was this idea that we should handle the payments . . .' Lewis stopped talking again, theatrically looking at Holgate as if worried he was going too far. The lawyer said nothing. The fat man continued in a different gear.

'You familiar with the term proprietary company?'

'I think so,' Newman replied. 'But don't assume anything. You tell me what it means.'

Lewis explained it was a polite way of saying a CIA front.

'Miami had problems with a couple of existing proprietaries they used to pay agents and move funds around. So they brought me in, and I did it for them. Simple as that. As well as running the public side of the business, like any ordinary investment corporation.'

Lewis began a long and, Newman thought, dull explanation of how the two sides of the company were supposed to be kept separate for security reasons, but financially the funds had to be what he called 'commingled'.

'The commingling of funds was there from the start,' Lewis said. 'Had to be. We were taking money from private investors, and we were taking money from the Agency and other government

129

operators. We had to mix the funds, otherwise it could not provide the cover that we needed.'

Newman was lost, but DeVos looked up from her notes directly at Lewis. 'You were money laundering for the Agency,' she said bluntly.

'Yeah,' Lewis replied, matter of factly. 'Sure. If that's the way you want to put it. We were pursuing legitimate investment opportunities for clients across the Caribbean, Central and South America, even in the Far East and Pacific Rim. While we were doing that, and moving funds, we also moved them for the US government. Nothing illegal in it, just that we had to keep it secret so that who we were paying didn't lead to questions about why we were paying it.'

'So how come the whole thing went bust?' Newman wanted to know.

'A very good question,' Phil Lewis replied grimly. 'And one that has given me considerable grounds for thought.'

He swigged back the last of his water, then pulled the pitcher towards him, working his arm awkwardly round his belly to pour another glass.

'The best I can tell you is this. Most of the private money we had came from government people – retirees, military people, some former intelligence officers. Hey . . .' At this the fat man became animated and sat up in the chesterfield. For the first time Newman thought he could see colour pumping back into his bulky pale cheeks.

'Hey, d'you know who the fuck was – 'scuse my language – do you *know* who we had on our board, for Chrissake?'

Lewis ran through the litany of diplomatic, military and intelligence names on the Winston, Hamilton board.

'Just because you had some big names,' Newman interrupted. 'Doesn't mean much. The prosecution are saying it was a Ponzi scheme. The oldest con in the book.'

Lewis looked positively flushed. He sat forward, balancing his belly on his knees.

'Look,' he said, pointing one ham of a hand at Newman. 'Look. I don't know how many times I gotta explain this. A Ponzi scheme is what we used to call in Britain a pyramid selling racket. You offer ludicrous rates of interest, so high the greedy bastards flock in, paying off the old investors with the new money until the whole thing goes phut! It takes maybe a few months. We were in business for ten years, right through the Contra war in Nicaragua, right through Irangate, which never touched us. Ten years! And how the hell d'you think I'd con a buncha people like those who were on our board, eh? You think I'm so smart I could con the local CIA chief and half the US military? Then, my friend, you really do have one helluva story for your paper. And you can print that. We're on the record now. You got me?'

The effort of sarcasm pained Lewis and he flopped backwards on the chesterfield like an exhausted whale, sighing heavily in disgust.

Newman sensed Holgate would soon try to stop the interview. They had been going for about an hour, and he had more questions than answers so far, and even more questions coming from the answers Lewis did give. He asked about the supposed suicide attempt and Lewis recounted what he could remember of the two Latinos in the Sheraton Hotel.

'I'm no quitter,' Lewis protested. 'Suicide is not for me. I wanted a few hours alone to think about the mess that was raised by that television programme, that was all. To work out what I should do, because there was so much at stake here. A financial scandal could expose operations, put in jeopardy the lives of real people working for this country. I had to think how to handle it. And while I was dealing with that, these bastards tried to kill me.'

There was a pause for a few seconds, until DeVos could keep silent no longer.

'Do you think it was the CIA?'

Holgate pounced. 'We have no idea, Miss DeVos, and neither have the police. We can make no such allegations.'

Now she had begun, Helen DeVos was not easily put off.

'It would be convenient for the CIA if you were dead though, wouldn't it?'

Lewis shrugged and said nothing.

'What kind of CIA operations have been put in jeopardy?' she continued.

Lewis thought for a moment. 'For background, not for quoting. We were extremely active down here throughout the 1980s – all across Latin America, all coordinated and paid from here. We used

Panamanian banks, the Caymans, Aruba, Curacao. The same methods and same places as the drug money launderers use. Only we did it in a good cause.'

'So you bankrolled Deep Blue,' DeVos said, a statement not a question.

There was an embarrassed silence.

'I think,' Tom Holgate said, looking at his watch, 'that Mr Lewis has said enough for today. We're going to have to finish now.'

But Lewis interrupted, more animated than at any time in the conversation. He wanted to reply in such a way that it would be an unmistakeable extended middle finger right up Vince Terrelli's nose.

'Let me answer it, Tom. The lady's asked a good question.'

Holgate shrugged. It had taken him two weeks to learn from Lewis about Deep Blue, and he resented the fact that everyone else appeared to know about it.

'Deep Blue,' Lewis said, 'was just some dopey name they gave to a whole series of projects. Somewhere up in the White House I think they have a special department of assholes who think up goofy names. Desert Shield and Desert Storm for the Gulf crisis; Operation Just Cause in Panama. Total bullshit. Anyway, if you want it a simple way, yeah, sure, I bankrolled Deep Blue.'

'On the record,' DeVos said. 'For quoting?'

Lewis looked at Holgate.

'I don't see what difference it makes, Tom,' he said. 'Our defence is that everything I did was ordered or authorised by the Agency. The name "Deep Blue" is part of Agency folklore. As long as I don't go into specific operations I don't see what harm it can do.'

Holgate shrugged again. He did not like making up defence strategy as he went along, and he had only agreed to Lewis's demands to give this interview because he wanted to see how his client might handle the American press if it became a high profile trial.

'We're winging it, Phil,' Holgate warned. Then to DeVos: 'I suggest you just quote informed sources or somesuch. Whatever you like, but not Phil directly on this.'

'Sure,' Newman agreed, anxious to appear helpful. 'If it causes you problems, we'll just quote sources close to the case, and I am sorry we had to press you on details after all you have been through,

Mr Lewis. Just one thing . . .' He looked around to make sure he was not seriously overstepping the mark.

He thought he had better address his comments to Holgate.

'Just one thing. Do you have any documentation to back up what you have just been telling us, and if so can we see it? And could you quickly explain any theories you have for the company going bust?'

Holgate nodded. 'Documents,' he said. 'Sure. We'll do what we can. We have the evidence. It's just a question of what might be appropriate to release at this point in time. We have to be able to establish the CIA connection without imperilling national security. We think we can do that. On the money, they say my client skimmed – well, think of a number – up to $200 million to pay for what they're calling his "champagne playboy lifestyle". We think not a penny is missing, though the paper trail is going to be hard to follow. They're just pulling figures out of the air.'

Holgate then explained how he believed the initial television report and the panic which followed precipitated a run on an otherwise sound financial institution.

'And when this is over,' he grinned at Lewis. 'We're going to carve a slice out of that reporter on Channel Six News.'

With that Holgate stood up abruptly and motioned Helen DeVos and Alex Newman towards the door. They shook hands with Lewis who then slumped heavily back into the chesterfield.

'I like your animals,' Newman lied, gazing at the stuffed sheep or goats around the room. They were about as gross as anything he had ever seen. 'Very interesting.'

'Yeah,' Holgate said stroking the fur of what Newman had assumed was a sheep. 'This one's a mountain goat from Alberta I shot a couple of years ago. In fact I'm trying to shoot one of every type of wild goat known in the world. Maybe it's my purpose in life. I got two left. One's in Mongolia, which could take a while to organise, though the way communism's collapsed you never know. The other's in the Atlas mountains of Morocco. Hope to go there next spring, God willing.'

Newman tried to look sympathetic. Holgate led them across from the gentleman's club to the high tech portion of the office.

'Hope we might meet again soon,' Newman called back to Lewis, who nodded impassively.

Holgate took them out into the ante-room and shut the office door.

'Look,' he confided. 'He's gone through a hell of a lot. I hope you can understand that. He's a personal friend of mine as well as my client, so I should know. The prosecutor's office has frozen all his assets. I can't even get paid. Then I hear some big gun is coming down from Langley to seal all the files on the case. Should be interesting.'

Newman nodded. 'How can they say there's no intelligence dimension if the CIA is sealing the files?'

'You got it,' Holgate said. 'We're going to force the CIA to appear in public on this. They are taking a sledgehammer to this guy, and I don't know why. There are things about this Deep Blue he won't even tell me. Secrets, national secrets that could explode in everyone's face if they get out. That's as much as he said. People's lives hanging by a thread.'

Newman nodded forcefully. Whichever way you looked at it, it was a great story.

'Why,' he tried as a parting shot. 'Why do you think the CIA were prepared to put so much confidence in someone who is not even American?'

Tom Holgate smiled. 'Tradition, maybe,' he replied. 'Trusting the Brits. Old Allies. Special relationship. Or maybe Phil Lewis just happened to be in the right place at the right time. Marriage of convenience. Who knows.'

Holgate shook hands and began to move away.

'Documentary evidence, Mr Holgate,' Newman tried again. 'Proving CIA involvement. To make the story work. Then we'll rattle a few cages.'

Tom Holgate smiled, perfect white teeth appearing in a suntanned face.

'Sure,' he answered. 'I'll see what I can do.'

When they left it was all Alex Newman could do to stop himself grabbing Helen DeVos and kissing her in the elevator as they descended to the parking garage.

'Bloody good story, this,' he said, beaming. Helen was pleased.

134

They climbed in to the Chevy Beretta and Newman insisted they drive to Cape Florida State Park on the tip of Key Biscayne.

'I think we deserve a walk on the beach. To celebrate maybe I'll buy you an ice cream.'

As they crossed Rickenbacker causeway Newman realised he could now assert definitively that the company which was at the centre of fraud allegations was – 'sources close to the company say' no, 'authoritative sources . . .' – at the heart of one of the biggest CIA operations of the past decade.

'I wonder,' DeVos interrupted his thoughts, 'what Lewis is playing at.'

'Meaning?'

'Meaning why did he talk to us? What's in it for him?'

Newman shrugged. He did not much care what Lewis's motives were.

'Maybe like Holgate said, he expects fairer treatment from the British press.'

'Hmmm.'

The sun was dipping low and the worst of the afternoon heat had passed. They parked and Newman took off his jacket and tie, rolled up his shirt sleeves and shed his shoes and socks.

'The Englishman abroad,' he said wryly. 'Always looking his best.'

They began walking along the beach at the water's edge, stepping in and out of the warm ocean, excited, happy. A dozen sailboards were skipping light waves a mile out to sea. The beach was almost deserted, small knots of people soaked in the sun or strolled along the cooling sand.

'What did you make of the warning,' Newman asked, 'that lives were at risk if this whole thing was blown apart?'

'Not our problem,' DeVos answered immediately. 'I have been publishing these kind of things for years in *Combat*. If people fear exposure, they should not do mean and underhand things while on the government payroll.'

'You think we should print anything – agents' names, for instance – if we happen to find them out?'

'Sure,' DeVos said. 'Having a government engaged in some cocka-mamie scheme to spy on and subvert governments all round this

135

hemisphere and in the Pacific is not what I pay my taxes for. If I find it out, I'll publish it in *Combat*, whatever your paper decides to do. We're in the disclosure business.'

Newman was silent for a moment.

'Seemed like a nice guy,' he said, eventually. 'Lewis.'

Helen DeVos looked at him and blinked.

'You ever read *The Quiet American*?' she asked.

'Graham Greene? Yes. Long time ago.'

Newman struggled to remember. DeVos was now at her most serious.

'You remember the CIA agent, Pyle, is supposed to be hopelessly naive,' she said. 'Blundering about in Vietnam until he gets himself killed.'

'Sure,' he said, vaguely recalling something of the book. 'Great novel.'

'Well it's not like that any more. In fact, I don't think it ever was. It just seems that way to outsiders. Especially the English. These guys are not naive, Alex, Lewis and the people behind him. Trust me. Naiveté is not their sin. At their worst they are venal and duplicitous and self serving. Sure, they dress it all up in idealism and patriotism. They like it when you dumb Brits think they blunder about the world waving the star spangled banner and talking about freedom. But that's just another cover. It's American interests they are serving, not American values. And at bottom it's just their own interests.'

She stopped walking and put an arm on his, looking straight in his eyes.

'Lewis is one of them – British, American, it doesn't matter. Take nothing he says at face value. He's working an angle. We'll probably never know what it is. We can use the story, of course, but there's a smell here. Believe me.'

They had reached a patch of large rocks at the end of the beach and, almost in step, turned for home. Maybe she was correct, but Newman did not really care who was naive and who was duplicitous. He had his story, and that was enough. And there was something else. Something important about Helen that he was just beginning to realise. Out at sea the sailboards were tacking southwards, sweeping

136

close to shore and then back out again, fluttering colours on the blue ocean in a hypnotising dance.

Newman listened to her speak, paying scant attention to the details. What he realised was that for the first time he was truly happy in her company. The story had gone well, but it was more than that. He looked at her face, her serious eyes squinting in the sun, small freckles across her nose. She would probably be appalled if she could read his mind. In her politically correct way she might regard any advance as sexual harassment in the workplace, even if the workplace for now happened to be the beach. Embarrassed and confused, he ran a hand through his blond curls and dropped his gaze to the sand in front of him as they retraced their footprints side by side up the glistening shore, listening to her voice melt over him, a slow flowing wave.

11

The curve of the bay at Santa Maria del Mar was gentle, yet it left the back of the beach-house facing almost due west across the Florida Strait towards Havana and the setting sun. There were orange and gold tinges on the water as half a dozen pelicans flew awkwardly westwards, bobbing in the air a few feet above the sea's surface. As the sun sank, the noise from the cicadas increased, echoing around the darkening sand. All the bathers and tourists had gone home to shower and avoid the mosquitoes. There was talk of a dengue fever outbreak and the Ministry of Public Health announced there would be spraying between the Playas del Este and Havana in the morning. The ministry's old single-engined bi-plane would sweep low over the palm trees and rough ground, loosing a stream of insecticide, and health workers would continue the latest programme of draining ditches and small ponds.

General Oscar Padilla Sanchez sat alone in a white painted wicker rocking chair he had been given by a Sandinista officer in Nicaragua, rocking gently and smoking his cigar behind the protective bug-screens at the rear of his beach house. He was thumbing absent-mindedly through a magazine, looking at the pictures, reading a headline, trying not to think. He had made a pitcher of *mojitos*, filled with sugar and mint and topped up with ice, determined, without any real enthusiasm, to get drunk. Eventually Padilla stopped rocking. He pushed aside the magazine, refilled his glass from the pitcher and put it back in the large old-fashioned Soviet refrigerator, which began a low moaning and laboured hum every time he opened the door. He walked back to the rocking chair again and sat facing the ocean.

The air was beginning to cool and a gentle evening breeze crept over the water surface, a breeze which might be enough to keep the mosquitoes away. Padilla opened a coloured wooden box. There were five cigars left, Romeo Y Julietas that he had been given as a farewell present a long time ago by the East German military attaché. Keep them for a special occasion, the attaché had said. It was special now. The attaché had gone; East Germany had long gone, swallowed up in a Europe which seemed to Padilla to be a new and increasingly strange continent, re-inventing itself in ways he could only guess at. If he was going to get utterly drunk, and that was likely, Padilla decided he might as well smoke his way through as many cigars as possible in one final flash of self indulgence. He was tired of a life in which enjoyment was something he could have tomorrow or yesterday, never today. He breathed deeply, cheered that despite his sense of impending crisis he was cool and disengaged. *El Tempano*. The Iceberg.

There was now greater paranoia than ever at the Defence Ministry. Three more air force officers with supposed links to the Oriente rebels had been arrested. Everyone looked over their shoulders to see who was next, who might be paying off old scores, who the true counter revolutionaries might be.

'All of us,' Padilla wanted to tell them, 'every one of us is tired of the Revolution. Though not all of us are prepared to betray it.'

There were now rumours of an American spy 'at the highest levels of the military' some in the Political Bureau said. 'In the Politburo itself', according to army officers, in a spate of mutual dislike and suspicion. Padilla trusted no one now, not even old friends like General Fernandez.

If someone told him Fernandez had been arrested as an American spy, it would simply be the suicide note of a Revolution determined to devour itself. He doubted if Fernandez could possibly be a traitor, but he did not doubt the hysteria within the Direccion General de Inteligencia, the intelligence service, to make examples, to ensure loyalty. At the moment, a DGI spy or secret police informer would see nothing through the netting of the bug screen except a distinguished Cuban military officer calmly enjoying the cool evening air. But Padilla felt a thrill of excitement as he realised that there was an impending moment of crisis for the revolution and for himself.

The waves were gently lapping as a breath of wind rose in the east and swirled across the bay. A few hours earlier Padilla had driven back from Varadero, content that the next cargo of cocaine was to leave for Florida on schedule. The arrangements were set. His role, he kept telling himself, had nothing to do with the morality of the drugs trade. It was logistics: fuel, aircraft, boats, finding couriers and pilots. All the grubbier ends of the negotiations were handled by others. Padilla took a swig of his drink, savouring the rum and mint and sweetness on his tongue, pulling an ice cube into his mouth and crunching it. The rum tasted fine. There had been problems with cloudiness in the dark brown seven-year-old Havana Club Anejo. Like the cigarettes, everything was getting worse.

'Drug of choice,' Padilla muttered into his glass, looking at the half-empty Havana Club bottle sitting beside the *mojitos* pitcher. 'That's what the Americans call it. Cocaine. Heroin. Marijuana. Rum. Drug of choice.'

Padilla sniffed at his drink. He took another sip and gave up the pretence of reading, throwing the magazine sideways across the table.

Try as he could to forget the details, his mind was on that night's shipment, 500 kilos scheduled to take off at midnight. However often he organised it, Padilla could not relax. Each time the tension was higher because the Americans were more alert. Of the most recent shipments by air two had been captured, four turned back, and simple economics might lead him to concentrate more on small boats instead. Whichever method was used, Padilla had instructed his junior officers to ensure that not a single item of Cuban origin was on board the aircraft or boats: no soda, bottled water, chocolates, Cuban money or the fancy silver coins the mint sold as souvenirs. Certainly no rum. Nothing that could link the business with Cuba or the revolution. Some of the pilots had asked what the searching was all about. Dumb mules.

'*Securidad,*' Padilla's officers would always reply dismissively, and the Colombians or Panamanians or Nicaraguans would either under-stand immediately whose security was at issue — Cuba's, not their own — or they would nod dimly as if this was a predictable and legitimate Cuban habit. When the first flights had taken off Padilla waited at the Varadero hangar, worried that something would directly link the drug shipments to Cuba, and wanting to hear for himself the first word of the capture of any aircraft. It finally happened on the tenth flight, a float plane which landed near an uninhabitable island north of Key Largo. Everything that could go wrong went wrong. The drugs were offloaded to a powerboat, which ran into a Coastguard trap, and the float plane could not take off due to a mechanical fault. The pilot was seized shortly after dawn, taken to Miami and interrogated.

He told the whole story, of course, fully implicating Cuba in the hope of saving his own neck. But there was good news, as Padilla quickly discovered.

Any US government statement that Cuba was involved in drug shipments was believed only by the American right wing and dismissed by almost everyone else as typical of US propaganda against a small and independent-minded neighbour. Statements from pilots that they had landed in Cuba to refuel or change planes were largely disregarded as the fraudulent confessions of worried men, prepared to say anything to please the Yanqui Bully. After an initial flurry of interest and publicity, the US authorities had stopped saying anything substantive about the shipments at all.

'In a society like that of the United States, driven only by money not moral principles,' Padilla once told Major Rico Herrera, his protégé and operational commander at Varadero airport, 'I think one can assume corruption in every part of political life. If a country like Cuba can seal its borders against that tide of filth, why do you think a superpower is failing?'

Herrera nodded and agreed. He could not understand why a great power like the United States allowed itself to be so corrupted by drugs, unless there was some perverse reasoning behind it.

'Maybe they want to kill off the blacks,' Herrera responded. 'Aren't they the ones who are most involved in drugs?'

Padilla shrugged. That was not his business. What was certainly true was that sometimes the US military did track the incoming Cuban aircraft but failed to intercept. Since they stopped short of shooting down the light planes, a really daring pilot could outwit them, refuse to be intimidated and turn back towards Cuban airspace.

'One day they will wake up,' Padilla thought, cutting the end off a cigar, rolling the leaves under his fingers. 'One day they will use AWACs against us, and F15s and live ammunition, and then maybe the pilots won't think $3,000 a trip is such easy money.'

He put the cigar in his mouth, licking the end. He lit it and pulled on it, feeling the smoke circle in his mouth. It was all such a dirty affair. It was not right for any true military man or revolutionary. It was a business for criminals. He supposed that from the start the Revolutionary Coordination Unit had disgusted and intrigued him in equal measure. Now the intrigue was gone, but the disgust remained like a bad after-taste, and he was left with no choice but to act. Padilla remembered his day of corruption as he did his own wedding or loss of virginity: a pleasant morning in May a couple of years before, standing in the Havana Defence Ministry while the sun shone strongly through the windows, staring out across the Plaza de la Revolucion at the statue of Jose Marti, the moral spirit behind Cuba's fight for independence. It was one of those gloriously cool and sunny May days when it was great to be alive, to be Cuban, to be home away from Africa. The telephone rang in his old Defence Ministry office and Luisa – slimmer, sexier, worth having around in those days – told him the Minister of Defence wished to see Padilla. He remembered how, despite his age and experience, he had straightened his back and stood erect listening to Luisa speak of the Defence Minister, and when she had finished, Padilla turned, put on his jacket and insisted she check for fluff.

He had walked smartly to the end of the corridor, told the guard at the elevator he was going to the fifth floor, and wondered what on earth he had done to deserve such favour or blame as was now about to be heaped upon him. Apart from formal parades, he rarely saw the Minister. No one did. He was a man who exercised his considerable power at a distance. Padilla entered the Minister's outer office and found the internal door was open.

He could see at the far end, some twenty metres away, the Minister sitting behind a desk which was raised on a stubby dais. The Minister beckoned him to enter.

'Take a seat,' Padilla was told, and offered a coffee. 'How are things?' the Minister's easy chatter began, as if summoning the hero

142

of Angola for a little small talk was all in a day's work. 'Have you settled in back at home?'

Padilla could not remember exactly how the conversation had developed. He assumed he had responded in a perfunctory manner. He was relieved to find there were three of them in the room: Padilla, the Minister, smiling benignly from behind his short moustache, and General Juan Antonio Fernandez who gently stirred his coffee, sat back and smiled in an old brown leather chair. Fernandez had the look of an American movie star from the heyday of Hollywood. He was more than six feet three inches tall, white wavy hair, ramrod backed, with a fine Roman nose which had somehow been broken and almost perfectly mended, so its straight thin lines had a slight and not unattractive kink. Fernandez was, the Cuban press always said, the 'Lion of Playa Giron', the bravest of them all in repulsing the American-backed invaders at the Bay of Pigs, three decades before. The Lion had become commander of Cuba's most important region, the Western Military District which covered Havana.

'I am very well,' Padilla had said, sipping his hot, sweet coffee. 'And pleased to be back home. Among friends.'

There might have been a little more amiable but pointless chatter, then, Padilla recalled, the Defence Minister rose, shook his hand abruptly and said he had work to do elsewhere.

'General Fernandez has something he wishes to discuss with you,' the Minister said. 'It is a matter of grave importance to the Revolution. I wish you to give it every consideration. The revolution needs loyal men like you, Padilla Sanchez. Listen well. Goodbye.'

With that, to Padilla's astonishment, the Minister left his own office, called out something to his secretary in the ante room and disappeared. Maybe, Padilla thought at the time, maybe things have changed a little while I have been in Africa. There was a minute or two of silence, while Fernandez finished his coffee and placed the cup on a sidetable. Then the Lion of Playa Giron, a man whom Padilla had always found to be direct and uncomplicated, began to offer him a cigar. As he rolled the fine tobacco in his fingers and they both lit up, Fernandez began to explain in the most elliptical fashion why the meeting was being held.

The Direccion General de Inteligencia had come up with an idea (puff) . . . after much reflection the DGI decided . . . The Defence Ministry was asked to approve (puff) . . . he himself consulted . . . someone of impeccable character required to co-ordinate . . . important and sensitive task (puff) . . . vital to the well-being of the revolution . . . Padilla Sanchez the obvious choice (puff, puff) . . . outstanding record . . . name on everyone's lips . . . clinching argument . . . Fidel had personally asked . . . Fidel had said . . . Fidel concluded . . . Fidel . . .

At that moment, while the subject under discussion was still covered in the camouflage netting of smoke and embarrassment, Padilla worked out that he was being offered some kind of job, one which – he assumed from the obfuscations – might not necessarily appeal to him.

The pain was eased because the offer was made by one of the very few Cuban soldiers for whom he had absolute respect. He remembered how the coffee was sweet and strong, but the office was chill and false with its processed atmosphere, one of the very few air-conditioned buildings in the whole country, in which a Cuban could breathe the sterilised and homogenised air of high technology.

'It is to be a new unit,' Fernandez said, losing patience with his own embarrassment and at last getting to the point. 'Composed entirely of the most trusted of our Angola veterans. Those who, like you Comrade General, have struggled and sacrificed to extend the revolution. It has been given the highest security priority, clearances higher than any members of the Political Bureau and even of the Central Military Committee, with the exception of the Defence Minister, the head of the DGI, and myself.'

'A cosy little threesome,' Padilla thought, but Fernandez was still speaking.

'Cocaine,' he intoned the word as a Moslem might invoke the name of Allah. 'Cocaine, Oscar. White Gold. That most corrupting drug will become Cuba's secret weapon. It is a weapon which we do not even have to possess, and which because we will not possess it cannot taint us. But it can destroy our enemies. It will undermine the Americans where nothing else – not even Russian missiles – has come close.'

It was then that Padilla first heard the English phrase which had

144

haunted him ever since, rolling around in his mind like some foul Satanic prayer or perverse ritual.

'It is the Americans' drug of choice,' Fernandez said, the last phrase in English. 'And we intend to help them obtain that choice. It is the drug which is undermining the will of their young people. It has destroyed their inner cities, and it is so much in demand that one small shipment by light aircraft can earn as much as two million dollars in untraceable cash, money the revolution can put to good use.'

Padilla was struck dumb. He assumed he must have looked strange because despite his coolness he was not much of an actor. This word 'cocaine' was somehow unclean, not fit to be heard in such an office at the heart of the revolution, spoken by such a man. General Fernandez creaked a little as he moved uneasily in his chair, sensing Padilla's bewilderment. The two men were directly facing each other. Padilla crossed his legs, trying to think of something to say. In front of him was Fernandez' dirty coffee cup and a small pot, a jug of iced water and three glasses.

'I see,' he said, and stretched forward to help himself to the iced water. Fernandez flicked ash from his cigar. 'I see,' Padilla repeated. There was a pause, as if Fernandez was waiting for a further reaction. Padilla picked up his glass and took a sip, playing for time. He looked up at Fernandez, who had become so uneasy he decided to speak again.

'You must know they want you to succeed me,' Fernandez explained lamely, 'in command of the Western Army. When the time is right for me to go, which may be a year or two. That is what they have in mind. That is why they want you to help them now.'

Padilla flushed. It had been by far his greatest ambition, perhaps his only remaining ambition, to be put in charge of the troops which were responsible for the defence of Havana itself. Commanding the Western Army, he repeatedly told himself, was far more important than trying to export the revolution to the people of Angola.

'Not yet, you understand,' Fernandez laughed nervously. 'I'm not quite ready to hang up my rifle. I have a couple of years left. But they want you as my successor, and so do I.'

145

'If they ask,' Padilla replied with modesty, 'then I should be honoured. When the time comes. And if they ask.'

Fernandez eyed him carefully, his face impassive.

'Which,' Fernandez said, returning to his over-rehearsed speech, 'leaves the question of what you do until my boots are ready to be filled. Have you thought about it?'

Padilla admitted he had not. At that time the Nicaraguan war was still continuing, but the Sandinistas no longer needed advice. They needed guns and money, that was all. Advice they had in plenty. Padilla was too old to be of much use to the FMLN in Salvador or M19 in Colombia.

'The reason I mentioned cocaine,' Fernandez said, the words coming out in a steady stream now, 'is that we have a special project underway. And we want you to be in charge of it.'

Fernandez quickly said, as if fearing Padilla's objections, that he knew there would be problems. It was manifestly a dirty job Padilla was being given, there was a moral dilemma, but the arguments were clear, and it was as important as anything he had ever achieved for the revolution in the jungles of Africa or Nicaragua.

'Drugs,' Fernandez said, 'to you and me, mean only one thing. Dirt. Corruption. Betrayal of principles. Everything we stand against, everything the revolution stands against. But our enemies have an appetite for such things which exceeds the understanding of those of us who believe in certain moral virtues and certain historical processes.' Padilla shifted in his chair. The unaccustomed chill of the air-conditioning increased his discomfort. Fernandez was still talking.

'Some light aircraft and small boats from Colombia and elsewhere carrying drugs en route for Florida have been intercepted by the American coastguard. They have headed towards Cuba for safety, which means the US planes are forced to turn back, or risk an international incident and a conflict with the Soviets on our side. So what are we to do? Turn away those who seek shelter from the Yanqui military just because they are feeding the American desire for self-destruction through drugs? The American war against drugs is not our fight.'

Fernandez poured himself a glass of iced water. He then answered his own question.

146

'No, of course not. The people who are smuggling cocaine are the victims of American economic power and perverse desires just as we are victims of their political and military power and equally perverse desire to smash our revolution. Since we are unwilling to hand these people over and help them into the jails of the Americans, the DGI has suggested, and it meets approval from this Ministry, that we now profit from the inevitabilities of the trade, that we charge for our services and use the money to bring in technical supplies banned by the American boycott. You understand?'

Padilla nodded. He understood. He just did not believe.

'You will be in charge of this operation, what we are calling the Revolutionary Co-ordination Unit. It goes without saying that it is of the utmost importance that all aspects are kept secret. There are those who would not understand that the end of aiding the revolution justifies such means as these.'

The lack of irony in Fernandez's voice, the way this grand old man just rattled out the words, made Padilla laugh.

'General,' Padilla said, deciding it would not be wise to show how absurd he felt this conversation had become, 'I have known and admired and loved you for thirty years, and yet you cannot expect me to say yes to something when you have so far failed to tell me precisely what the job is. What exactly are you asking of me?'

Now it was time for Fernandez to laugh.

'I am sorry. Let me be clear. You are to supervise the landing and transshipment points for the drugs, both by air and sea, and work out the best routes for evading the Americans. None of the planes or boats must have any Cuban features – Colombian, Venezuelan, Panamanian, American, whatever, but not Cuban. You are then to liaise with the DGI's people in Panama to ensure that the money is efficiently laundered, and that we can buy the things we need, principally high technology items, computers and the like, through Panama, Mexico, wherever we can.' The old man smiled again, putting his cigar in the ashtray and stubbing it out. 'Do you understand your commission, Padilla Sanchez?'

Padilla felt his jaw had quite literally dropped.

One of the achievements of the revolution, of which they were all proud, was that drugs were not a problem in Cuba. There was some marijuana, some drunkenness on rum. But no hard drugs.

'It has approval from the highest levels, Oscar,' Fernandez repeated, not waiting for a reply. 'All we do is facilitate the shipment from Colombia to Florida, or wherever you decide, allowing them to pass through our airspace in specially designated corridors, or to land and re-load the drugs on small boats which head for the Keys. We are merely a transshipment point. Nothing comes to Cuba permanently except the money, and the quantities of cocaine will be strictly limited to ensure far more travels by other routes than through here. The risk of exposure will be minimised.'

In his astonishment Padilla said very little. He was perplexed, even scared, that he had been asked to become involved in something so alien to his character. He was also intrigued that anyone should contemplate such a scheme, but by the time he might have objected, the Defence Minister came back to reclaim his office.

'Thank you, General Padilla Sanchez,' the Defence Minister said formally, before Padilla had a chance either to greet him or reply to Fernandez. 'Thank you for everything you have done for this revolution, and everything you are now about to do.'

Padilla stood up – that was clearly what was demanded – saluted Fernandez and the Minister, and walked out. In the years since, he had re-played that most peculiar meeting again and again in his mind, trying to see why they had chosen him and whether there had ever been an elegant escape route.

He had become convinced there was none. The following day Fernandez called down to Padilla's office, and suggested they go over the details. They walked out of the Defence Ministry and across the Plaza de la Revolucion towards the Ministry of the Interior where the massive 1960s mural of Che Guevara smiled down.

'You will need,' Fernandez had said, as they strolled side by side in full uniform, 'to open a series of bank accounts which will be in your name, or rather in a name we shall decide upon. The money will be paid directly from Colombia. They will ferry cash – mainly $100 bills – to Panama, where it will enter the banking system. You may then seek to transfer it to other accounts in, say, Mexico. All at your discretion, Oscar. The DGI Technology Unit under whose wing

148

you will be operating already has its own list of high technology goods we need, software, small computers. You may also be called upon to launder other money, from the shrimp boats perhaps.'

Padilla looked puzzled.

'Our boats sell their catches in Panama as if it were Panamanian shrimp. It ends up on the dinner plates of Texas and New York and nobody knows the difference. But believe me, the new business will be more profitable.'

It was all so relaxed they could have been discussing anything. Eventually, Fernandez stopped walking and patted Padilla on the shoulder.

'I know your moral scruples, Oscar,' he said, eyeing him carefully. Padilla looked at the fine nose, the unbending discipline of the man. 'If you did not have those moral scruples you would not have been our choice. It is dirty and sticks to everyone who touches it. You were chosen because you are above corruption. You can be trusted with the burden of a secret as foul as this. I know it disgusts you, but I think you can see it is necessary for our survival. The paradox is that only someone disgusted by the moral compromises necessary to make this work is fit to do the job.'

Padilla nodded. 'I see, General Fernandez, that what you want is merely a new kind of chemical warfare. I am a soldier and Cuban patriot and I will do my best.'

Fernandez laughed heartily. 'Chemical warfare,' he said. 'I will repeat that to the Minister. He will like it.'

He would indeed, Padilla thought. A good joke, with a somewhat limited audience, if only a handful of people knew about the creation of the Revolutionary Coordination Unit. At first Padilla was so busy that his moral qualms took second place to the simple logistical problems of creating a new, sophisticated and extremely secure military unit. He gathered together a core of personnel who had served with him in Angola and whose loyalty he could depend upon, beginning with Major Rico Herrera. The site at Varadero was the most obvious, easy access, a fine airfield, a substantial tourist trade in the margins which could explain some comings and goings. He decided the incoming aircraft would file flight plans as if they were bringing rich tourists from the South American mainland.

The unit would then find a second mule and alternative aircraft or boat to complete the journey. There were two Colombian link men based in Havana. Padilla had told General Fernandez they were 'the Ambassadors of Medellin,' and the General had laughed his deep belly laugh and again promised to pass on the witticism to the Defence Minister.

'If I don't get command of the Western Region,' Padilla thought, 'maybe they'll give me my own comedy show.'

It was now completely dark at the back of the beach house and Padilla lit an old kerosene lamp. By its glow, he could see the night's insects piled up on the bug screen round the porch. He went back to the refrigerator and poured another refill from the pitcher of *mojitos*.

Then he sat back in the chair and lit another cigar. Looked at through the bottom of his rum glass, the past few years had been the most unhappy and unsettling part of his life, the moment when he felt so much struggle and sacrifice had resulted in nothing. The DGI had provided a skeleton team for the money laundering, plus contacts in Panama and Mexico. Padilla had found radar specialists and military intelligence advisers. No more than forty men in all at the core of the operation, plus about a hundred and fifty more to provide the muscle: guards for the transshipment warehouses at Varadero, a small naval and coastguard team under the direct supervision of one of two navy vice-admirals.

Now, in the night sky over the beaches, there was no moon. Somewhere a few miles away on the secret end of the Varadero airfield in the back road of the Via Blanca on the Laguna de Paso Malo, the pilot would be making his final checks for the evening's flight. He would be nervous, tight in the gut with fear, knowing he faced a life sentence if caught by the Americans. The alternative, for a successful trip, was a payment equal to two years' wages. It was not a bad risk. Padilla put down his glass, and somewhat awkwardly opened the back door of the porch, walking out on the sand westward along the ring of palm trees that fronted the bow of the beach. He took off his sandals and walked barefoot, enjoying the feeling of sand between his toes and drinking in the cool air, puffing his cigar in the darkness. Every hundred metres the lights of houses guided him, lights bright

150

enough to make it difficult to see the stars, though the night was clear and cloudless.

He would barely admit it to himself, but the latest wave of paranoia made him sense fear for the first time. It was not the fear of combat, or of being arrested and shot or tortured. It was the fear of disgrace and humiliation. The only superior officer with whom he had ever discussed the operation of the Revolutionary Co-ordination Unit was Fernandez. Of course Fernandez seemed to operate with the authority of the Minister of Defence, and indeed claimed authority from Fidel himself. Padilla had no proof, however, no proof of anything, except that he personally had organised the network, had worked with the DGI agents sent to him through Fernandez, had created a working organisation from nothing. It was all a matter of idealism and trust, and his idealism was long gone and his trust had evaporated. He recognised what it meant.

If at any time they found him embarrassing or troublesome or over-ambitious, it would be easy to demonstrate his corruption as a *narcotraficante*. To be a counter-revolutionary, given the moral bankruptcy of the revolution, was dangerous but almost acceptable. To be a drug dealer would place him as a symbol of the regime's degeneration, not as someone leading a new Cuba towards a better future. He would lose his life, and also his place in history, forfeiting his past as well as his future. The fine beach sand gently massaged the soles of his feet and spilled between his toes. He was not drunk exactly, just anaesthetised in the warm night, listening to the sound of the cicadas and the frogs in the ditches behind the ocean and the lapping of the smallest waves. What really unnerved Padilla was a deep suspicion about the motives of everyone he now worked with, including General Fernandez himself. Since dealing in drugs subverted every moral principle of the revolution, who was not a traitor now? Fernandez? Padilla himself? The Defence Minister? It was too disgusting to contemplate. They were all traitors, betraying their consciences to hold on to power.

Padilla threw his cigar butt deep into the darkened ocean. The truth was that when the United States sent its troops into Grenada, or mined the harbours of Nicaragua, Padilla found it easy to maintain his own morale. The less the United States acted as the regional bully, the more difficult he found it to see the point of his personal dirty little war. He reached the end of the beach where it became rocky and a small creek cut him off from the rest of the coast as it wound towards Havana. He turned back to the house, catching a glimpse of his own kerosene lamp hanging from a hook. He supposed there were family matters to think about, but they did not bother him much.

Eva, his wife, was just an old friend who happened to be mother of his children, nothing more. Inevitably she found out about the girls down at the beach house and there had been broken crockery on the walls. He shrugged it off and moved out of the Havana house into the beach bungalow. When he reached the beach house again Padilla emptied the dregs of the *mojitos* into his glass. He noticed the electric light in the refrigerator did not come on. He tried the wall light. Nothing. A power cut.

He looked down the beach towards the next house, a hundred metres away. No lights there either. He cursed, and returned to the porch, sitting under the glow of the kerosene lamp in the corner, slumping in his chair. A few weeks before he had thought contentedly that when he was in his twenties his women were in their twenties. Now he was fifty, his women were still in their twenties, stretched out as the general requested from Cuba to Panama to Mexico. And yet beyond his pride in his conquests, the truth was he saw nothing but vanity and emptiness, no purpose in anything he did. He swigged back the last of the *mojitos* and crashed the glass down on the table. He was suddenly filled with a sense of conviction he had not felt since the days in the Sierra Maestra. He was absolutely, definitely going to wind up the drugs trade – or at least his part in it – in as spectacular a way as possible. They could do as they damn well pleased, but Oscar Padilla Sanchez was finished. He stood up unsteadily and yelled full throated into the night sky an old slogan he had not used for years.

'*Venceremos! Venceremos!*' he shouted drunkenly, his head spinning with rum and emotion. 'We shall overcome! We shall overcome!'

12

When Lula Martinez first got the call from Kiki Mendoza he could not figure it out.

'You know, Kiki,' Lula said, 'it's like this does not compute. Like it's, well, you know, weird, even for someone as permanently freaked as *La Tortuga*. What's the Turtleman thinkin'?'

So Lula started thinking about what the Turtle was thinking, until he got a sore head and gave up.

Kiki the Bear had called Lula to say he wanted to know about the two of them spending a weekend with some Puerto Rican girls up in Jorge Lopez's waterfront house in Palm Beach. Not the remake of the White House that the Turtle normally lived in, but the one Lopez sometimes used at weekends when he wanted to impress people or get away from his mother, take in a bit of the ocean action out near where the Kennedy family have their place. It was the classy end of town, where some of the big time Wall Street people went for winter vacations, where local bars charged seven dollars for a beer and ten for a cocktail. Anyway, it was summer and hot, so Lopez didn't want to go there.

The crazy Turtle was running yet another big Republican fund raiser, another five hundred dollars a plate dinner, this time to help keep the president in the White House. The way Kiki told it, Lopez called him up and said, 'Hey, Bear, you want to spend a weekend at my place at Palm Beach? Take Lula. Check it out. Have some fun.'

'So how come,' Lula asked, puzzled. 'So how come I'm flavour of the month again? One minute he's pissed at us, me for sure, because we fucked up with Phil Lewis, and I won't take none of his crazy

Turtle-headed bullshit. And you tell me I'm way out of line. I should go chill out someplace. And the next I hear the Turtle's offering us his beach house for the weekend. So what's happening, Kiki?'

The Bear's voice was reassuring, gentle.

'Hey,' he said. 'Seems like *La Tortuga* has been having second thoughts 'bout the way he treated us. Says he was too heavy, you know. Should have recognised that we'd have been better just blowing Lewis away. Not pulling nothing fancy. Waste a time. So he says while he's still trying to locate Lewis for us to finish what we started, maybe the two of us could use a little vacation. Sounds good to me, eh?'

Lula admitted it sounded good to him also. A few days away from Miami. Check out the shopping malls up in Palm, grab himself some new clothes, silk shirts, a new pair of Nike trainers.

'We'll pick you up late Friday afternoon,' Kiki said. ''Round four thirty. At your place. Plan to stay till Monday.'

'We? You and who else?'

'Miguel Morales and Antonio Montoya. They're the ones who're setting us up with the chicks.'

There was silence while the Bear let the bomb drop. Lula was learning to think for a moment before he spoke. So he thought. Then he said: 'So we're working with the child molesters, Kiki. Is that it? I thought you was telling me you wanted to work with Miguelito and Tony like you wanted a dose of herpes. Whadthefuck, Kiki. Eh, whadthefuck. So we're doing like the Turtle says, eh? Is that it?'

Kiki began to explain, but Lula was heating up again.

'Is this Lopez's idea, eh? Well, Tony's okay, I suppose. If you like that kinda thing you'll like Tony. S'just I don't like that kinda thing. But how'd you hook up with Miguelito? I mean, Kiki, you and me go back a long ways, and you always said he was some kind of sicko. Some kind of pervert. We're talking serial killer here, man.'

'Yeah,' Kiki the Bear said reflectively, when he could get a word into the conversation. 'Yeah, but I guess business is business. And Lopez wants them to be part of the action with Lewis next time. And with The Turtle trying to make the peace with us, this is no time to pick another fight, Lula. That's just the way it is. We work together with Tony and Miguelito. We have fun together. Maybe they don't much like us either. Maybe they think your aftershave sucks. But the Turtle says we go and have fun, so that's what we're gonna do. You know. Orders. Teamwork. All that shit.'

Lula was far from convinced, but what the hell. In a house as big as the Lopez beachside mansion there would be plenty of room to lose the creepy bastards. Friday afternoon Lula packed half a dozen beach shirts and some shorts. He was wearing a hot pink tee-shirt and a beige linen Rodier suit, white loafers and no socks. He picked up his automatic pistol and wondered whether he should take it or not, whether something might break with Lewis and he might need it. He packed and unpacked it then threw it back in the tote bag one last time, along with a couple of spare magazines.

'Decisions, decisions,' Lula said out loud, thinking: who knows what the Turtle might want? Or when. Best prepare, huh. Keep him happy, like he's trying to do for us.

Friday, it was hot like an oven with a wisp of a humid wind from the sea. Then late afternoon it started to cool, with the wind turning to the south and the WTVJ weatherman calling for showers. It would cool them off and they could sit in hammocks and drink beer. Have some fun with the Puerto Rican girls. Lula figured to take his video camera, record the fun. Play it back later. Keep himself amused. He knew Miguelito would take a camera. The stories went that he liked to video everything – with women, or when he and Tony Montoya were beating the crap out of some poor sucker who wasn't making his payments on time.

'Must check out Miguelito's tape library sometime,' Lula giggled to himself. Right on time the Bear rang the bell at Lula's apartment and they took the elevator down to the garage where Miguelito was driving a Toyota van with heavily tinted windows. Tony Montoya was in the back and the Bear shifted his bulk in beside him telling Lula to sit in front.

'Hey Lula, you gotta sit there and be the dee-jay. Otherwise you'll only bitch at the rest of us about playing the wrong CDs.'

Lula smiled and climbed in the front, throwing his tote bag in one of the spare seats beside the Bear and carefully laying his Sony handicam beside it.

'How's it going, Lula,' Miguelito said, offering what passed for a smile, rolling back a slack unshaven lip to show new dental work. Maybe someone busted his teeth, Lula thought. Would be about time.

'*Eh, bueno, Miguelito. Como estas?*'

'It's been a long time, Lula,' Tony Montoya said slowly, leaning forward to shake hands. 'You're looking good.'

'Too long, Tony. How've you been? Doing well for yourselves, last I heard.'

'Doin' okay. Doin' okay.'

As Miguelito turned the van around, Lula slipped on his Ray Bans. The sun would soon be setting and there was a strong orange tint to its rays as it beat in from the west just above the level of the horizon, into their eyes until they turned northwards. Lula selected an old Gloria Estefan CD and pushed it into the player. Miguelito nosed the van on to I-95 heading north towards Palm Beach.

'*No hay que temer,*' Gloria Estefan began to sing, and Lula cranked it up loud.

'*Si sola no estoy*
La vida nunca es facil
Pero se a donde voy
Siempre llena de preguntas . . .'

In a few minutes they were on I-95, speeding in the overtaking lane at seventy-five miles an hour, gazing around them through the tinted windows which cut out the worst of the sun's glare. Big Kiki the Bear was sitting directly behind Lula who chewed gum and was thinking of starting a conversation with Miguelito about whether he had brought his video camera too, and whether together they might get the Puerto Rican girls performing from every angle. Suddenly behind him the Bear's paws moved with astonishing nimbleness.

The Bear's left hand went to the base of Lula's skull at the point where it met the top of his neck. He could feel Lula's neatly gelled hair sticking to his palm. At the same time the Bear curled his right hand in front of his face and grabbed the chin in his stiffening fingers. For an instant Lula saw the quick-moving hand sweep in front of him, but before he had time to turn or struggle, the Bear rapidly and violently twisted his hands counter clockwise, snapping Lula's neck like a dry twig with such a crack Miguelito sat bolt upright in the driver's seat.

156

'*Bueno, Oso,*' he said, with something approaching awe in his voice. '*Eh, bueno!*'

Lula's body slumped down on the seat, held by his safety belt. The Bear wiped the grease from the hair gel off his left hand onto the cloth of his own seat, then he leaned forward until he could push the button which allowed Lula's body to slide back from the vertical position to the horizontal.

'Undo the safety belt,' he hissed at Miguelito who released the catch and the belt slid back onto its reel.

'Hey,' Miguelito said with a grin. 'I thought safety belts were supposed to prevent people getting hurt.'

Nobody laughed. Tony Montoya helped the Bear pull the body backwards into the rear of the still speeding Toyota van, as Miguelito looked for the signs to I-75 west, turning away from the Palm Beach road and taking them instead along Alligator Alley. Kiki the Bear pulled the body beside him on to an old blanket. He took off the Ray Bans which were hanging sideways on a bright pink cord.

Lula's vacant face was clean shaven and the Bear could smell the strong Paco Rabanne aftershave competing with the odour from the hair gel. The Bear sniffed his left hand and tried again to wipe the remains of the gel off his fingers and on to the seat. He looked down at Lula's face which hung at an obscene angle from the broken neck. He put his large fingers on the forehead and gently closed Lula's eyes, picking up his arms and folding them across the corpse's chest. Then he wrapped over the blanket and tied it tightly with cord at the neck and feet. When the Bear finished, he was sweating despite the strong air-conditioning. He wiped his forehead with the palm of his right hand and sniffed cautiously at the fingers of his left. They still smelled of perfumed hair gel and he tried one more time to wipe them clean, knowing that it would be of little use. He would need a proper wash with soap and water.

Miguelito still could not believe what he had seen, and more especially what he had heard. When Jorge Lopez told them he wanted Lula disposed of because he no longer trusted him and thought he might turn him in to the Feds, Miguelito had sneered.

'Maybe you want us to get rid of the Bear too, Don Jorge. Two for the price of one. As a favour to you.'

But the Turtle shook his wattled head.

'Kiki Mendoza is loyal. And to prove it, I want him to pull the trigger.'

Lopez had not said anything about the Bear wanting to do the job with his hands, but when they began to plan it the big man insisted and nobody wanted to argue. Miguelito couldn't care less. The way he looked at it, whatever worked was good. But when he saw it with his own eyes, he was awed by the power of the Bear.

'Hey, *Oso*,' he called out. 'That was some performance, Bear. What you do for an encore? Bite the heads off live chickens? What you say?'

'Shut the fuck up,' was what the Bear said. He was in no mood for Miguelito, no mood for anything. Lula might have been a loud-mouth who liked to think he knew it all, but he was a decent-hearted kind of guy, not like the skinny rattlesnake in the driver's seat or the big dummy Tony Montoya who had not said more than six words in the past hour.

'Slow down, for Christ's sake,' the Bear growled. Miguelito immediately eased back on the accelerator. 'What you trying to do? Trying to attract the cops like you dialled 911? You got no sense, Miguelito, with a stiff in the back and you carrying the kind of shit you put in your bag.'

The part about spending the weekend in Jorge Lopez's house in Palm Beach had been true. The Puerto Ricans girls were also sched-uled to arrive. Only Lula's plans were to be changed at the last minute. But the Bear noticed Miguelito stuffing six small coke bags and a Glock pistol into his own tote bag, and the Bear was not especially impressed at what the other two clearly thought might make a good weekend party. The Bear knew coke heads were losers, simple as that.

'Sorry, *Oso*,' Miguelito grunted, slackening back on the accelera-tor until it tipped the legally permitted fifty-five mph. He did not like to admit it, but what he had just witnessed scared him. He made a mental note. Don't fuck with the Bear, he thought. Unless maybe with a Glock 17.

Miguelito lit a cigarette and threw one backwards to Tony Mon-

158

toya. Then he racked up the volume on the CD player. Gloria Estefan was beating out the final chorus of the song.

'*Desde la oscuridad veo el sol de un nuevo dia*
Naciendo en mi
Desde la oscuridad el amor que me a salvado
Ha sido de ti . . .'

Musical Spanglish, the Bear thought. Just right for Lula.

'Lula, if you only knew how pissed you made Lopez with that attitude of yours. Goddamn attitude. And that mouth. Never could keep it shut. Calling him *La Tortuga*. Shit. Always said that mouth would get you killed one day, Lula. If you only listened instead of talked, maybe we could have avoided this.'

The sun dipped completely below the horizon, and Miguelito switched on the lights of the van. They drove in silence for a further thirty minutes, the Bear preoccupied, Miguelito a little scared, Montoya about as interesting as the corpse beside him. Then eventually Miguelito pulled off the freeway, made another couple of turns, slowed down.

'Okay,' he said. 'Looks like we're here.'

'Here' was a side road which ran along the back of the Tamiami Canal between Copeland and Ochopee, a track used only in the day by fishermen and occasionally at night by courting couples, if they could not find anywhere better, which was difficult to believe.

Miguelito had driven along Alligator Alley then south past the Big Cypress National Preserve. The last of the day's fishermen had long gone, and the first of the courting couples probably would not arrive for hours.

There was a rough parking spot where a crude and shallow lake pushed backwards from the side of the canal. In places it seemed little more than a swamp but Miguelito and Tony Montoya appeared to know precisely where they were going.

'Tony,' Miguelito ordered. 'Bring the weights.'

The Bear watched Miguelito pull the Glock pistol from his bag and stuff it into his belt. For a split second it crossed his mind that maybe this was another double cross, that Lopez wanted him dead too and Miguelito was going to do it. That was the trouble with breaking the rules. Once you did, you never knew who you could trust, and the idea of being smoked by this coke sniffing son-of-a-bitch made the Bear angry.

'Hey,' he hissed, pointing at the gun. 'Where the fuck you going with that?'

Miguelito looked surprised.

'What if we got company down here?'

'You afraid, Miguelito?' the Bear spat out with contempt. 'If we got company, then I tear their fucking heads off. You take the gun down here and start firing it, then I tear your fucking head off. You reading me, *amigo*?'

Miguelito pulled the Glock from his belt and put it in the van's glove compartment which he locked, then he walked round to the back and pulled out a flashlight. Kiki the Bear hoisted the blanket-covered body over his shoulder while Tony Montoya picked up a couple of weightlifter's fifty-pound weights, a chain and a simple padlock.

Following Miguelito they walked in single file along the track away from the canal. In less than five minutes they reached what looked in the dim moonlight and under the beam from the flashlight like a man-made spit of land which jutted out into a lake.

The lake seemed to widen as it swept away from the reeds of the swamp. On one side it fed into the canal through a concrete spillway. On the other it stretched back into the darkness with what the Bear could vaguely make out as trees half submerged at the water's edge. He could feel the sticky night air hang on his clothes, and hear the sound of half a dozen types of crickets and cicadas calling from the rushes and grass. Bugs were flying round his head, mosquitoes, fire-flies, moths. He ignored them. There was a concrete arch which formed part of a massive pipe linking the lake and swamp and canal, the whole system of drainage in a slow moving river of water and reeds from Lake Okeechobee in the middle of the state to the Ever-glades in the south and the sea down at Florida Bay. It was a vast, uninhabitable swamp stretching through hundreds of miles of track-less wilderness, impassable except by a few raised roads and the man-made waterways.

The Bear remembered some seventh grade lesson in geography when the teacher told them how the state of Florida had been almost impossible to live in until after World War Two when the invention of DDT killed off the bugs, and air-conditioning made the heat and humidity bearable. There were some bugs that he guessed they had missed, but somehow they had carved civilisation even from this unpromising frontier. The Bear pushed apart the brush to keep the tangle from slowing his progress. Perversely, he did not want any of the overhanging branches to hurt or bruise the body of the man he had just killed. At the end of the spit, on top of the concrete pipe the Bear could make out the red glow of a cigarette. There was the outline of a man standing up, the barely discernible silhouette of Miguelito who turned as the Bear and Montoya approached, labouring under the burdens they carried.

Miguelito switched on his torch and pointed it at the ground.

'Put him there for now. Strap on the weights, Tony, while we look for the dump site.'

'The water here at the pipe's about thirty feet deep and as brown as shit,' he explained to the Bear. 'It feeds back to wherever. The canal I guess. Anyway, me and Tony have lost one or two unwanted items down here in the past. They ain't come back yet, if you know what I mean. The way we do it, we stick the weights on his legs and throw him in over this ledge. There's suction here from the canal and that pulls him down and in. We get Fat Phil Lewis, we got room for him here also. No problem.'

Miguelito shone his torch on the dark brown water which seemed to swirl in wide desperate arcs, as it was sucked under and drained away.

'This is the best place,' he said. 'I guess the 'gators get them. In this heat, as long as they don't float to the surface, they don't last long.'

Montoya had finished chaining the weights round Lula's legs. He and the Bear carried the body between them to the spot where they could most easily throw it into the deepest water.

'Wait,' Miguelito said. He pulled a flick knife from his pocket and slid out the blade. Hearing the noise the Bear took one step backwards, ready to rip Miguelito apart if he tried anything. Instead he knelt by the body and cut open the blanket near Lula's head.

'What the fuck you doing, man?' the Bear growled.

161

'Letting out a little blood. You made it too clean. He ain't bleeding. I'm gonna slash him a bit. Help the 'gators find supper.'

The Bear turned away in the darkness. When Miguelito finished, he wiped the bloodied blade on the blanket then stood up and lit another cigarette. He put the knife back into his pocket and switched on the torch to help the others see what they were doing.

'Watch the blood,' Miguelito said. 'Don't get it on your clothes.'

The Bear pushed both Montoya and Miguelito aside and picked up the blanket himself, carefully keeping the slit end and the blood away from him. Then with an almighty groan he heaved Lula out into the water. There was a splash which resounded across the swamp, and by the time Miguelito shone his torch on its surface there was nothing to see except widening circles of tiny brown waves closing over the corpse. They returned to the van in silence and darkness, and when Kiki the Bear sniffed the fingers of his left hand he could still smell the sickly perfume of the dead man's hair gel.

13

Helen DeVos had spent thirty-two years having better days than this one. She could not remember ever being bedevilled by such frustrations. With what they thought was an excellent story almost sewn up, Newman had flown back to Washington leaving her to pick up the documentary proof substantiating Lewis's allegations, but so far all the promises made by Lewis and Holgate had come to nothing. Her suspicions that Lewis was using them in some deep game returned with a vengeance. Finally her patience snapped. She delivered an ultimatum to Holgate's secretary: no documents, no story.

'I am catching the six o'clock flight back to Washington and will check out of here in two hours if I have not heard from Mr Holgate or Mr Lewis by then. Please pass on the message.'

Either Lewis was lying to them, she reasoned, in which case nothing could be lost by hanging tough, or he was telling the truth. As an intelligence officer he would be a manipulator by profession. That meant the ultimatum was a language he would understand. Within an hour everything changed. There was a telephone call, then another, then another. The first two were from Tom Holgate asking her again for specific details of the kinds of documents she might need to make the story stand up for publication, then checking once more. The third call came from Lewis himself. He wanted to meet her, would not reveal where he was, but offered to send a driver to bring her to him. There was a knock at her hotel door within half an hour. DeVos looked carefully through the spy hole at a tall, thick-set, handsome Latino wearing baggy khaki trousers and a green and white striped cotton shirt, open at the neck to show a thickly hairy chest.

He called himself Steve Ortiz and said he was sent by Lewis. Still suspicious after the lousy day, she said he should return to the hotel lobby and she would meet him in five minutes.

'What's your role in this?' she asked Ortiz cautiously.

'I'm a friend of Phil's.' Ortiz had no trace of a Hispanic accent. He looked her straight in the eye. 'He says you have to come right away. He cannot wait for long.'

Outside Ortiz escorted her across the hotel car park to a beaten up red Jeep Cherokee. The windows were dark smoked glass so no one could see inside. She felt her heart beat in panic and almost decided not to travel with him.

'Strange windows.'

'Yeah,' Ortiz said, opening the doors. ' I guess.'

DeVos took a deep breath and climbed in. She half expected to be raped and murdered. As they drove in the Miami twilight she watched Ortiz nervously. He turned the radio on loud, tuned it to a Latin music station and tapped the steering wheel to the rhythm of the drums.

'Like a cop,' she thought. 'But not a straight one.'

Ortiz was just over six feet tall, late thirties, jet black hair receding at the sides. He had a droopy moustache with a wisp of grey which gave him an air of deep sadness, and wide-staring brown eyes which would suddenly lock on like a missile finding a target. When he stared at her she looked away, unnerved, wishing he would just watch the road and drive. Ortiz changed lanes past the airport and followed the signs to Coral Gables. Still he said nothing. Helen was curious about him, but felt it unwise to talk. In the end the burden of silence was too much.

'How'd you meet Phil Lewis?'

'Oh,' Ortiz replied as if bored, the sad moustache quivering only a little. 'Everyone around here knows Phil Lewis. I've been working with him for years on various projects.'

That made DeVos even more curious. She wanted to know what kind of things.

'This and that,' the droopy moustache said helpfully. There was a long pause. He cracked first. 'I'm a licensed private detective. Do a lot of divorce, insurance, you know the kind of work.

164

That's the reason for the van and the windows you like so much.'

So he had noticed her nervousness. Another pause.

'Don't get you,' DeVos said. 'How does the van help?'

Ortiz told her his usual assignments involved checking personal injury claims for the big insurance companies, or husbands and wives cheating on each other.

'Y'know what I mean,' he said with a smile. 'Some woman driving up Route One gets tailgated at twenty miles an hour. Then some smart ass lawyer says she could sue for millions. So she starts thinking about it, and discovers she's got this stiff neck and bad back which means she can't have sex any more, can barely walk, quality of life permanently impaired. That kinda thing. I prove otherwise.'

'How?'

Ortiz smiled at DeVos again.

'Well,' he said. 'Like last week there was this woman who was trying that kind of scam. She couldn't walk, couldn't have sex. No interest in men. Frigid, after some car accident over in Broward County.'

Ortiz began to snigger so the moustache quivered on his lip. 'Boy is she gonna be pissed when it comes to trial and they show the pictures I got of her Sunday, playing tennis in Fort Lauderdale and stroking this guy like she wants him right there in the court.'

Ortiz laughed a strangled kind of laugh which DeVos did not entirely like.

'Anyway, I help Mr Lewis out when he needs it. Looks like he needs it now. Needs all the friends he can get.'

'How do you help him out?'

Ortiz looked at her.

'At the moment I help him not get killed.'

DeVos was becoming so interested she was almost sorry when Ortiz pulled off the freeway and into a small residential area. He stopped outside a large ranch-style house behind a high wall. She noticed the security camera. Ortiz stepped out of the Jeep and talked to someone on the telephone. The gates swung open and they drove inside.

Phil Lewis was drinking beer from the bottle while playing pinball.

165

His wrists were still covered in pink tape. He wore a bright blue Ralph Lauren sports shirt distended by his large gut and his trousers tightened underneath it with a leather belt.

'Hi,' she said. 'Good to see you again, Mr Lewis.'

He smiled and began talking with more of an English accent than she remembered.

'Nice to see you again, Helen. May I call you Helen? And do call me Phil. There are no lawyers present this time, so we can be a little less formal. Good of you to come at such short notice. Like a drink? 'Fraid I have only got beer.'

'Beer would be fine.'

'Steve, three beers.'

Ortiz grunted something, and turned towards the kitchen. DeVos noticed now he had taken off his blouson jacket, that he carried a gun, a big revolver in a heavy leather shoulder holster.

'Well, look now, Helen,' Lewis said. 'I have managed to put together files which I think back up the main points I have been making.'

He walked over to a coffee table topped by three piles of papers each approximately nine inches high. 'These,' he said, pointing at the first pile. 'All personal. May be of some interest.'

DeVos scanned the files and noticed they included photocopies of newspaper and magazine articles about Lewis's company and his supposed business successes. There were *Investor's Journal* and *Business News Monthly* reports praising the extraordinary philanthropy and entrepreneurship of 'the kind of Englishman who could help put the Great back into Britain.' The pile also included Lewis's own company reports on the Argentine economy and banking system, the prospects for democracy remaining strong in Brazil, and other economic research papers.

'This second group,' Lewis said, 'contains legal documents, including some parts of my sworn affidavit and other material which we obtained under the discovery procedure. You should find all that quite interesting.'

Then Lewis became quite excited. 'The third pile is what you really need. It establishes beyond any doubt that the CIA was heavily involved in Winston, Hamilton, Bellingham, Lewis and Lopez. And

166

equally it establishes that we were a vital resource for the Agency and other parts of the US government. I suggest you have a look at that pile now.'

DeVos skimmed through the papers.

'Yes, Mr Lewis,' she said with a smile. 'That will do for now, I think.'

Alex Newman was becoming increasingly anxious. He stood at Washington DC National Airport trying to dodge the thousands of travellers who seemed intent on taking off his kneecaps with their heavily loaded Samsonites, overstuffed garment bags and sharp cornered attaché cases. Newman should have been in a good mood. His London office had expressed enthusiasm when he briefed them on the Lewis story.

'The way we see it, Alex,' the foreign editor, Mike Holroyd had droned in his nasal Lancashire tones. 'The way we see it, it could be a strong summer feature on the decline of the Greed-Is-Good generation. You know, after BCCI and the Guinness affair, a kind of epitaph on the *Bonfire of the Vanities* type of people set down in Florida with an English lead player. You follow my drift?'

Newman had barely a clue what Holroyd was talking about, but that was no real problem. He was of the opinion that if he ever did understand one of Holroyd's conversations it would be the worse for both of them.

'Precisely, Mike,' he enthused. 'Exactly. On the button. Not forgetting the CIA angle of course.'

'Of course,' Holroyd said.

Now, standing in the airport terminal building waiting for Helen DeVos, Newman's anxiety was less to do with the story than with DeVos herself. He had missed her. To his surprise he had found her exceptionally tempting in Miami, and to his astonishment he had done nothing about it. She seemed to frighten him, or subdue him. That was more like it. She was a colleague, he supposed, and also a kind of friend who could presumably manage to catch a cab to the *Tribune*'s offices all on her own.

Yet here he was standing like some long separated and much devoted lapdog waiting for his owner to step into the terminal

167

building, so he could bound along, tail wagging, and greet her. Sickening. Their last dinner together in Miami had been in a seafood restaurant in Surfside, north Miami Beach. They sat close together in the romantic candle-lit darkness, talking about anything except work, anything except Lewis and the CIA. Helen had answered defensively when Newman began fishing for details about her true relationship with Chuck Lowell, and Newman felt adolescent in his clumsiness, unable to find the correct vocabulary. He was so embarrassed he even prayed once or twice disconsolately, which made him even more uncomfortable as he wondered why he was seeking spiritual guidance on how to get a woman into bed from a Supreme Being whose very existence he doubted.

Newman stood at the airline gate waiting for Helen DeVos, thinking he was now the oldest adolescent in town. As he shuffled his feet, the crowd from Miami swelled suddenly, men in loud beach shirts, young women in the shortest of skirts or large flapping sun dresses showing off as much of their tans as they dared; a crowd of Salvadoran workers speaking in thickly accented Spanish; businessmen in sharp suits; and then near the end – somehow Newman knew it would be at the end – with the last of the stragglers came Helen DeVos. She looked suntanned and fit, smiling in such a way that as she stepped into the baggage hall Newman felt immediately cheered. He pushed through the crowd, helped her with her garment bag and gave her a hug and a brotherly kiss on both cheeks. She did not object, parting her lips in a wide smile.

'Good trip?' Newman said lamely, looking into her eyes. 'You sounded excited last night.'

He had been wakened at two in the morning when she arrived back at her hotel. She had apologised, saying at a gallop that she felt they had to talk, that there had been important developments. Then, irritatingly, as Newman sat up in bed opening one eye and struggling with the other, she had refused to tell him anything of significance over the telephone, except that she had been given copies of some of the documents they sought. As they spilled out of the airport with the crowds Helen began to speak quickly, her eyes wide with pleasure.

'I was excited last night, and so will you be after you hear what I

168

picked up. It's exactly what we wanted. I think we have a great story.'

Newman hoped so.

'Where are you staying?'

'With you.'

Newman blinked in amazement, his heart thundering as they walked towards his parked car. He looked at her and wondered what exactly she meant, though it seemed obvious. Then he blinked again thinking maybe she was saying she trusted him enough to want to sleep in his apartment. They were colleagues, remember. Friends. She was not offering to sleep with him.

'Just for one night. Then I'm off to New York tomorrow. That's unless you think the *Tribune* would like to pay for a hotel.'

Newman did not think so, and he had more than enough room in his Georgetown apartment to fit in with any arrangement. It was settled then. He was employer, chauffeur and now hotel keeper.

'Fine with me.'

Newman threw the garment bag in the back of his ageing Pontiac and opened the door. He never locked the car, hoping that one day an unfortunate car thief might be seduced into stealing it. As Newman drove Helen talked about business, punctuating her sentences with the tinkling laughter that Newman had most missed over the previous three days. He smiled, and looked across at her, at the freckles on her nose, at the way the sun had tinged her skin. As they sat in heavy traffic trying to turn into Georgetown Newman blurted out that he was glad to see her again. She looked at him and smiled.

'Thank you, Alex,' she said, her voice low and clear and her tone making him blush. She knew that he wanted her. He could read it in her eyes, in the way she spoke to him. He had broken the code. 'It's good to see you too.'

'Well,' he said, trying to dissipate his embarrassment by talking of work again. 'What did you make of the files?'

'I think there is no doubt Lewis is – was – CIA. Nor is there any doubt about the kind of things he was up to. He was bankrolling Deep Blue. We have not got specifics on any of the individual operations or names of agents, but we have enough to go on. He was the key link in all the covert operations in Latin America for years, financed through a company which has gone belly up leaving all kinds of people without their life savings. The CIA was in this, and we can demonstrate that. The only doubt in my mind is whether Lewis is a crook as well as a spook. Probably. The trouble is, those two professions are so close it's hard to tell them apart. But that's not our problem. It's the jury's. We have our story. That's enough.'

Newman parked the car in the garage under his apartment block.

'You did bring copies of these papers,' he said as he lifted the garment bag from the rear seat.

'Of course,' she said almost in despair. 'What do you think is making the bag so heavy? Souvenirs of Miami?'

Newman opened the door of his apartment and wondered yet again what she meant by this decision to stay with him for a night. He brought her inside and thought about whether he should dump her garment bag where he slept in the master bedroom, get to the point, stop wasting time, but his courage failed him, and he put her luggage in the spare bedroom next to the study.

'Drink?' he called to her, as she unpacked.

'Please,' she yelled back. 'White wine if you've got it.'

He went to the refrigerator and poured himself a Quibell, no ice, with a twist of lime, then opened a bottle of chilled Australian chardonnay which he kept for guests, and as a temptation to be resisted. He sniffed it gingerly. It smelled wonderful. He sniffed it again. This secret vice was permissible, as long as he did not drink it. It smelled of fruit and hay and alcohol, and of happier times. Newman looked at his own glass, then back to the chardonnay, the dull amber light shining through the condensation on the outside. For a moment he thought he was going to take a sip, then he steeled himself against it. DeVos showered and changed into a light blue cotton skirt. She sat with her tanned legs folded underneath her on the couch in the main room of the apartment, looking very much at home. Her hair was long and wet, straggling down her head as she ran her fingers through it.

'Did you do any work in Miami,' he said, handing her the wine glass. 'Other than getting a suntan?'

She laughed, and sipped her drink.

'Wait,' she said, then hurried back into the spare bedroom, returning with three thick folders containing what looked to Newman like two thousand pages of files. She handed him one page. It was a formal CIA secrecy agreement, signed and dated by Lewis, the standard form for recruits. Newman had never seen one before and began reading aloud.

'I,' and here Lewis's name was hand written in capital letters, 'Philip Andrew Lewis hereby agree to accept as a prior condition of my being employed by, or otherwise retained to perform services for, the Central Intelligence Agency, or for staff elements of the Office of the Director of Central Intelligence (hereinafter collectively referred to as the "Central Intelligence Agency") the obligations contained in this agreement.'

There followed a total of seventeen paragraphs outlining the various duties in respect of secrecy. At the very bottom on the left hand side there were spaces for witness signatures. Two had signed and dated the form, Walter Creschi and Richard Boone.

'Who are they?'

'Walter Creschi, formerly CIA chief of station in Chile, now supposedly retired and a board member of Winston, Hamilton. And Richard Boone. I don't know what he was back when Lewis signed the forms, but I know what he is now. He's deputy National Security Adviser. He's the White House specialist in charge of coordinating intelligence policy.'

Newman whooped with delight.

'Paydirt,' he yelled. 'We got the bastards.'

For the next three hours Newman and DeVos worked together in the sitting room reading and re-reading the files. There was so much detail Newman was not absolutely sure where to begin. There were secrecy agreements relating to a dozen or so other members of staff. There was a full board list going through the various military personnel connected to the company, and a photograph showing the company team – Lewis and Jorge Lopez standing together at the front, beside them a strikingly beautiful Latin girl identified as 'executive assistant Ileana Del Cid,' and around them company workers and one

171

or two board members. There was a whole series of legal documents concerning other companies, one based in Panama, the 'Ayala Investment Corporation', with three directors, Lewis, Lopez, and someone – presumably a Panamanian – called Ricardo Alarcon. There was a mound of other information. DeVos handed Newman three thick reports bound together by large bulldog clips.

'If you had any doubts,' she said with a smile, 'read these. I think this clinches it.'

Newman picked up the reports. The pages were photocopies, and on the front page each had the CIA seal and the words 'Bureau of National Estimates'. He turned the page on the first report. It was dated June 1991, just before the Moscow coup. 'The impact of Perestroika in Eastern Europe and the Soviet Union on the economy of Cuba', the report said. He flicked through the pages. It could have been an academic report from any university, except for the seal on the front. There were tables and graphs showing different types of Soviet economic support to Cuba, outlining how much Soviet oil Cuba was able to re-sell on the world markets, and demonstrating the links between Cuban state owned enterprises and those in Eastern Europe. Newman turned to the Executive Summary. It said that the Castro regime had overcome shortages and inefficiencies before, but never had there been such a sense of malaise within Cuba and pessimism about the future.

'Because the Soviet Union remains a superpower with global ambitions,' the report concluded, 'it will retain an interest in Cuba. But even if the Kremlin wishes to continue an extensive programme of aid to Havana, the fact that Soviet enterprises will now be expected to operate at a profit means there is little appetite to offer the kind of aid which has characterised the past thirty years. Our conclusion is that the economic conditions in Cuba will worsen drastically in the early 1990s, leading perhaps to the achievement of all Deep Blue objectives without any further active engagement by the middle of the decade and possibly sooner.'

Newman sipped his Quibell, trying not to look too impressed.

'I think we have one hell of a story,' he said calmly. DeVos nodded and grinned.

'I think so too.'

'Leading to the achievement of all Deep Blue objectives,' he repeated aloud. 'Without any further active engagement by the middle of the decade . . . Looks like they were planning to wind it down.'

'If Castro fell they would have to,' DeVos replied. 'The map would be shaded blue from Baffin island to Tierra del Fuego. The only left wing regime left in the entire hemisphere would be Massachusetts state legislature.'

Newman shook his head in disbelief. He felt they had uncovered – she had uncovered – an astonishing amount of information. He was proud of her.

'I suggest we work on this late tonight,' he said. 'Try to piece as much of it together as we can, fit the parts and decide what to concentrate on, whether we need anything else, start writing. There's a lot to do.'

Helen nodded again. Her eyes seemed so alive and happy, it made Newman smile. He felt his heart beat quickly and he began to think this was the time. She had asked, demanded, to spend the night in his house. She was smiling at him now, her face upturned towards him. He wondered if he dare do as he wished, and then flushed again and panicked.

'Maybe we should order pizza,' he said, thinking how banal the words sounded. 'Have something delivered.'

His heart was really pumping now. His words were coming out wrong, all of a jumble.

'Good idea,' Helen said, staring straight back at him, smiling widely, as if amused that he was flustered and talking about food. 'Pizza would be fine.'

The blood was beating so strongly Newman could feel a tightening in his throat so that he could barely swallow and an awkwardness in his limbs as if he only half controlled them. He put his glass of mineral water to one side. It had to be now. He stepped over to where DeVos was sitting and carefully took her glass of chardonnay, setting it down on the table beside him. Every moment he watched her, looking for a sign to make him change his mind, searching for a flicker of disappointment or alarm that would make him think again. She had stopped smiling now and looked up into his eyes. At the moment he knew absolutely she wanted him, Newman bent his neck towards her and ever so softly pulled her chin upwards until his lips gently met hers.

'What took you so long,' she murmured.

14

For reasons of good health and in the hope of keeping his heart pumping a year or two more, Vincent Terrelli had cut back on cholesterol and croissants, ham, eggs, high-sodium sodas and caffeine. Unfortunately for his health plan, the Deputy Director of the CIA found it impossible to cut back on anger. He was sure it was his mixture of New York Italian blood and fighting Irish. The eruptions, when they came, hit with spectacular fury, volcanic rages which blew open and filled the air with soot and fog and ash. Today, Vesuvius erupted early. It was shortly after six in the morning. Terrelli was drinking orange juice, standing in the back porch looking at the Potomac Valley, feeling refreshed after his morning run. The telephone rang. He picked it up, listened for four minutes without speaking, then yelled a string of expletives his wife Liz Terrelli found adolescent as well as vulgar. She watched his face redden. He slammed the telephone receiver into its cradle, as if the plastic handle burned his fingers.

'I thought,' Liz Terrelli said, languidly, 'that you hot shot administration types believed in not getting mad but in getting even. What is this tomfoolery, Vincent?'

Terrelli grunted some primitive noise. His wife detected he was cooling down but the lava was bubbling beneath the surface. She hated to see him like this, twisted with stress for reasons she could barely guess at.

'Maybe,' he said with a struggle, moderating the urge to yell at her because she happened to be in the direct field of fire for his rage. 'Maybe you are right, but getting mad helps some of us poor benighted folk get even.'

Liz Terrelli had risen unusually early and joined her husband for breakfast. She planned to fly to New York for the day, do some clothes shopping, which she found almost impossible to accomplish satisfactorily in a small town like Washington. She'd stay overnight in Manhattan, eat a little dinner with friends. Vincent, of course, could not make it. He never could. He had chosen to be part of an exclusive cult, which she vainly hoped might have faded with the end of the Cold War. The CIA had its own peculiar monastic code, Liz Terrelli explained to friends. And having a husband in a senior position might sound important but was really rather dull, like being married to an enthusiastic freemason or senior member of a stuffy gentlemen's club. It was presumably interesting if you could take it seriously, but she could not manage that. She surveyed his swept back black hair and good Italian features distorted by bad humour.

'Well,' she said. 'What is the news that has put you in such a state so early? Let me guess. Something really serious. Perhaps you are to be kept on as Deputy Director after the election, or even worse: that president of ours has decided to promote you to Director of Central Intelligence. Is that the big secret? A complete disaster?'

Terrelli glared at her. 'Huh,' he snorted, part of him thinking maybe she was right. Maybe they both had had enough of his job, and especially of the chimera of promotion. Why should he bother? Someone else would take up the torch, or the whole thing might come crashing down. What did he care? The trouble, damn it, was that he did care that whatever service they ended up with was effective and so not led by a choirboy like Cabot. More especially he cared that the morning's bad news had boosted Cabot's chances immeasurably. The ash began to settle, the sulphurous vapours were clearing.

'It's no big secret,' Terrelli said. 'That's the problem. It is something I would have liked to keep secret, only it has been shared with a few million people in Europe. The secret is that some dumb English newspaper has just published a whole lot of our material in its morning edition. God, they make me sick.'

'Oh, dear,' his wife said with exaggerated sympathy. Vincent Terrelli shook his head, the anger returning. He continued speaking in a voice dripping with sarcasm.

176

'No problem, I guess. Just an attempt to undermine operations dating back years. Maybe it will lead to the deaths of people who have risked everything for us. What would you expect? Have newspaper people no sense of morality, of what is really important in the world? All they care is that they sell their goddamn newssheets. I do not exaggerate, Liz. People could die because of this.'

Liz Terrelli shrugged. Careless talk costs lives was her husband's current favourite dinner party theme: how even after the Cold War the press and television constituted one of the gravest dangers to democratic society. Vietnam was lost on television; the Gulf War won because journalists were kept at the greatest possible distance and fed the least amount of information. And so on. She considered it to be a little more complicated than that.

'I thought all your spying was with satellites and microphones nowadays,' she said. 'Isn't that what you're always telling me? So how can this be such a big deal? I expect it is more political embarrassment than real national security. It always is. And I'm sure you'll sort it all out Vince. You always do.'

She rose and began to get ready to leave. Terrelli kissed her goodbye, his lips pressing briefly against hers in a return of an old routine, his mind utterly distracted by the impending political tidal wave which might yet sweep them all away.

'Enjoy New York,' he called to her, his mind racing in another direction, thinking he might have to go to Florida and begin to clean out the Augean stables himself.

'Don't worry,' she replied, leaving. 'I will.'

Terrelli heard the telephone bell ring on the fax machine in his study. He had ordered the Chief of Station in London to send him a copy of the newspaper report immediately. He had never even heard of the *London Tribune*, and wondered if it was one of those slimy tabloids that in America were sold in supermarkets to the intellectually retarded but in London were considered to be real newspapers fit for general consumption by millions. Regrettably the London Chief of Station informed him that the *Tribune* was one of the new, supposedly 'quality' papers which had surfaced in what had once been Fleet Street. Terrelli pulled the fax impatiently from the machine. He felt the lava about to flow again as he scanned the headlines. In the covering note the London CoS described the *Tribune* as 'an upmarket, non partisan, well respected paper with a circulation of 700,000.'

'CIA in alleged $200 million swindle,' the headline read. 'British born CIA agent says "I did it for the Free World." By *Tribune* Washington Correspondent Alexander Newman.'

The story outlined in detail the Lewis case, including a picture of the fat man beaming from behind a desk in the company offices. There was a group photograph of the Winston, Hamilton, Bellingham, Lewis and Lopez board including what were enigmatically described as 'key consultants'. This picture had been blurred by the fax but the caption made clear the general drift of the story.

'British born CIA agent Philip Lewis and exiled Cuban multi-millionaire Jorge Lopez pose with key consultants,' it read. 'But Winston, Hamilton and Bellingham do not exist.'

The newspaper recounted Lewis's biographical details and his association with 'military and intelligence figures'. It asked if Lewis had swindled the CIA – in which case, an unnamed Florida police source said, 'the initials stood for Confirmed Incompetent Agency' – or whether the CIA had 'merely' been involved in a shady financial operation which had 'simply collapsed under the weight of media scrutiny'. Neither question was answered. 'But one thing is certain,' the main section of the article concluded in bold type. 'This is precisely the type of scandal the White House could do without in an already tough election year. The evidence points unmistakeably to the fact that America's Central Intelligence Agency used this British born agent and his complex financial dealings to bankroll a series of Cold War operations in the Caribbean and Pacific codenamed Deep Blue. All this was part of the great push to turn back the tide of communism begun in the presidency of Ronald Reagan. The collapse of yet another CIA dirty tricks operation seems certain to lead to a new row over whether the Agency – led by political appointee Bill Richardson and his powerful deputy, career intelligence officer Vincent Terrelli – is again out of control. And this time the United States might decide it can do without the embarrassment by doing without the CIA.'

For a moment it looked as if Terrelli might tear the fax to pieces.

It was such . . . such . . . crap. Instead he shook it wildly in the air.

The Chief of Station in London had neglected to read him the final paragraph, no doubt anxious to convey the gist of the story without risking the possibility of Terrelli angrily assigning him to a new posting as CoS, Mogadishu.

'Sons of bitches,' Terrelli snarled, his cheeks reddening again. 'Now I *am* going to get even.'

Terrelli quickly decided he was not going to allude to the story in that morning's eight o'clock White House intelligence briefing. His instinct to cover his back by alerting the president came second to the realisation he would need to give a full and complete account this time. He was not ready yet. Terrelli knew that even someone attempting to tell the whole truth would probably only manage to get it about ninety per cent right, because of mistakes or misperceptions. Even the world's biggest liar had to build on the truth or the lies would not be credible, telling the truth maybe seventy per cent of the time. Somewhere in that twenty point spread was where all the fun was going to take place. The story might need twenty-four hours to be picked up on the White House radar screen. In the meantime, Terrelli would nail Boone, who sat in the middle of the web of Deep Blue operations and was the only one who seemed to know fully what was going on. For a moment Terrelli felt a spasm of fear. He thought of Boone sitting behind his desk flexing his biceps and grinning at some secret within Deep Blue that he was withholding even from Terrelli, something about Lewis or the money or the fate of Columbus. Terrelli shook with tension.

If you could not trust those on your own side, true believers like Boone, then the game might as well be over. He gulped down a mug of coffee, his mind racing at the possibilities. He thought of everything he knew about the Deep Blue operation, of what the president knew, Cabot knew, the newspaper knew, and then what Boone and Lewis might know. They were like layers on an onion and the British newspaper had just pierced the very outside skin. Warren Cabot and the president were one more layer inside, knowing that the last relics of Deep Blue were being sustained by the existence of a valuable asset in Cuba: Columbus. Then, Terrelli thought ruefully, came his own layer of knowledge: the true nature of Columbus and what he had been permitted to do. Terrelli put down his coffee cup and felt his heart beat hard.

He knew in his guts there were more layers, somehow linking Boone and Lewis in ways he could only guess. Lewis was sending them all a signal by doing this, that had to be it. The crazy bastard really was willing to risk it all to grab his best deal. Terrelli was sure of it now, and he tried not to panic at the thought of what further ghosts might leap at him if he probed too deeply into the heart of Deep Blue. Maybe he should not be too curious. If it all fell apart they would haul him before Congress and ask him the Watergate question – what did you know and when did you know it? And for now he could answer, not much, ever, nothing.

Terrelli began to calm down. He was too busy to scare himself with the possibility of failure. There were two definite jobs ahead of him. First, he had to ensure that nobody started unpeeling any more layers of Deep Blue. Nobody. The newspapers had to be kept out, making no progress beyond the vague whispers of a CIA connection.

The president's spy Warren Cabot had to be kept from finding out about the compromises they had been forced to make to guarantee the survival of Columbus, otherwise Terrelli's chance of making DCI would evaporate. In this case 'secret' meant not telling the president. He might understand, but he would not forgive. Terrelli's second task was to solve the Lewis problem. Permanently. From his speeding limousine on the way to the White House Terrelli called Warren Cabot at home on the secure telephone. It was seven thirty and Cabot switched down the volume of a classical music radio station to hear Terrelli's cold anger, as the DDCI briefly read selections from the *London Tribune* newspaper. He made it clear he blamed Cabot for every word.

'Your job, Warren,' Terrelli said coldly, 'is to ensure that nothing sensitive leaks out of Miami. And my job is to ensure that nothing sensitive leaks out of Langley. Not even to you. So I am restricting your further access to the Deep Blue files. I am going to do my job properly even as you fail to do yours. Now I am sure you want to verify that everything we have done since the Stone Age has been ethically correct, but before you start any further crusades I want

180

you to do something useful. You will go down to Miami again and liaise with the FBI investigation team. You will inform me within forty-eight hours whether in your judgement the case against Phil Lewis is watertight. If it is, we will fry the bastard. If it is not – if there is any reason for doubt, or serious concerns about the degree of public disclosure – then we may have to think of another way to silence him. I want you to remind Lewis's lawyer that we have copies of secrecy oaths, letters of confidentiality signed by his client. If Lewis talks to the newspapers again, I want you to tell me what legal way we have of putting him back in jail until the trial. You got that? The message is, we're playing hardball now.'

Cabot, sitting in the study of his Georgetown home, had barely managed four words during Terrelli's verbal barrage. (And as he told his wife immediately afterwards, three of them were 'yes', and the other was 'hello'.) He was not going to take this.

'But I need to know,' Cabot insisted, 'why Deep Blue operations were kept running at such a high level right into the 1990s, when the communist threat had collapsed. Why were we still running such a big operation from Miami when, with the exception of Cuba, all the major Deep Blue objectives had been fulfilled?'

'I thought you were going to ask Boone.'

'I did.'

'And?'

'And he said to ask you.'

'Well, that's an end to it,' Terrelli said in exasperation. 'Boone ran it out of the White House, not me. If he has nothing more to say, nor do I, Warren. You do not need to know any more.'

'And who is Columbus?' Cabot shot back.

'It would be better for you, Warren, better for all of us if you forgot you ever heard the name Columbus. And if instead of worrying about my job and Boone's job, you worried more about your own. Any more leaks from Lewis, and I will not see the point in retaining you as legal counsel. I intend to inform Richardson and the White House of that fact, is that clear?'

Terrelli slammed the telephone down without waiting for a reply.

That should shut Cabot up. Keep him on the defensive, knowing the failure in Miami could now be presented as his failure.

'Heads I win, tails you lose, Warren,' Terrelli muttered, as his black limousine entered the south west gate of the White House.

He delivered the morning intelligence briefing – Middle East, unrest in the Islamic republics of the former Soviet Union, threats from China over Hong Kong – with his usual polish. The president seemed distracted. The chief of staff told Terrelli the latest private opinion polls showed he was neck and neck with the Democratic candidate, a piece of political intelligence far more riveting than anything Terrelli could deliver.

'We're losing them on the economy and health care. We're going for a big domestic policy speech at the Convention at the end of the month.'

Good, Terrelli thought. Keep them focused on domestic issues for a while, until I can get this fixed. After the briefing he walked through the White House grounds to the Old Executive Office Building. The morning was already hot and humid, the clouds beginning to build to produce one of Washington's spectacular summer thunderstorms. He could feel the blood throbbing in his temples and a tightness round the back of his neck, the start of a headache. Richard Boone's secretary showed him into the deputy National Security Adviser's office. Boone sat at his desk with a grim smile, as if he already knew the bad news. His hair was as spiky as ever, and Terrelli wondered how he could keep it so short, not-quite-bald but not-a-haircut.

'Hi, Vince,' Boone said cheerfully. 'How're ya doin'?'

'How am I doing?' Terrelli replied. 'Read this and see what you think.'

He handed Boone the fax. Boone's thick neck turned from side to side as he scanned the *Tribune* article. Terrelli could see his right hand clenching and unclenching into a tight fist.

'Yeah,' Boone said as he read down the page. 'I heard 'bout this.'

He finished and put the fax down on his desk. 'Could've been worse. It's obvious they don't know diddley squat about what we're doin' down there. Even the stuff about Deep Blue coulda been picked up from newspaper cuttings. Nothing much here.'

Terrelli could not believe his ears.

'Nothing much here?' he exploded. 'Direct links between Lewis and the Company. Quotations from the Bureau of National

182

Estimates on Cuba . . . nothing much here! The only thing missing is the fact that the operation has been run out of your office, not out of Langley. Maybe if I started leaking that you would wake up.'

'So would the pres'dent,' Boone replied. 'He'd wake up real quick if he knew it touched the White House. But look at it this way: Phil Lewis did not mention any of that. It is a min'mum damage op'ration from his point of view. We may not like it, but I figure – despite what he told Cabot – he wants to make a deal. This is just his opening pitch to show he has some leverage, that's all. The Cuba stuff they published was hardly high grade intelligence. It's barely even news. "Cuban economy in deep shit." We're not talking some awesome state secret here. The whole report coulda come from some George-town Un'versity professor. I tell you Vince, there's nothing in it.'

'Nothing much maybe,' Terrelli admitted, cooling down and recognising the sense in Boone's interpretation.

'Except it did *not* come from any Georgetown University professor. It came from Lewis, and I thought the goddamn Boy Scout had sealed all the files to make sure he could not pull this kind of stunt. Even Richardson's beginning to take an interest now. The president'll be on my case before long. I need cover. I'm sending Cabot down to Miami again to make sure Lewis realises if he talks any more we'll throw him in jail until the Second Coming of Christ. Violation of secrecy oath. We'll think of something. And we're going to gag his goddamn lawyer too.'

Terrelli began pacing across the room, thinking fast. He knew he had to ask Boone to come clean.

'What I want you to do, Rich, is make sure there is nothing – nothing – about your involvement with this operation that we need worry about. We've got to clear it up now. Every last bit of this . . . this manure. No trail leading to the White House, to you or me. You know Lewis well. You have had a long term . . . relationship with him. I want you to tell me how we can guarantee he keeps silent.'

Boone rocked in his chair, pursing his lips, trying to work out what Terrelli suspected by the gentle innuendo. It might be bluff. He decided to play it lightly.

'Come on, Vince,' Boone said, with a back-slapping air. 'You don't need a masters degree in psychology to figure this out. Lewis's pissed at us. He's a stubborn limey son-of-a-bitch who thinks we shoulda stood by him even though he ripped us off. One for all an' all for one. That's the way he thinks. Like we're in *The Three Musketeers*. He believes we tried to have him term'nated. God knows what he thinks. But he's like that. Ornery, mean, vindictive bastard who does not handle rejection or threats very well. I know because I'm just the same kind of son-of-a-bitch. He's positioning himself so we will make a softer deal with him. Whaddya expect?'

Terrelli stood erect in front of Boone and began speaking in measured tones which were more chilling than his volcanic anger.

'What I expect is that former employees abide by the terms of the secrecy agreement and do not compromise the integrity of the Agency in any way. What I expect is the lawyers in Miami shut Lewis up and stop this mess – your mess, Rich, yours as much as the Company's, though we are going to be tarred with it – stop your mess from causing us trouble in court. And what I expect from you, is the complete winding up of any National Security Council involvement in Deep Blue, because if any of this starts becoming a campaign issue, we're dead meat. All of us.'

Terrelli nervously rubbed his jaw and paced again across the room.

'There has to be nothing here when the president starts to ask about it, and he will. There has to be nothing which exceeds any intelligence finding signed by him or his predecessor. I'm not going to go through another entrail searching like we went through twenty years ago. I'm not having it again in the last few years of my career, Rich. Believe me.'

Terrelli stared fixedly at Boone throughout his tirade, then he walked to the window which faced the White House. He could see the top of the Stars and Stripes flying limply over the White House roof.

The president was planning a Rose Garden ceremony with the Veterans of Foreign Wars, then he had a state visit from the Queen of Denmark, followed by a speech to a teachers' association on education in the next century. The Marine Band was gathering, the flags and bunting drooped in the humid air.

Boone gazed at Terrelli, wondering what had spooked him so much. He ran his right hand quickly backwards over the stubble on

184

his head, thinking it was that he saw the DCI appointment slipping from his grasp.

'So the president doesn't know the whole story yet?' Boone asked, trying to work out whether Terrelli had fatally damaged his hopes of promotion by this kind of irrational anger at the intelligence briefing. 'About the Lewis affair.'

'He knows,' Terrelli said glumly, still staring out the window. 'Not everything, but enough to see the potential for a problem. I talked him through some of it a month ago, after it first broke. I kept it simple. He just nodded, wanting to know how embarrassing it might be if it were to come out before the election.'

'What did you say?'

'That the operation was started under different rules. Under Hughes-Ryan procedures, I guess. That we had almost wound it up, but we had at least one very important asset in Cuba to protect. That the White House could say, if necessary, that the unfortunate occurrences in Miami, while peripherally connected to the CIA, did demonstrate the wisdom of the president's own decision to ensure that the Agency is firmly switched towards intelligence gathering and away from these other kinds of activities. That Warren Cabot would conduct an internal inquiry.'

'And what might Cabot come up with?' Boone asked. 'In this internal inquiry?'

'Who cares? I've told him he is now personally responsible for ensuring there are no more leaks on Deep Blue. If there are, then it's his butt that gets kicked.' Suddenly Terrelli turned round from the window and stared straight at Boone.

'I take it you have no worries, Rich, about Cabot finding out things that could rebound on you for the way you handled this? Any little hidden secrets you kept from me?'

Boone stared back, assessing what lay behind the question, what Terrelli had learned or guessed. He was now very cool.

'Nothing I can think of, Vince. Cabot will not want a public scandal. If the arrogant son-of-a-bitch really thinks he can make it to DCI, he won't want to blow the president's re-election chances by allowing any of this out in the open. I think we've got him bottled up, as much as he's got us. He's part of it now.'

'Huh,' Terrelli responded. 'Maybe. But we also have the problem of how to protect Columbus, if such a thing is possible. I'd guess he's in real danger now. If he's still alive. You hear anything?'

'Nothing. Except he's still in Havana. No contact for three weeks.'

'Maybe we should assume the Cubans will pick him up,' Terrelli said.

'The worst they can do is attempt some kind of show trial, make him squeal. We can handle that. No one will believe what they say. I'll get the president's people to talk about Cuban black propaganda, how the communists are trying to get a weak Democrat elected.'

'You can write your own script. Not a problem. Could even help the re-election campaign.'

'It's a problem for Columbus, though.'

'Sure,' Terrelli agreed. 'But there's not much we can do about it. Unless you got some ideas?' Boone shook his head. Terrelli kept talking.

'Anyway, the other task is to make sure the journalists who are digging around don't upturn any more rocks. Maybe I'll get Cabot to fix them. Make sure they realise what's at stake. See if they can be brought round. Anything you can think of on that would also be appreciated.'

Boone rocked gently in his chair. He rubbed his hand over his hair stubble and smiled.

'Yeah. I got some input. I figure we can make life real difficult for them. At least as long as the American press don't start a feeding frenzy. Let's just see if there's a follow up. My guess is Lewis will lie low now. He's made his point.'

Boone again picked up the faxed article in his big fist. It was spread over two full pages with a series of interconnecting small stories enlarging on the bigger theme: that the CIA in the 1990s was back to the old kind of dirt of the 1960s, only this time it was also proving that greed was good. The correspondent, Alexander Newman, had interviewed Philip Lewis ('Philip,' Boone said in an aside to Terrelli. 'Can you believe these Brits with their "Philip".')

'I suppose you could call us the CIA's bank,' Lewis was quoted as saying. 'We paid those they wanted paid, hundreds of people in sensitive positions all over Latin America. We took good care of

186

those people and our customers. Now there's a money problem, and unlike a bank which squeezes its customers, this time it's the CIA, the customer itself, which is doing the squeezing.'

And there was one more interesting part which caught Boone's eye.

'Additional reporting by Helen DeVos,' it said at the end of the main text. The name sounded familiar. He would check on it.

Terrelli had calmed down completely and was now sulking.

'As far as it goes it does no real damage,' he finally admitted. 'I guess you are right. But I feel like one of those goddamn English kings, Henry the Something. I just want someone to rid me of this turbulent priest, this son-of-a-bitch Lewis.'

Boone looked at Terrelli carefully, rubbing his hand across the stubble on his head and down his face, stifling a yawn.

'Y'know, maybe we've got to think of the kind of deal that would buy Lewis off. Whatever we think of him, if he shuts up and disappears maybe we should drop the charges.'

Terrelli was shocked. If Boone was right that Lewis had encouraged the publicity to ensure a better deal, then they might be prepared to talk. But dropping charges completely meant the Agency he hoped to run was prepared to turn a blind eye when intelligence officers stole from it. The suggestion was ludicrous.

'But he skimmed the money,' Terrelli said, hearing in the words echoes of Warren Cabot's legalistic bleatings. 'We can't just drop charges against someone who has swindled millions of dollars. What would that look like when Congress started asking questions?'

'Your high morals are touching,' Boone shot back. 'I suppose you would rather go to trial and run the risk of him dragging us all through the slime just so you can feel you have done the right thing. Real nice.'

'Isn't that what we are here to do?' Terrelli snapped. 'Act within the law, punish those who break it?'

'Sure, Vince,' Boone said with a sarcastic laugh.

'Sure. But if you're right then you better start thinking how to explain to the public the whole Columbus story. How we never cracked down on the drug shipments just so he could maintain his credibility. How we let the Cubans launder their drug money. And maybe you could also explain how we preferred to let the cocaine come in to Florida so Columbus could continue to tell us real important Cold War information like what Fidel had for breakfast and whether he had a bowel movement. Yeah, Vince. You're good at explaining things. You'll enjoy explaining that.'

Terrelli flashed with anger, but said nothing. There would be newspaper commentaries about how drugs killed more young Americans every day than the entire war with Iraq; how the CIA was out of control and out of touch, and yet Terrelli found it hard to face allowing Lewis to escape punishment just because it would be more convenient not to pursue the case against him. Terrelli watched Boone's round face and muscled neck. There was a light pulse where the carotid artery beat under the skin. Both men knew this was a moment of crisis as Boone's words spelled out what neither wanted to confront. Eventually Terrelli began to speak again, thinking aloud.

'I have considered every possible way of handling this,' he said slowly. 'Everything from letting Lewis go, to prosecuting him, to . . . to hoping the people who tried to deal with him in the shower have a second chance. There are practical or legal or moral difficulties with each solution. Even if we decided to block the charges against him, how would we pay off the investors? The money would have to be appropriated by Congress which would allow them to stick their noses in the trough. Just about every way is full of difficulties. And . . .' He paused then decided to say it straight one more time.

'And I confess to you I'm worried that there may be parts of your relationship with Lewis which you have not told me about, and which could be damaging.' They stared at each other in silence, Terrelli looking at the way Boone's muscles filled his suit, Boone wondering whether Terrelli could hold his nerve. Outside, Terrelli could see the stars and stripes still hanging limply in the fetid air. He walked over to the window again, looking for inspiration. 'Is there anything more about Deep Blue you want to tell me, Rich?' Terrelli repeated. 'Anything more I should know?'

Boone took a long breath. 'You know all you need to know about it, Vince. And just as important, you know more than Cabot or anyone else will ever find out.'

188

Terrelli turned away from the flagpole and looked at Boone behind his desk. 'You sure, Rich?'

Boone sighed again. 'I'm sure of one thing. That I can shut Lewis up. I'll need a little leeway. Maybe I'll be out of town for a few days, but nobody'll miss me in August. I'd put it this way: this is Lewis's last chance. If I can't make him keep quiet and accept some kind of reasonable deal, I'd say some of the Mi'mi Cubans trying to find him might expect to have more success. All I'd ask is that you look for ways of being more flex'ble on a deal with him. If we try to punish him too much, the people who'll suffer will be ourselves.'

Terrelli nodded.

'Okay,' he said hoarsely. 'Do what you can.'

When Terrelli left, Boone paced backwards and forwards across the office. He stopped by the window where Terrelli had gazed at the flag on the White House roof. The clouds were now thick and grey.

The humidity outside would be unbearable, and a thunderstorm was certain. It was obvious that Terrelli could smell beneath the surface of Deep Blue, and yet Boone felt curiously unafraid. It was hang together or hang separately for all of them. Lewis, Terrelli, himself. Even Cabot. Maybe Lewis was right. Once you started breaking the rules it was one for all and all for one, or else everybody lost out. The only important thing now was to screw the lid down tight. Boone heard rumbling thunder in the distance and watched as the first raindrops spilled on the green of the White House lawn. The Marine band would be soaked. The president would have to greet the Queen of Denmark inside. There was more thunder and he saw a fork of lightning to the south, over by the tidal basin and the Jefferson. He turned away and sat at his desk. He also had in his mind a way to fix the journalists who were asking too many questions. Maybe Jorge Lopez could be called upon to perform a patriotic chore. But first there was something more urgent he had to take care of himself. He picked up the telephone and hit a series of buttons with the index finger of his right hand. The Florida number rang five or six times until Boone almost despaired of an answer. Then there was a man's voice.

'Is that Philip Lewis?' Boone asked cheerfully. '*The* Philip Lewis

189

who is so much in demand in the British newspapers? Well, this is Richard Boone. And this time we have to meet.'

There were a few mumbled words from Florida.

'No, Phil,' Boone replied. 'You do not understand. Either you agree to meet me now, or the next time I see you, I'll be in my dark blue funeral suit and you'll be in a casket. It's meet me now or I'll see that somebody does to you what the Cubans are going to do to Columbus.'

15

The worst moment came when General Oscar Padilla Sanchez shook suddenly from a nightmare and realised for the first time in his life he feared the sound of a knock on his door. In the atmosphere of sudden betrayal Padilla now believed everything was corrupted by failure and treachery. There were no values except survival. Signals of an impending purge within the military, the renewed whispers about spies, had dissolved even the instinctive trust between old comrades. Without that, there was nothing.

Late in the afternoon General Juan Antonio Fernandez strode up to Padilla's desk, ramrod backed, and signalled that Luisa should leave the outer office so they could talk alone. Padilla dismissed her and looked into the eyes of the Lion of Playa Giron, sad, worn, old. For a moment he wondered what this was that stood before him. A hero once, now shambling and distraught. Under suspicion, presumably, like the rest of them, a secret conspirator or traitor in his heart as tired of it all as Padilla himself. The purge was claiming them as the revolution became a demented sow eating its own litter. The old man stood rheumy eyed, scanning the face of his one-time protégé. He began talking in a low voice. He said the DGI was excited by reports from London that a bankrupt Miami investment corporation with which Padilla had placed some of the drugs money was linked to American intelligence.

'Some of the names, Oscar,' he said haltingly. 'People you met in Panama. Mexico. I'm not sure. The DGI are very suspicious. I wanted to warn you. There is a perverse hunger. The revolution needs blood to survive. You may be next.'

Padilla was stunned. He stuttered that he might have been duped but he knew nothing of links with American intelligence.

'I know, Oscar,' Fernandez said sympathetically. 'I know. But be careful. The DGI have already contacted the Defence Minister for permission to speak to you. He agreed. You are in grave danger. Even if they can prove nothing, even if you are above suspicion, there are some who will try to use this to destroy you. You have the capacity to command loyalty and inspire people. It used to be valued here. Not now. You could become an alternative leader. They fear you for it.'

Padilla did not know what to say. He could see Fernandez was close to tears, curiously more alarmed by the prospect of the imminent arrest than Padilla himself. He hugged the old general warmly.

'There are some things,' Padilla said, 'which they cannot kill. Decency. Inspiration. Loyalty. Friendship. Thank you for taking the risk of warning me.'

The old man nodded, turned on his heel and left the office. Padilla wanted to be able to say that he was ready. That night he stood upright on the patio at the beach house, staring across the sea. He prepared his full military dress uniform, his medals, his star as Hero of the Revolution. There would be no fuss while he scrambled into suitable clothes, no tearful farewells, no clinging children. There were no affairs to be put in order. The General would merely await the knock, stiffen and go. He went to bed late and tried to sleep, waking shortly before dawn, washing and shaving carefully. When the time came the first thing Padilla noticed was movement to his left, down behind a small stand of palm trees and low scrub on the sand's edge. At least a dozen men blundered through the brush, attempting to hide themselves.

'Dead men,' Padilla muttered, 'in Angola.'

The incompetence of their approach angered him more than anything they could threaten him with, as if thirty years after the revolution he might have expected something better. They reminded him of Batista's men: targets. Padilla knew that the driveway would be blocked, that all the men would be pre-positioned and with the appropriate degree of theatre the chosen officer would knock and the arrest would take place. He stared over the sea, for what he was sure would be the last time. He regretted the waste of his life rather more than he feared pain or execution.

'*El tempano,*' he said proudly. The iceberg.

They would shoot him as they had the air force officers who had caused trouble in Oriente province. The officers, the official tribunal found, had conspired to overthrow the revolution and to defect to the United States taking their MiG fighters with them. What a coincidence. Internal insurrection and external escape at the same time. A clever trick if you could manage it. A fist beat on his door three times shaking Padilla from his thoughts.

'Oscar Padilla Sanchez,' a voice boomed from the front of the house. 'You are under arrest . . .'

There was more, but Padilla tuned out the extra words. He could do without rhetoric now. If hot air had been oil, Cuba would be wealthier than Saudi Arabia. Unfortunately an accident of geography had given the Arabs hydrocarbons and the Cubans political theorists. He gazed over the sea once more, watching the small cumulus clouds gather on the horizon, hoping for a thunderstorm to clear the humidity, to sweep away all their arrogance and hypocrisy in a second flood. There would be rain later, he was sure of it, lashing rain to cleanse spilled blood.

He opened the door and they led him away, rough peasant hands on his arms. At that moment as Padilla smelled the sweat on their bodies, the fumes from the diesel trucks, he recognised that the revolution was not what the hoaxers and theorists said. It was not some historical process based on quaint laws from the nineteenth century. It was just people, people like him. And the counter-revolution was not some Yanqui plot. It was people like them, people with ordinary faces and dull private lives and lovers and children and terrible secrets and vices, not hollow names like 'proletariat' or 'state' or 'counter-revolution'.

Padilla screwed his face with disgust, sneering at their boorish incompetence. They pushed him into the back of a large unmarked truck and drove away from the sea and the freedom of its lapping waves. He sat squeezed between four armed soldiers who shifted their eyes constantly to miss his gaze as they rumbled towards Havana. At that moment General Oscar Padilla Sanchez felt like a saint among demons, ready to burn at the stake if necessary, to sneer at the sound of his own flesh sizzling in the flames and to mock the emissaries of the Anti-Christ.

Padilla's interrogators treated him with every courtesy. He assumed such orders came from the very top, the Defence Minister or Barba-roja, the head of the DGI. Despite the official denial of the significance of individuals, the arrest of the man earmarked to take over command of the western army on suspicion of treason would – especially after the executions in Oriente – redouble the shock waves through the upper reaches of the armed forces once it was made public.

Military officers would become restive, wondering who was next. There would be alerts, fears of a coup, and then the DGI would release some hastily concocted intelligence about an imminent Ameri-can invasion and mobilise voluntary forces to bury every doubt under a wave of patriotism. Padilla assumed they would keep his arrest quiet until they figured out how best to control any backlash. His occasional disappearances were normal. His wife Eva and the rest of the family would only begin to miss him after two weeks. Lucia would assume he had gone to Mexico or Panama at short notice. Herrera would continue with the donkey work at the RCU. And it would take time for rumours of his arrest to leak out, maybe two or three weeks. The interrogators were polite but determined. They had a task to perform, and their own careers depended upon it. They did not allow Padilla to sleep for more than an hour at a time over three or four days in a windowless cell. Once his body patterns turned upside down and he was unable to guess whether it might be day or night, the interrogations gathered pace and became more intricate. From the start he recognised there was little point in hiding what they already knew, and naturally they gave the appearance of knowing everything: the bank accounts that had been authorised by the DGI, extra and unauthorised ones he had used for himself. They quoted to him the names of Panamanian intermediaries and their links to the Americans; the use of the Panamanian registered Ayala Corpor-ation as a funnel for cash which then disappeared on a paperchase they had been unable to follow. On this Padilla was especially unen-lightening.

194

'The Panamanians were the experts. They handled the money. As long as I channelled cash from the Colombians and was able to spend it or hand it over to the DGI when they needed it, I never saw any problems. I did not follow everything exactly. I'm a soldier not an accountant.'

The interrogators were inexhaustible. There were six in all, three teams of two. As Padilla grew more tired, unable to shower or shave, disliking the rank animal smell that he knew was him, he was convinced he would choose one interrogator to whom he would unburden himself in a spectacular catharsis, and who would therefore have an interest in championing the truthfulness of a confession he had so painfully extracted. Padilla was mentally prepared for everything except physical violence. He was sure they would never even slap him, knowing his stubbornness would make their job more difficult, perhaps impossible. At the first taste of violence he would shut tight as a clam, coolly withdraw any cooperation and prefer to die silently than physically be forced to speak. There was one refuge for the defeated. That was to hope for no salvation. *'El Tempano,'* he thought, repeatedly. The iceberg.

Almost from the start Padilla knew it would be Colonel Cesar Fonseca Hijuelos of all the interrogators who would deserve his confession. Fonseca had short grey hair swept back from his forehead, a thin, clever face and wiry body. He chain smoked during the interrogations, and treated Padilla with exaggerated courtesy, as if it pained him to ask a Hero of the Revolution such appalling questions.

'When did you begin to spy for the Americans?'

'I never spied for the Americans.'

'You met American agents frequently in Panama. You admit that.'

'I met drug dealers frequently too. Does that mean I spied for the Medellin cartel?'

'You used banking facilities provided by the Americans, and now the western press tells us these banking facilities were front organisations for the CIA.'

'But we never believe the western press. Or do we? Maybe you do. In which case perhaps you are the spy. Why don't you confess?'

Part of Fonseca's charm rested in the very dull and methodical

195

way he questioned Padilla. No jokes or sarcasm disrupted the steady progress of his questions. He spoke firmly but sadly.

'You cannot expect us to believe, Comrade General, that you really did not know these were CIA organisations.'

Padilla had a headache from being held too long without light and fresh air. He wanted to walk on the beach again at his house, looking at the sea and sand.

'Listen,' he said wearily. 'I was forced into dealing with two kinds of contamination – the Colombian drug dealers, who are the scum of the hemisphere, and the money launderers in Panama, who are no better. Then I dealt with higher-class and better-dressed scum operating from the Cayman Islands, Mexico, and Europe. The fact that we were so naive not to realise the Americans would be heavily involved in money laundering for intelligence-gathering purposes confirms that we are still fighting the wars of the 1950s, still hiding behind the jungles of the Sierra Maestra. Our revolution is frozen like a prehistoric monster caught in the glaciers of the past. You may believe what you wish about me, but neither I myself nor the DGI of which you are no doubt a distinguished member, were aware of the corrupt activities of American intelligence.'

Fonseca pulled another cigarette from its packet and tapped it hard on the desk. He lit it and stared at Padilla.

'We all know there are shortcomings in the revolution, Padilla Sanchez,' he said. 'We have been cut off from our natural trading partners for three decades.'

He paused for a few seconds, and Padilla watched the smoke curl above his head. His eyes nipped from tiredness. He would have liked a cigarette, but it was not offered and he was too exhausted to ask. He felt himself nodding to sleep again. Then Fonseca grabbed his attention.

'You know how to make a dog vicious?'

It was not a question to which Padilla had given much thought. He shrugged and looked away. Fonseca's eyes bored into him.

'You make a dog vicious not by beating it,' Fonseca said. 'That's how an idiot might do it, or a sadist. You make it vicious by feeding it once a day yet otherwise ignoring it – no contact with other dogs or humans; no commands, no love, not even a beating. The dog

196

goes insane from loneliness and starved of affection it becomes so aggressive it will fight its own shadow.'

Padilla turned back to look at him. Fonseca's thin face was animated now, orange coloured in the sharp light.

'So?'

'So, Padilla Sanchez, if this revolution has turned to viciousness – to drug trafficking – it is for that reason. That like a dog they wanted to make mad, the Americans cut us off from everything – everything – until we cracked under the pressure. Not the economic pressure they thought would work, but being ignored, being left alone without the full contact of others. If we are perverse then it is because they have made us so.'

Fonseca had come to the end of his cigarette and a half inch of ash fell on the table between them. He stubbed out the butt harshly in the ashtray.

'The only ones to be corrupted were the old revolutionaries like you.'

Suddenly Padilla felt very bored with these games.

'If you want me to plead guilty to something, I will do it. For the sake of the revolution. If it is felt to be necessary. There is nothing in my life which I love so much that I would not give it up for something important. If you want me to appear in a show trial and confess according to a script that you devise, I will do that too. But, *companero*, please do not treat me like a fool. You are almost of my generation, maybe a few years younger. You know this revolution has lost its way, has achieved little in the past ten years, and while the rest of the world killed off the stupidities of Marxism, we pursued them as if they were still better than the truth of God. You cannot blame the Americans. We chose, or at least some of us chose, to become involved as *narcotraficantes*. No end can justify that means. None. No matter who says so. If you want me to plead guilty to something, then I will. But not to treason. Not to helping the Americans. These are false and stupid charges. If I am a traitor then you are too. Or General Fernandez. Or the Defence Minister. We have all betrayed the revolution, which is why it is in such a mess. Purge us all. Kill everything back to Year Zero. Start again.'

The effort made Padilla sweat hard and his head swim. He changed his tone and began speaking more softly.

'If I must plead guilty to a crime to suit your convenience, so I may be removed without threat of military unrest, then I will plead guilty to drug trafficking, because that is a crime unworthy of this nation and the Cuban people, and I am guilty. The only trouble is I was ordered to do it in the name of the nation and the Cuban people. Maybe we should all be indicted, convicted, sentenced to remain trapped on a prison island with no contact with the outside world.'

Fonseca interrupted. 'Why was it a waste of time to try to free people from the old colonial powers? Why was it a waste of time to help people down the road we have travelled? What happened to set you against all we stand for?'

'Fidel was and is a great leader,' he said. 'But he is not Jesus Christ. He is not to be worshipped. Not by me, at any rate.'

Fonseca looked on impassively.

'Oh yes,' Padilla continued. 'Some say Fidel has this marvellous way of cutting through the bureaucracy and the stupidity of the petty party officials. But who created the bureaucracy and who keeps the petty party officials in their jobs? Is this something else we can blame on the Yanquis? For thirty years I have watched this great man grow old, watched his revolution – and ours, and mine and yours – fail to renew itself.'

Padilla thought he was beginning to ramble. He stopped for a moment and heard the clatter of the stenographer cease with him.

'Look,' he said, using up the last of his energy. 'If we must have a Jesus, then let us at least have the real Jesus, but do not pretend that Fidel stands for all good things and that our problems come from the Martians or the CIA, or God. They seem to be about much the same thing in this country. Sacrifice me if you want, but do not treat me like a child.'

Padilla's voice trailed away. For some reason his mind turned to Africa and the bush war, the thumping of heavy artillery in the jungle, the hit-and-run enemy using classic guerrilla tactics against the soldiers of a Cuban government which had employed the same methods to come to power in Havana all that time ago. He muttered some-

198

thing about the stupidity of the campaign, the arrogance of what they had tried to do.

'And the waste,' he whispered through cracked lips. 'The waste of time and of lives.'

Fonseca interrupted. 'Why was it waste of time to try to free people from the old colonial powers? Why was it a waste of time to help people down the road we have travelled? What happened to set you against all we stand for?'

Padilla smiled and shook his head.

'Nothing happened, that was what made me realise the revolution had failed. Nothing changed by the time I returned from Angola. That was the point. While the world continued to turn, we stopped moving. You must change or die. That is all there is to know.'

Sometimes during the interrogations Padilla felt lucid and in control. When they scared him most, he was at his most acute. But increasingly as the days wore on he would dream while awake, hallucinations of the past and nightmares of what was to come. Fonseca wanted more details of the people Padilla met in connection with the money laundering. Padilla described them for the hundred and fifteenth time, his voice a monotone, his mind on autopilot. He rehearsed the names and biographies of the Panamanians, Jorge Lopez and his colleagues, and then Phil Lewis, the fat American, whose life in Miami was now being quoted back at Padilla from the cabled report sent by the Cuban embassy in London.

'What did you think of Lewis?' Fonseca asked again. 'Were you impressed by him?'

Padilla explained patiently how he met Lewis, how the Panamanians offered the initial banking facilities and first introduced him to Lopez. After a while, Lopez set up accounts for Padilla in the Caymans, Florida and the Bahamas.

'That's when Phil Lewis appeared,' Padilla said. 'The difficult thing was getting the large quantities of cash into the banking system. You can't walk into a bank with a million dollars in a suitcase and expect people not to be suspicious. The Lewis company got the money into the system for us. They must have guessed where it came from but did not care. Maybe they were monitoring it for the CIA, I don't know. But once it was in the system it was easier to move it around

199

into other accounts. As far as I could tell, money was the only thing Lewis and Lopez were interested in.'

'Did they talk about the possibility of you leading a military coup in Cuba?'

'No. As I told you, they thought I was an expatriate Nicaraguan using the cover name Ricardo Alarcon.'

'How can you be sure they did not know your real identity?'

'I can't. But they never betrayed they had any CIA connection. They never suggested I do anything for them.'

Fonseca decided to change the subject. Yet again he tried to push Padilla on details of where the money had gone, and Padilla admitted he was overwhelmed by it.

'It was manageable at first,' he said. 'Even for someone like me who is a stranger to all this. When we merely provided protection for the Colombians we were pulling in thirty million dollars a year. We were doing little more than levying a tax on the cocaine cartel. And if allowing the drugs to get to the United States and gathering in the proceeds was justified, then extending the supply network to make more money must be justified too. It's simple logic.'

'So that's when you began buying and selling,' Fonseca said. 'Even though that clearly exceeded your orders.'

'Exactly,' Padilla replied. 'Except I do not see how you can say I exceeded my orders. I gave the orders. It was up to me. My decision was for Cuba to take a bigger cut. The Colombians had little choice but to accept. We smoothed over some of their problems in Panama with Noriega, and they were very grateful. Then I told them we wanted to buy and sell on our own account, as well as allow them to transship through Cuba.'

'What was their reaction?'

Padilla laughed.

'Rather like a monopoly supplier from the bourgeoisie being told the government is about to take over part of his business. But they knew there was very little choice. It multiplied our profits tenfold. And, in case you have forgotten, *companero*, profit was the main reason I was pushed into this business in the first place. The only problem was not moral but practical. The money was coming in so fast there was the question of what we do with it. That helped push

200

me deeper in with Lewis and his company.' Padilla admitted that he was naive not to suspect the Americans would be watching money trafficking as much as drugs trafficking. 'Lewis once explained to me,' he volunteered, leaning forward as if confiding in Fonseca, 'that they recognised the cocaine business was only partly about drugs. It's really about money. Separate the dealers from their drugs and they become angry, but separate them from their money and you kill them off.'

Fonseca nodded.

'Very profound,' he said sarcastically. He wanted more details from Padilla to confirm the data they had already seized from the files in his beach house. Padilla could not remember.

'I was never very good with the money, as you can see.'

Fonseca laughed, a bitter laugh which tore at Padilla's flesh.

'Neither were the Americans, *companero*,' he said, jabbing a finger towards the cable from the London embassy with its summary of the *Tribune* story. 'Otherwise your friend Mr Lewis might still be one of the pillars of Miami society and you might be commander of the western military district.'

Padilla smiled grimly at the thought. Fonseca signalled to the subsidiary interrogator that the session was now at an end.

He stood up, and so did Padilla who immediately felt dizzy and thought he might faint. He gripped the front of his chair, suddenly very tired and old, hoping that this time Fonseca and the others might let him sleep.

'Tell me,' he said as they prepared to escort him back to his cell. 'What will happen now?'

Fonseca shuffled his papers together on the desk, and picked up the half empty packet of cigarettes. He turned from Padilla, stood up then looked him in the eye.

'Our investigations continue,' he said flatly. 'And will conclude with a lengthy, detailed report. Either you will appear innocent but disloyal, in which case you will be forced to resign your command and be left in retirement where you can do no harm. Or your guilt will be established. And your treason. In which case you will be tried, you will confess, and be shot. This revolution cannot tolerate drug smugglers and thieves.'

16

The bruising row with Terrelli left Warren Cabot especially hopeful as he took a cab to Washington National Airport for the flight, once more, to Miami. He considered Terrelli clearly rattled, exploding with the anger of a guilty man. That meant, a loser, and with luck Cabot would be able to judge within forty-eight hours whether the Lewis affair might be damaging enough to guarantee that he himself became the next Director of Central Intelligence. He chuckled with satisfaction, though he felt ghoulish at the thought of profiting from such adversity. Of course Terrelli's bluster, ordering him to go down to Miami and claiming it was Cabot's errors that had allowed the disclosures in the British newspapers made it all the easier, all the more necessary, to exploit the situation. Panic, Cabot thought. Terrelli displayed justifiable panic, because he was not up to the job and had not given the correct degree of moral leadership. Where there is no vision, the Agency will perish.

Cabot checked in for the flight full of optimism that his career was on some kind of cusp; that within days, hours, everything might change for the better. Every time he telephoned the FBI investigators in Miami it became clearer that Lewis had been sitting on top of a rotting garbage heap of investments with interests halfway round the world and it would take months to sift through the debris left behind. That was good news. It meant no trial could be contemplated until well after the presidential election and the inauguration. The delay caused by the technical difficulty of assembling evidence did not restrict Cabot in what he might choose to do privately.

It seemed to him absolutely in the public interest (and his own, a

202

pleasant coincidence) that he use whatever information came his way.

Cabot spent the journey considering his next moves. He had a few days before the planned summer vacation at his wife's ranch in Montana. He would of course do absolutely as Terrelli had ordered in Miami, make sure Lewis and his lawyer Holgate realised there could be no hope of them mounting a defence based on classified documents if they talked to the media. The Classified Information Procedures Act would make sure they were hamstrung, coupled with Terrelli's threats which Cabot was more than happy to deliver. But he would go further, and use the trip to pump the FBI on what had really gone wrong with the operation. He arranged to spend time talking to Lewis's former assistant, Ileana Del Cid to see what she might come up with about the relationship between Boone, Terrelli and Lewis.

When the flight landed, a tall Hispanic girl in a bright blue mini-dress was waiting near the gate holding a piece of cardboard with 'Warren Cabot' written in laundry marker pen. She was stunningly attractive, with long and shiny black hair, perhaps a little too much make-up for Cabot's taste. Even though she wore low heels she stood a full inch taller than Cabot himself.

'I'm Cabot. Warren Cabot.' He beamed behind his glasses.

'Ileana,' she replied, shaking him firmly by the hand. 'Ileana Del Cid.'

Ileana threw her cardboard sign away and shepherded Cabot through the main terminal building towards her car. He was not what she had expected, much more diffident and bookish than those who had worked for Phil Lewis. But, she told herself, that was because he was just a lawyer, not from the Operations Directorate.

Cabot gazed around the airport terminal watching the Latin American bazaar of Salvadorans returning home clutching electrical goods, Nicaraguans and Costa Ricans, squads of thick set Colombians, pretty young girls with sleazy fat men in open-necked shirts, gold Rolex watches strapped round the ends of their suntanned arms, well dressed Caracas businessmen, harassed families trying to get to Bogota and Mexico city.

'It's been a long time since I spent a vacation in Florida,' Cabot said, trying to make conversation. The truth was he never much liked the state, and now in August found it detestable. He admired the energy and drive of the Latino population but for the rest, it was too flat and too hot and too full of tourists and emigrés from the north. It reminded him of New York without either the culture or the shops, which is to say, a zoo.

'With the exception of the short trip I made to seal the files when this broke, I guess I haven't been here for ten or twelve years.'

'You will find it has changed a lot,' Ileana said, parting her perfectly lipsticked lips and looking down on him with a stiff smile. 'Full of Haitians and Nicaraguans, Salvadorans and Panamanians now. Used to be just Cubans. Not any more.'

Cabot nodded. The heat was stifling as they walked to the car park, even worse than Washington.

'Did you have any luck trying to contact Lewis?'

'No, Mr Cabot,' she replied, somewhat perplexed. Everybody wanted Lewis and thought she must know where he was. She did not. Then her uncle Jorge Lopez had suggested that Cabot would know, so if Ileana was nice to him maybe she might find out. Now the CIA's own lawyer was professing ignorance. It was too complicated.

'I have tried through Phil's lawyer, Tom Holgate,' she said. 'Then through all the contacts we used in Washington. Richard Boone at the White House. Nothing. Or nothing yet. Mr Boone said, maybe sometime soon. He would let me know. But wherever Lewis is, he has not contacted me. The lawyer, Holgate, says he passed on the messages to Phil, but I just don't think he wants to talk to me, Mr Cabot. Which is a bit hard to take from someone I worked with for seven years.'

She unlocked the car, a black Mustang convertible. Cabot thought it nice enough to be called 'Mr Cabot' once in a while.

'In fact, Mr Cabot, I was hoping you might know where he is and tell me.'

'Oh, what do you want with him?'

'To check on the safety of a mutual friend,' she blurted out. 'In Cuba. Perhaps you know about it, Mr Cabot. And perhaps you do not, in which case I have gone too far.'

'Columbus,' he said. 'Mutual friend.'

'It's better we do not talk about it. But you must know there are people in danger over there as a result of this mess. People I care about very much.'

'I understand, Miss Del Cid.'

If she knew about Columbus, the beautiful Ileana might be more helpful to Cabot than he had realised.

'I suggest we go straight to the Federal Building,' she said, pleased to change the subject. 'It's getting late if you want to talk to the FBI. They will still be working, but if you prefer we can put them off until tomorrow, and check you in to your hotel.'

'No, tonight will be fine. I'm anxious to get working.'

He looked across to her as she drove. With the hot Miami air whistling through his grey hair, speeding along in a convertible with a pretty young woman beside him, Warren Theodore Cabot felt like loosening his tie. He stiffened. There would be no point. He would merely have to re-knot it before meeting the FBI team.

'You been with us long?'

'Seven years,' she replied, looking at him sideways. 'Like I said. Seven years since I was recruited to work with Phil Lewis.'

'What do you think of him?'

She smiled, showing her teeth, and Cabot thought how white they were against her skin.

'Have you ever met him?'

Cabot shook his head.

'I've read his files. Or some of them. Not having automatic access to operations material I suppose what I know about him is a heavily truncated version of the truth. I guess that is always the way. You know something and you guess some more, thinking you have the whole story. In this case I'm aware that every one of us only has a limited grasp of what we're sitting on here.'

Ileana laughed. 'Everything you know about Phil Lewis will always be a heavily truncated version of the truth. In seven years I never fully figured him out. He was one of those men who constantly say they are acting out of patriotism or the national interest. That was very important for him, I guess, as a Britisher and immigrant to this country.'

'And was he?'

'Was he what?'

'Acting out of patriotism and in the national interest?'

Ileana laughed again. 'For Phil Lewis patriotism, like charity, began at home. The best way of explaining him is as one of those television evangelists for whom God's will and their own personal profit always seem to coincide.'

Cabot blinked. She was sharp, this young woman. He liked her. They were sweeping towards the city and Cabot watched the lights of the skyline spreading along the ocean. The signs carried exotic names like 'Coconut Grove' and 'Coral Gables' and 'South Beach'.

'Is it not possible to do both?' he wondered aloud. 'To serve your country well and fulfil your own ambitions?'

'Sure,' Ileana said. 'But I guess what I'm saying is, looking at the way the pack of cards came tumbling down here, that when there was a choice, Phil acted mainly on behalf of Phil. He fooled all of us into helping him because we figured it was for the good of the country. I guess he really believed that what he did and what the country needed were the same things. But that's what made him so convincing and so dangerous.'

They turned off the freeway and at the first underpass a dozen black youths stood at the street corner eyeing them contemptuously. Cabot could see two of them with portable telephones, one talking heatedly as he paced up and down.

'Dealers,' Ileana said, noticing Cabot's curiosity. 'Taking telephone orders.'

'For what?'

'Crack to go. Cocaine. Heroin is making a comeback. Anything you want, I guess. Except pizza.'

There were a few street people wandering in grubby knots through the centre of town.

'It's the same in Washington, too,' Cabot said. 'Five hundred murders a year in a city of seven hundred thousand people.'

Ileana shrugged. She pulled the Mustang into the car park under the Federal Building, flashing her pass at the security guard. When they stopped, Warren Cabot ran his hands through his hair to try to make some order out of the chaos caused by the wind. He checked his tie and put on his light blue seersucker jacket.

'The people you are going to meet,' she warned, 'have been eating and breathing Phil Lewis fifteen hours a day for the past five or six weeks. They normally start work at seven in the morning. This time of night, you'll find they have fairly strong opinions. I suggest you take it slow, Mr Cabot.'

'Thank you for the advice.'

The air-conditioning had been turned down to its night time level and the offices were above eighty degrees. On the sixteenth floor Ileana used a key card and a code pad to open the front doors. At the security desk Cabot was presented with an FBI visitor's pass which he clipped awkwardly on his tie. They moved to a large open plan office. In the corner, four men were still working, sifting through mounds of paper. The four stood up as they approached, nodding at Cabot, eating up Ileana in her tight blue dress.

'This is Warren Cabot,' she said, then introduced them one by one. 'Leon Kramer, head of the Lewis investigation whom I guess you've talked to a lot on the telephone. Julio Cardoza, his number two, and from the fraud side Bill Spence and Joe Donahue.'

Cabot looked into four pairs of tired eyes.

'We better go in the tank,' Kramer said, gesturing towards a side office with a metal security door.

They picked up their papers and Kramer gestured to Cabot to follow him and take a mug of coffee.

'We won't be long, Ileana.'

Kramer hit a key pad at the side of the metal door, then slipped in his own electronic pass. The door popped open, and the five men, each carrying a coffee mug, strode inside. Even before they sat down, Kramer asked Cabot what he needed to know beyond what they had discussed nearly every day on the telephone over the past few weeks.

'Well,' Cabot said. 'What more can you tell me? Let me put it this way, every time I ask you what I think will be a simple question, can we nail Lewis in court, you dodge and weave. What's the problem?'

Kramer sipped his coffee. He liked Cabot's directness but did not show it. He was, as always, professionally unimpressed. Kramer was a middle-aged New York Jew who had tried for years to get some kind of posting in the sun. He wanted San Diego, but as soon as the Bureau heard he was angling for California with the perverse logic of all bureaucracies they posted him to Florida to work alongside the Drug Enforcement Administration. No, Kramer could not figure it out either. Nor could he fully figure out the Lewis case. The more he burrowed into it, the more it was some kind of bad joke.

'Look, Cabot,' he said. 'We're simple folk down here. We don't play Washington games. We don't understand them, and we don't have the time. So here's how we do this. You tell us precisely – precisely – what you want. We tell you what we can. How's that sound?'

'Sounds good,' Cabot replied. 'Sounds fine. Then let me ask again. I want to know how strong the case against Lewis is likely to be.'

Kramer shrugged, looking at his assistants and rolling his eyes. 'Well,' he finally began, 'it's strong if you mean do we have evidence of money pouring into Lewis's company and some of it pouring out again into Lewis's own bank account as supposed interest payments on investments he never had. But it's like one of those Russian dolls. Every time I crack open one of them, there's another inside with a different kind of smile on her face. Lewis was skimming money. There's no problem with that. But the case has got one fatal flaw in it, Mr Cabot.'

Kramer paused for effect, noisily sipping his coffee.

'Which is?' Cabot asked, irritably. 'The flaw, I mean.'

'Which is that as soon as we present the evidence in court Lewis will do what he's already done in the newspapers. Start hollerin' that everything was ordered by and for the benefit of the CIA, sanctioned by Uncle Sam in the name of God and Country. Then either the judge allows into evidence the files you just sealed a couple of weeks ago, or his smart ass lawyer tells the jury the reasons why you sealed the files. The CIA was so obviously in this like a pig in shit I'd say then your chances of a conviction slip below fifty fifty.'

Cabot nodded.

'Bad news travels fast,' he said. 'About the newspaper story.'

'Sure,' Kramer replied. 'I'm up to my neck in telephone messages from the *Miami Herald* and every television news show from Pensacola to Key West. They're following up something from a British

208

comic. The Brits say Lewis is claiming the Nazi defence, that he was only following orders. Like the rest of us, I guess.'

'In which case,' Cabot said, 'is it worth the trouble to pursue a case with so little chance of securing a conviction?'

'Depends whether you're a Democrat or a Republican,' Kramer said with a grin. 'I mean, you're asking me questions above my pay grade. But some of this stuff doesn't look so good. It's like you took crime off the streets and put it in Langley. So we find out the CIA was using the methods of the money launderers to pay its agents. That's no big deal. But then it set up a front company taking investments, and the company goes belly up. So Agency headquarters decides not to prosecute because it would be too embarrassing for one of its own to be found guilty of swindling people. I'd say that if you do not prosecute you're in bigger shit than if you do. Speakin' personally.'

Joe Donahue chimed in. He was a dumpy curly-haired Irish American. 'Mr Cabot,' Donahue said, in a thick New Jersey accent, pronouncing the first word 'mista'. 'Mista Cabot, don't you get the wrong idea here. This company was full of sleaze. Only maybe it wasn't the kinda sleaze you're thinking. We're only right now getting to grips with all this, and we're not working at it day or night 'cause we think this is one you should forget about. The way it's looking, wherever the paperchase goes, in the end we got one clear picture. The picture's this: Agency operatives or former operatives invested their money at highly preferential rates through Lewis's investment companies.'

'So?' Cabot asked. 'So what?'

Donahue scratched his curly mop of hair. 'So we think the deal was to use CIA intelligence to provide information on the performance of corporations, economic information on trade and the activities of foreign governments, the way the foreign exchange markets were gonna move, like an Agency within the Agency kinda style. And –' Donahue tapped Cabot on the knee to make sure he got the point. 'And we think the centrepiece of the scam was that profits were raked off for a whole group of intelligence officers behind the operation.'

Kramer broke in impatiently. This was the best bit, and he wanted to say it.

'Look, Cabot. I don't think any of us understood what is at stake here. The way I read it, this was the sweetest insider trading scam there could ever be. The best. We reckon, maybe thirty or forty big players in or around the Agency, plus military brass, all guaranteed the money would be safe thanks to Uncle Sam. All raking in the cash. This was a real financial turkey shoot. Nobody who was in could lose. I mean, it was all phoney names. One of these mothers pulled in over four million dollars. Apple something.'

'Appletree,' Donahue chimed in. 'David Appletree. Four million four hundred thousand. And still counting. There were a dozen others who scored more than a million. An' they're just the ones we've found out about.'

Cabot took off his glasses and rubbed his eyes.

'I don't think I fully understand,' he said. 'Did Phil Lewis steal money from Winston, Hamilton, Bellingham, Lewis and Lopez or not?'

'He did,' Donahue replied.

'And you've got the evidence to prove it?'

'Yes we have.'

'Then we should prosecute him. Second question: are you telling me this goes a lot further than Phil Lewis? Is that what I'm hearing?'

Kramer laughed. 'Look, Mr Cabot. Whatever you think Lewis was into, he was into it ten times over. Whoever you think was involved, multiply it by ten. Bottom line? This is like an abscess filled with pus. We've just made the first cut. We don't know how deep it goes, whether we can save the limb, but we know it's bad. Real bad.'

The shock of what Kramer was saying began to sink in, but Cabot was not thinking how deep it went. He was thinking high. Either Boone or Terrelli did not know, or did not want to know what had happened. Maybe that explained why the Lewis operation had survived unscathed long after Deep Blue outlived its Cold War mission. It was making so much money for so many people it was virtually self financing. Cabot was lost in thought trying to work out the implications for the Agency, and for himself, his face knotted in a heavy frown. Kramer could see he had hit Cabot with a blackjack. He drained his coffee and put it to one side.

'It's real simple, Mr Cabot,' Kramer said, 'though the details are complicated. We can prosecute Lewis, but if we do, we open up the abscess to public view. If we don't, in effect we're all part of a cover up. Whatever else is in there, we know it points to serious corruption in the national security establishment. I have informed the Attorney General's Office, and we'll just have to see where it runs now.'

Cabot looked at Kramer, feeling a twist of panic in his stomach and recognising the reason behind the near hysteria that seemed to grip Terrelli. Whatever he had hoped to find or exploit for his own advantage, Cabot realised this was too grim. He felt a chill in his bowels.

'I need you to run that by me slowly, one more time,' he said to Kramer. 'So I am sure there is no mistake. I'm just a dumb lawyer, remember. Are you telling me that Lewis and others used Agency expertise to make money for themselves?'

'Yeah. And to bankroll operations. They did their patriotic duty too.'

'And that Lewis's Miami operation was virtually self financing because it made so much in profits?' Cabot attacked.

'Yeah – if you include some government money which had been budgeted to pay agents and expenses.' Kramer was now spitting out the words at dictation speed. 'It was a self-standing, independent, intelligence-gathering operation which also paid handsome profits to those who were part of the loop. This was a private enterprise for CIA profit. Which is why that investor Scott Lehtinen was so pissed. He knew somehow of the money to be made, only he wasn't part of the action. But all we got now, apart from Lewis, is a string of phoney names, aliases, running bank accounts in Panama, the Caymans, Aruba and Curacao.'

Warren Cabot thought he had heard enough. He thanked Kramer, shook hands all round and left abruptly. He asked Ileana Del Cid to drop him at his hotel at Coconut Grove, and then claiming he was tired did not, as he had planned, invite her to dinner.

'We'll meet before I go,' Cabot said, desperately wanting to be alone to think. 'We have a lot to discuss, but it will keep. Thank you for your help today.'

As soon he reached his hotel bedroom Cabot undid his tie and rolled up his sleeves. He needed fresh air to think. He walked downstairs and out into the hotel grounds. The swimming pool was lit up and there was a kind of boardwalk which ran out to a marina with a few dozen yachts and power boats bobbing in the darkness. Cabot almost could not believe the conversation with Kramer. He was struck by his description that it was like opening up a series of Russian dolls, with a new one inside every time you thought you had reached the inner chamber. And he was struck too by something Ileana Del Cid had said: that Lewis had the happy knack of pretending that actions which were really in his own interest were also in the national interest.

It was the habit of government. If Kramer was right about Deep Blue, that habit was also the guiding principle of more than a decade of covert action in the hemisphere. Cabot sighed. He had a stick the size of a baseball club to beat Terrelli and Boone with, bludgeoning his way to the DCI job, if he still wanted it.

Cabot looked at the boats bobbing in the darkness on the calm bay, the lights reflected in the water. The enormity of what Kramer had said made him shiver with anxiety despite the heat. He felt a vague fear ripple through his body. It had all seemed a game, this ambitious career in public service, trying to push others to one side because he was the best man for the job, sniffing power like a pig after a truffle. But now he was faced with a world in which he did not belong.

Cabot was on the edge of the violent frontier, the moral wilderness which made him shake with worry. The opportunity and the danger he had seen in this crisis were reaching a point where he had to take an inescapable decision. The country's best interests would not be served by another great scandal, either before or after the election, weakening American intelligence and inevitably ending at the White House. If it was exposed in the next few weeks it would wreck the president's already troubled progress towards re-election. And if it came out later, after he was re-elected, it could turn him into a lame duck president, a second Nixon, with the CIA being dismantled underneath him.

For the first time he could remember, Cabot saw a clear difference between what was right for the country and what was in his own personal interests. He could scream what he knew of the scandal

212

from the highest roof top, advancing his own claim to be the straight arrow capable of reforming the Agency.

Or he could shut up, as Kramer said, in effect become part of the conspiracy, and bide his time until after the election. Cabot began to walk back to his hotel. He felt pained and alone as if everything he stood for in public service had become tainted by a creeping cancer which touched all of them, a lingering disease from the Cold War.

Warren Cabot stood on the boardwalk where the yachts at their moorings creaked and groaned. He pulled off his glasses and polished them clean, gazing around him in the blurred night hoping for inspiration, praying that the hand of God might touch his shoulder and turn him one way or the other. There was not even a breath of wind. After a few moments he slipped the spectacles back on his nose and the world, such as it was, came back into focus, sharp and desperate.

17

Helen DeVos stood in the heat outside Miami Federal Courthouse for two hours. She wore a broad-brimmed hat as shade from the beating sun and drank from a bottle of lukewarm Perrier water – Alex Newman would be proud of her. She was determined to carry out the old threat: you can run, but you just can't hide, even if in this case 'you' happened to be the special counsel to the Director of Central Intelligence. She had missed Warren Cabot on his way in to the closed hearing; he had turned up two hours early, according to a friendly police officer on guard duty. Holgate had alerted DeVos and the Miami media that this was the day on which the CIA's lawyers were formally trying to extend their gagging order, while Holgate himself was seeking to un-freeze Lewis's bank accounts. DeVos flew down from Washington, having persuaded Newman she had a slim chance of speaking to Cabot and could at least include the hearing in a possible second feature for the *Tribune*, while he saw to more routine matters like the presidential election campaign.

During the boring hours of her wait DeVos tried to keep amused by thinking of lovemaking with Newman. From the moment they kissed he began to undress her, and she found herself grabbing at him in an adolescent dash to strip one another naked. Newman had pulled her towards him from the chair to the floor and they made love in a frantic combat.

'I think,' she had said, when they recovered their breath, as she stroked his hair and he kissed her gently on the neck, 'I think we might be more comfortable on your bed.'

Newman laughed. 'Maybe we should take off all our clothes as well.'

214

He switched on the ceiling fan in the bedroom and they lay under its waves talking and laughing, as if a few minutes of sex was a liberation from all previous misunderstandings between them.

'I thought you talked too much,' he said with a grin. 'A know-all.'

'Insecurity,' she said, 'in the face of your hostility.'

'Maybe I just wanted to impress you, to be decisive, and it came across as hostile. Pathetic, isn't it?'

'Only because we think we're old enough to know better. But we're not. Nobody is. When it comes to things like this, everyone acts . . . well, pubescent.'

Helen told him the truth. That from their first meeting in New York she found him interesting but stuck-up in that peculiarly superior way she thought a British national characteristic.

'You resented my expertise on this story and I guess some Brits just can't handle women in positions of power,' she had said to him after one especially vicious dispute.

'I suppose that's why we elected Thatcher as Prime Minister three times in ten years,' Newman shot back in a tone which confirmed her worst suspicions.

'I'd hardly call her a woman,' Helen replied, confirming his.

Now it seemed so ridiculous, especially when she told him that she knew for days they were going to end in bed together.

'Why didn't you tell me?' Newman protested. 'We could have got on with it quicker instead of wasting time with me being so careful not to upset you. I thought you were so politically correct the first time I laid a finger on you I'd hear screams of date rape.'

She sniggered. She could not really imagine him as the supposed Modern Man, anxious not to offend, understanding, kind.

'You would not like me that way anyway, Helen,' he said. 'I think you prefer Cavemen to Quiche Eaters.'

'If that was the only choice, then yes, you're probably right.'

When the tip off from Holgate came about the court hearing, Newman seized upon Mike Holroyd's enthusiasm for the first story to cajole him into paying DeVos's fare to Miami a second time plus a few days' research fees to try to dig up more files. Now as Helen paced up and down the courthouse steps and read for the hundredth time the list of names of federal judges inscribed on the wall, she wondered whether Holgate's anxiety about unfreezing the funds was because he was anxious about his own three hundred dollar an hour fees. Suddenly Holgate strode out of the courthouse. His tanned face was darkened thunder. He walked up to the dozen or so reporters and three television crews and stood sweating gently in his dark grey three piece suit yelling about the injustice that had just taken place. He recounted how the private hearing had ended with confirmation that the files he needed to make his defence case had been sealed, a more stringent gag order was now in place, and Phil Lewis's funds still frozen. Strike three.

'I have to be very careful what I say,' Holgate bellowed. 'So much of what I would like to tell you is covered by the gag order. It's like a growing police state in this country, the arrogance of power. Who gave American intelligence the right to destroy a man's life without a trial? Who said the CIA could now act as prosecution, judge and jury, determining what is or is not in the national security interest, and sealing a private citizen's bank accounts? We're on the brink of the twenty-first century and what have we created here – the American Empire's Gestapo?'

Unluckily for Warren Cabot he chose the moment of the loudest yell to appear from behind the courtroom doors into the news scrum. Holgate caught a glimpse of his patrician figure, awkwardly trying to clear a path to his waiting car.

'And that is the leading lawyer for the police state,' Holgate bellowed enthusiastically. 'Coming to court on behalf of a clandestine arm of the US government, an Agency so secretive we do not even know how many employees it has, so out of control it can seize files which happen to embarrass it.'

Cabot tried to push through the crowd but they refused to part before him. The television cameras turned to Cabot's embarrassed face, though they could still pick up Holgate's yells on the sound track.

'How can you threaten to jail my client before the trial takes place Mr Cabot? How can you claim he has violated the CIA secrecy oath when you are telling everyone publicly you do not accept Phil Lewis was part of the CIA? What the hell's going on here?'

The gag order covered classified information but not, apparently,

216

abuse. Helen DeVos tried to hold back her amusement as she pushed her cassette recorder under Cabot's nose.

'What's the CIA's response to that, Mr Cabot?' she asked, but he pressed his way more firmly now towards his waiting limousine. DeVos was delighted. She knew that when the scene was replayed on the local evening news he would look less like a Boston brahmin than a thief making a guilty escape from a mob of the justifiably outraged.

'What about the investors' money, Mr Cabot?' another reporter yelled. 'Will the CIA pay it back?'

'Who were you spying on in Miami?'

'Yo, look here willya? Yo, hey man.'

'Sir, just one comment.'

Grim faced, his grey hair wet with perspiration, Cabot finally pushed through into the air-conditioned cool of the limousine which sped away. Helen DeVos, flushed with success, called Newman immediately from a pay phone. It was difficult now to have a business conversation with him. While she spoke about Holgate and Cabot she was thinking about sex. While he listened politely, he was thinking about the same thing. It was less fun but more efficient when they barely liked each other. He said he was sure there was enough for a follow up story. Holroyd reluctantly agreed to think about it, the most lukewarm commitment imaginable. Helen said the theme might be that James Bond at the CIA these days carried a briefcase and legal papers rather than a pistol and a licence to kill. Maybe he could call the British Embassy for a comment on this type of American justice for a British citizen.

'I miss you,' Newman said when she paused.

'I miss you too.'

'Especially last night.'

'I'll be back soon.'

'I know. When do you think you'll be finished?'

'Probably tomorrow. Holgate's so spooked by the gag order I don't think I'll get anything more out of him. Lewis has disappeared again. Holgate claims he's not even in Miami.'

'He would say that, wouldn't he.'

'Sure.'

'Call me again tonight.'

'I will . . .'

As soon as she finished the conversation Helen drove back to her hotel in South Miami Beach.

Now the *Tribune* was not paying expenses, only research fees, she took an inexpensive room in the Art Deco district, at the Aztec Hotel. As soon as she arrived, she changed into her yellow swimsuit. She threw her clothes to the floor then stood for a moment, naked, gazing at the mirror. It wasn't such a bad body really, not that of a teenager, but firm enough for a thirty-two-year-old. She ran her hands down from her breasts to her hips, trying to pinch the flesh between thumbs and forefingers. No excess fat. Well, perhaps a little, but none that mattered. She pulled on the swimsuit, smoothing it over her breasts, and padded down the corridor to the elevator. It was almost six o'clock and there was no one in the pool.

She guessed that all the tourists were eating in one of the seafood restaurants, stuffing themselves with jumbo shrimp. She was delighted because she hated trying to swim laps through a bunch of kids, or worse, hippopotamus-sized adults lumbering in their first exercise for months. She slipped off her beach shoes and looked east over the ocean.

The palm trees were almost completely still, just the hint of a rustle in the air. The pool lay before her shimmering in the fading rays of the sun. It had a hypnotic effect, the orange sheen, the sparkle, the blue. Helen dived in gracefully, delighted as the shock of coolness washed over her, fresh on her skin. She began swimming an easy, rhythmic crawl. There were loose ends to be tidied up. Chuck Lowell, for one. It was over, and she would have to tell him soon, but she did not want to do it on the telephone. She could imagine the sad, beagle eyes as he stood crying and begging her to change her mind, but that was pointless.

However things worked out with Newman, Lowell was part of the past. Like the magazine *Combat*, Lowell belonged to a different age, and she was not prepared to live with someone merely for reasons of sentiment. When she finished in Miami she would fly to Washington for a few days more with Newman, then to New York to end it with Lowell. It was one of the easiest decisions she had taken in her life. Helen felt her muscles settle as she cut through the water, and began thinking again of Newman. She wanted him. She liked him, but was not ready to become too excited about what might happen. He was an odd mixture, this Britisher. Brittle on the outside, arrogant and distrustful, and yet behind the blond curls there was something far more interesting. A repressed sweetness, maybe. Decency. She was not sure there was any right word. One moment he would complain how she lectured him – 'Oh, do shut up, Helen' – and the next he would launch into a lecture of his own, normally a variation on the theme of what was wrong with America. She thought it funny that sometimes he irritated her so much she defended her country like the most rabid member of the Daughters of the American Revolution. And then. Then he says to me that the British Empire was run by people who read Catullus and Plato and the American Empire is being run by people who think Catullus and Plato are cities in Mexico. And I laugh and want him again, and he knows it.

DeVos grew tired of swimming crawl. She rolled over on her back, staring at the palms at the end of the pool. The sun was beginning to set behind a stand of trees and low flowering shrubs as the sky slowly darkened. She was feeling good now, her muscles fully relaxed. As she reached the far end of the pool, her right hand arching over her head on the final stroke before the turn, a tough man's fist grabbed her wrist, pulling her brutally towards the side as an angler might reel in a fish.

She was so surprised she opened her mouth to yell, but swallowed water instead, warm and heavily chlorinated. DeVos coughed and twisted to try to look at who or what held her wrist so tightly she knew it would bruise.

'Miss DeVos,' a man's loud voice said, pulling her face up until it was only inches from his own. It was a round, dark face staring down at her, a Latin looking man in his early thirties in a white shirt and tan trousers. Behind him in a light grey striped seersucker suit stood a bald man who held up some kind of badge.

'Miss Helen DeVos?'

'Yes,' she coughed water, catching her breath.

'Miss DeVos,' the bald man said. 'We are from the Drug Enforcement Administration. We have reason to believe you may be in possession of controlled substances, narcotics. We have a court order granting us the right to search your hotel room. Please get out of the pool put on a towel or clothes and come with us. Now, please.'

The voice was formal and insistent. She pushed her wet hair back from her face and coughed again to get rid of the last of the swallowed water. She could see behind the DEA agents three or four uniformed police officers, one a woman, and a gaggle of tourists rubbernecking at the action. The Latino was reading her Miranda rights. The bastards were arresting her for drug trafficking. She pulled herself from the swimming pool, picked her towel from the sun-lounger and dried her face.

'There must be some mistake,' she said. 'I don't do drugs. I have nothing to do with drugs.'

'That's not our information, Miss DeVos. Please hurry along.'

'What information?'

'Please hurry along.'

She walked towards the elevator past the tourists and the gawking hotel staff. She was clean. Drugs were for losers. This was crazy. Crazy. How could they make such a mistake? How could they . . . A chill crept over her. It was obviously no mistake. Someone had decided she was trouble. The elevator doors opened and Helen DeVos walked towards the hotel room, feeling each barefoot step like a thudding pulse. Two more Dade County officers in uniform stood by the door. DeVos realised that if someone really wanted to ruin her life then a few grammes of cocaine planted in her luggage while she was staking out the courthouse would do. If the Agency was really hurting over the Phil Lewis disclosures and the *Tribune* article, they might stop at nothing. It would be easy to destroy her, Newman, and the credibility of everything they had written. Helen DeVos held out the key to the door of the room and turned it gently in the lock. She could feel the light hairs stand on end down her back and arms in the chill.

Inside the air-conditioning was beating out full blast, though she was sure she had never turned it up so high. Ever. She often switched it way down or off before going out to save electricity. She was certain she had done precisely that before taking the swim. Someone

220

had been in the room. Had to be. A stranger. She felt the blast of cold air hit her wet body, still dripping in the bathing suit. While the DEA agents and uniformed officers pushed past her she stood cold and alone. They began a methodical search through her property. She shivered as they unpicked her room and her life, naked and helpless.

18

Ileana Del Cid parked the black Mustang convertible in front of the pastel pink towers of Cabot's hotel. When her uncle Jorge Lopez found out who she was having breakfast with he demanded she ask Cabot yet again where Lewis could be found.

'He must know,' the Turtle insisted. 'You can't tell me that with all its power the CIA does not know where Phil Lewis is hiding out?'

'But, uncle, Cabot seems to know even less than I do. Besides, he has already delayed meeting me three times since I picked him up at the airport. After the way he looked when he was surrounded by the reporters on television last night I think he'll stand me up and catch the first flight back to Washington.'

Jorge Lopez snorted and shook his red Turtle cheeks. His last words were that she had to help him find Lewis, and that was an end to it.

Well, how was she supposed to do that? Clairvoyance? Hire a private detective? Pick up a couple of bloodhounds at the Bal Harbor Mall and set them loose with a sniff of one of Lewis's suits? She had had enough of the whole damn thing, the bizarre telephone calls from Richard Boone in Washington, from Vince Terrelli, from her uncle, from the media. Then this oddball Cabot demanding to see her so she could tell all about Lewis, then ducking out of dinner after he met Kramer and the FBI guys, then skipping breakfast, and saying he'd call her. Now making another demand that she come round before he had to go back to DC. She was ticked off. Everybody working some different angle. And now her uncle wanted her to pump for information a man who either knew nothing or gave a

222

convincing impersonation of someone who knew nothing. Absurd.

Ileana Del Cid ran her fingers through her long black hair and checked her dress in the hotel lobby mirror, then she called Cabot's room. To her surprise he was still there, and this time there were no excuses. When he arrived in the lobby he looked like he had slept badly and was dressed in a rumpled white shirt without a tie, and check trousers. His grey hair was mussed up and his glasses could do with a clean. The old guy was worn out.

'How's the hotel?'

'Oh, it's fine.'

'Sleep well?'

'Sure. I mean, no not really. You know, strange bed.'

'Shall we eat here?'

In the breakfast room he seemed preoccupied, more distant than when she picked him up at the airport just three days before. She wondered what Kramer might have said to upset him. Or maybe it was being attacked by the press pack. Cabot began asking her questions about Lewis but in a way which lacked the fire of curiosity he had shown before. She explained again that she had worked in Winston, Hamilton ever since graduating from Georgetown University. She was everything from office manager and secretary to Lewis's confidante and part time party hostess or 'facilitator' as the fat man called it. She would put on an eight hundred dollar black silk dress she'd bought up in Palm Beach, spend an hour making sure her hair was just right, show off her legs, smile, have a few drinks, have fun at the parties on the 'New World', facilitate her butt off. The job was to introduce the Venezuelan oil men to the Florida mayors or the Panamanian bankers to the Winston, Hamilton investment portfolio directors.

'Like being a hooker,' she told Cabot.

He blinked into his orange juice at the ugliness of the thought.

'Only I did not sleep with the clients. Just rubbed up their egos till they get off on it. Rub 'em up for a price. That's all.'

'You are clearly very angry.'

'Yes. I am. I feel I wasted the past seven years working for something I believed in, you know – freedom, apple pie, motherhood, the American way. And I just realised Lewis betrayed everybody. Especially me.'

'It was not all wasted. I hear there were many achievements.'

'Huh,' she snorted. 'You really think what we did won the Cold War for Uncle Sam? Forget it.' Ileana ordered more coffee and pushed her almost untouched fruit plate aside. 'I'm just not hungry.'

'I understand. Tell me some more about Lewis. What was he like to work with?'

Ileana explained that however blunt the various parts of Lewis's large body might be, the brain was sharp. It worked well, with a rapidity which always surprised her. If she had to guess, she would say his strongest asset was the fact that people underestimated him, until he somehow sucked them dry of whatever in the way of favours or investments or information he wanted. As she spoke Cabot watched the delicate mouth, the carefully applied make up, the rich brown eyes.

'Mr Cabot,' she asked eventually. 'What will happen to Phil?'

Cabot explained the public line, that he would be prosecuted for fraud, and perhaps also for breaking his secrecy oath. He would go to jail, perhaps for a long time.

'I hope so,' she said bitterly. 'I've heard rumours from Kramer and the FBI people of deals being made. Politics. Deals to let him off the hook. That would be terrible.'

'Why?'

At the end of three days in which he had heard the worst Kramer had to offer and been ambushed by the press rat pack at the court-room, he could not understand why anyone would find it so terrible to bury the whole thing.

'Well, because it would be unjust. He's stolen money from people. People who trusted him because he was connected with the government. Doesn't that count for something?'

'Of course it does,' Cabot soothed. He was perversely cheered to be reminded he was not the only taxpayer who believed in crime being punished.

'And —' she stopped abruptly.

'And what?'

Ileana thought carefully for a moment, then decided to say what was on her mind.

'And there are those here who will not forgive him. If Phil Lewis

224

is allowed some kind of soft deal other people will try to punish him in their own way.'

'What other people?'

Ileana sighed.

'The same other people who have already tried to kill him, who are desperate to find out where he is now. One way or the other, Phil will be punished. Either by the government or other people. I'd prefer it was the honest way, by the law. If that doesn't sound too naive.'

It sounded fine to Cabot. He drained his coffee, determined to get back to Washington as soon as possible. He had a lot of thinking to do. There was, however, one question he was desperate to have answered if only to gratify his own curiosity.

'Can I ask you something, Ileana?'

She nodded.

'Of course.'

'Who is Columbus?'

Ileana Del Cid stared at the man in front of her, nearly thirty years older than she was, with his intelligent eyes studying her from behind thick spectacles. She sighed.

'I am sorry, Mr Cabot. But if you do not know, then that can only be because you are not supposed to know. That's all I can say.'

'But you know who Columbus is, don't you, Ileana?'

'Yes,' she said softly, her eyes losing focus. 'I suppose you could say that. Columbus, he's the discoverer of new worlds.'

'And is he in danger?'

'Everybody is in danger who stands for freedom in a tyranny.'

After that they said a rather strained goodbye, and while Cabot caught a taxi to the airport, Ileana drove home to her two bedroom condo facing the ocean at Bal Harbor. There were two messages on her telephone answering machine, both probably from Uncle Jorge demanding to know where Lewis was holed up. She decided to ignore them. Instead she prepared sweet Cuban coffee, her mind racing, trying to work out how someone as important as Cabot could not know the identity of Columbus, and why he was so desperate to find out. What was happening to them all? Her former boss was a crook, her uncle was on the point of insanity trying to track Lewis, and now

225

the chief counsel to the Director of Central Intelligence was asking questions that he must know were none of his business. She made the coffee especially strong, poured it into a small cup and sat down in a hanging wicker chair facing towards the sea. She sipped slowly. To her right she could see in the distance the towers of the Miami Beach Sheraton where Lewis had supposedly tried to kill himself.

The caffeine was beginning to jolt her awake. She drained the coffee, then took a sip of iced water. She sighed, deeply. Memories were nagging at her like a toothache, keeping her from doing anything – finding a new job, having a good time, anything. A few months after Lewis first recruited her he took Ileana to Panama where he was arranging what he called 'secure banking facilities for high value clients'. As far as she could tell that meant the Panamanians were so corrupt he could stash any kind of money there, no questions asked. In Panama City Lewis introduced her to a middle aged but handsome Latino who called himself Ricardo Alarcon. Afterwards Lewis said enigmatically that 'Alarcon' had a different name and a grand title in his own country.

'So?' she said, determined to be unimpressed.

'Well,' Lewis replied as they sat together in the back of the Lear Jet flying from Panama City to Colon, 'I'd like you to get to know him.'

Ileana did not like the innuendo.

'What I mean is,' Lewis recovered, 'his native land happens to be Cuba. We've been cultivating him for months. He's part of their money laundering team, selling Cuban produce in Panama, passing it off as Panamanian in order to break the US boycott, then taking the money to buy high technology goods for shipment back to Havana.'

As Lewis explained how the Cuban organisation worked, Ileana Del Cid realised it was almost a carbon copy of their own operation.

'Small world,' she said, 'when the Cubans and ourselves end up in the same few countries laundering money for our intelligence services.'

Lewis laughed.

'You cannot buck market forces,' he said.

Lewis explained that he and two of the Panamanian bankers who worked for Winston, Hamilton, were now sure 'Ricardo Alarcon'

226

might be turned. 'One unhappy Cuban,' Humberto Arias, the chairman of the Panamanian Caribbean Security Bank said. 'When he gets drunk, which is frequently, it begins to spill out. His unhappiness, the unpleasantness of life in Havana. How he hates his wife. How his kids have no future. Real bad case.'

'Your job is to cheer him up,' Lewis told Ileana, believing that the company of a young and attractive woman of Cuban background might help 'Alarcon' make the right decision. Ileana remembered how she had desperately resisted any idea of finding him attractive. She especially resented the idea of being instructed by Lewis to be 'friendly' towards him, as if the fat pimp was trying to set her up for his own convenience. Yet somehow over a few days she found herself more and more in 'Alarcon's' company, actively seeking him out at barbecues and on the beach as they shifted from friend to friend in Panama, drinking and swimming and partying. The Cuban had rented a house near Quarry Heights, the American Southern Command military headquarters which overlooked the Panama Canal. A crowd of them had been invited to spend the afternoon by the pool, and she agreed to go even though Lewis and Arias and all the others said they would be delayed. 'Alarcon' and Ileana lay on sunloungers, dappled in shade from the overhanging trees, talking inconsequentially until he identified himself properly as Oscar Padilla Sanchez, General in the Revolutionary Armed Forces. As he talked he moved from the dry details of his life, the clipped sentences from an intelligence report, towards revealing an eloquent and humane man somehow bereft of hope, his optimism destroyed now the revolution he had worshipped was irredeemably tarnished.

They lay together for what seemed like hours, talking about his time in the Sierra Maestra, in Angola and Ethiopia, talking as if she had burst through a thick-walled concrete dam which once separated them but now allowed a flood of truth to break through. In this new intimacy she spoke of her own family and the curious ironies of history that put them on opposite sides of the Florida Strait, ninety miles and a world apart, different sides of the Cold War barricades, like the Koreans or the Berliners. She told him of the bitterness of her uncle and their pride in being Cuban but American too. She remembered the strange electric numbness which beset her all that afternoon, as if every moment held a significance she could barely guess at. And she remembered the gentle way in which he had finally moved to her, putting her drink to one side, slipping her sunglasses from her nose and gently pressing his lips upon hers in a deliciously tender kiss. The Cuban general drew her from the sunlounger to the ground by the pool so softly it was as if she floated on air. He was kissing her neck and her shoulder, his hand slowly stroking her hip until she shivered despite the heat, arched towards him. He slipped down her bikini, and she remembered him gently moving on top of her, kissing her constantly.

Now in the main room of her apartment at Bal Harbor Ileana Del Cid looked down at the dregs of her coffee and shuddered. There was a peculiar pattern left by the drying grounds in the cup. She wished she could read the pattern since everything else had fallen apart and nothing made sense, now the people she had trusted were being branded as criminals. She stood up quickly to allow the memories to disintegrate, haunted by her fears of danger sweeping towards Padilla for reasons she did not quite understand, but knew to be real.

She opened the sliding balcony doors and felt the sticky air hit her as she stepped outside. She slid the door shut behind her to keep the air-conditioned room cool, and stood gazing over the water in the vague direction of where she supposed some ninety miles away the island of Cuba lay. Ileana Del Cid knew if she telephoned the Fat Man's lawyer one more time she could pass a message to Lewis, ask him about Padilla, tell him about her fears. She would do it not because her uncle had asked her but because Lewis was the only one who might know if Padilla was safe. Phil Lewis, failed businessman, failed spy, crook, overweight Englishman, was the only one she could think of who might be able to do something, because out there beyond the horizon Oscar was in danger, and the thought made Ileana Del Cid tremble as much as his kisses the first time they made love by the pool in Panama City.

19

Richard Boone was not in the mood for jokes, especially not ones originating from Phil Lewis. He smiled cadaverously, put his Corvette convertible into first gear and pulled away from the other traffic heading west on C Street. He accelerated quickly, changing gears, catching a red light, ignoring it, foot hard down. No cops. Good enough. The sports car hit sixty miles an hour in seconds, and he eased back. The trouble with the Corvette, Boone thought, as he shifted his eyes back to the mirror to make sure there were still no traffic police, was that in the Washington summer it was too damn hot to run with the top down. When he tried it, the humid air hit his face like a hairdryer. He yawned, rubbed his left hand over the stubble on his head. He hoped the mountains would be cool. It was early Friday afternoon and the weekend traffic was thickening. Boone had arranged to meet Lewis on the Blue Ridge Parkway at the north end where the Appalachian forest of Skyline Drive begins. He was to check into the Skyline Drive Lodge under a name suggested by Lewis.

'Just my little joke, Rich,' Lewis said.

The kind of little joke that gets people killed. The way Boone felt, he'd rather rip the Fat Man's head off than make a deal. This time Lewis had gone too far.

As he hit the freeway Boone calmed down, delighted to feel the Corvette throb to his touch and escape the city. Working in Washington was the price you had to pay for exercising the power of the presidency, and Boone was in no doubt where that power lay – with him, and a few dozen others like him. Certainly not with the president himself. He was too busy.

229

Boone flickered his eyes back to the mirror as he touched seventy miles an hour. Nothing compared to the all-American muscle car.

'Like the country,' Boone thought. 'Still the greatest, but it's tough hanging on.'

He was satisfied he had done more in two days to confuse and upset the reporters who were making things difficult in Miami than a decade of Warren Cabot's lawyerly ways. Neither Alexander Newman, nor his subversive-loving friend, Helen DeVos, would know what hit them. But they both would get the message. Boone was sure of that. The traffic began to thin out. Boone blipped the accelerator and hit ninety-five, then slackened back to seventy.

'Careful,' he told himself. 'Just because you have the power, you don't have to use it.'

Owning a Corvette had been Boone's ambition ever since he was a teenager in the mid West. He remembered staring through the showroom window until his nose made marks on the glass. The guys back in junior high in Kansas or those in his Marines unit would never have guessed that he'd have an office right next to the White House and a red Corvette convertible that drove like it had wings. Boone had changed into a white Ralph Lauren Polo knitted shirt with light blue trousers, his thick arm muscles distending the shirt elastic to its full extent like a leg of Virginia ham. He had worked out hard that morning, adding one extra circuit because there would be little physical exercise on the weekend, unless Phil Lewis, unless Lewis what? Unless Lewis pulled another of his little jokes and got him so mad he decided to beat the crap out of him. The thought was incomplete because Boone did not know exactly what Lewis had to do to make his own life bearable again. Stop making waves. Had to go bury himself in a hole somewhere.

Had to get out of Richard Boone's face. Boone's eyes narrowed as he thought how it might have been if the knives that slashed Lewis's wrists had been more successfully applied. Maybe just a little more skill, more pressure, a fraction of an inch deeper, and he, Terrelli, the Agency, and ultimately the entire administration and the nation might be spared all this angst over some renegade foreigner.

Boone sighed. There was a twenty ton Mack truck pulling out in front of him. He flashed his lights, blipped the accelerator and passed

230

before he had time to think. The truth was it was all coming apart. Terrelli was turning as crazy as Lewis, losing his nerve because he was sure his job was on the line, because he could see it all unfold in a series of scandals in the newspapers, then in Congressional hearings, maybe even in criminal proceedings. Cabot had ducked out of sight, seemed to be having an emotional crisis, behaving more and more like a Georgetown faggot. It was all: 'I don't advise this', and 'We should consider the downside of that' kind of inactive talk which made Boone want to throw up. If Cabot had been as good at keeping Lewis quiet as he was at explaining the precise nature of the mess they were in, they would not be in the mess in the first place.

And then Lewis, Boone thought. Lewis. The ultimate goddamn looney tune. Boone's threats to force a meeting provoked Lewis into yelling down the telephone that he was going to tell the newspapers everything – *'Everything! Goddamit you gotta believe me, Rich, every fucking thing!'*

'Calm down, Phil,' Boone ordered. He would cheerfully have shot Lewis to put them both out of his misery. 'Calm down. We gotta work this one through together. Play as a team. Like we shoulda done earlier.'

Lewis agreed. Teamwork. He liked the sound of that. All for one. One for all.

'A little help at the start, Rich, and it'd never have come to this.'

'Okay,' Boone reassured him. Talk positive, talk up. 'Okay, Phil. Now remember what Warren Cabot told your lawyer. It's real important you don't start mouthing off again. You do it one more time, and there's nothing I can do to help you. Okay, Phil?'

'Okay.'

'Now it's gonna take a little more leverage to put Humpty Dumpty together again, but we can make it. First you gotta trust me and tell me where the hell you are.'

'Forget it, Rich.'

There had been silence for a few days, then Lewis began calling again, short calls which were difficult to trace. Boone did not even try, playing it cool.

'Yes, Phil,' he would say. 'Sure, Phil. Yeah, I understand perfectly,

231

Phil. Yep, just another snafu, Phil. No problem. Clear it up, Phil.'

And Lewis would ring off and call back from some other dreary shopping mall on the road from Florida through Georgia along the Appalachian mountain chain towards Washington DC. Day after day he called sounding increasingly neurotic, isolated and afraid. Boone would calm him down, as Lewis vowed to fight to gain back his reputation.

'More than the money, Rich,' he bleated, weeping on the line. 'More than anything, my good name.'

He was unpredictable. One minute he would be threatening to blow the whole thing open, the next apologising for talking to the British newspaper in the first place.

'Tell Terrelli,' Lewis sobbed on his most recent call at two in the morning and in a way Boone could do without. 'Tell Terrelli, Rich, he'll listen to you. Tell him I wanna make his deal.'

The fat man whined that Terrelli and Cabot held all the cards.

'I can't pay Holgate any more, what with the funds being frozen, and I think he's gone sour on me. I might end up with a public defender, which means they'd fry me alive. I'm prepared for anything, but you gotta help me.'

A public defender would be fine if you happened to be innocent, Boone thought. But Lewis would need a little more help. Boone had one call to make before he set off for the rendezvous in the mountains. He steered the Corvette into the CIA grounds and showed his pass. He was escorted through the reception area, past the carved stars on the wall and the quotation from St John, into the elevator and up to Vincent Terrelli's office. Boone very rarely had cause to travel to Langley and after casual greetings with Terrelli, he gazed round the Deputy Director's office, at the Navajo war shield and blanket and the cowboy bronze of John Wayne on a bronco.

'I never knew you did this stuff, Vince,' he said. 'You the first Italian cowboy, or what?'

Terrelli smiled.

'It's from Liz's folks. Her family's all from Arizona and Colorado. They think there's a cowboy in everyone. Me, I'm strictly spaghetti western. Anyway, before you see Lewis I wanted to show you this.'

Terrelli pushed across the table two printed sheets, columns of

232

figures, from the FBI investigation into Winston, Hamilton, Bellingham, Lewis and Lopez.

'It's the latest from the accountants,' Terrelli continued. 'It shows that greedy son-of-a-bitch personally skimmed more than five million. Every week the goddamn figure goes up. And Lewis just banked his own salary. His expenses included supermarket till rolls. Can you believe that? He charged the government for his groceries. This guy has some kind of greed sickness.'

Terrelli was really angry. Boone wondered whether that meant he had flipped so much he had now switched off the idea of a deal with Lewis, which could make things extremely awkward. Terrelli stood up and poured them both coffee. 'As if there was not enough in the trough for him already, he has to push it all too far. We set him up in the sweetest kind of life imaginable, and it's not enough. He starts to skim even more. Then there's maybe up to ten million that's disappeared into other private accounts in Panama and the Cayman Islands for people who don't exist. And' – Terrelli picked up another sheaf of paper filled with close typed columns of figures. 'And who the hell do you think David Appletree is?'

Boone shrugged. 'No idea, Vince, never heard of him, until you mentioned his name to me the other day. One of the big benefactors of the scam.'

'Yeah,' Terrelli said, handing Boone more figures. 'He's one of the names we're still trying to track down. He's paid into a Nassau bank. Then the money goes to Grand Cayman. Then we lose track. Whoever he is, he's a lucky son-of-a-bitch. Lewis paid him something over four million that we can definitely account for. Then there's the other names we talked about – eight hundred thousand dollars for someone calling himself Anthony D. Stewart, and six for R. David Dalton. The same for Dwight R. Petty, and four hundred and fifty thousand for Peter S. Kalish. You think all of these are Phil Lewis?'

Boone shook his head.

'How would I know, Vince? I'm an old leatherneck, 'member, not an accountant. You want me to go storm a beach, I storm a beach. You want me to un'erstand this business with the money laundering. Forget it. Ask me something I know. Like what we could do about it.'

Vince Terrelli asked.

'We got two choices,' Boone replied. He held up his left hand like a large fleshy disc, the thumb erect. 'One, Phil Lewis does somethin' helpful. Like dies. The word is that Jorge Lopez was the genius behind the slit wrists in the bath tub. Maybe old Don Jorge might still be angry at Lewis, the two of 'em find a way to come together again. I'm not talking right or wrong. I'm talking possible here. Okay?'

Terrelli said nothing, no lectures about Agency policy or the Executive Order on assassinations. Nothing. Just two volcanic Italian eyes staring back at Boone.

'Two,' Boone said, raising a second finger. 'As we discussed, you put the inves'gation on hold, stop trying to chase down the paper. Call off Warr'n Cabot. He's done enough, scaring the shit out of Lewis with his contempt of court talk and class'fied information proceedings. I talk to Lewis tonight. Maybe tomorrow if he's late. Put it to him he's going to take a fall one way or the other. In jail or outside, he's sliced pork. His one chance is to plea bargain. We'll beat down the sentence provided he gets the hell out of the US. Maybe goes back to England, serve Queen and country, whatever he likes. And wherever his money is, he turns it over. That'd be real punishment for a guy who is so sick with greed. The first way's tidier, but this oughtta work.'

Terrelli took a deep breath.

'Listen, Rich,' he interrupted. 'I have to think of the Agency. I have got the Justice Department breathing down my neck asking if any of these payments to Appletree and all the others might be legitimate, or if they are all false names for Lewis, or if, as the FBI in Miami suspect, there's a wider pattern of corruption within the Agency. I don't know the answers to these questions. I just don't. But I need to know.'

Boone interrupted savagely.

'Don't start sounding like Warren Cabot again, Vince. If you think I'm driving all the way out to the Blue Ridge just to tell Fat Phil there's no deal, forget it. You want to be rem'bered as the guy who caused the end of the CIA, go ahead. Act like some goddamn stiff. But you gotta decide now, Vince. Right now. Which side are you on?'

234

Terrelli weakly protested that Boone misunderstood what he meant.

He was worried there might be a serious problem of corruption which they could not ignore, and if they did try to cover it up Cabot would wreak havoc.

'All he has to do is go to the White House and spill the whole story. We'd look like dirt while Cabot takes over as DCI. I'm just trying to do my best, Rich, that's all.'

Boone nodded. That was the problem. Some days Terrelli just wanted to get the job done. Other times he wanted to preach a daily sermon. Today's sermon was pointing in the direction of Terrelli's best interests. Didn't God move in mysterious ways? But for the first time the Deputy Director was looking truly beleaguered.

'Sure, Vince. Sure. Punishment. I got it. But let's keep a sense of pe'spective here. Punish Phil Lewis, but be prepared to deal so we don't end up punishing the Agency as well. And ourselves. It's likely Lewis used Appletree and the other names to hide away his own money. Even if he did not, we find out anybody else was corrupt, they get fired 'mmediately. We deal with this exec'tively, not by smearing everything in dirt.'

Terrelli shrugged.

'I suppose,' he admitted. 'Cabot is unlikely to do anything before the election. That would be dumb. And because I knew the Justice Department might make waves I've already begun preparing the White House by dropping hints about his ambitions.'

'Like what, Vince?'

'Do I have to spell it out?' Terrelli repeated, the old fire returning. 'I've made sure the right people know Cabot wants to take over as DCI and thinks the job is his after the election. That doesn't go down too well with Richardson or the Chief of Staff. If Cabot tries to heap dirt in our direction, his motives will already be under question.'

Boone sniggered. Terrelli had balls after all. Got his retaliation in first.

'Well, Vince. I guess you have just dem'strated to them that the Boy Scout is just like the rest of us. Talks about morality and the national interest, pursues his own.'

'Yeah,' Terrelli replied. 'I guess so. As for you, Rich, I suggest you handle Lewis whichever way you think is best. Whichever you think cleanest. Tell him you need me to sanction it. That'll give us time. Find out what he wants and how hard he's prepared to play. But remember, in the end he can't be allowed to profit from this. People we trust can't use the privileges we give them to break the law, otherwise everything falls apart. Everything.'

Boone shook hands with Terrelli, then sped out of Langley and hit the Interstate north towards Front Royal. When he reached the edge of the Blue Ridge he looked to his left and the sweep of the mountains as they hung over the Shenandoah Valley, the tree-lines of Skyline Drive. He turned the Corvette towards the National Park and stopped at the gate, paying the entrance fee. He rolled down his window and turned the air-conditioning off. The air was warm and slightly humid, pleasant enough for high summer. Boone rested his thick left arm on the window ledge and set off again towards the Skyline Drive Lodge, about thirty miles down the parkway. When he arrived he turned the Corvette on to the gravel drive and pulled up near the hotel reception. The Lodge was a massive log cabin, with a dozen smaller cabins in the grounds serving as individual rooms. He took his overnight bag from the car and walked up to the receptionist, thinking again about the thing that made him most queasy, Phil Lewis's little joke. It was the kind of joke that might mean Lewis would have to be punished after all. Punished very severely. It was a joke which, whatever Terrelli wanted, deal or no deal, meant that Lewis might be better off dead.

'My name is Appletree,' Boone told the receptionist, using the name Lewis insisted upon, the little joke Boone thought Terrelli might not find amusing. 'David Appletree. I have a reservation. One night. I'll pay in cash.'

20

In the hot Georgetown night a few Friday evening drunks were yelling in the backstreets off Wisconsin Avenue. A car door slammed, a screech of tyres in the sticky darkness. Police moved in as a dozen black youths on roller blades skated through the traffic where Wisconsin met M Street. The kids were raucous and cheerful, full of margaritas and pork ribs from a long evening at Houston's all-American restaurant a block further down towards the Potomac, dodging the police and skating their way back to the other side of town. Alex Newman looked at his watch for the third time in twenty minutes. It was shortly after 11.30 P.M. and Ted Koppel, the ABC television news anchor, was interviewing three men with beards, fretting about the danger of America turning inward away from its full role as a world power now the dangers of the Cold War had passed.

'Well, Ted . . .' the first beard explained, the mundane presented as calamitous. 'As we reach the climax of the presidential election campaign, the war on drugs instead of the war on communism . . .'

Newman was uneasy. He looked at his watch again, switched off the television and prepared to go to bed. He sipped ice cold Saratoga Springs water with a twist of lime, nervously padding around the apartment in bare feet, sure he should go to bed, equally sure he would not be able to sleep. Helen still had not returned his calls, several of them, all with calm-sounding non committal messages, asking her please to call him when she had time. Please. Puh-lease call when you have the time . . . I know, I have called before, but . . . He picked up the telephone again and dialled the Aztec Hotel.

The receptionist yet again politely listened as he spelled out his name and number and a short message.

'Yes, Mr Newman,' she repeated. 'I will certainly see she gets that message. And the others.'

He put the telephone down and felt impotent and unhappy. Jealous was the word which came to mind, though it embarrassed him even to think it. A solitary vice. What right had he? But why not? What could she be doing until this time of night in Miami? Who was she with? It struck Newman as an adolescent way to behave, and consequently in keeping with his attitude to Helen. He reassured himself there was also a protective impulse. Maybe she had been in a car accident. Maybe she had been mugged. He said a few words out loud which he realised amounted to more talking with God, hoping that God, if he existed, would look after her.

'Shit,' he said out loud. 'I'm cracking up. Doing this praying thing again.'

He began to undress, smiling as he recalled how she had described American television as ninety-eight per cent kids' stuff and two per cent anal retention. She had giggled, he had laughed. She would have enjoyed tonight's two per cent performance on Nightline. Newman switched off the television, slipped into bed and checked his watch. 11.45 P.M. For the first time in years he was no longer happy to be alone. It was a shock to discover that the last few days with Helen meant he looked to someone else for his contentment. It worried him, but not as much as the fact he could not talk to her now. Newman sighed, and tossed on his pillow, listening to a few more cries in the darkness as the last of the drunks bundled themselves into taxi cabs and headed home.

Eventually he fell asleep until some time in the middle of the night, when the air had cooled down and the ceiling fan made him clutch a sheet around him. The telephone rang. He woke immediately, reached for it, blinking in the darkness.

'Hi,' he said tenderly, not showing his anxiety, and hoping it was not Mike Holroyd. 'It's about time you called.'

When Helen DeVos began to speak her voice sounded strangled and tense.

'Hi,' she said, struggling for control. He heard the alarm and sat

238

upright, swinging his feet to the floor and switching on the bedside light.

'Helen? What is it, Helen? What's the matter?'

She choked a little then caught her breath.

'Something happened . . . I . . . was . . . arrested.' She forced the words out in what was almost a sob. 'By the DEA.'

Newman blinked his eyes wide open. 'What?'

She repeated the sentence and recounted for him how she was swimming when it happened, how they had taken her to the hotel room, how she trembled with fear at the ease with which someone could have planted cocaine in her luggage.

'Was there anything?'

'Any drugs?' she said. 'No. Otherwise I guess I would not be talking to you. Except from jail.'

'Where are you?'

'In the hotel. Whoever set me up did not go the whole way. At least, not this time. The DEA agents took me away for hours of questioning before letting me go. That's why I am so late. I just got back. They were polite. Suspicious as hell at first, then they seemed to think it was some big joke. Brought me back to the hotel in their own car. I'm still shaking.'

'Did they give you any reason why they picked on you?'

'Oh,' DeVos said, beginning to feel more in control, as if speaking to him helped dispel the ghosts which haunted her. 'They told me they had a tip off. On the drugs telephone hotline. You know the thing, you dial 1 800 BIG HERO and you tell the volunteers who's pushing in your area. They take no names from callers, nothing. Except you can leave a false name in case you want to call back for a reward. Anyway, someone called in with a perfect description of me, where I was staying, what my rental car looked like, details that checked out and made it seem credible. Like some accomplice decided to turn me in. So the DEA followed up, along with the Dade County sheriff's department and God knows who else. It was like I was Al Capone. I asked if they often got bum information like this, and they said it sounded for real, that's why they jumped me. In the end one of the sheriff's deputies, a redneck from Alabama, looked me over and said, well, sugar, it looks like someone out there doesn't really care for you.' She took a deep and uneven breath and Newman thought she was going to cry, but she held back. 'You can say that again,' she said.

'I called you,' he said. 'I care.'

'I know. And I guess they thought you were an accomplice or something. The hotel was told to say nothing.'

'How are you now?'

'Okay, I guess.'

They talked for an hour and he wished he could be with her. He said so, and she cried. When the New York toughness disintegrated she was surprisingly vulnerable, which made him want her more.

'There's more research to be done,' she said stubbornly when he told her to catch the first flight back. She did not want to let him down. 'I still have to try to dig out the rest of the military people who were on the Winston, Hamilton board. Lewis is providing us with no help. Disappeared. I think he's out of town. Holgate's told him since the CIA lawyer was down here that they are not bluffing. That if he talks they will put him away, and maybe Holgate too. Says their only chance now is a full Classified Information Procedures Act hearing to declassify some of the CIA documents but if Lewis talks before the hearing, they will get nowhere.'

'Forget it,' Newman said decisively. 'It looks like the story has gone cold. And we need to re-think the whole thing after what happened to you.'

Newman did not like to tell her that the *Tribune* could not care less about the story. They were spending too much money in Eastern Europe and wanted him to concentrate on the presidential election campaign. Whatever had happened to Helen would make no difference. '*Tribune* freelance researcher wrongly arrested then released on drug suspicion,' was not much of a headline, and there was no point taking risks for nothing.

'Come home, Helen. I've missed you. We have things to talk about. And no story is worth this. Come home to Washington.'

'Okay. But there's one thing I should tell you. Once I convinced the DEA I was clean I asked them who could have given them this information.'

'And?'

'And they said they never discuss it. That if they did not ensure confidentiality nobody would call with a tip off. So I got real mad and I said they had violated my civil rights on nothing more than an unchecked rumour and now they were not even going to let me know what was behind it. That it was goddamn outrageous and I was prepared to sue the hell out of them once they let me go.'

'You don't take "no" from anyone, do you, Helen?' Newman blurted out.

'So they kind of gave in,' DeVos said. 'At least they checked and discovered it was some fake name, a call sign for someone who wanted the reward.'

She paused and he could hear her take another deep breath.

'What was the name, Helen?' he asked, trying to make his voice sound calm.

'The name,' she said, breathing hard as the shock took over again. 'The name the caller gave was Phil. He was most careful that they took a note of it. He repeated it several times. "Fat Phil" was what they had written down. Whoever set me up wanted them to mark the reward down for Fat Phil.'

21

The horse trail wound slowly past Whitefish Lake through the Flathead National Forest and then took a low ridge towards the north west. It had been months since Warren Cabot and his wife had made it to the Montana family ranch Robyn Cabot inherited from her father, and the two of them talked almost obsessively on the flight from Washington about the prospect of a week of peace in the clean air of the west. This was a place where the real Americans lived, Robyn Cabot was fond of saying. Not the freaks and weirdos who gravitated towards Washington, District of Columbia.

'If this job is going to make you so unhappy, Warren,' she repeated several times during the course of the journey, 'then give it up. Why put yourself, put me, through this? We don't need the money. And if you were as bored as I am with all this inside the Washington beltway nonsense, then we could spend time managing the ranch like we are always saying we will one day. We could do something useful.'

'One day,' he repeated ruefully. 'One day.'

Robyn Cabot was ten years younger than her husband, an attractive brunette of forty-two, who had fallen in love with Cabot when he was married – though at the time he did not know quite how unhappily – for the first time. Her own background, born and raised in the west though schooled in the east, meant she had a healthy disrespect for the notion of power and government. At least, it had no mystique.

She thought his ambition to run the CIA and co-ordinate US intelligence in some 'new order' bizarre to the point of eccentricity. Her own father had once run for Congress then dropped what he called that 'foolish notion'.

242

'Papa believed,' Robyn Cabot used to tell dinner party guests in their Georgetown home, 'that one of the reasons he deserved to be elected was because he did not want to serve in government in Washington at all. He thought the most important duty of a Congressman was to dislike his job. That way he would neither become too attached to power nor end up as the government's representative in Montana rather than the other way round.'

After thinking carefully about the implications of what the FBI had told him in Miami, Cabot was beginning to share the old man's disdain. His confusion and unease helped make up his mind to spend the week's vacation in Montana rather than attend the Republican National Convention in New Orleans, which he knew was merely Washington politics transplanted south for the sake of photogenic presidential theatre. Cabot knew he had to pull things together in his head. He would spend four or five days at the ranch, riding and fishing for cut-throat trout, cooking them in the open air, eating the fish hot while he sat watching the sun set over the mountains of Montana's big sky, and confronting the choices that lay ahead of him like a deepening fog. That first night he went through the motions of discussing with the ranch manager the price of beef cattle and how many sheep the upper pastures might hold the following spring. The summer night was mountain cool and they lit a log fire in the ranch house, cooking trout which neighbours, knowing of their arrival, had put aside for them. As the sun set, Cabot went for a stroll around the yard, bidding a good evening to a couple of wranglers who sat talking and smoking at the rear of the barn.

'Good evening, Mr Cabot.'

'Good to see you again sir.'

'Good to be here, Paulie, Joe. Can't tell you how good.'

The air up here, Cabot thought, was so pure it hurt the lungs with disinfectant cleanliness as he stretched and breathed hard. He looked about him with fresh eyes and saw an owl hovering in the twilight, sweeping into the woods on silent wings, searching for prey. In an hour or two he might hear coyotes or a wolf's howl. Robyn was right. This was the real America. The heartland of the republic.

In the end it came to this: how ambitious was he for the job of

Director of Central Intelligence, and how committed to doing what was right rather than what was convenient? He had always believed this was what distinguished him from Boone and Terrelli and the others. That for him there were non-negotiable moral values guiding conduct between people and nations which should not be bent or twisted to suit short term ideas of success. The president, Cabot was sure, had recognised that ethical sense in him, which was why he had been appointed special counsel to the CIA. He knew the president saw his role extending beyond advice about the law to offering some kind of pure light for intelligence gathering and covert action. But now the smart move would be to turn the guiding light off, at least for a while. For days, ever since Leon Kramer had led him to the corruption at the heart of Lewis's empire, Cabot had realised that the safe thing to do was to become part of the cover up. He could close down Deep Blue as he had been instructed by Terrelli and Boone, and in acquiescing Cabot knew he could guarantee no public scandal. Even now after the first journalistic exposure, the full story would be difficult for any newspaper to crack – no one talking, no Congressional inquiries because no appropriated money had gone astray, Lewis and his lawyer effectively gagged.

A safe presidential re-election would follow, and Cabot could name his terms with Terrelli and Boone, insist they recommend him to the White House, DCI by acclamation. Neither of them would cause him a moment's grief ever again. And yet he was tortured by a simple doubt. However he dressed it up, it was wrong. Once he started making compromises he knew he would slip into the slime, become as bad as Terrelli, or worse, as bad as Boone. Descend eventually to the level of Lewis himself, so devoid of value he could not recognise the difference between his own pocket and that of the government and people of this country.

Cabot began walking back to the ranch house thinking that at least he had done his duty. Before he left for Montana he briefed Bill Richardson in vague terms for the outgoing DCI's next encounter with the Senate Intelligence Committee. The important thing, as Richardson always recognised, was to tell the Committee precisely those things they were bound to find out anyway, and do it early enough so that, like small boys everywhere, they were grateful to be allowed to share in the Big Secret. Richardson guessed that in briefing them with a few sanitised snippets on the links between Deep Blue and the Lewis financial scandal – plus added warnings from Terrelli about CIA agents 'in grave danger' in Cuba – he would have an easy summer. The Intelligence Committee might read the occasional news story, but they would be convinced the whole thing was in safe hands.

And yet Cabot wondered whether he had made one potential error of judgement. He had attempted to speak directly to an old friend about Deep Blue and had been turned down. The old friend was now president of the United States.

The White House chief of staff listened to Cabot's vague words about something 'of great importance, a strictly confidential matter' then told him it was impossible for the president to make time before the convention.

'He'd love to meet with you, Warren, I know he would, but if what you want to discuss is as serious as you say, then he will need to give you undivided attention. He can't do that until after New Orleans. You can imagine how it is. Sorry.'

Cabot thought carefully and then called back. He asked to meet the chief of staff alone. This request was granted. They spent forty-five minutes together inside the White House beginning at six in the morning, while Cabot rehearsed his fears and his doubts.

'One,' he said. 'I think there is evidence of serious corruption emanating out of the Miami operation and at least tolerated by senior officers in Langley or perhaps even in the White House. The CIA liaison here had direct control of the Winston, Hamilton company, acting as Phil Lewis's boss.'

'Boone?'

'Yes, Boone. And two: there will have to be an inquiry into all of this whether we decide to halt the prosecution of Lewis or not. We have to find out who is clean and who is not, though I suppose you are about to tell me we must prevent it falling apart before the election.'

The chief of staff nodded.

'That's exactly what I'm telling you, Warren. The Democrats are hurting for an issue. The president has tried his darnedest to make

245

sure nothing like this happens on his watch. It would be so unfair if this were to damage him now, after all he has done to run things clean. Why should he be tarred by something he did not know about and which began before he took office? I want you to say nothing to anyone. Take your vacation. Leave it until after November. Opening this up would be like opening up your own guts to check whether your heart's beating, pointless and dangerous.'

Cabot looked up at the big Montana sky, the stars stretching endlessly in the clear night. Here, he thought, there might be a sense of perspective to help him make the right decision. Inside the ranch house Robyn Cabot was sitting in front of the log fire watching the convention live on television from New Orleans.

'The president is about to speak,' she said. 'Fix me a drink, will you please, Warren.'

Cabot poured her a weak gin and tonic and gave himself a small Glenlivet malt whisky, no ice or water. He sat by the fire and waited, sipping the Glenlivet. There was a trumpet fanfare and the crowds went wild in the usual spontaneous cheering, standing ovations and Hail to the Chief. The president climbed to the podium and began to speak. It was, from a man for whom oratory was always a trial, not bad. It was a definition of the way ahead, now the world had lost the certainties of the struggle against communism. He quoted a galaxy of stars from the nation's past, comparing the next century to John Winthrop's vision of America as a shining city on a hill. He spoke of an America which dared to care about its less prosperous citizens, and about its role in the 'complex world where America is valued as a friend and feared as a foe, where our moral leadership is matched by our military might, where liberty has triumphed because the price of peace is eternal vigilance.'

Cabot sipped his whisky. He looked at the president's face, glowing under the television lights and rising to his great moment, the party nomination certain, victory in November likely. He could undoubtedly scent the chance to accomplish what he really wanted to do over the next four years when he would no longer be a prisoner of the electorate. Then there was a change of tone. Suddenly sombre, the president warned against complacency in the campaign and, quite remarkably for a man who now was some eight points ahead in all

246

the opinion polls, warned against 'unfair tactics by our opponents'. Cabot sat up and put the whisky glass down.

'Beware of an autumn surprise,' the president said, gravely. 'Beware of our opponents trying to use the last lap of the campaign to discredit us unfairly. Beware of dirty tricks and foul jibes. Beware of those who do not engage in this contest with our own sense of fairness and justice. Beware of those who do not feel comfortable with the ethical administration this president has brought to the White House, and will try anything, reach into any gutter to discredit us.'

Robyn Cabot looked across at her husband.

'What's all this drivel, Warren?'

Cabot thought for a moment, as the president wound up his speech with the customary cheerleading slogans, booming out God Bless America, the band playing and tens of thousands of red, white and blue balloons descending from nets in the ceiling on to the heaving patriotic mass of delegates holding their state placards aloft.

'Well,' Cabot said. 'It could be nothing. Or it could be that the worm that has been eating away at me for the past few weeks has finally gnawed its way right into the heart of the Oval office.'

The following morning Cabot rose at six, his body still on east coast time, his mind troubled by Deep Blue, and now even more confused by the president's speech. Cabot drank a little coffee then ordered his old appaloosa stallion, Cloudy, to be saddled. He was ready to set off alone on the trail through the forest. Robyn said she had to call on the neighbours and thank them for the trout they had delivered.

'I've retained some of my country politeness,' she chided gently. 'Even if you've lost yours.'

He smiled and said to invite them to dinner. 'Tell them I'll be sociable,' he grinned. 'I'll act like I'm a real American. Not a Washington stuffed shirt.'

Before he could leave the telephone rang and she answered it, then handed it to him with a grimace.

'The White House chief of staff,' Robyn Cabot said flatly, arching her eyebrows. 'For you.'

'This is Warren Cabot.' The conversation was short. The chief of staff managed his own time with the rigidity he used organising the president. He wanted to know if Cabot had seen the previous night's speech and the warning of an 'autumn surprise'.

'Sure.'

The chief of staff explained it was an attempt to forestall accidents.

'You did well to warn us. I think you should continue to conduct your investigations into this Deep Blue mess, Warren, so if it starts leaking out we can say there's an inquiry underway. We don't want your report until . . . let's say February. A month after the inauguration. In the meantime, the president has taken the moral high ground, and if the Democrats find out enough to open up the issue, believe me, we'll play hardball. We'll make it seem like it's political dirty tricks at work. Unpatriotic. I think we can handle it.'

Cabot did not doubt that. He could hear a chuckle at the other end of the line, as the chief of staff relished the idea of a political bar room brawl. At times Cabot wondered how his old friend from Princeton could stomach the kind of sleaze he had to tolerate to get elected.

'The president asked me to thank you for the warning,' the chief of staff concluded, but in such a tone Cabot suspected the president had not been informed. 'So thank you, Warren.'

'Good,' Cabot said. 'But does he want anything done immediately?'

The chief of staff was a man who thought small minds asked small questions. The telephone call to Cabot had already lasted ninety seconds longer than budgeted.

'No,' he said. 'There will be a reckoning at the appropriate time. But right now there is no substitute for victory, Warren. Remember that. No substitute. You understand?'

Cabot understood. There was a final chuckle on the line. The chief of staff was about to make a joke.

'So Deep Six it, will you. This Deep Blue trash. Bury it, Warren. Till the spring. Or the next Ice Age. Whichever comes later.'

Ten minutes later Cabot was sitting on the appaloosa, walking the trail. It forked, a lower branch snaking down to the lake and the river which turned south, the upper branch reaching above the skyline to a long ridge from which you could see the white mountain peaks of

248

Glacier National Park. Cabot gently turned Cloudy uphill. The horse was willing but he could feel him slowing with age.

'Like me, Cloudy,' he muttered. 'Past your best, boy. Past your best.'

The chief of staff seemed relaxed, but that only made Cabot feel as if he himself carried the burdens of the presidency on his shoulders, secrets which could gut the administration.

He was not sure how much, if anything, the president had been told. The lines could easily have been inserted in the speech without much explanation – 'just in case of accidents, Mr President.'

Cabot trusted no one now. As the horse settled into a rhythmic walk uphill he thought he could continue to demand – and he assumed, eventually receive – a meeting with the president somewhere on the campaign trail, and tell him everything in an unmistakeable way face to face. And then? Cloudy stopped and stiffened on the trail, his ears erect, sniffing the wind. Cabot looked to his left into a patch of huckleberries which moved just enough for him to see the tail of a small black bear scuttling downhill. As soon as the bear disappeared, the appaloosa picked up the trail again which had begun to flatten out as they reached the top of the ridge. He stopped the horse as the ponderosa pines and aspens thinned and there was a break with a view down the valley to his left. Cloudy began to pull on the reins to graze on the tussocky grass and Cabot dismounted, standing by the horse's side drinking the air.

A pair of grey jays bounced from tree to tree, squawking harshly, looking for food. He could hear the humming of insects and see beneath him in the clearings the berry patches where the bears would gorge themselves fat until the first snowfalls, then slink off to their mountain caves. Warren Cabot listened to his own regular, deep breaths, pulling the clean air inside his lungs as he gazed from left to right across the horizon of the big sky. Down towards Whitefish, Robyn would be drinking coffee and eating fresh baked biscuits with friends, discussing the old times and their exotic, alien lifestyle in the power circus of Washington DC.

On the streets of Whitefish and Kalispell families would stop at grocery stores, filling their coolers with Cokes and beers and ice and head down to the lake where the main weekend entertainment, a water skiing competition, was to begin at noon. Cabot felt the sun warm on his back and he loosened the top of his water bottle to take a swig. There was something in this America, this vast and rambling chaotic continent that he knew was worth defending. There was a basic decency of ordinary people who would be outraged at what had gone on in Miami. He despised Terrelli and Boone and Lewis and all of them for betraying these decent Americans, and he wondered whether, despite his loyalty to this administration, it was right to keep silent. All this was going on in the name of national security and paid for by the good honest folk who were picnicking by the lake or fishing in the stream down below. They deserved better. He screwed the top back on his water bottle and slipped it into the saddle bag. He ran his fingers down the carefully crafted leather. The saddle had been a present from his wife on their tenth wedding anniversary, and now felt worn like a comfortable pair of shoes. He mounted Cloudy again and spurred him along the ridge and then began the slow descent on the loop trail down to the river valley. It would be tricky for the old horse, easy to miss a step and fall.

Cabot knew the right thing for his country, its citizens and under God, was to throw open the windows on the filth that had been uncovered in Miami, throw them open and let the president dismiss and humiliate those responsible. The self-inflicted wound might cost him the presidency, but the whole history of fifty years of Cold War had been like that, losing sight of what was right for short term gains. Now here was the chance for penance.

Suddenly Cabot remembered how he had learned in school of the first fathers of the American Revolution, those who believed that like the Roman leader Cincinnatus they could fight in the wars against the British or serve in public office and then retire back to their farms, with no love for permanent power or glory. That was a core value.

Those men who admired Cincinnatus had always been Cabot's ideal – capable of exerting power, but not fooled or seduced by it. He would be like the Cincinnati, throw it all away, return to the land, leave Washington to the poweraholics, the Boones and Terrellis – even if he was convinced they were precisely the people who should not be placed in charge.

Cloudy had done well. He had puffed and pulled his way down

the trail, stumbling a little, yet recovering. There was life in the old horse yet, and while Robyn's friends were always trying to sell Cabot something younger and more active, he resisted. He was loyal and valued loyalty in return. The old horse seemed to sense it, doing his best in some kind of intuitive arrangement. When they reached the river Cabot allowed the horse to stretch its neck and drink. He sat high in the saddle, unscrewing the top of his own water bottle again and drinking deeply. There was a rhythm to life here that was so real he could almost reach out and grasp it. They would go to church on Sunday and nod and exchange pleasantries with families he had not seen for months. Sunday night, he would take Robyn to the steak house on the edge of town and they would meet the same good folk from the church, eat too much, drink iced tea. Monday, they would meet them on main street, struggling with supermarket shopping or taking their kids to the lake.

Cabot turned the appaloosa on to the trail and headed back to the ranch. He checked his watch and it was almost lunchtime when he tied the horse at the back of the barn and called for one of the stable boys to unsaddle it. As he approached the house he saw his wife on the porch rocking gently, reading a book and sipping iced tea. She looked up and smiled, her face without make-up, freckles dappling her nose like a schoolgirl too long in the sun.

'Sun tea. Like some?' she asked, and he nodded. 'How was your ride?'

'It was fine,' he said, as she poured the tea over ice cubes. 'Gave me a chance to clear my mind.'

'It does that up there. Clears away the city dust.'

'I wonder,' he said to her, sitting down on the swing and putting his arm round her shoulders. 'I wonder what you think of what I've got to tell you.'

'Oh,' she said, looking at the sweat on his brow and the reddening of his nose and cheeks. He had caught the sun and for the first time in months looked healthier and younger than his years. The grey had gone. 'Anything important?'

Cabot sighed.

'Important? Well, it could decide whether I become Director of Central Intelligence. Or whether I even want to. And it could change who is the next president of the United States. But I've been thinking that the great thing about this country is that it has character enough to survive whoever ends up in the White House. So important? I guess not.'

22

Alex Newman woke early, shortly after six, and went for a run around the deserted Georgetown streets. As soon as he arrived back in his apartment, sweating from the humidity despite the hour, he called the *Tribune* foreign desk to speak to Holroyd.

'Saturday, old son,' the duty desk editor reminded him. 'In fact it's Saturday all day today. Maybe you forgot. Or it's different out in the Colonies. But we still don't have a Sunday edition. You'd better try him at home.'

Newman called Holroyd and told him what had happened to DeVos.

'Bad luck,' Holroyd said. 'Sorry to hear that. Must have upset her. Still, no damage done.'

Jesus, what an idiot, Newman thought, standing in the main room of his apartment, sweating and angry.

'Well, maybe not, Mike. But it looks as if we have another story. I mean the caller said it was Fat Phil who set her up. Now obviously it was not Fat Phil Lewis himself. At least I would not think so. But someone is trying to warn us off the story, and I think . . .'

Holroyd interrupted. He had better things to do with his Saturday morning and fell back on that peculiar English habit of always apologising when he was being most rude.

'I am sorry, Alex. I'm really sorry. But the people who are warning you off this story are not the drugs enforcement people. Or the CIA. It's your editor, Alex. And your foreign editor. Remember us? The people who pay your salary? And we have had enough of it. It is not going anywhere.'

Newman pulled the telephone away from his ear and stared at it, wishing he could crush it in his fingers.

Holroyd was still lecturing him.

'I've told you about this before. It's becoming an obsession with you, God knows why. It is simply not that interesting to the rest of us. And I don't want this . . . this unfortunate incident with the researcher to start encouraging you again. I'm sorry, Alex, but we do not want any more stories about the CIA down in Miami, thank you very much. What we want are some properly presented ideas on the presidential election campaign. In case you have forgotten it, Alex, the election has not been standing still while you've been off chasing spies. I'm sorry, but we just do not want to hear any more about it.'

Newman slammed down the telephone.

'Bloody arsehole,' he yelled out loud, his face red with anger. What Holroyd simply did not understand was that it had become personal now.

They had tried to hurt Helen – whoever 'they' were – and he was damned if he would not find out why. Newman showered quickly and changed, clipped on his skypager beeper, and picked up his portable telephone. Just in case. It should be a quiet weekend but the *Tribune* would never forgive him if something broke and they were unable to get in touch. He stormed out of the apartment into the elevator and gunned his car from the parking garage towards the airport. By the time the first Miami flight arrived, Newman had paced up and down the arrivals hall as often as an expectant father. Helen DeVos walked off the aircraft with a carry-on bag over her shoulder, her brown hair streaming behind her, skin glowing from the Florida sun. She smiled nervously and Newman could see she had the strained and cautious eyes of a mugging victim. He took her bag and kissed her quickly, then hugged her, thinking how beautiful she was. Her body felt good, thinner, firmer than he remembered. She was shaking, unsure of herself for the first time since he had known her.

'Let's go to the apartment,' he whispered, and she smiled. 'I want you.'

She ran her hand down the side of his face. 'I can't tell you how glad I am to see you, Alex.' She smiled again, happy to be with

254

someone she could talk to, happy it was him. 'I think it has to be the Agency,' she said as they crossed Key Bridge into Georgetown. 'Has to be, unless you believe in wild coincidences. Why else would someone use the name Fat Phil? It's a warning. They're trying to scare us off.' There was a long pause, and then she added: 'And I think they have succeeded.' Newman told her about Holroyd and how little interest there was in pursuing the story further.

'He may be right,' Newman added reasonably. 'We got an exclusive. So what? How do we take it on? The answer might be, we don't. They want economic stories, domestic agenda pieces, mainstream politics, and nothing more. And I don't want you getting hurt.'

Helen shrugged. They could talk about it later. She just wanted to be with him, to relax, to pretend she was not frightened any more. Newman parked the car and picked up her garment bag from the back seat. They took the elevator to his apartment. He put the garment bag against the door as he tried to pull the apartment key from the half-dozen he needed to enter the *Tribune*'s office every day, through the burglar alarms and elevator security. As he fiddled, and before he could find the key for the lock, the gentle pressure from the garment bag pushed the door of his apartment open with a long, slow creak that cut through him like a knife. He looked up in astonishment at Helen, then put his finger to his lips. For a moment he wondered whether to go inside or turn around and call the police on his portable telephone. He dialled 911 but it refused to connect. He tried the operator. Nothing.

Then he tried calling the National Press Center to see if they would have any better luck, but again it stubbornly refused to work. The battery was either too low or the telephone would not work from inside the building.

'Fuck,' he whispered, feeling the rush of adrenalin pumping through his body. 'There's a phone at the Seven Eleven on the corner,' he said to Helen. 'You go. I'll stay here.' Helen wanted to argue, but saw there was no point. Newman's once cherubic face was reddening, his muscles tense. She looked at his eyes and saw nothing but determination to go into the apartment, and she was too shaken to try to argue. She turned and ran down the stairs towards the Seven Eleven store. As soon as she had gone, Newman listened for sounds from inside the apartment but could hear nothing. He put the portable telephone in his right fist like a club, reasoning that it might at least prove good for something. Then he took a deep breath and gently pushed the apartment door fully open. Inside it was open plan, a narrow hall opening out to a living and dining area, with a balcony and two bedrooms above. He heard every creak of the boards, every whisper of air leaving his lips as he tried to move soundlessly inside. The craziness of what he was doing half crossed his mind. People who liked breaking into apartments, Newman thought, were the kind who also liked guns. But he was angry now, angry and feeling violated, demanding the revenge of bringing the weight of his fist crashing down on the bastards who were doing this to him and to Helen. He turned and swept his eyes across the sitting room and dining area – nothing. No sign of anyone having been in the apartment except himself. For an instant Newman wondered whether he carelessly had failed to lock his own front door as he left that morning, beset by worries about Helen, angry with Holroyd, tired after just a few hours' sleep. Maybe.

It would not be out of character. And his mind had been so filled with Helen, there was little room for anything else. He began climbing the stairs towards the two bedrooms and bathroom, thinking how foolish he would feel when the police arrived and he would have to admit his own stupidity in failing to lock the door. Then he felt a chill of fear. He listened to every creak of the stairs as if they sounded klaxons signalling his arrival. As he reached the upper floor, Newman decided to check first the smaller bedroom which he used as a study. He pushed the door open and felt his heart pump to his throat. He saw the figure of a man standing over his desk holding his laptop computer in one hand and two boxes of diskettes in the other. Newman did a double take. It was as if he had stumbled into the study of a computer salesman, smartly dressed in blue jacket and grey trousers, white shirt, red striped tie, ratty face. Little guy. Ugly. Olive complexion. Maybe Hispanic or something. Looking like he owned the place. Newman was utterly transfixed, staring at his property in the man's hands and dropping his own right fist a little, still clutching the telephone like a caveman holding a rock, uncertain whether he should try to club the intruder or run for help. The man

256

smiled, a wolfish grimace, drawing back a slack lip. Newman blinked, still unable to understand exactly what he was looking at. He heard a rush of air behind him and what sounded like an explosion shattering the right side of the back of his head just behind the ear. There was a sudden warmth and a crushing silence as Newman fell towards the smiling Hispanic, gripping the useless portable telephone in his fist as he smashed to the floor. His head was a buzzing numbness, the blood spilling from the side of his face and dripping a dark stain on the beige of the carpet.

23

At first Boone wondered how Phil Lewis had come to hear of the place. It didn't look his style, all wood and stone flagged floors and outdoorsy and too many National Park people in Smokey the Bear hats taking kids for a walk in the woods to show them the difference between bluebells and black bears. There wouldn't be a yacht harbour, Hispanic waiter or *mojitos* drinker within fifty miles.

'There you go, Mr Appletree,' the receptionist said. 'You're all set. Cabin A7. The porter will show you the way, or you can take the Bald Eagle loop. Yours is the fourth cabin on the right.'

Boone walked about fifty yards down the loop, wondering if this was some kind of set-up. Lewis was capable of anything under normal circumstances, and now appeared to have freaked completely under the strain. The thought made Boone's hair bristle on his neck. Maybe the son-of-a-bitch had decided to become a government witness. Nail us all. Everybody who made money out of Deep Blue. Boone felt his muscles tense. He was ready to punch the nearest tree. He took a deep breath as if he had just pressed two hundred pounds high in the air until the moment of panic passed.

'Calm,' he told himself. 'Keep calm.'

It was more likely that Lewis wanted to unsettle him, show him the power he might use if they did not come to a deal. The fat man kept babbling about 'mutually assured destruction' and 'deterrence'. By recalling the 'David Appletree' pseudonym Boone had used for his Deep Blue investments, Lewis was conducting a test explosion for propaganda purposes.

'Fuck him,' Boone thought. 'I'll deny everything. Who will they

258

believe, a foreign swindler from Miami or a senior member of the White House staff, eh?'

The Skyline Drive Lodge cabins were made of rough hewn logs, like a pioneer settlement on the edge of the frontier, though each had individual air-conditioning and a minibar inside. Boone threw his bag by the side of the bed. As he did so the telephone rang.

'Mr Appletree,' a voice said. 'I'm sorry. I should have checked your messages when you arrived. Your English co-worker Mr Jackson said to let you know that he is in cabin A3. To dial it you call 713. Thank you for staying with us, and have a nice weekend.'

Sure, honey. Mr Jackson and Mr Appletree are going to have one hell of a weekend. Boone rubbed the back of his neck with the palm of his hand. The muscles were stiff from the drive. This was one pioneer who'd like a shower or maybe a jacuzzi. His stubby fingers punched out 713.

'Hi,' the voice said.

'Phil? It's me. Rich. I mean, Appletree. I'm in A7. Want to meet here or the bar?'

In the bar fifteen minutes later Boone barely recognised the fat man.

He had aged greatly, lost a little weight and stood blinking nervously like some nocturnal creature dragged unhappily into sunlight.

'You're dropping a pound or two,' Boone said, pointing to Lewis's belly.

'Yeah,' Lewis replied. 'Shed twenty pounds and aged twenty years in two months. I got a secret diet.'

'What's that?'

'I don't eat,' he laughed sarcastically. 'Or sleep. Being scared shitless is quicker than all those diet milkshakes. I can still shift beer though. Want one?'

Lewis ordered a Molson. Boone took a Jack Daniels on the rocks, sipped it while they exchanged small talk, family talk.

'If we want to speak privately,' Boone finally suggested, 'then maybe we should go for a walk.'

Lewis knocked back the rest of his beer in a few seconds. Some things never change, Boone thought. The man still eats and drinks

259

like a pig. Real English class. Boone pushed his Jack Daniels to one side.

'I can get it later. This is more important. Let's go talk.'

Phil Lewis led the way across the car park, past Boone's red Corvette.

Boone noticed a battered Jeep Cherokee with Florida plates and dark tinted windows.

'This yours?' he asked. 'You drive up all the way from Miami in this piece a shit?'

'Sure,' Lewis replied. 'I took a week. On the Blue Ridge parkway it was fine. At least I felt safe for the first time since everything fell apart.'

The sun was beginning to dip behind the hills to the west over the Shenandoah Valley. The path was marked with blue diamond signs, a two mile loop and nature trail. The first signpost stood by a large white oak and detailed how the forest pattern had changed after European settlers arrived. Lewis looked at it listlessly. Boone came to the point.

'I don't know what games you think you're playing, Phil, checking me in as David Appletree. Fuck with me and you'll be sorry. If you're thinking of setting me up, then you're thinking like a dead man. Nobody's playing this to lose, Phil. If I lose, I'll kill you.'

Lewis smiled. Another threat or two from Boone just added to his collection. It cheered him to think that he was still able to irritate the deputy National Security Adviser.

'Oh, yeah. Sorry, Rich. I told you it was just my idea of a joke. Won't happen again. Promise.'

Boone would not leave it be.

'You sending some kind of signal here, Phil? 'Bout maybe turning me in?'

He was looking his most aggressive, tensing the muscles in his shoulders and arms so they bulged under his Ralph Lauren shirt. They had walked slowly and were standing near a sign which said 'Plants of the Swampy Ground'. Lewis smiled again.

'I don't do signals, Rich. If I wanted to get you, don't you think I would have done it by now? Just let slip the word to the Feds or that tight ass lawyer you keep sending down to Miami, Warren Cabot.

Or to the thousand and one assholes I've had to deal with over the past couple of months? Well, I haven't betrayed you so far, and I've no plans to, and I'm not making any threats. I don't have to. You know if they break me I could start naming names. I could get them interested in how you afforded the Corvette, for instance. Or maybe start asking what you're doing with a ski lodge in Park City, Utah, on your salary. Or the condo down in Puerto Vallarta. I mean, you inherit the money, or what?'

Boone looked at him grimly, the head and neck bending forward a little, aggressive, wary. Lewis began to laugh. 'Listen you dumb fuck, I'm not going to turn you in, Rich. There's no point. All I'm trying to do is take you up on your invitation to fix a deal that closes Deep Blue. Deal, you remember. That's when two sides negotiate. Work together on this.'

'I remember,' Boone hit back bitterly. 'I remember most things. Like the night we discussed how in this country they expected talented people to go into gov'ment but refused to reward them for it. How we figured everything worked better in the private sector. I remember how this bright, impressive Englishman – you were lean and hungry once, Phil – persuaded us with his fluent Spanish and business contacts round Latin America that he could play our games better than we could ourselves, less s'picious, able to move in and out of Cuba and Nicaragua without any trouble. The ideal solution, we thought. Freelance, off the shelf, self-financing. Now a pain in the ass.'

As Boone talked Lewis kept his distance, out of range of any punch that could tear his head from his shoulders. Lewis watched the thickness of the arm muscles swelling angrily under Boone's shirt.

'What are you telling me, Rich?' Lewis broke in. 'That you were some kind of virgin in the 1980s corrupted by me? Fuck off. You took your chances. You could have stayed on the outside of the Deep Blue investments like Terrelli. He must have suspected what was going on, but he didn't ask too many questions. Never part of it, never closing it down. Or you could have gone all moral on us and turned us in. But what you did was put your snout deep in the trough just like the rest of us. So say what you have to say but don't start whining. Don't start a moral lecture, or I'll throw up.'

261

Boone looked at the shambling, angry fat man thumping his weight down the trail beside him. He was reminded of a moment a decade before when the two of them were walking round Congressional Golf Course side by side, just like this, discussing Deep Blue.

Lewis had explained how they could profit from patriotism.

'You invest money in the company, we put it in sure-fire things based on our expertise and our contacts. I'm doing the same with the budgeted funds anyway. I don't see why you shouldn't share in our success.'

'So what happens if it comes apart?' Boone remembered asking.

'How can it come apart?' Lewis replied. 'Our job is to avoid banking and other regulations, move funds according to operational requirements. That means far from the law taking it apart, we *are* the law, Rich. All you have to do is come up with the name you want your investments run under. Anything you like. Johnny Appleseed. Jimmy Appletree, Rhyming Simon, whatever.'

And so, by the eighteenth hole, David Appletree of Grand Cayman was born, to proud parents Richard Boone and Philip Lewis. A mixed marriage, an easy birth.

They were now in a clearing by the river which fed into the Shenandoah, then curled round to the Potomac and the sea at the Chesapeake Bay. Boone thought he could cheerfully strangle the fat man, throw his body in the river and drive off as the police searched for the phantom David Appletree. But he supposed if his mission had been murder he would have planned it without the striking red Corvette. Despite the pleasure it would give him to strangle the fat bastard, that was a job best left to someone else. And not now. He would save Lewis's fat ass, in the hope, not entirely incidentally, of saving his own.

'The deal from Vince Terrelli is this, Phil, and you'd better listen up because it's simple, non negotiable, and the best you're gonna get.'

He had the fat man's full attention, standing face to face under the oak and whitebeam and hazel and pine as the sun cooled down. 'The deal is you plead guilty to a couple of specimen fraud charges, details of which are to be agreed between our lawyers and Holgate. You are offic'lly declared bankrupt, and all your pers'nal assets, those which can be traced, and those of the company, go to pay off cred'tors.'

Boone looked at the round face in front of him, sweating in the heat. Now he came to the best part.

'The thing is, we expect to have a cash injection of around twenty million dollars from a private source which will ease the pain and get rid of the worst cases.'

'Which means?'

'Which means nobody's gonna be screaming for you to be fried, providing you continue to do what you're told and not go blabbing to journalists, not here, not in England, not anywhere.' He looked straight at Phil Lewis, wagging his finger under the fat man's sweating jowls. 'We've got just a few weeks left not to screw up before the election. You cause trouble and you're a corpse, I swear it Phil. As sure as I'm standing here looking at you. I'm talking to a dead man if you even think about working us over. Me and Terrelli decided it's a carrot and stick policy as far as you are concerned, Phil. The carrot is, we won't use the stick. You understand?'

Lewis nodded. He understood. There was a long pause while Boone let it all sink in. Then he started to explain the rest of the deal.

'Your sentence will be two years, to be spent in a minimum security jail, with maximum remission. You'll be out after eight months. My guess is you might even decide you like the climate better in England from now on.'

'Why England?' Lewis wanted to know.

'We don't care,' Boone snapped back. 'England. Tahiti. Borneo. So long as it's not here. You got friends who're pissed at you because they lost money, like old Jorge down in Miami. And you got friends like me who're pissed because we made money and maybe would like it kept quiet. One of these days, Phil, some of us friends are gonna get together and take you warmly by the throat and beat the crap out of you, first because you fucked up the investment company and second because you talked about it.'

The two men stared at each other. Phil Lewis looked at the thickset face in front of him, the close cropped head and bull neck. There were beads of perspiration on Boone's hairline and patches staining his Ralph Lauren shirt. Boone stared back, just inches between them.

He could see a twitching in Lewis's right eye, a minor nervous ripple as the fat man digested his words. Lewis suddenly turned away, closing his eyes and holding his head in his hands.

'I know you are capable of it, Rich. I know it. Oh, God!'

For a moment Boone thought the fat man was going to cry, but he only rubbed his face and sighed, recovering his composure.

'You don't think I've wondered ever since they tried to carve me up in the hotel bathroom whether it would not have been better to have died? You don't think I've wondered that? Every waking minute. But I tell you, if I look back at all we achieved, I'm proud of it. Proud. For eight, nine years we never appeared as a blip on the Congressional radar. Instead we made the taxpayers some money. And ourselves. We were the Stealth team, and it worked. It was people like us that put this country where it is today.'

Near where they stood was a bend in the trout stream, a long, slow curve where the water's glassy surface was puckered by the fish rising for flies. Half a dozen rings could be seen where trout languidly picked up food in a summer of plenty. Boone noticed the fat man was sweating more now, not complaining, but clearly wanting a pause in the walk. He sat down on one of the big boulders by the riverside. Boone stood a few yards away. He rubbed his two hands backwards over the stubble on his head.

'Sure, Phil. It worked for a while. But now it's hist'ry. And people in this country'll tol'rate anything so long as it's a success. It has nothing to do with right or wrong. If we'd won at the Bay of Pigs we'd have been heroes. We lost, so it's a fiasco. Deep Blue is now fucked up, and I'm trying to get all of us out from under the wreckage. What do you say?'

Lewis shook his head, trying to think. Boone looked to his right and saw a large trout take a fly a few inches above the water surface and hit the river with a splash.

'So it's all wrong now is it, Rich?'

'All wrong, Phil. The whole thing.'

'Columbus?'

'Especially Columbus. They've probably shot him by now, Phil. All that shit is in the dustbin of hist'ry. Finished.'

Lewis took a deep breath. He was saddened but not surprised.

264

'Just a foreigner,' Lewis began to say. 'Like me. Some goddamn foreigner who tried to help this country. Now he's been wasted, and I've been abandoned. Jesus. What a fucking mess.'

Boone again thought Lewis was near to tears. He decided to snap the fat man out of it.

'What do you want, Phil? A medal? Sure it was beautiful. Sure it was. Now it's a li'bility. What if they put Columbus in the dock for some kind of show trial? We've got to be prepared for everything. In a way, that might lance the boil. Once the Cubans start making all'gations about the drugs, that will kill the story forever. Nobody would believe we'd do something like that. Nobody. Communist prop'ganda. Trying to influence the election. Dirty tricks. Typical of the pinko Democrats trying to benefit from it. You can write your own script. But whatever way you write it Phil, it's over. The game's over.'

Lewis stood up from the rock and turned to face the river, composing himself, watching the shimmering surface flow down towards the Shenandoah Valley. Boone was looking at the way two spare tyres of flesh fell over the top of the fat man's pants.

'Deep Blue is finished,' he repeated. 'All of it.'

'But the good guys won, Rich. The good guys won.'

'Sure, Phil. Sure. This time the good guys won. The map's all in one colour now, except for Cuba, and that's bound to fall. We got there Phil. We got there. Deep Blue.'

Boone could hear a mockingbird sing in the trees on the other bank, a short delightful song over and over again, a trill of notes somewhere in the foliage. He turned round and looked back at Lewis. The fat man was following the diamond direction markers back towards the Lodge.

The mountains to the south had that smoky, purple glow in the last light from the setting sun, the hazy colour which gave them their name, the Blue Ridge and the Smokies, the spine of the Appalachian chain. Boone was anxious to finish.

'So do we have a deal, Phil?' he asked as they neared the Lodge.

Lewis held out a pudgy hand.

'Yeah, I guess we do. I'll want to discuss it with Holgate, but I guess we do.'

They shook hands and Boone patted him on the arm, then they walked back inside.

'Maybe I won't stay the night after all,' Boone said, with relief, looking round the main Lodge reception area and smelling dinner being prepared in the restaurant kitchens. 'Our business is done, Phil.'

Lewis nodded. They had said enough.

Boone fetched his luggage from the room, told the surprised receptionist that Mr Appletree had unfortunately been called back to Washington, and a few moments later stood next to the Corvette with the fat man. Neither was fond of goodbyes, and this could hardly be especially tender. Boone settled in to the car's leather seats, undid the roof catches and let the top of the Corvette roll back. The evening was cool enough to drive with it down.

'Oh, there was one thing,' Boone said. 'One thing I forgot to tell you. About your suicide. The word down in Miami is your two helpers were a pair of Latino goons, whose names I don't remember but whose employer I do recall. Your good friend and partner Jorge Lopez. I thought you should know. We think that Cuban woman who worked for you . . .'

'Ileana.'

'Yeah, Elena. We think, seein' she's Jorge Lopez's niece, that one of the reasons she's so keen to find you is so you and Jorge's goons can get acquainted again. I wasn't sure if anyone had cared to mention it.'

Lewis nodded impassively. Like Boone said, he knew who his friends were.

'Are the police gonna nail him? Lopez, I mean.'

'I doubt it,' Boone replied, opening the door of the Corvette. 'They have all got alibis. The Turtle was at some Republican Party fundraising event. Black tie dinner up in Cocoa Beach. So I guess that's solid. The two goons were down in Little Havana drinking beer in the company of half a dozen of their pals. One of them, Lula Martinez, has gone missing. Maybe he's gone back to Cuba. Who knows. Anyway, no forensic, no witnesses except you. And you said you could not recognise them, right.'

'Right.'

266

It was now a pleasant summer twilight. Boone started the car and switched on the lights. The engine growl excited him. He rubbed his hand across the stubble on his head, eager to be done.

'We can't meet again,' he said. 'Ever. It would be too dangerous.'

'I know.' That was fine with Lewis.

'Take care of yourself, Phil. And good luck. I guess you'll need it.'

'Just don't fuck with me over this, Rich,' Lewis said. 'I've gone through enough. And there was one thing I forgot to mention. If anything were to happen to me now, anything like an accident, or some surprise to do with men with knives. If anything like that were to happen again, it would just excite the kind of media curiosity you and Terrelli and all of us could do without. So I've taken precautions.'

'Such as?' Boone asked suspiciously.

'Such as making sure a lot of people are on the mailing list in the event of my sudden death.'

Boone looked at him angrily. 'Mailing list for what, Phil?'

'Names, dates, times, places. My life story, I guess. Posthumous autobiography of the deceased. I think you know the kind of stuff. It goes to the *New York Times*, *Washington Post*, *LA Times*, *Miami Herald*, the networks, that British newspaper, the *Tribune*, the BBC . . . someone else. I forget. Oh, yeah. The Democratic National Committee. Yeah, the DNC. That just about covers it, I guess. Unless you can think of anybody I left out. I just figured that way you'd have a vested interest in taking care I make it okay through the next few difficult months. All for one, one for all.'

'Goodbye, Phil,' Boone snarled, turning the Corvette round and driving hard into the night, barrelling towards the interstate while the cool mountain air rushed at him through the darkness. As soon as Boone left, Lewis walked across the car park. He stood beside the battered Jeep Cherokee with the Florida plates and looked around him. The woods were silent except for the sound of the crickets at the beginning of night in the Virginia mountains. Lewis tapped three times on the back door of the Jeep and it opened. The face of Steve Ortiz showed from the side of the heavily tinted windows.

'How'd it go?'

'Okay,' Ortiz replied. 'Woulda been better if you'd worn a wire so I could get sound of what you were talking about. But I got good video and stills of the two of you.'

'Good,' fat Phil Lewis said. His old optimism had started to return. He had even more leverage now. They were coming round to his way of thinking, now he'd shown them the strength of his deterrent. He could hope to go off to a new land of opportunity – England, maybe – and reinvent himself one more time.

It was not the country which made you what you were, it was the men who made the country. It was spirit that created the pioneers who conquered the rough frontier, and Lewis knew he had that right stuff. He slapped the private detective on the back, beaming at Ortiz's face.

'C'mon, amigo,' he said. 'Let me buy you a beer, my old friend. I think we got David Appletree by the balls now. All we have to do is decide when to squeeze.'

24

The interrogations lasted eight days and Padilla was as pale as a corpse from which blood and life had been methodically drained. He wanted to close his eyes and dream of a paradise full of slowly lapping waves and capacious hammocks and wide, soft pillows on which he would bounce himself to sleep and sleep forever. He thought intermittently about Ileana Del Cid, about his family, about his men, his comrades, his friends. At no time did he think of the revolution or patriotism or other abstractions, and more recently Padilla thought of nothing except himself, of the dull throb in his aching head and his unquenchable need to dissolve the pain in sleep. They had taken him back to his cell: white staring walls, freshly covered in cheap paint, a wooden bed frame and mattress without covers, two enormous fluorescent lights which never dimmed.

'The only place in Cuba,' Padilla thought, 'where the electric power never fails.'

They told him the day's sessions were over, but they lied. They always lied to him now, as if no truth were possible any more. He lay on the bed, closed his eyes and slept for what seemed like a few seconds, enough to befuddle his brain with thoughts of whether a day had passed or a month or a minute, or whether it was the same day, or the next day, or a week before. He lost all sense of time except for a here and now of bright lights and rough voices and exhaustion. Then he heard shouts again and the boots on the concrete, the shaking of peasant hands on his shoulders.

'General,' they always called him politely when they shook him awake. 'General! General! Rouse yourself! It is time!'

A time to sleep, a time to dance, a time to die. It mattered little now. He would stagger to his feet and they would carry him like a cross on which the revolution's sins might be nailed, along the green walled corridors, half dragged by the guards because his step was so uncertain and they feared he would fall asleep in mid stride. It seemed that seconds after he had left he was back in the interrogation room for the next session with the next team, with the same questions until his body shrieked in pain and his mind swam and bubbled.

'Oscar Padilla Sanchez,' one of them would bark, in the familiar routine, impressing upon him the formality and the seriousness of it all. And the other would be softer, offer cigarettes, coffee, a little gossip, day after day.

'General Padilla,' Colonel Cesar Fonseca Hijuelos said to him this time. 'We wish to bring your case to a close as quickly as possible. We are going to be busy over the next few weeks with other matters.'

'Why?' Padilla asked wanly. 'Other matters?'

'We have more problems in Oriente province with a small clique of troublemakers in the air force,' was all Fonseca would say. 'I thought we had cured the problem, but it appears there is some serious counter revolutionary activity which we have yet to deal with.' Fonseca lit a cigarette. This time he did not offer Padilla one. He blew smoke in the air and arranged the files on his desk. 'And there are also those who wished to leave Cuba through the Peruvian and Czech embassies who have now decided, for patriotic reasons to renounce their treason and return home. We have to deal with them too. So I cannot spend any more time on this case with you. They have to be seen to immediately.'

Even though Padilla was half asleep it sounded rather lame.

'Oh,' he asked. 'Why?'

'Why what?'

'Why did they renounce treason . . . return home?'

Fonseca laughed.

'Because we persuaded them of the error of their ways, and the revolution likes repentant sinners.'

Then he explained with some amusement that the DGI had developed a new trick in dealing with those who wished to defect by entering foreign embassies to demand political asylum. The DGI had taken to sending in its own men, each claiming to the Peruvian or Czech diplomats that they too were trying to escape from Cuba and demanding asylum. Once inside the embassies the DGI agents hectored, cajoled and intimidated the genuine refugees into leaving, threatening to murder them, to persecute their families in Cuba.

'They will be sent to the sugar fields,' Fonseca said. 'To help with the harvest. And many more to come. Until they are re-educated. But all that means there is little time left to spare you.'

Padilla was too anaesthetised by fatigue to play games about his own future. He assumed it meant they were about to shoot him. The matter of his own death or imprisonment was of so little consequence compared to the chance of rest, he did not bother to ask.

'You will be released,' Fonseca continued. 'By order of General Juan Antonio Fernandez, confirmed by the Minister of Defence. They will instruct you of your new orders within a few days.'

Padilla blinked his dry, tired eyes. There was danger here, he sensed, but he was too exhausted to figure it out. Fonseca continued.

'The Revolutionary Co-ordination Unit is to be disbanded and your operations wound down. You are to oversee the destruction of the Unit, the handing over of all funds to the DGI. You will be expected to announce your retirement from the armed forces. When that happens I am instructed that no further action is to be taken against you.'

Padilla blinked again. The lids hurt in his reddened eyes. He wished he could cry to ease the pain. Fonseca said his case had been considered at the Tribunal of Revolutionary Justice where Padilla's disillusionment with the revolution and unauthorised contacts with American intelligence had been weighed against his past service and the inconclusive nature of much of the evidence against him. Fonseca was still talking but Padilla was lost, his head drowning with fatigue.

'The most telling point in your favour,' Fonseca said, grimly, 'was that Cuba does not need any more bad news. A case against you would have to demonstrate your clear guilt to the armed forces and the people. It would have to be a public humiliation. The political purpose such a trial might serve would be outweighed by the harm it would also cause to the state. Public morale is very fragile right

271

now. Such concerns have to be weighed in the balance. The greater good.'

Even in his exhausted state Padilla could understand the code. With the problems in Oriente, and all the economic difficulties, they feared a military rebellion if they moved against him without clear and conclusive evidence. It did not exist. Even a confession, which he was now prepared to sign, admitting to anything including his complicity in the murder of Abel by Cain, would not be enough.

People knew about confessions.

He was being spared, he knew, only thanks to political exigencies. The greater good and his own safety appeared to coincide. Fonseca pulled another cigarette from his packet, lit it, and then as an afterthought offered Padilla one. Padilla took it and unsteadily accepted a light.

'So you are lucky, General,' Fonseca concluded, leaning back in his chair and blowing smoke clouds carelessly in the air. 'The revolution needs live heroes to encourage the people more than it needs executed traitors to instil discipline.'

He blew another smoke ring above his head.

'For now,' Fonseca said.

'For now,' Padilla echoed faithfully.

Within an hour of being dismissed by Fonseca, Padilla was driven back to the beach house by two DGI officers. He had fallen asleep before the car had moved a hundred metres. He slept all the way, his head tossing from side to side as if his neck were broken. They arrived at the house and tried to wake him, without success. They were forced to carry him to the bedroom where they placed Padilla carefully on top of the sheets. He slept fully clothed for sixteen hours, drunk with exhaustion. When he awoke it was daylight, mid morning by the height of the sun. He pulled himself from the bed and into the bathroom, filling the sink with water and ducking his head several times beneath the surface. He dried his eyes and let the water drip through his clothes, cooling his body, then walked to the kitchen and opened the door of the refrigerator which clicked into a loud hum as the motor restarted. Inside there was no rum, no food except a papaya and a half a pineapple. There were two dark Cabeza de Lobo beers, and he opened one and began drinking from the bottle. It was good beer. Black. Strong. They had not managed to destroy the quality. For now.

The words came back to him like a dismal mantra. For now. He remembered a little of his talk with Fonseca like the last part of a nightmare before morning. He was to wind up the Revolutionary Co-ordination Unit, though it was quite possible market forces had already wiped them out. The Colombians had complained they were losing too many aircraft for too little profit. They wanted to switch more to small boats and to land transportation through Mexico. Cuba was becoming less important anyway, in this as in everything else, floating to the sidelines of history. Padilla thought vaguely he would try to learn the truth from General Fernandez, the truth about his own future. It would be difficult. The Lion of Playa Giron might have more sense than to talk to him again. Padilla gulped down the beer, then stopped suddenly, his random and tired thoughts interrupted by a sudden yet hyper-realistically clear vision of his future. They would close down all his operations and gently ignore him, pushing him to one side as a broken traitor, a piece of flotsam from a time they now despised.

They would declare he was ill. Mentally unstable. He would become one of the Undead, the spectral figures of formerly high officials now disgraced for reasons never made public. He would be condemned to join the Undead in their haunting of the dreary cafes and parks of central Havana, neither disgraced nor trusted, bereft of a career, or meaning or life. He would spend the last of his days waiting for the counter revolution like an ageing spinster waiting for a husband, playing chess or engaged in morbid discussions with the other former high officials now disgraced. He walked back to the bathroom, suckling the beer from the bottle like mother's milk. He stripped naked and washed the grime and the odour of the prison from his body.

He shaved carefully walking back to the bedroom to sleep some more. As he lay on the bed an idea began to carve itself in his mind, drilled on his brain by the brown eyes of Ileana Del Cid laughing by the pool of the house in Panama.

Ileana's naked body was dancing before him with every firm curve slowly turning in delight, her breasts cupped just out of reach of his

273

hands as she moved backwards away from him, her outstretched fingers curling at the tips demanding that he go to her now, and give her pleasure.

'*Todo sera mejor,*' she called to him, as the sleep came again. Everything will be better.

25

So he was dead now. Alex Newman had not expected to wake up. He had not expected anything any more. He supposed what he had heard was a bullet blowing his brain all over the inside of his study, little pieces spread like dust among his books and personal effects. He remembered thinking that death seemed so banal. Not painful. Not interesting. Then at some point he was shaken violently by Helen DeVos who was hysterical with grief and so relieved when he groaned that she shook and hugged him until his eyes opened and he could see the blur of her face smeared with blood. His blood.

There was pain now, and dreaminess. Newman vaguely recalled a number of large black men in dark uniforms, the District of Columbia police, and paramedics and ambulances and a quick scream of the siren through the hot streets towards Georgetown hospital. All of this made him feel he was in the middle of some made-for-TV movie, a spectator on an overwritten scene, as they rolled him on a trolley through corridors and under machines where they X-rayed and scanned his brain and shaved his skull and tried to put him back together again. When they decided he might be able to think, they told him the good news: that he had not been shot, and he was not going to die. Yet, anyway. Then they told him the bad news: that his skull was fractured. It had been chipped at the base behind the right ear where a large blunt object – the butt of a gun, or, Newman thought wryly, maybe a portable telephone, the new Georgetown weapon of choice – had smashed into him like a half brick. They told him it had been wielded by a heavyweight bear of a man over six foot three tall with an exceptionally strong right arm.

Fine, Newman thought. That narrowed it down from about two hundred and fifty million Americans to oh, say, to about twenty million. The pain made him want to fade away behind the drugs they pumped into him. He had a ringing noise in his ears and was bored with staring into the eyes of doctors who looked as if they had stepped out of a soap opera, who smiled and were cheerful and filled him full of painkillers, until he could not separate one buzz from another. They told him that as skull fractures went it was 'relatively minor', but then he supposed on a scale of ailments he would rather have relatively serious haemorrhoids or chronic athlete's foot. And instead of recovering instantly as they did in the cartoons, Newman wanted to stay in bed forever, to be cosseted by Helen who held his hand and stroked it and cried by his bedside until he too began to weep.

'I thought you were dead, Alex. And I wanted to die too.'

'What a dumb idea,' he replied, then he realised that was an American, not an English, expression. 'I must be brain damaged,' he told her. 'I'm beginning to talk like an American.'

She assumed that meant he was recovering. A bunch of flowers had been delivered by the *London Tribune* with a note from Holroyd. One or two of his colleagues sent 'Get Well Soon' telegrams. DeVos bought a huge potted plant with thick waxy leaves which she insisted on putting on his bedside table, throwing everything else to one side. On the fourth day he told her he could not remember much of the man he had seen, and nothing at all of the one who hit him, except he thought he remembered gutteral Spanish as he lay on the floor with his head smashed open.

He wasn't sure. Some kind of muttered conversation echoed in what was left of his brain.

'It doesn't matter, Alex,' she said, trying to comfort him. 'It doesn't matter now. The *Tribune* sent someone to cover for you. I took a telephone call at the apartment from Holroyd. He said you just had to get better. Think about nothing else until after the election. Don't worry about your work.'

Helen had been concerned how he might react. He had mellowed from his worst workaholic phase, but she was not sure he would accept the idea of another correspondent taking over his patch when

276

the presidential election was becoming the most significant story of his time in the United States. To her surprise he did not seem disturbed.

'Good,' Newman said. 'That's exactly what I want. Not to work. At least, not to work on the election story. I have other ideas.'

Before she could respond, Newman sat upright in bed and grabbed her arm, pulling her towards him. There was a fierceness in his eyes that she had not seen before, and it frightened her almost as much as seeing his body lying bleeding on the carpet. 'Listen,' he hissed. 'I don't exactly know what we've done, or who we have angered, and I don't care. But I know this. I am going to find out who cracked my skull, and why. And I am going to find out who tried to fit you up with the drugs, and why. And if it means I have to track down fat Phil Lewis for the next ten years I'm going to do it. And I'm going to talk to that smarmy CIA lawyer Warren Cabot that you saw down in Miami, if I have to camp out in his offices for a month. I am not going to be smacked around and intimidated by these people. Not going to take it.'

The effort seemed to exhaust Newman and he fell back on the pillows, releasing his grip on Helen DeVos's arm. She looked at him, his head partly shaven, the rest swathed in bandages. She thought at first she had better humour him, agree with whatever he said however fanciful. Then she realised he was serious.

'Don't be crazy, Alex. There's nothing in this for us any more. There's no story here. No one wants it. Lewis knows if he talks he is finished. And why should the CIA lawyer help us? We're in a dead end.'

'Doesn't my cracked skull count for something?'

'Well, it made a few lines in the *Washington Post* Metro section. I showed you yesterday: Journalist Investigating CIA attacked during break-in at home. That's about it.'

'Yes, yes, I remember,' he said irritably. 'I've got a cracked skull, not Alzheimer's disease.'

'Well, you asked me what it counted for, Alex. And I'm telling you. An inconclusive story in the *Post*. Another in the *Miami Herald* and a few lines on the local television news.'

Newman put his arm out to her again, gently this time. She took

277

it and looked down at his fingers, playing with them one by one, nervously.

'I just don't want to see you get hurt,' she said. 'Nothing is worth that.'

Newman smiled.

'Look, for a start there's probably a book in this. I don't know exactly what, but it might be possible to persuade Lewis to talk, maybe when the court case is over. Tell the whole story. Maybe it's some kind of epitaph for the Cold War.'

He saw flickering fear in her eyes. 'I thought you were the crusader, the one who wanted to expose these people for what they do?'

'I am,' she replied. 'But not if it means they try to put me in jail and nearly kill you. For God's sake, Alex. It hardly fits in to your idea of a story. There's no fun in it; it won't be good for your career, and nobody's told you to do it. In fact I'm telling you NOT to do it. It's crazy.'

She raised her voice enough to disturb some of the other patients who looked across at them. One of the nurses appeared to be on the brink of coming over and telling her Newman had to rest. But he did not want to rest.

'Listen,' he said. 'This isn't a story any more. It's not something I can stand over with objectivity and put together. It's something I am part of and I have to find out what it means. I have to. There's no choice, whether it's a book or an article for *Combat* or just to satisfy my own curiosity.'

He sat up and pulled her towards him fiercely again, rattling out questions like water down a drain.

'How can I find out what is so dreadful about what we have printed that someone tries to kill me? What is there about this which leads someone to set you up for a drugs bust? What is there which allows the CIA lawyers to claim there is no CIA connection with Phil Lewis and yet seal all his files? Where is the key that turns all this stuff into sense?'

Now he was truly exhausted and Helen did not want to argue with him any more. She leaned over and drew her fingers gently down his cheek as he stared back at her, the blond curls either shaved away near the wound or covered by a bandage, the eyes moist with strain.

278

'I love you, Alex,' she said, tears beginning again. 'That's why I want you to be careful.'

'I love you too,' he whispered back, unashamed. 'That's why I want to know the truth.'

26

It was seven in the morning and there were two of them, smoking by a dark green Lada at the end of the driveway. General Oscar Padilla Sanchez stared towards them without animosity. The older one was mid-thirties, grey flecks in his thick beard.

'Baby Fidel,' Padilla muttered.

The younger, clean shaven, nervous, maybe late twenties. Neither had been born at the time Padilla had begun the struggle in the mountains of the Sierra Maestra. The younger one had probably not even been conceived when they had marched behind Fidel victorious into Havana, drunk with success. They were DGI agents, the most visible of however many he realised were to dog his every step from now on, to remind him he was balanced on the edge of the precipice.

'Children of the revolution,' Padilla repeated to himself. 'Which now must eat its own.' Then: 'Buenas dias, companeros,' he called out cheerfully, strolling towards them. 'Que tal?'

The younger one immediately stubbed out his cigarette and shuffled anxiously at the great hero of the revolution moving towards him. Baby Fidel looked back with a level gaze.

'Good morning, General,' he said, straight backed and wary. He too dropped his cigarette to the ground.

'Good morning,' the younger one echoed.

'Look, friends,' Padilla said. 'Let's make this easy on each other. I can guess what your orders are, and it is your duty to obey them. It is not my intention to make any difficulties for you. I am now going to my office in Havana. Then I will take coffee and maybe a little lunch. I have attempted to persuade our comrades that I am guilty of no crime. They have released me, so I assume they agree. But as is obvious from your presence, they are persistent and I am still under suspicion. They may have told you I am expected to wind up a major project I have been working on, the Revolutionary Coordination Unit. Later I plan to return here, and I will have work to do this evening at the base in Varadero. If I'm lucky I'll have time to spend with a woman. I hope that makes things easy for you.' The two men grinned and nodded. 'And don't worry,' Padilla said. 'You will be aware of my every move.'

Padilla drove to his office in central Havana, arriving shortly before eight o'clock. It was his first day among the Undead. Word of his detention and release had obviously spread. There were formal salutes from junior officers, and guarded words from the civilian staff. Padilla could only guess at the problems he was causing Barbaroja, Fernandez and the others.

The DGI suspected everything and could prove nothing, though of course they could assert he was a drug trafficker and have him shot anyway. His brother officers would not be tempted to rebel if they believed he was a *narcotraficante*. But he assumed the DGI shrank from finishing him off not from residual guilt and the vestige of decency, but because the prospect of a rebellion remained serious. That meant they had calculated the story that Padilla was a drug trafficker would be regarded as incredible.

He tried calling General Fernandez at his office but the secretary stonewalled. Padilla assumed that in offering his initial warning the Lion of Playa Giron figured he had taken enough risks. Luisa had not yet arrived at the office and Padilla desperately wanted a coffee. He called the orderly at the end of the corridor who made *café con leche* and left it with a bowl of sugar in the middle of his desk. Padilla thanked him, and when the orderly left he pulled his dress uniform from behind the door. It was newly cleaned and neatly pressed. He sipped some of the hot coffee and felt its warmth jolt him completely awake. Then he turned and put the uniform back on the hook, thinking how good he would look in it later. Luisa arrived some time after eight and Padilla checked her face for signs that she had been told he was now a suspect. Nothing.

'Do you know where I have been for the past two weeks, Luisa?'
She stared at him without embarrassment.

'They told me you were in Panama. But everybody knows you were arrested by the DGI.'

Padilla waited for her to say more.

'Well,' he asked finally.

'Well what, General?'

'Well, what do you think of it?'

She looked puzzled.

'There is nothing to think, Oscar,' she said. 'You have been released, and so there must have been a mistake. If they decide to re-arrest you and you are shot, then you will be guilty. That is all there is to know.'

Padilla looked into her heavy brown eyes. He knew she had been ordered to watch over him, to report back.

She carried an uneasy burden, being ordered to prove her own loyalty by spying on her boss and former lover.

'Luisa,' he said quietly, 'whatever you have been instructed to do, you must do. That my future will be grim is not in doubt. It is your future you must think of.'

She smiled a little, embarrassed. There was a long silence in which they looked calmly at each other, understanding as former lovers do what each needed for survival. He knew she would not treat him as Undead. Eventually Luisa spoke.

'What I have been instructed to do is to help you close the Revolutionary Coordination Unit and prepare for your early retirement. Correct?'

'Correct,' Padilla replied. 'That means that I have some work with the files to do today.' Luisa laughed.

'This must be serious, Oscar. If it means you are to do filing they are punishing you severely.'

He began by searching through the main cabinet, pulling out neatly organised lists of how many kilos had been brought in and by which methods. Fonseca's people had been through every one of these files trying to build their case against him, but as far as he could tell there was nothing missing. He wondered how much Luisa really understood, as she typed the lists, what 'Consignment 20: 440 Kilos'

282

might mean, or the profit and loss columns, or the 'expenses' which included details of every aircraft that had been captured and two which had crashed. Padilla pulled half a dozen folders from the racks and carried them into his office, closing the door. It took two hours to gather the simplest records of how much had been shipped from whom and to whom, how much Cuba had taken as profit for the revolution.

One of the delights of the operation (which he remembered had most intrigued Phil Lewis) was that under the old Soviet-inspired system of accounting – which Moscow had long abandoned but Cuba still embraced – there were literally no overheads. The entire military operation was free, paid for by the state, not accounted for in any way. That meant all the hard currency that was obtained was profit, a remarkable kind of economics. By the time he finished Padilla had extracted about two hundred pages of papers. He clipped them together, put them in a separate file in his briefcase. Then he returned the remaining papers to the filing cabinet. True to his word to the two DGI officers, Padilla went for mid-morning coffee, two coffees, black, strong and sweet, washed down with iced water, and smoked two cigarettes while reading the newspaper. There were reports of further oil shortages and another planned 'power emergency' for the end of the month. The idea was that all centrally generated electricity was to be turned off for eight hours to give the emergency and defence services a chance to learn how to cope. More than thirty years since the triumph of the revolution, Padilla thought, three decades of sacrifice, and now we are being expected to do without energy to cook or see by. The Havana bread ration had been cut to three ounces per person per day.

'Pathetic,' he muttered into his coffee, pushing the newspaper to one side.

There was one other story which caught his eye: confirmation that twenty-three 'counter-revolutionaries' who had tried to leave Cuba by seeking sanctuary in the Peruvian embassy had now 'recognised the futility of their plan' and 'left the embassy to face revolutionary justice.' The revolution was so successful, Padilla thought, that people had become one of their best exports.

He stared across the bar at the two DGI goons, the younger one grinning inanely, the older eyeing him in return. The evolution of the human spirit had taken them five hundred years and three thousand miles from the wharves of Seville and Cadiz, the conquistadors and the Inquisition, to this grim cafe and his cadaverous company. Always the Dark Ages, he muttered into his coffee, thinking of the DGI goons as Roman Centurions who poked spears at the man on the cross or Torquemada's assistants who burned and tortured; the same dreary functionaries who beheaded Louis XVI and shot the Romanovs and gassed Jews or bombed Hiroshima and Nagasaki. They had evolved from spears to bombers, but neanderthal morality was constant, and it disgusted him.

Padilla nodded at the two goons to indicate he was leaving. He returned to the office and telephoned one of his current girlfriends, a translator in the National Tourist Office. He made a date for late that night, offering to take her to a very expensive restaurant at the end of the Malecon called '1812'. The girl was delighted, and so was Padilla. He assumed the telephone was tapped. The line sounded clearer than it had been for months. There could be only one explanation. Padilla picked up his full dress uniform and walked out of the office, telling Luisa he expected to be late the following day.

'I have meetings at the Defence Ministry,' he called over his shoulder. 'They could take me some time. Tell people I will probably not be back until late afternoon tomorrow.'

She nodded sadly.

'Of course,' she said. 'Take care.'

And before he could stop her Luisa put her arms round Padilla, hugging him tightly.

'Oh, take care, Oscar,' she repeated, a matronly hug. 'Take care.'

He called for his Lada, and began the drive back along the Malecon, the drive that after a week in Panama or Mexico he wanted to come back to, and which after two weeks in prison made his heart beat faster than he could have imagined. He took the road towards Santa Maria del Mar, wondering if this was to be the last time, convincing himself it would not be. Nothing was 'forever', not the revolution, not exile, not disgrace.

As he neared Santa Maria del Mar, he slowed to let the DGI car close on him. He wanted the boys to feel good, that they were on

284

top all the time. He watched as they stopped at the end of his lane, park and jump out of their vehicle. When they were safely on guard he walked inside the beach house and telephoned Varadero airfield to confirm that the schedule he had agreed with the Colombians was still being followed. Major Rico Herrera, a stiffness in his voice, said there had been no changes.

'Though we are to cease operations entirely next month,' Herrera said grimly. 'Is that not correct, general?'

'I believe it is, major. Those were the instructions handed down from the Defence Ministry.'

Herrera confirmed that General Fernandez had instructed them to maximise the number of shipments until the final closedown. Yes, there would be one tonight, as planned. No, he did not foresee any problems.

Padilla showered and shaved again, patting his face with cologne. He pulled on his full dress uniform, buttoning the collar primly at the neck.

Then he took his dress leather holster and pistol and strapped it to his waist, checking it was loaded and that he had a spare magazine.

He was more surprised they had left him the pistol than that they had released him from jail, until he came to the conclusion they were sure he would shoot only one person with it: himself. Who else might he turn it on? Suicide would rid them of the agony of decision over what to do with him, confirming the DGI in their suspicions he was a traitor; reinforcing the counter view from the military that he was but a loyal officer who cracked under the strain of unfounded charges, and yet giving his comrades no pretext on which to cause trouble. He drew the pistol from the holster and held it in his hands, passing it from left to right. It felt good. Smooth. Unlike some of his fellow officers who appeared to think a gun was now merely a part of the dress uniform, Padilla recognised it might have its uses. He walked into the darkness at the front of the beach house, and opened his car door, calling out briskly over his shoulder.

'I have business at Varadero airport.'

As he started his car and drove off, to his great amusement Baby Fidel and the younger one had to scramble to follow. They caught up before he had travelled a mile. At Varadero the guards on the gate sprang to attention when they saw him arrive, saluting even more formally than usual as they noticed his full dress uniform. Inside, in the main operational hangar Major Herrera looked surprised at all the formality.

'Special occasion, General?' Herrera asked. Padilla could see in his eyes the same embarrassment he noted in Luisa.

'Oh,' Padilla replied. 'I suppose you could say so. Just something I have arranged for later tonight. A reunion with an old girlfriend.'

'Ah, very nice.'

There was an awkward silence between the two men. Padilla looked at him – mid thirties, dedicated, efficient. Something about Herrera made Padilla desperate to explain.

'You know I was arrested,' he said. Herrera nodded.

'I know.'

'And that I am not guilty of betraying revolutionary principles.'

'I know.'

'Even though I think we are dangerously on the wrong course.'

Herrera nodded again and said nothing. They stared at each other for a full ten seconds until Padilla was sure Herrera understood.

That night's pilot was a slim faced young Nicaraguan with a small moustache and a worried look. He had been in the Sandinista airforce until the collapse of the Ortega government and now was trying to trade flying MiGs for something more profitable. Cocaine paid better than killing contras, but he was having second thoughts.

'First time?' Padilla wondered, noticing the look he had seen so often before combat.

'Yes, General.'

'Well, it's not so bad. You'll get used to it.'

The Nicaraguan did not think so. His load was three hundred kilos of cocaine in black plastic bags divided into two lots. There were now two principal buyers in Florida with whom they most frequently dealt. The buyers were business rivals, of a sort, but had taken to cooperating rather than killing each other – at least for now.

'Where's your target site?' Padilla asked. 'For the drop.'

The Nicaraguan was sweating gently, and Padilla could see small beads on his moustache. Padilla, on the other hand, had never felt more relaxed in his life, as if he had stepped from a sauna and massage.

286

The Nicaraguan produced a map.

'The route takes me out to the west first,' he said. 'Then back towards the Florida coast here, near Everglades City. The landing strip is in scrub and swamp. That's not too difficult. I landed on just about everything, sometimes under fire, during the contra war. But . . .'

'But you're worried about the Yanquis?'

The man nodded.

'And the weather. It could be rough and wet, low cloud, turbulence. Maybe that will help me. But I'm still nervous.'

'Well,' Padilla reassured him, 'that's natural. We would not want any pilot not worried about the Yanquis to take off with a load like this, would we, Herrera?'

They laughed and tried to encourage the Nicaraguan to do the same.

'Cheer up. At least unlike the contras they will not shoot you.'

The Nicaraguan smiled grimly.

'I should have introduced myself. I'm General Oscar Padilla Sanchez. What's your name?'

'Juan Luis Echeverria,' he said. 'I'm pleased to meet you, general.'

'Are you ready for take off?'

'Completely. But the schedule says I have to wait another hour.'

'Ah,' Padilla said. 'We must always stick to the plan. Like all good socialists. Even though we are winding down our operations here and I thought I should watch the last few take offs. For old times sake. I'll look forward to you making a safe trip. Let's drink some rum when you return.'

'Thank you,' Echeverria said.

Padilla wandered through to the officers' room and for a few moments took coffee and chatted.

He assumed that like Herrera they all knew of the disgrace which had fallen upon him, though he doubted they would have learned anything specific. They probably deduced that if, like the Oriente mutineers, he had truly committed treason, he would already have been shot. He looked around the room at the officers as they smoked and laughed together. He liked them all, Herrera especially. If this was the best of Cuba's future then it might not be so bad. They

287

fought bravely in a thankless war in Angola. Now they performed a dirty task cheerfully and loyally at home. Padilla drained his black coffee to the dregs and told them goodbye, he would not come again. Their work was almost at an end.

'Keep up your standards,' he said. 'The country is proud of you. And no matter what you hear about me in the future, I have behaved properly as befits a Cuban. And I am proud of you too.'

As he turned to go they began to applaud in spontaneous appreciation. Then they stood up, one after another, scraping their chairs backwards as they gave him a standing ovation. Padilla retreated, surprised, embarrassed. He climbed into his car knowing this was the moment in which all would be won or lost. It was his only throw of the dice, and he felt his heart beating harder than in any action, in any combat, ever.

'*Tempano,*' he whispered to himself. 'Iceberg.'

He drove to the gate and was about to leave the base when he stopped.

The Lada containing the two DGI men had parked outside.

Baby Fidel and his colleague were leaning against the body of their car, relaxed, smoking, chatting to the guards.

'Damn,' Padilla said, so everyone could hear. 'I forgot my files.'

He turned the car around and drove back across the airfield to the Revolutionary Coordination Unit hangar. Juan Luis Echeverria had supervised the last of the fuel loading, and was walking round the aircraft trying not to look nervous.

'I want to talk to you in a moment, Juan Luis,' Padilla said, halting the car for a moment by Echeverria's aircraft. 'There is something of a security problem, which you need to know about. Make ready to leave as soon as possible. Tell no one. I will be back in five minutes to instruct you whether you must go early or not.'

The Nicaraguan looked startled, but stood his ground by the aircraft.

'Of course, General,' he said, straightening his back and almost saluting the voice of command.

Padilla spun the car round and parked next to the officers' room.

He had only one order left to give as a Cuban general to his troops and it would require all his authority to have it obeyed. If his courage

288

failed him now he was dead, which at least was a marginal improvement on being Undead.

'Major Herrera,' Padilla called out bursting into the room where the men were laughing among themselves at some profanity. Herrera stood up, as did the others, and snapped to attention at the general in his full dress uniform suddenly returning to bark out new orders. 'Major Herrera, we have an emergency. There are two men at the front gate acting suspiciously. I saw them on my way out. They claimed to the guards they are from the Ministry of the Interior, but the guards on the gate are suspicious, and so am I. If they are spies detailing take off times for the Americans they could be one reason we have been losing so many aircraft. Find them, hold them, and if they resist, shoot them. I will ensure the aircraft takes off on schedule, and then immediately inform the DGI of the arrests. Now spring to it!'

Herrera was like a hound chasing a hare, out of the door with the other officers, heading for the guard post. Like the snap of excitement from an incoming artillery round, the orders catapulted them into action. Padilla watched proudly as the men raced towards the gate ready to round up the intruders. Calmly he pulled a cigarette from his pack, stubbing it to try to keep the tobacco inside. He lit it and walked across to where the Nicaraguan pilot was standing open mouthed at the scene.

'Let us get into the plane immediately, Juan Luis,' Padilla said. 'We have no time to lose. It could be a long night.'

As the twin-engined Piper Aztec prepared to take off to the west the bewildered Nicaraguan was not sure what to make of his passenger, the commotion at the base, or the coolness with which the general ordered him to get airborne.

'We have enemies,' Padilla hissed at him. 'We must move quickly, or else all is lost.'

Juan Luis Echeverria had been nervous when he flew Nicaragua's defence minister, Humberto Ortega, from Managua across the country to Bluefields on the Atlantic coast in the middle of the contra war. But that was nothing compared to the nervousness which now gnawed at his belly as he started the engine and began taxiing towards the end of the runway with his cargo of cocaine and this rather splendid but peculiar Cuban general coolly giving him orders. He sweated with stress, fearing he might be sick.

As they watched the Piper Aztec move out to the runway, the Varadero air traffic controllers bellowed on the radio at Echeverria to respond.

But Padilla insisted the pilot say nothing until they reached the take-off position.

'Papa Alpha Four-One, why are you moving early? . . . Four One this is Varadero tower . . . Four One you are not authorised . . .'

'I must talk to them, General,' Echeverria pleaded.

'Prepare for take off first,' Padilla replied coolly, unbuttoning the leather flap on his holster and putting his hand on the grip of his 9mm pistol. 'Then when we are ready, I will tell you what to say.'

Padilla sat directly behind Echeverria in the first of the Aztec's passenger seats, and slowly pulled the pistol from his holster. When they reached the end of the runway, and watched the lights glow in a long track leading westwards, Padilla ordered Echeverria to speak to the tower.

'Tell them Major Herrera has gone to deal with two suspected intruders at the gatehouse. He is worried about the security of the mission and has ordered you to take off immediately. Do not say I am on board.'

Echeverria turned his head and looked back at General Oscar Padilla Sanchez, and Padilla saw the wide eyes of a nervous rabbit. He lifted his pistol into view.

'Juan Luis,' he said quietly. 'I think you already have your orders.'

The rabbit blinked. Echeverria called the tower and told them word for word what Padilla had said. The tower said they would check with Herrera.

'Tell them there is no time. Tell them again that Herrera fears a major breach in security.'

Echeverria swallowed hard. He had gone through in his mind every single complication that could befall him – the aircraft developing mechanical trouble, arrest in Florida. But nothing prepared him for the unnervingly calm man who held a pistol just behind his back.

'Juan Luis,' Padilla continued. 'Please do not force me to shoot you. It would be very inconvenient for both of us.'

Echeverria relayed the message, and requested immediate clearance for take off, making his own final preparations.

'Negative,' the tower said. 'Until we check.'

Over to his right, by the hangar where the Revolutionary Coordination Unit was based, Padilla could see headlights and some kind of movement. It looked as if Herrera and his men had returned from the front gate with their captives. There was a further pause while the tower contacted Herrera.

'Negative,' the tower repeated. 'You are to return to the hangar immediately. Repeat, you are to return to the hangar immediately.'

There was a new urgency in the voice from the tower, and Padilla thought he could see the lights of two vehicles to his right speeding from the hangar towards him. He pushed the snout of the pistol to the back of Echeverria's head, cold metal on the sweat just beneath the hairline. The pilot twitched.

'Take off immediately, Juan Luis. And switch off the radio. There is nothing we need to hear from them now.'

Among Herrera's men everything was now a mass of confusion. They had raced to the front gate and quickly surrounded the two DGI officers, AK47s cocked and ready. The younger one dropped his cigarette. Baby Fidel blinked with surprise until Herrera ordered them to turn round with their hands above their head.

'We are from the Ministry of the Interior,' Baby Fidel barked.

'Shut up,' Herrera ordered back, and as the soldiers disarmed them the younger one felt fear pass a shock wave through his gut so intense he thought he might lose control of his bowels.

'What are you doing here?' Herrera snarled to the younger one, face to face, inches apart, as the soldiers roughly searched them. 'Do you not know this is a prohibited zone?'

'Yes . . . but . . .' he stammered. The soldiers pulled a pistol from the younger one's shoulder holster, and another from the older agent with the Fidelista beard.

'We were following General Padilla,' Baby Fidel answered, regaining his confidence.

'Orders from the Comandancia,' the younger one added, finding his own courage return. 'The general is still under suspicion. Did you not know this? We were to follow his every movement until he finished his business with you . . .'

Herrera took a pace backwards and breathed deeply. One of the soldiers showed him the two DGI identity cards he had found in their wallets, but Herrera did not need to see them. In one foul instant he recognised everything – Padilla's trick, his own predicament.

'Back to the hangar,' he yelled, and they clattered into their vehicles, bundling the DGI officers inside.

They arrived at the main hangar in time to hear the increasingly anguished calls from the tower asking for an explanation of the security emergency. Herrera blurted out what had happened as best he could. The two DGI officers, still at rifle point, rolled their eyes skywards.

'Then does Papa Alpha Four-One still need to bring forward its take off?' the tower asked.

'Negative,' Herrera said. 'Repeat, negative. Tell it to return to the hangar.'

When the Aztec refused to comply, Herrera's suspicion that Padilla was on board was confirmed. There could be no other explanation. Herrera knew he was in trouble now, betrayed by Padilla yet somehow reluctant to believe the truth. A perverse part of him wanted Padilla to make his getaway, but his own instinct for survival drew him to act.

'Hold these two here,' he yelled, pointing at the DGI officers. Then Herrera pushed his driver from the side of the jeep and started up, speeding towards the runway, angry at his own stupidity, surprised, confused. He wanted to see it for himself: General Oscar Padilla Sanchez, Hero of the Revolution hijacking an aircraft filled with cocaine to fly to the United States. And when Herrera saw it, he was too late. Inside the Piper Aztec Echeverria swallowed hard, turned off the radio, increased revs and released his brakes. Padilla watched the two military vehicles on his right change direction to try to intercept them, but the Aztec had already gained too much speed. It bounced down the runway until the landing lights that led to the west blurred on either side, and Padilla looked away from Cuba, towards where he hoped his future might lie. As the Aztec's nose eased off the tarmac Herrera braked, coming to a halt in the middle

292

of the airfield apron. He stepped out of the jeep and watched the small aircraft climb slowly into the cloudy night, a butterfly in the storm.

'*Buena suerte*, General,' Herrera whispered. Good luck. Then he turned round and slowly drove back to the hangar, seeing himself as they would see him: an accomplice to Padilla's treason, needing his own good fortune.

A few miles from the airfield Padilla ordered the pilot to turn north.

'Take the shortest route towards American airspace. And keep low.'

Padilla glanced at his watch trying to work out how quickly they might be intercepted. In test trials run by the Ministry of Defence, MiG interceptors could be airborne within a few minutes. But this was not a test trial. And it was not in response to an incoming intruder. The efficiency of the military apparatus had to be weighed against the inefficiency of the decision-making structure. There would be panic and confusion and no one would know what to do. No one would want to take the initiative, unsure whether Padilla was on the aircraft or whether Echeverria had panicked, or even if the Nicaraguan was simply being prudent.

For the first time in his life, Padilla thought that the Cuban bureaucracy might actually help him. That meant, if he calculated correctly, at best a fifty-fifty chance. Padilla thrust a packet of cigarettes through into the cockpit and right in front of the pilot's nose.

'Smoke, Juan Luis,' he said, making it sound more an order than a question.

The Nicaraguan took a cigarette, and in his nervousness let the first half-inch of tobacco fall on the floor. Padilla lit both cigarettes, catching a glimpse of Echeverria's anxiously twitching eyes.

They were a few hundred feet above the water's surface, thick cloud above, cutting out all light from the moon. The Aztec bounced and pitched over the waves until even Padilla felt he might be sick.

'We should take it higher, General,' Echeverria said.

'Stay where we are, Juan Luis,' Padilla replied. 'Keep it low.'

'It eats fuel this way, General.'

Padilla laughed. Maybe Echeverria still had not figured out that there would be no return trip.

'Just keep it low,' he insisted.

Padilla pulled back the hand with the gun and let it rest on his hip. He looked at his watch. They were seven minutes gone. Padilla drew on his cigarette until it glowed in the cabin. If it came, he assumed it would be a quick death. It was not a matter to which he had given much thought.

They would see the fighter and it would signal them to turn around, and Padilla would have a choice to make: he could either allow them to be shot down, or he could tell Juan Luis to turn the Piper Aztec back towards Cuba as Padilla shot himself. That way only one would have to die. No more wasted suffering. No more unnecessary sacrifices. That was the way Padilla wanted it. The cigarette was finished and he pulled another from the packet. He could, of course, allow Echeverria to switch on the radio again, but that might panic the Nicaraguan even more, confuse him with conflicting instructions from the general with the pistol or the MiG with the air-to-air missiles and heavy cannon.

Eleven minutes gone. They were well into international airspace now. Padilla supposed that in the end he would allow the Nicaraguan to turn back. If he had learned nothing else over thirty years, it was to deny their hollow pretence that individuals do not make a difference. He was now sure that no man had the right to sacrifice anyone else for abstractions like the common good, and he would not sacrifice Echeverria. Not in the name of the revolution. Not even in the name of his own freedom. Padilla looked down towards the pistol in his hand, but the night was so dark he could barely see it.

When the time came he would have to rely on touch to place the barrel in his mouth pointing upwards, squeezing the trigger and spattering his brains and blood around the inside of the Piper Aztec.

'*Socialismo o muerte*,' Padilla muttered. Socialism or death. So that was the choice after all.

In the Varadero hangar there was now an interesting dilemma. For obvious security reasons the Revolutionary Coordination Unit worked as a highly secretive team. If something went wrong with a flight, Herrera was to go directly to General Oscar Padilla Sanchez. However, Padilla was presumably otherwise engaged. Even so, there was still the chain of command, and every member of the Unit had repeatedly been indoctrinated in the same procedures: by-pass all normal military channels; only deal with other RCU personnel; do not discuss or refer to senior officers outside the RCU chain. The only other senior officer in whom Herrera was supposed to confide was General Juan Antonio Fernandez. Herrera immediately telephoned him for instructions, but the Lion of Playa Giron was (of course) not at his Ministry of Defence office, nor was he at home. The minutes began ticking away, and Herrera felt the stippling of sweat along his forehead. The DGI officers were now becoming most insistent they be allowed to telephone their headquarters and Herrera had no choice but to agree. He had already delayed as much as possible without confirming any suspicions about his complicity in Padilla's defection. Herrera checked his own watch.

Fifteen minutes gone. Now the intelligence service would have to think quickly, which was a political oxymoron. With every minute Baby Fidel was on the telephone, arguing, discussing, insisting, justifying, blaming, Padilla was a minute nearer American airspace and safety.

In the Piper Aztec Padilla offered Juan Luis Echeverria yet another cigarette. He looked again at his watch, the glowing numbers staring out at him through the darkness, as the aircraft bounced under the gathering clouds. Nineteen minutes gone.

'They say,' Padilla mentioned in a conversational tone, 'there is a tropical storm deepening off Hispaniola. Could even turn into a hurricane.'

'Not tonight,' Echeverria said with a throaty rasp, his nervousness making his tongue stick to the roof of his mouth. 'And not coming this way. I checked the meteo thoroughly. Everything, I do thoroughly.'

Padilla now thought he had better explain to the Nicaraguan what was to happen in the unlikely event they made it to US airspace

'We are going to land at a place called Boca Chica,' he said. 'Do you think you can find it on your map, or shall I point it out to you?'

There was some shuffling in the front seat, which Padilla did not like. He raised the pistol again and gently placed its muzzle on the back of the Nicaraguan's neck.

295

'No, General,' Echeverria panicked. 'I'm only looking for the map. In all the rush I . . . it fell or something . . . look, here it is.'

'Ah,' Padilla replied affably. 'I am sorry to seem so suspicious. But things may happen rather quickly from now on, and I want to be prepared. I will keep this pistol behind your head not because I intend to use it. Merely to concentrate the mind, in the event of a crisis in the next few minutes. Just remember, whatever others may do, I will not miss. Is that clear?'

'*Si, claro.*' It was abundantly clear.

Padilla switched on a small flashlight and leaned over to look at the map.

'I think you will find Boca Chica . . . here. On the Keys. See?'

Juan Luis Echeverria found it with his finger on the map.

'It's marked as an American airbase,' the Nicaraguan called out in alarm. Padilla laughed.

Major Herrera had by now apologised to the two DGI officers, returned their pistols and identity cards. He had been forced to waste vital minutes relaying something of the story again to their controlling officer at DGI headquarters, explaining what the aircraft carried, and giving a rough account of the flight plan in a way which seemed to him utterly redundant. By the time he finished he looked again at his watch. Twenty-three minutes. At a cruise speed he estimated of 330 km/h, if they flew a direct course, the Aztec might now be impossible to catch, unless the Cubans were willing to risk an armed conflict in US airspace.

'You can switch on the radio again now,' Padilla ordered. He was curious to hear what kind of trail of devastation lay behind him, but the radio remained stubbornly silent. Juan Luis Echeverria checked and re-checked the new course for Boca Chica, his sweaty hands sticking to the controls. For all his own coolness, Padilla was also wet through his uniform.

'*Tempano,*' he thought to himself. 'An iceberg which sweats.'

He pulled the pistol back up towards his head and pushed back his cap. The metal felt good on his forehead. He let it slip down to his side, and was beginning to relax, feeling the seconds tick away towards Florida, knowing there was land not far ahead. They were safe, on the edge of reaching a foreign shore full of new promises.

296

Suddenly from far to starboard a fully armed fighter travelling very fast and low swept across the sky in front of them. Echeverria sat back startled and his nervousness in the fighter's wake caused the Aztec to bounce violently in the air. The radio began to crackle as the fighter dashed to the left and turned. Padilla knew it would circle and within seconds be behind them. He felt a rush of adrenalin and fear, bracing his body for the shock of cannon fire that would rip them to pieces in seconds, spreading the wreckage like dust on the Florida Strait.

27

Warren Cabot's Washington offices a few blocks from the White House were functional and dull, which was pretty much how Newman assumed he would find Cabot himself. As well as his work for the Agency, Cabot still kept a foot in his private practice in an old fashioned Washington partnership which specialised in advising corporate clients how best to lobby Congress. Being allowed to retain his old office was, Cabot thought, so much more convenient than trudging all the way out to CIA headquarters in Virginia, and it bolstered his treasured fiction that he was part of the real world as well as government.

Newman realised as he came upon the address that he had walked past it a hundred times, but this was shapeless commercial Washington and one utilitarian office block was much like any other. He took the elevator to the fifth floor and walked in to a wide reception area full of ferns and greenery. There were two rows of defending receptionists before Newman was finally led through to meet Cabot. He noticed infra-red security devices in each of the hallways and a metal-bolted door barring the way towards one end of the office.

'Mr Newman for you sir,' the secretary said and withdrew, leaving Newman gazing across a room filled with male trinkets and knick-knacks. There was an oar across the ceiling painted with the words 'Princeton 1958'. To the left, Newman saw a startled twenty-pound Chinook salmon mounted with a fly in its mouth in a mahogany case with an engraved brass plaque – 'Kodiak Island 1986' – and a series of photographs round the walls taken by Cabot himself, mainly mountain views near the family ranch in Montana, with his wife, children, and horse, a grand-looking appaloosa.

It reminded Newman of eighteenth-century British oil paintings of the landed gentry surrounded by their possessions. To his right along the wall Newman saw another series of photographs: Warren Cabot with singularly important-looking people, signed by those same important people in the requisite style of politesse oblige.

'To a very dear friend,' one said, signed by the current National Security Adviser. 'And a Great American.'

'To Warren, who helped make it all possible,' from the man who was now president of the United States of America.

'Best wishes, Warren, from one who admires you greatly,' showing Warren Cabot being presented with what looked like a medal or award by a grinning Bill Richardson, in front of a seal which read 'Central Intelligence Agency'. Big grins, backs slapped and egos stroked all round. Cabot sat stiffly upright behind a black wooden desk of modern design. He came to his feet, tall, dignified, with a benign smile, sweeping back his long grey hair with his left hand, beaming from behind his golden spectacles. Cabot extended his right arm and they shook hands. As Newman continued looking round the room trying to take a measure of the place and the man, Cabot stared directly at the reporter's head. If Newman was amused by the lawyer's little treasures, Cabot was appalled by the way Newman looked – the pink surgical collar, the white bandage, the shaved head.

'Ah,' Newman said, catching Cabot's gaze. 'You're wondering about my appearance. Well, so am I. I have a fractured skull, as you may recall from the fax I sent your office.'

Cabot blinked and Newman heard him draw a deep breath. The fax was simply a short covering note and the most recent story Newman had filed for the *London Tribune* plus a few paragraphs from the *Washington Post* metro section.

The *Post* story said: 'A Washington based British journalist investigating alleged CIA links to a Miami investment company was hospitalised after being beaten by intruders in his Georgetown home. The intruders stole papers and computer files relating to investigations being carried out by Alexander Newman, forty-two, of Prospect Street NW who was beaten unconscious as he tried to tackle two men. A friend of Mr Newman's, journalist Helen DeVos, said . . .'

Newman decided to twist Cabot's obvious discomfort even more.

'A fractured skull,' he said, 'is, in this case, less dramatic than it sounds, thank goodness. As the stories I sent you show, I was cracked over the head by one of two goons undoubtedly working for the Agency you serve who were searching my study when I disturbed them. They did a better job of ransacking my files than they did of breaking my skull, otherwise I wouldn't be here to boast about it.'

Cabot looked concerned. He suggested they move to what he called the soft area – a settee and two easy chairs beside a small coffee table. As they sat down Cabot asked Newman in an avuncular tone what precisely he was suggesting. Newman replied that it was obvious what he was suggesting, and as additional evidence he recounted in full the DEA arrest of Helen DeVos and the burglary at his own apartment.

'They stole my lap top computer, with research notes on various stories including the Winston, Hamilton story, in the hard drive. They took my back-up diskettes, though not, I'm pleased to say, all of them since I'm a belt-and-braces man. I always back up everything twice and still have copies. And they stole all the files they could find relating to Phil Lewis in Miami, everything which we obtained to provide credibility for our story. My wallet, money and valuables were untouched. Not exactly the normal Washington burglary.'

Cabot said nothing, looking at Newman as a psychiatrist might regard an enigmatic patient.

'It strikes me, Mr Cabot,' Newman continued, a patronising edge in his voice, 'that there can be no explanation other than that these events are connected to the Lewis affair. No one would benefit from the burglary or the scare tactics used against my colleague Miss DeVos except the CIA. And since you are supposed to be the guardian of the CIA's legality I thought I should talk to you about it. What do you think?'

Cabot rather liked the British as a rule. He was easy in their company, shared their sense of irony and understatement, believed the two sides of the Atlantic had common values and often identical interests. Yet since the Lewis affair broke, he had for obvious reasons avoided discussing any of it with Newman or any other journalist trying to cover the story. The allegations contained in Newman's fax made him change his mind. Cabot had checked through Terrelli and

Boone that no intelligence officers had entered Newman's home; that there had been no crude attempt to scare off DeVos. Terrelli had been adamant and incendiary in his denials.

'Do you think we're crazy?' he yelled down the telephone. 'Do you think we want to encourage publicity? If you believe we'd do stupid things like that, then you might as well believe we put a contract out on Phil Lewis. Which we did not, Warren. And if we damn well had, he'd be history.'

Cabot asked Newman if he would like a coffee and told his secretary to bring a fresh pot.

'I have quite a lot to say to you, Mr Newman,' Cabot began. 'Some of which may be unpalatable, most of which I consider to be very important and all of which is off the record. The CIA does not give interviews to foreign journalists, and it never will. You can say however that the first part of our conversation is under what you British I believe call "lobby terms". This meeting in other words does not take place, but as background may inform you of our position.'

Cabot switched on a pocket tape recorder and placed it on the table in front of him.

'I have one comment for you which you can quote,' he continued. 'It is to be attributed to a CIA spokesman, should you choose to use it. The quote is merely an extension of what we told the *Washington Post* and numerous other newspapers following the vicious attack on you. Let me read you the statement, and then provide you with a copy, so you need not take notes.'

Cabot took off his spectacles and began to read in a clear, deliberate voice.

'No officers or agents acting for the Central Intelligence Agency played any part in the attack on British journalist Alexander Newman or the break-in at his apartment. The CIA rejects the false accusations and innuendoes with which Mr Newman has tried to link the Agency with such activities. Further, the CIA disputes the contents of a story published by Mr Newman in a British newspaper claiming the CIA played a major role in the Miami investment corporation Winston, Hamilton, Bellingham, Lewis and Lopez. Lawyers acting on behalf of the CIA have sealed certain files of the corporation for reasons of national security, however these files play no part in

301

the upcoming trial involving the corporation. Statement ends.'

Cabot put his spectacles on again and studied Alex Newman's face. Newman was unable to hide his laughter. He had planned to be polite, but being beaten round the head and now this obvious contempt left him hovering between anger and bemusement. He drew his copy of the statement towards him like a soiled tissue.

'You have sealed the files for national security reasons,' he scoffed. 'But there's no CIA role in the company. You played no part in the burglary of my apartment, but everything stolen relates to the CIA. Come on, Mr Cabot. You'll really have to do a bit better than this. It reads like something from the bad old days of *Pravda*. You know, record wheat harvest yet again this year, that kind of complete baloney.'

Cabot looked at him carefully.

'Do you agree to our conversation from this point being completely off the record?' he asked, as the secretary arrived with coffee on a tray. Cabot poured. 'That we talk frankly to each other, no notes?'

Without waiting for an answer Cabot switched off his tape recorder.

'Is there an alternative?' Newman said with a smile.

'No. It's that or nothing, which could be a little socially awkward,' Cabot laughed, passing a cup to Newman. 'You would then have to have your coffee in silence and leave, which would not be American hospitality. Now please put your notebook away.'

Newman bristled. He did not like to be steam-rollered, and the crack on the back of his skull entitled him to a little more than this.

'Very well,' he said, accepting the inevitable with as much good grace as he could muster, pocketing the notebook. 'I will listen to what you have to say, but I will also pursue this story to the best of my ability. I think there's enough dirt in here on which to base a book, and I intend to write one. And, needless to say, I think your on-the-record denial is nonsense.'

As Newman spoke he eyed Cabot coldly. He thought he recognised the type: New England, old money, Anglophile, one of the rocks on which the American empire had been built. Cabot was the sort of goofy patrician some Americans would mistake for a wimp, but Newman recognised that behind all the wool there was steel, and in

302

the end it would prove tougher stuff than whatever was in those who played the wild west cowboy.

Cabot too thought he recognised the type: a pushy British journalist who believed he had uncovered a good story even though he had no idea what it was really about; the initials CIA had excited him, and his editors. The rest was innuendo and guesswork which could damage the Agency, the presidency and the country in the weeks left before the election. But Cabot was now so nagged by his own doubts that he was almost willing to believe anything: the frame up of one journalist, burglary and beating of another.

'I am very sorry about the attack on you,' Cabot said with what Newman thought was sincerity. 'Truly sorry. But I have to repeat that the CIA has absolutely nothing whatsoever to do with it. I can say that with the authority of the Deputy Director.'

'Vincent Terrelli?'

'Yes, Mr Terrelli himself gave me his word. It is unusual for anyone involved in the Agency to discuss such allegations, but he feels very strongly about it. And he also said he knows nothing of any attempt to scare off Ms DeVos. We have checked with the DEA and what you say is correct. There was a tip off about her being involved in drug trafficking. Naturally they followed it up.'

'Naturally,' Newman sneered. 'Look, Mr Cabot. I don't know what kind of nonsense your people tell you to tell me. I am sure you are a decent man trying to do your job. But please do not patronise me. When a couple of goons break in to my apartment and steal nothing of value except documents, files and computer records relating to Phil Lewis in Miami, what do you expect me to think? The link is clear.'

'Precisely,' Cabot said, in a decisive tone that surprised Newman. 'Precisely my point. If you do not believe the word of the Deputy Director, then at least please explain why we would be so stupid as to encourage even greater media interest by staging something so dumb witted as you describe?'

'I don't know, Mr Cabot. Except it might be that the CIA is full of ruthless but dumb witted people. I would simply ask you to examine your conscience and tell me whether this story of yours is anything other than the usual convenient fiction. What you are telling me is not the truth. It is what your people hope will serve as the truth: whatever works to their advantage.'

Cabot persisted patiently. 'Let me be frank. Lewis is an embarrassment because he is using his former relationship with the CIA to try to get away with a massive fraud. He will not succeed. But he might severely embarrass the Agency in an election year, and he risks uncovering sensitive operations. The combination of his actions and your story means key agents are at risk in hostile countries and some might possibly be picked up and executed. Lewis has offended many people in Miami. He has caused them distress and cost them money. He now accepts that one of them tried to settle old scores – nothing to do with the Agency. In my view your case is similar. You are fishing in murky waters, and someone wants you to stop. You face dangers but they do not come from this Agency. You have my word.'

Newman's head had hurt for so long he was now used to the dull throb across the back of his skull.

'Are you threatening me, Mr Cabot?' he asked. 'When you tell me that unnamed people want to stop my researches, it sounds like a threat.'

His bluntness pushed Cabot to the point of panic.

'Oh my goodness, no,' he blurted out. 'Please don't think of anything so ridiculous. I am merely stating the obvious. Lewis was involved with all kinds of Latin American exiles down in Miami. The trail of his misdeeds may very well lead to drug money and money laundering, where even a million dollars is just loose change. It is entirely up to you whether you continue to report on this story, and for goodness' sake do not leave here with the mistaken view that I'm warning you off. You want to write a book, then write it, Mr Newman. But the fact there are dangers should be self evident.'

Newman thought for a moment.

'You believe all this stuff, don't you?'

Cabot looked perplexed.

'What stuff?'

'Oh, you know,' Newman said. 'My Country 'Tis of Thee type of stuff. That when Vincent Terrelli tells you he could not possibly have been involved that he would never lie to you, and so you faithfully

304

repeat his instructions like any lawyer passing on what his client has to say. My country right or wrong, the oldest lie.'

'Mr Newman,' Cabot said with some amusement, 'I have been around Washington for long enough to know there can indeed be a difference between what people say and what the facts truly are. But in this case I promise you the logic is that this administration has nothing to gain and a lot to lose by involving itself in the kind of nonsense you are suggesting. *Cui bono*, Mr Newman. *Cui bono*.'

Ah. Now Newman was impressed. An American who does not split infinitives and has at least two words of Latin. There was hope for the country yet.

'Oh, well,' Newman laughed, beginning to relax. 'If you're asking me who might benefit then maybe it is all a plot got up by the Democrats to smear thc president in the closing stages of an otherwise tranquil re-election campaign.'

Instead of laughing, Cabot sat stony faced. When he spoke he enunciated each word with great precision.

'Very little about this country would surprise me, Mr Newman. And during an election campaign, nothing at all. You must remember that we are now very *professional* about the exercise of our democracy.'

Cabot looked away, his attention taken by a hidden train of thought.

There was a profound silence which Newman sensed was his cue to go. He drained his coffee and stood up, feeling strangely cheated as if his cracked skull had deserved more. With the boldness of someone who was not a journalist on a story but a citizen who felt justifiably aggrieved, Newman fired a parting shot.

'I am glad we talked, Mr Cabot,' he said, 'because I suspect that you are doing your best for your country and your president. But I know what you are passing on to me is a farrago of lies. You are not being told the truth. Somewhere in Deep Blue and the Lewis affair the jigsaw makes sense, but not to me and maybe not even to you. I intend to find out what is going on, and when I do, I will let you know.'

Cabot recognised the arrogance behind Newman's words, and also the dismal truth that neither of them could piece together the jigsaw.

'If you are right,' he said sadly. 'Then I am appalled and angry. I have no evidence to sustain the inferences you draw. And I have categorical denials from honourable people in a position to know. If you have any evidence – not gossip or speculation but real evidence to back up what you think to be true – then let me know. I will see it gets as far as the White House itself. Whatever the consequences. I promise you that.'

Newman shrugged, they shook hands and he walked out into the sunshine leaving Warren Cabot deep in thought. After a few moments Cabot stood up and began pacing across the room. He halted at the window and watched the street crowds moving about their business. He had one more telephone call to make before he finally took a decision which he would either regret forever or be proud of for the rest of his life. He dialled the Deputy Director of Central Intelligence on his private line.

'Terrelli.'

'Vince, it's me. Warren. We need to talk about Deep Blue and Lewis.'

'What more do we need to say, Warren? It was all taken care of.'

Cabot said if that was true, it was not in a way he could understand. 'I want to know whether you are serious in agreeing to the plea bargain Lewis is demanding. We're letting him off, Vince. We're pretending he did no more than fail to complete his income tax returns. A suspended sentence, that's what he's holding out for. A promise that he will cooperate in future investigations. And a lifetime gag order. It's not even strong enough to be a slap on the wrist. It's not a slap at all.'

Terrelli was not in a mood to argue.

'I am not having you unpick this now, Warren. We have to close the case without inflicting further damage. I think most of the investors can be paid back. If you have problems with the plea agreement then I will put it in the hands of a lawyer who does not. The agreement stays. Whether you stay or not is another question.'

Cabot thought for a moment. Both men were icily calm and correct. It was as if Terrelli recognised that losing his temper was only possible when matters were not truly serious. Now was the final

306

moment of crisis between them. When Cabot began to speak it was in a grave tone as if he were about to bury the dead.

'I thought we believed in the rule of law, Vince. I thought that was what we stood for in this country. I thought that was what we took oaths to protect.'

'I know what you mean by rule of law,' Terrelli said viciously. 'What you mean is that if this is all cleaned up the way we have agreed with Lewis then you will not make it to Director of Central Intelligence. That what you need is a nice fat scandal to ensure that you can come in as the outside lawyer who tried to blow the whistle on all the bad guys out at Langley.'

Cabot protested that this was not what he meant at all.

'Don't patronise me, Warren,' Terrelli shot back angrily. 'I know behind all that Ivy League bullshit you're as ambitious as anyone I've ever met. People like you don't kill for the big jobs, because you don't have to. But the mentality is the same. You are prepared to cheat and connive. Why else would you be passing all those secret messages to your pal the president?'

Cabot was now alarmed. Only the chief of staff, his wife Robyn, and presumably the president knew he had contacted the White House.

'The gossip's all around town, Warren,' Terrelli continued. 'About how you tried to manipulate the Deep Blue mess to further your own career. Well, I'm telling you, friend, it's backfired. There's not many who have respect for someone who uses a national security difficulty to further his own naked ambition. Everyone knows the game you're playing now. Everyone who needs to know anyway. It's over, Warren. You're finished.'

Cabot was stunned. How could anyone portray what he had done and what he tried to do in such a perverse light? And he did not expect his most confidential attempts to clean out the corruption to be presented as the talk of every Washington cocktail party.

'I . . . I . . . I . . .' Cabot spluttered, but Terrelli cut in again.

'From now on, Warren, you do as you're damn well told. I did not spend twenty-five years in this game without making friends. If you think Deep Blue can help you, you're crazy. You've wrecked

307

your credibility, permanently I think. No one likes to see naked opportunism, Warren. It's disgusting.'

Cabot was shaking, pale with rage. He stood up from his desk and bellowed down the telephone.

'Now you listen, Terrelli. I don't care who climbs to the top of the Agency any more because it's just a question of who inherits the garbage heap. I doubt if even you know where the slime stops and the good work begins. And if people are questioning my motives and my personal ambition then I'm going to make it easy for them. I quit. Get yourself a new special counsel and a new set of excuses. The old ones have worn thin.'

Before Terrelli could reply Cabot threw the telephone down and sat back in his large leather armchair quivering with anger.

He could not think when he had last lost his temper. He regarded such outbursts as immature and out of character. Yet now he felt a quietness and a release. There was a strange peace. He picked up the telephone again. Whatever lay ahead – and it might be to aid Alex Newman in his lonely quest to assemble the Deep Blue jigsaw, or a retreat to the mountains of the real America – he would begin again like Cincinnatus to lead a decent, useful, normal life.

Cabot wanted to call his wife. She would be pleased with his news. The Central Intelligence Agency would be starting the next millennium and the new order without him.

28

Vince Terrelli prepared for his early morning jog shortly after six. He was thinking that he would happily have left his next task to someone else, but there was no one else. He had to fly to Miami and put the final pieces in place to ensure Deep Blue was buried forever. The way things were coming apart, there were few he could trust, maybe only himself. That was the trouble when people began suspecting each other. Nobody knew when to stop. Warren Cabot had telephoned again from some goddamn log cabin on the frontier – Montana, Wyoming, God knows – apologising for losing his temper but saying he was sure his desire to quit was the right one, 'because the whole thing is so dirty, Vince, every time I touch any of it I feel I'm covered in slime.' He had put the resignation in writing and decided to take leave of absence until it was made public after the November election, now just four weeks away.

'It might damage the president if it was made public now.'

'Sure, Warren,' Terrelli said, magnanimous in victory. 'Whatever you say. Take a few months rest.'

Terrelli began the run, loping down his driveway where the rhododendron bushes shielded the house from the road. Suddenly he pulled up short. There was a man facing him, standing just outside the gate of his house wearing a blue business suit, shirt and tie and calmly staring at him. Terrelli stared back, puzzled. He felt a burst of fear realising that while he varied his routine as much as possible, his own arrogance had prevented a full security detail being available to him as appropriate for his rank. The man in blue was motionless, scrutinising him carefully.

Terrelli thought for a moment about opening the gate and sprinting past him, then of turning back to the house and calling the police. Before he could decide, the man began to shout.

'Mr Terrelli, my name is Alex Newman. I'm a British journalist who was assaulted by CIA operatives while working on a story connected with Deep Blue. I want to talk to you about it.'

Shit, Terrelli thought. Goddamn Looney Tune time. In part he was relieved it was not a terrorist or kidnapper. This was the psycho journalist who called the CIA every day asking to do an interview with him. He ran back to the house.

An hour later as he was about to climb into his limousine to be driven to his aircraft for Miami, Terrelli was called by the Secret Service who said they had begun to interrogate Newman and he was cooperating fully. He was unarmed, except with a notebook, and had broken no law they could think of.

'He has a White House press pass, Mr Terrelli, which we threatened to pull. But the truth is he has committed no offence. He's fully cooperative. He has no history of mental instability nor a prison record. Under the First Amendment . . .'

'Screw the First Amendment,' Terrelli yelled back. 'For Christ's sake, I'm the Deputy Director of Central Intelligence and I don't expect to find dogshit like that on my doorstep. Is that understood?'

The Secret Service said they would begin a twenty-four-hour stake-out of Terrelli's house with immediate effect but they could see no way of preventing Newman from standing at the end of his driveway hollering questions.

'But what about my early morning runs,' Terrelli began to say, then realised it was a dismal bleat. 'Aw, never mind.'

He climbed aboard the Lear Jet for Miami in a sulphurous mood thinking journalists were no more than a big number of small time whores working for a small number of big time whores. The trouble was he had no leverage with the big time whores, the proprietors and network owners, if they happened to be foreigners. He just hoped this particular small time British whore at the end of his garden would find the weather and the Secret Service increasingly hostile. Cabot had mentioned the journalist's visit to his office. He claimed to have been impressed with Newman, believing he was telling the

310

truth about the assault on him and the burglary of his apartment. Terrelli thought that statement told him more about Cabot's own state of mind than anything else. If the Agency had been involved, Terrelli would know about it. Right? Unless . . .

As the Lear Jet made its descent towards Miami International Airport, Terrelli could see power boats and yachts sailing up and down the coast, automobiles running along the north-south highway beside some of the finest beaches in the world.

'Boone,' Terrelli muttered to himself, gazing at the sunshine playing on the gold sand and blue sea. Unless it was Boone. Boone who was out of town according to his secretary, who was still brokering the deal with Lewis. Boone who was on the dark side of the moon, and who, Terrelli had decided, no longer fitted in to his own plans for the future. When he made it to DCI Terrelli would make sure Boone was removed from the National Security Council staff. The man was out of touch and out of time with his attitude. They needed new blood.

'Boone,' he said again, convinced he knew where the key lay to the worst of Deep Blue.

In the lobby of the Miami Beach Sheraton Lindy Bishop thought she recognised the distinguished dark-haired man walking across the bright pink carpet. She could not be sure. There was something familiar about his face, the way it was with some of the more frequent guests. The only thing was that he stared at the macaw in its cage scraping its beak on a cuttlefish as if he had never seen it before, and he kind of allowed the bell boy to lead him to the reception desk. Maybe he was a famous person whose face she remembered from *People* magazine.

Lindy Bishop gave him the registration card and her big smile when she saw he had reserved one of the four large suites on the penthouse floor, and pulled out an American Express Platinum Card to pay for it. This was the type she could go for – late forties, born to money, black hair greying at the temples, handsome Italian face. Lawyer, could be. Something professional. She thought she had it on the tip of her tongue. Gynaecologist. Bedside manner. Lindy Bishop looked at the Amex Card but the name rang no bells, though Italian was right. Maybe he was leader of the Mob. Takes all sorts. She cut the computerised key and listened to the beeps and whistles from the machine, then turned back with the big smile to the *capo di tutti capi*.

'There you go, Mr Terrelli. You're all set. Room 2004 on the top floor. The bell boy will show you to the elevator. If you have any questions, don't hesitate to call. My name is Lindy and it has been a pleasure to serve you. I hope you enjoy your stay with us at the Sheraton Miami Beach, and have a nice day.'

Vincent Terrelli took the key and attempted a smile back, but could not quite manage it.

'Messages?'

'Please wait while I check.'

She hit a few more taps on the computer.

'None right now, Mr Terrelli. But I'll see that any are delivered to you right away.'

'Thank you.'

The trouble with hotels nowadays, Terrelli thought grumpily, as he followed the bell boy through the lobby foliage, was that they were always making goddamn speeches at you. Used to be when you telephoned a hotel they would say something useful like, 'Good morning, Sheraton Hotel.' Terrelli knew this was the kind of place where it would be: 'Good morning, thank you for calling the Sheraton Hotel Miami Beach. My name is Lindy. How may I direct your call?' He shook his head in irritation. The country was falling apart because everybody was on the telephone or standing in hotel lobbies listening to the same kind of bullshit, so nobody had any time to get the job done. Which was why he was here. To get the goddamn job done.

The penthouse was large and airy, a corner room with two double windows, one of which looked towards the sea, the other south to the city of Miami. Terrelli had decided on the Sheraton because he wanted Jorge Lopez to have to call him there, a signal to Lopez that he knew the kind of things the Cuban organised in Sheraton bathrooms. It was not that they had any hard evidence against the Turtle. Terrelli heard that the FBI interview with Lopez had already attained folkloric qualities within the Bureau. It had been a bizarre

312

encounter in what the lead agent, Leon Kramer, called 'the Oval Office of the Cuban White House', and what another agent called 'the interrogation of the president of Disneyland'. Lopez made it plain he was not about to make any statement on anything to anyone at any time, least of all to the FBI. His hard case Cuban American lawyer kept answering awkward questions with variations on a theme.

'My client wishes to help in any way possible but he has no significant information to share with you on the subject of Mr Lewis. And I have to ask, do you suspect him of some involvement in a crime? He is, after all, extremely active in fund-raising for the president's re-election campaign and it could be embarrassing to all concerned if a cloud of suspicion hung over his head at this time.'

Embarrassing to all concerned. Right. Lawyerspeak for butt out. So with little solid to go on, the FBI backed off. At least that's what Kramer told Terrelli, though he was not sure whether they regarded the CIA as a help in getting to Lopez or as a group of individuals potentially involved in the wider scam. Whichever it was Terrelli and Kramer circled each other warily. They had a community of interest only the way poachers have with gamekeepers. Terrelli informed Kramer officially he was travelling to Miami to see Lopez, knowing the Bureau would be sure to find out anyway.

'I need to talk to him about Lewis,' Terrelli said. 'Ongoing Agency operations which need delicate handling. I think Lopez might well be of use to us. If he gives anything on the attempted murder, I'll let you know.'

Leon Kramer sounded grateful, as if Terrelli was doing them a big favour. Maybe he was. The more Terrelli thought about it, the more he realised he was doing all of them a big favour.

When he first set up the lunch with Lopez 'at my hotel' the Cuban laughed cheerfully.

'Certainly, Mr Terrelli. Which hotel would that be?'

'The Miami Beach Sheraton.'

He could feel Lopez swallow hard, but he did not miss a beat.

'Sure,' Lopez replied breezily. 'The place where Phil Lewis nearly breathed his last. Ha, ha. Good choice, Mr Terrelli. I hear they carve a nice turkey out there. Ha, ha, ha. I like your style.'

Yeah, Terrelli thought. I like my style too. Lopez called at one thirty and said he was in the lobby. Now this was a face Lindy Bishop definitely recognised, ugly Jorge something-or-other, the heavy hitter from Little Havana who had made his fortune in real estate, this-and-that. He was always appearing in the *Miami Herald* as a big time Republican party supporter, organising one thousand dollars a plate dinners for party funds. She also remembered his strangely hooded eyes and the extra folds of skin in his neck which gave him an appearance like . . . well, some kind of, yeah, reptile. It was weird. Like one moment he would just flick out a long tongue at you or something. Terrelli and Lopez had never met, but there could be only one Turtle in the hotel lobby and this was as close to a Turtle in a light blue cotton suit as Vincent Terrelli cared to see.

'Mr Lopez,' Terrelli said charmingly, holding out his hand. 'Delighted to meet you.'

'And I, you, Mr Terrelli. You do me a great honour travelling all this way to see me. I should have been most happy to come to Washington if you had wanted. And please call me Jorge. All my friends do. Or George. That's for those who can't get their lips round the Spanish.'

The English had a Spanish tang, and the Turtle somehow managed to smile throughout his little speech.

'I'm Vincent – or Vince,' Terrelli said. 'Let's eat, Jorge. I didn't have time for breakfast. My morning routine was interrupted by a journalist in pursuit of his First Amendment Rights. Dumb son-of-a-bitch spoiled my day.'

He explained about Newman. The Turtle laughed so heartily and Terrelli thought the sound so unpleasant he decided to cut the jokes for the duration of the meal. They chose a table by the window overlooking the sea. There was only a handful of other diners, and the nearest table was yards away. The waiter, who could have been Mexican with a strong Yucatecan or Mayan face, did his creepy 'My name is Enrique and I'll be your waiter today' number. Terrelli managed to send him away with a rapid order, conch soup, stone crab claws, large salad. Lopez ordered shrimp and the crab claws.

'Ah, you like *sopa de caracol*,' Lopez said, still smiling. 'Then you would love my mother's. She makes the best conch chowder you will

314

ever taste. Maybe some other trip you will find time to visit me at my home and we will treat you to real Cuban food.'

'I'd like that very much,' Terrelli lied. 'Now to business.'

Before he could begin the waiter arrived with the drinks, iced tea for both of them, a speech about the house dressing for the salad and some other information Terrelli did not want to know. As soon as Enrique returned to wherever it is waiters go when they are not hovering, Terrelli came to the point.

'I'll play it straight and fast with you, Mr Lopez, because I get the impression as a businessman you can rapidly size up the situation for yourself. Let me start at the beginning, even though you will be familiar with the first part of what I have to say.'

Terrelli outlined his version of how Winston, Hamilton, Bellingham, Lewis and Lopez had gone wrong, that Phil Lewis had exceeded his brief and allowed too much money to be pulled in from outside investors, that he had become greedy and arrogantly wrapped up in his own success, unable to distinguish between his own interests and those of the country.

And that Lopez himself was an innocent, patriotic victim, his reputation unfairly dented by the scandal.

'The fact that the collapse was provoked by a stupid and misinformed television report does not much matter. In my view the Englishman had so twisted our original idea that Winston, Hamilton had become an accident waiting to happen.'

'I agree,' Lopez interjected, sipping his iced tea. 'I agree completely with you.'

Terrelli said the important point was not simply to learn the lessons of the past but to push on from the mess that was left behind.

'The country should be very grateful to you, Jorge, for the selfless way in which you allowed your good name to be used in connection with this business. I am instructed that the administration is extremely pleased with everything you have done, and is conscious of the fact that Phil Lewis's errors have, unfortunately, tarnished your own reputation, by association if nothing more.'

The Turtle was nodding vigorously into his iced tea. He was thinking how busy things had become in Miami, how adversity had brought him together with all kinds of people. First there was this gorilla of a man, Richard Boone, who had come all the way down from the White House, contacted Ileana Del Cid and asked for a meeting with her Uncle Jorge. The Turtle had of course been delighted to help him out with the pestering journalists, and was still hopeful of some fresh information about Lewis in exchange. And now here was the Deputy Director of Central Intelligence sympathising with his problems.

'Yes, Vincent,' the Turtle said. 'Looks like we're all being burned by Lewis. He was like a brother to me. Now what he does, he hurts me. He hurts you. And maybe he hurts the government and this country with what he says. And all I ever wanted was the chance to show my love for the freedoms I'm allowed here. All I . . .'

Terrelli had been right. The patriotic line was the one to take. He thought Lopez was about to have a star spangled orgasm. The waiter arrived with the appetisers, which allowed a little time for Lopez to calm down.

'I am very pleased,' he said, 'to hear that my contributions have been recognised.'

Now it was Terrelli's turn to nod vigorously.

'At the very highest level, I can assure you. Within the White House itself.'

Well, Lopez knew that. The big gorilla Boone had told him as much. But it was nice to hear it again. Terrelli took a spoonful of soup.

'What did you call this?'

'*Sopa de caracol*, Vince. Conch soup, or conch chowder.'

'*Soupa de caracol,*' Terrelli tried to repeat. 'It's very good.'

He looked from the restaurant window across the ocean. There was a lone windsurfer with a huge blue and white sail and the word DUFOUR written in pink letters skimming the wave crests towards the hotel then turning hard out to sea. The wind seemed to be picking up, but the boardsailor managed a quick turn, leaping nimbly to the end and bouncing the Dufour around. The right to pursue happiness. Terrelli looked back to the table, and broke a piece of bread.

'I understand, Jorge, there are those here who value your contribution to public life so much they are suggesting that you might

316

care at some point to serve the community directly by running for Congress.'

Terrelli was touched to notice that a gentle red colour spread across the Turtle's dry face. The man was almost embarrassed in his pride.

'It is true, some have suggested it.'

'And not only here, Jorge. There are those in Washington who have also formed the view that you could well represent vital interests in Congress, that you would act as a role model for others, especially Hispanics who are trying to integrate into American society, who might follow your path to become valued citizens, creating wealth for America. In short, you would demonstrate that the Republican Party is truly the party of inclusion.'

The Turtle was nodding again, nodding so hard the extra skin on his neck appeared to flap.

'It's true. It's true.'

'Of course the Phil Lewis affair is now attracting extremely undesirable headlines,' Terrelli continued, 'after some stupid attempt at burglarising the home of one of the journalists who have been writing about it. In fact the one who pestered me this morning.'

'Yes,' Lopez said cautiously. 'I read about that break in.'

'I suppose you have no idea what might be behind it?'

'None, Vince,' the Turtle said. 'I assumed from the newspaper reports that maybe your Agency would know more about it than I do.'

Terrelli looked at him angrily.

'No,' he snapped. 'We don't. And since my job is to keep the Agency in business I'd be a goddamn idiot to pull such a stunt at any time, especially just before a presidential election.'

'Of course,' the Turtle said soothingly. 'Of course. And even if people like the reporter do write lies, breaking in to his apartment is no way to handle it. Stupid. Real stupid.'

Terrelli calmed down.

'He's pestered me too,' Lopez volunteered. 'This Newman. He is always trying to call me, leaving messages. Says it is urgent. I am sure there are many people who think the guy has a bad attitude.'

Terrelli nodded.

'Me included.'

He went on to explain that in the mid term elections in two years time he understood there was one safe Republican district in Florida which might be opened up. 'I cannot go into details. You know the members of Congress here better than I do. But I am told that you will be offered the seat once the sitting representative chooses to retire. I understand it's a district with a large Hispanic population oriented towards business values. We would be very surprised if you did not win it.'

The Turtle's eyes widened with excitement. Maybe first prize was becoming president of a liberated Cuba, but entering the US House of Representatives as a freshman Congressman from southern Florida would be a very pleasant second prize. He rapidly thought through half a dozen Congressional districts trying to work out which might be his in the fullness of time. The waiter took the soup and shrimp cocktail dishes. Then he returned with two large plates of stone crab claws, and two finger bowls. The windsurfer outside was shooting up the coast, the wind picking up as he jumped over light waves on a broad reach. Terrelli envied him. He thought of sailing his Lightning out of Annapolis, racing at the yacht club in a stiff north wind. He shook his head to clear it of distractions.

'Even within the White House, as I say, your contributions have been recognised,' Terrelli continued. 'The chief of staff discussed them with me the other day, and said he personally would be delighted if you were to be offered a safe district.'

Terrelli then paused for maximum effect, looking at the reddened face of the Turtle, a smile criss-crossing the heavy folds on his face.

'There is, however, one obvious problem,' he said, bringing an end to Lopez's fixed grin, and dropping his voice. 'The Lewis business.'

Lopez nodded again, this time with little enthusiasm. Terrelli felt he did not really need to spell it out any more for the Turtle. A Democrat running against Lopez would be sure to dig up whatever he could about Winston, Hamilton, Bellingham, Lewis and Lopez. From being a mere sleeping partner, in the hands of an adept campaign strategist Lopez would become a major criminal with Lewis the peripheral figure in the Turtle's own vast conspiracy. Having given Lopez his bar of candy, Terrelli delighted in taking it away.

318

'It would be too risky to think of your candidacy while the Lewis business rumbles on, and unless it reaches a satisfactory conclusion it could continue to haunt your political career for some years.' He paused to let the point sink home. Then Terrelli turned upbeat again. 'And yet it would be ridiculous to allow such a thing in which you were at worst an innocent party, and more likely an injured party, to deny the people of southern Florida such a distinguished potential representative.'

There was a long pause in which Vincent Terrelli ate two stone crab claws, dipping them in garlic mayonnaise, and nibbling at his salad. Lopez looked confused. Was this supposed to be good news or bad news? Whichever, Lopez would like to get on with it.

'So what do we do about it?' Lopez asked, his eyes nervously scanning Terrelli's face for clues. 'What can we do?'

Terrelli liked that 'we'. It was the word he had been counting on. We were going to help each other.

'Well, my conclusion, Jorge, is that we have a strong mutual interest here, and the potential for an important friendship in the future.'

Lopez appeared to perk up a little, though he remained cautious. There was a hook in this bait somewhere and he could sense it. His private conversations with Richard Boone had not revealed anything along these lines. He was beginning to wonder who in official Washington knew what. It was as if the political world was divided into a series of little boxes, and nobody had access to them all. Maybe that was what the Constitution meant about checks and balances. You survived by knowing more about more boxes than other people. Lopez wanted to open a few now. Terrelli was outlining his own problems, how the Lewis affair had not yet damaged the CIA's reputation or morale but had the potential to do so; how he, like Lopez, had not been involved in Phil Lewis's corruption and yet would inevitably be tarnished by it.

And how publicity could destroy them both and the Agency just at the time Congress was asking why they needed a CIA any more. Most importantly, Terrelli said, they had to consider how it might derail the president's steady progress towards a second term.

'Look at what the bastards are saying, some of those liberal Democrats. They want to spend the peace dividend, whatever the hell that is, on more welfare. They think we don't need the same level of intelligence capability now the Cold War is over. And that the CIA could be cut back a little here and there. The Lewis affair is a gift for the kind of gutless liberals and backstabbers and second guessers in Congress who tried to ruin our country before and will do it again if people like you and I do not stop them.'

'How, Vince?' Lopez asked, prising open the box at last. 'How do we stop them?'

Terrelli said he thought that whoever tried to kill Phil Lewis might – though the act was wrong and misguided – might have done them all a great service. The Turtle stared impassively at Terrelli's face, not a flicker of discernible interest. It was like a distant echo of the message he had heard from Boone and he could not believe it was mere coincidence. For a second Lopez thought the Deputy Director was about to ask him to try again, to encourage him to kill Lewis. Terrelli was still talking.

'It is unfortunate the attempted killers did not succeed only in the sense that all these problems would have died with Lewis in his bathroom in this hotel. But we were not so lucky. It was not to be.'

Terrelli paused to pull a lettuce leaf from his salad, shake the dressing from it and put it into his mouth. 'And anyway I am only joking about the murder attempt. That is obviously not the way civilised men conduct business, and we cannot use methods like that. That was frontier justice. We gave that up a long time ago.'

The Turtle nodded, nibbling a crab claw.

'Of course, Vince. Of course.'

Terrelli said he was now attempting to strike a deal with Lewis in which he would plead guilty to fraud and make a statement ensuring he took full responsibility for all losses from the company. He would call CIA involvement with his investment corporation 'peripheral'.

'The crime was mine and mine alone,' the statement would read. 'If I have blackened the reputation of others then I am truly sorry.'

Something like that. The Turtle was almost beaming. He liked the idea of no messy court case. No trial meant no awkward evidence and therefore no guilt by association. And most importantly in the light of what Terrelli was offering, no problems for Lopez himself on the way to Capitol Hill. Terrelli smiled. He could see clearly that however astute the ugly Turtle might be, with flattery and threats Terrelli could switch him on and off like a light. He was beginning to enjoy his lunch enormously.

'The good news,' Terrelli continued, 'is that in one sense Lewis was correct. Beyond his own corruption, and the fact that he seems to have channelled a few millions into a string of bank accounts in fictitious names for . . . well, I guess, his accomplices . . . the basic system worked well. He played the currency markets shrewdly, made money, so that the long term military investors earned enough on dividends to more than compensate them. I do not think any of them can complain. Even with the loss of principal they have turned an average of four per cent over the past six or seven years. Which is fine.'

Lopez smiled. 'Not bad,' he said. 'Just like a checking account.'

They had all but finished their meal and Terrelli was about to make his final play when Enrique the waiter reappeared from behind the ferns, on cue at precisely the wrong moment.

'Yes the meal was fine,' Terrelli snapped at him. 'No dessert, just coffee.'

And with that Enrique took his strong Mayan face hurriedly back to the other side of the dining room. Problems remained, Terrelli was saying. One in particular. They needed extra funds to pay off some of the noisier creditors, the ones who should never have been involved in the company in the first place and who were a particular irritant, those who had not made as much money as the longer term military or former military personnel.

'So what we need to close the book on this,' Terrelli said, 'is fairly simple. First, an act of contrition from Lewis and his disappearance off the scene. Jail or somewhere like it. Maybe England. And that's lined up. Or so I understand. Plus a reasonable pay off to the non-military investors. The catch is we cannot use government money because Congress would have to appropriate it and would begin to ask all kinds of questions which would better be left unanswered, you follow? I don't intend to stand in front of the barracudas and let them bite strips off my ass.'

The Turtle was not laughing now. He had been in business too long not to get the point. His hooded eyes were fixed on Terrelli's in a way which the Deputy Director found discomforting.

'How much,' the Turtle said quietly. 'How much do you need?'

29

The fighter aircraft turned in a steep arc to put itself on the tail of the Piper Aztec. Padilla could hear Juan Luis Echeverria, the Nicaraguan pilot, praying softly as he tried to hold the Aztec on course. Padilla was not ready yet to make his own peace with God. He barely glimpsed the jet in the darkness. It moved so quickly he saw only a vague shape screaming across the night sky. Perhaps a MiG 23 scrambled from Varadero or Santiago de las Vegas. Whatever it was the end would be rapid: the tiny defenceless Aztec ripped apart by the MiG's cannon, disintegrating in mid-air as Echeverria and Padilla plunged towards the ocean, bleeding, unconscious, dead.

Padilla had never before tried to imagine the moment of his own death. It was not useful for a soldier. But now in these seconds over the Florida Strait, more than in the great adventure in the mountains of the Sierra Maestra or the jungles of Africa, he felt death coming and he shrank with fear at the pointlessness of it all. Dying for the revolution had once meant something to him. *La Causa*. The Cause. Dying now was banality dressed up as martyrdom. He felt sick and impatient, desiring death as he had wanted sleep in prison. He toyed again with the idea of turning his pistol on himself in a final act of defiance.

'That they could not even kill me,' he muttered.

'What?' Echeverria jumped nervously, turning from divine to more mundane guidance. 'What did you say, General?'

'Turn the radio on,' Padilla barked back.

Echeverria obeyed, more terrified by Padilla's eccentricities than the fighter aircraft.

'Hand me the microphone,' Padilla ordered.

He took it thinking that above all he wanted the MiG pilots to threaten him and order his return to Cuba. He would delight in refusing. No, he would say, I will not turn back to Havana – why should I face the same fate as your brother officers in the air force who were executed in Oriente province, eh, *companero*? I should rather kill myself. Padilla considered it amusing to imagine the discomfort of a pilot a few miles from US airspace being reminded about the purge within the ranks of the Cuban airforce. That should slacken the fingers on the triggers. He smiled, recovering his composure. He waited for the sound of a Cuban voice on the Aztec's radio.

He would taunt them, shoot himself and allow Juan Luis to return to Havana unscathed. The ultimate contempt. But there was still radio silence. Maybe they were now so near US airspace the Cubans could not risk talking to him, firing first. In which case, where were they? There was nothing on the radio but a gentle hiss of static. They could have been on his tail again in seconds, unless they chose to radio back for further instructions, or were confused by other light aircraft in the area. Where was death when you needed it? Rationed like life in Havana?

Suddenly there was a rush on the port wing of the Piper Aztec and then another to the right as this time two fighters streaked past. Padilla blinked.

'Are they talking to us, Juan Luis?' Padilla asked anxiously.

'Not on this frequency, General. And this is the . . .'

Echeverria was interrupted by a crackle of rapid Spanish.

They were being asked to identify themselves. Padilla pulled the microphone to his mouth.

'You know who I am,' he snarled. 'Why are you playing games?'

There was another crackle and more Spanish. Padilla recognised the tones of someone used to giving orders.

'This is Major Joe Diaz of the 113th Tactical Fighter Wing from Boca Chica, Florida. I'm in an F15 Eagle with enough weaponry to turn your flying food mixer to guacamole in three seconds. So what you're going to do is hold your course and put down where I tell you. You understand?'

Padilla understood. He just did not believe.

'Say again, Major Diaz,' he stammered. 'Repeat, please.'

Diaz said it one more time.

'You have entered US airspace without a flight plan. I am ordering you to put down in Boca Chica, Florida.'

Padilla was utterly silenced. He shook his head once, then clicked the microphone again.

'Que buen' idea,' he said. *'Que buen' idea.'*

Some twenty minutes later General Oscar Padilla Sanchez climbed from the Piper Aztec on to the tarmac at Boca Chica, watching the lights from the Humvee military vehicles come towards him. His uniform was wet with sweat and he stretched his back as he breathed deeply the air of the United States for the first time. Juan Luis Echeverria stepped warily from the cockpit, his initial cheerfulness at having escaped being blown apart by MiGs or shot in the back by Padilla giving way to deep apprehension. The Nicaraguan was not sure what the Yanqui reaction would be to a flight which contained one former Sandinista pilot, one Cuban general in full dress uniform and several hundred kilos of cocaine. He assumed the worst.

Padilla meanwhile was full of optimism. Behind them on the airfield they could hear the rush of two jets landing and they turned to watch the F15s taxi towards the stand. When the airforce guards leapt from the Humvees Padilla saluted and proudly introduced himself.

'My name is General Oscar Padilla Sanchez of the Revolutionary Armed Forces of Cuba,' he boomed above the noise from the Eagles. 'I demand political asylum.'

'You demand nothing, pal,' a voice in Spanish yelled back. 'Just put your hands above your head and keep them there. You too, shitface.'

'Check 'em out,' the sergeant ordered in English. A stream of soldiers clattered across the tarmac towards Padilla and Echeverria, pushing them to the ground and searching them, whipping Padilla's pistol from his holster and grinding his face into the tarmac.

'Yo, sergeant,' someone yelled. 'You wanna toot? We got enough to get the whole of south Florida blasted. You wanna scc?'

Two soldiers jumped from the Piper Aztec each holding bags of cocaine above their heads.

'What the fuck is it?'

'What do you think?'

'Maybe they're smugglin' Sweet 'n' Low, sarge.'

'Yeah, guess so.'

'Yo, we get our medals now man, War on Drugs. Frontline action.'

'Shit, you seen this stuff . . .'

'Who's the dude with the uniform?'

'Crack city.'

They took Padilla and Echeverria towards the base and split them up. The interrogations began almost immediately, in Spanish. Padilla was confused and angry. It was not the welcome he had predicted, though his anger was directed less at the Americans than at himself for not realising that drug smugglers, even those who have attained the rank of general in the Cuban army, might not be treated like important military defectors. It occurred to him that he was not the first man to arrive on the shores of north America and be disappointed.

'What happened to the MiGs?' he demanded, while they ignored him or insisted that they asked the questions and he answered. 'Why weren't we shot down?'

Eventually Major Joe Diaz himself came to see what kind of fish he had landed. Diaz told Padilla that two MiG 23s had closed in on him, but too late.

'They did not find you until a couple of miles from US airspace. Maybe they were worried about some kind of diplomatic incident. More likely our F15s scared them off. We'll see what the SIGINT says on their radio talk. Anyway, they turned tail back to Havana. And we got ourselves two live ones and a stack of cocaine.'

Padilla demanded that the authorities contact his 'two good friends' Ileana del Cid and Phil Lewis, who, he told them, worked for the CIA and so could explain everything.

'Tell you what,' replied the Spanish-speaking airforce intelligence captain who had been dragged away from a seafood cookout to help understand what the hell was going on. 'Tell you what, General. *You* explain everything. Then we call your good friends. That's how we play it with drug smugglers, okay?'

326

30

Alex Newman haunted the driveway of Vince Terrelli's house every day for a week. He watched in silence each morning as the limousine drove past, tinted windows closed.

'Mr Terrelli,' he called out. 'What's your connection with Phil Lewis?'

Or: 'What was the CIA's role in Winston, Hamilton?'

Today he was even more optimistic: 'What are you hiding in Deep Blue, Mr Terrelli?'

The Secret Service men sat in their car watching him carefully but doing nothing.

'What's all this for?' one of the agents asked affably when the limousine pulled away. 'You on some kind of mission?'

Newman explained as best he could, standing by the Secret Service car, talking through the window.

'But you're keeping the man from his morning run,' the agent said with a grin. 'It could amount to harassment.'

'Maybe he should sue me.'

'Maybe he will. See you tomorrow.'

Newman left and began his daily bombardment of phone calls beginning with Mike Holroyd – 'take a rest, Alex, for God's sake' – and Jorge Lopez: 'Mr Lopez is not available right now. May I take a message?'

Then, as was becoming increasingly frequent, Phil Lewis called. It was the highlight of Newman's day as the expatriate odd couple talked of everything from cricket to the court case. Newman stopped asking where Lewis was calling from, because the fat man always refused to say. But after the burglary and assault Lewis treated Newman as if they had a lot in common.

'Victims,' Lewis said, 'who're gonna get their own back. I got burned despite all my faithful service, and now I'm useless to them. You got burned trying to do your job, and I guess you're on the way out with your newspaper if they sent someone over to cover the election.'

'Thanks, Phil,' was all Newman could think of to say. 'Thanks for cheering me up.'

'Well, it's true isn't it. You have become as obsessed as I have about this. All your talk about writing a book on Deep Blue. And what's all this with Terrelli?'

Newman explained what he was trying to achieve by dogging him in the mornings, try to persuade the Deputy Director that his life might become less miserable if he would just grant a short interview for Newman's book.

'That'll make him real mad,' Lewis laughed. 'It won't work, but boy will he be pissed at you. Terrelli thinks life is just one big machine to be driven for his convenience, like his limo. You're throwing a spanner in the works.'

'I've got no alternative. I just want to know what's behind it all. There's meaning in here somewhere, I've just got to find it. I'm not obsessive about it. I just want to know the truth. Is that too much to ask?'

Lewis said if Newman was not behaving obsessively he was giving a terrific impression. 'It should only be a story for you, Alex. For me it's my life.'

'And mine too. The moment they hit me on the head or tried to fit up Helen on drugs charges. That's when it became personal. That's when I stopped being a spectator. You could help me if . . .'

Lewis interrupted, saying it was wrong to think there might be one explanation or one key which would unlock everything. 'That's crazy conspirator talk, Alex. In great enterprises involving thousands of people different men pursue different objectives. That's why Deep Blue is so complicated.'

'So what's your objective now? Why do you keep calling me?'

Lewis laughed bitterly. 'Who else would I call, Alex? Tell me? My wife who wants to divorce me? My former associates who want to kill me? Who do you suggest?'

Newman pointed out there was a gag order.

'About talking publicly on matters of national security,' Lewis said. 'Not just talking. It's not quite the Thought Police. Not yet, anyway, but it's going that way.'

'Yeah, but I'm a journalist, remember. Talking to me is talking publicly.'

Lewis sounded offended. 'Well, this is not for publication. And you are a journalist whose own newspaper won't publish his stories. That's like being a comedian who tells jokes which aren't funny. After a while you can't call him a comedian any more.'

Hearing Newman speak in the accent of England made Lewis feel both secure and slightly homesick. The fat man knew these were odd sentiments.

'Maybe you're also part of my insurance, one of my backstops. They will know I'm talking to you because they must be tapping your 'phone. The one thing they fear is disclosure. The one thing that scares the shit out of all cockroaches is bright sunlight. That's why they want me to keep quiet. And that's why I don't want you to get obsessive about what happened. Journalists are supposed to shed light on the cockroaches, not step on them. That's for others. You're getting too involved for your own good.'

'You mean, for your own good,' Newman shot back.

'Maybe,' Lewis said, adding that it was not publishing his story which was important. It was the threat of publication. 'If I tell all I know,' he continued runically, 'then everyone dies. They have nothing to lose at that point.'

Newman asked whether Lewis knew who had attacked him in his Georgetown apartment.

'Same people who attacked me in the Miami hotel, I guess.'

'And who are they?'

Phil Lewis thought for a moment. 'Probably a couple of Cuban American goons working for Jorge Lopez.'

'Why do you think that?'

'Trust me.'

'I do trust you. But why do you think that?'

'Trust me.'

Day after day as he kept his vigil outside Terrelli's house, Newman considered whether one last throw of the dice might be worthwhile. He could forget Terrelli, since Lewis was surely correct in assuming he would never say anything. Instead Newman might go down to Florida and find a way to confront Jorge Lopez Ibarruri. It was risky, but Newman realised that if he was not completely safe from attack even in his own apartment then the risks of annoying the Turtle could not be much greater. If Terrelli would not talk and Lewis, at least for now, could not talk, then the Turtle was his last best hope. He bombarded Lopez's office with calls and got nowhere. Then he persuaded Lewis to divulge *La Tortuga*'s unlisted home telephone number. When Newman tried it the telephone was answered by a gruff-voiced man who yelled at him in Spanish then slammed the receiver down. The number was changed.

'I have all the Evelyn Waugh qualifications for a journalist,' Newman told Lewis. 'Plausible manner, moderate writing ability, and ratlike cunning. So I guess I'm ready to face the Turtle.'

Lewis laughed again and the sound stuck in his mind. No one made him laugh any more, and he appreciated Newman for it.

'Yeah, but just watch him, Alex, he's a snapping turtle. Mean. Dangerous. By the way, I have a story for you if you are thinking of going to Miami, and in the unlikely event anyone will publish your trash any more.'

'Oh,' Newman replied. 'Does this involve me having my head beaten in like the last story we collaborated on?'

'Probably. But if you are determined to chase Lopez you'll have your head beaten in anyway, believe me.'

Lewis told him he might find it profitable to look into the rumours of a Cuban defector having flown into Boca Chica airbase.

'I think,' Lewis said, making his words as clear as possible so the eavesdroppers would be in no doubt, 'I understand this is no Cuban wetback. He's a very senior Cuban general, with strong connections to some of the things we were doing. Why don't you see where that trail leads?'

330

31

The way the golf course was built there were three serpentine ponds cut to cause maximum distress to anyone who sliced off the tee. The idea was to pretend to encourage as much natural wildlife as possible, stopping short, maybe, at alligators, within the well manicured and weed-killed greenness. There were a dozen or so white cattle egrets standing bolt upright on the sixteenth fairway, until a ball bounced among them and they scattered in all directions, a panic of white wings and awkward legs. An anhinga, a thin cormorant-like diving bird, had been slipping into the water in one of the ponds near 'Cabana 9', the best of all the resort hotel outbuildings. The cabana was large, three bedrooms, facing directly on to the pond and the expanse of the sixteenth fairway. On the wooden deck surrounding Cabana 9, General Oscar Padilla Sanchez sat in a white tennis shirt and shorts and sparkling new Adidas sports shoes. Beside him in a short dress which made the best of her figure and slender brown legs was Ileana Del Cid, disconsolate, moody. She poured him another glass of freshly made lemonade. Padilla took a Marlboro cigarette from a packet on the table and lit it. Ileana scraped her chair backwards on the deck so she did not have to breathe the smoke.

'If you want to settle in here,' she moaned at him in Spanish, 'you better quit. No Americans with any class smoke any more. Smoking is for poor people and dumb immigrants.'

'That's me,' Padilla smiled. 'Poor, dumb, friendless son-of-a-bitch.'

'Well,' she replied. 'At least you're one immigrant that didn't come here thinking the streets are paved with gold.'

Padilla laughed. 'In Havana we say that when Cubans go to the

331

north they realise that in American cities the streets are never paved with gold. In fact they are not properly paved at all. And it's the dumb Latino immigrants who are expected to pave them.'

Padilla continued to laugh long and hard at his own joke, though it did not seem especially funny to Ileana. She looked at him, roaring loudly and opening his mouth wide through the smoke so he showed the silver in yellowing teeth badly filled by his Cuban military dentist.

'Anyway,' Padilla said, 'stop calling me an immigrant. I'm no immigrant. I'm a refugee.'

'Oh,' she replied. 'Does that mean you might return to Cuba? Next year in Havana? The old lie?'

From the start the bureaucracy began its weary process of deciding who was in charge of what. US Customs, the DEA, the FBI and through them the CIA, were all informed of Padilla's capture. Each wanted a slice. Terrelli quickly established precedence. He decided to hide Padilla as far away as possible from every other investigation except the CIA's own. They moved him to the golf course hotel, secure, discreet, the kind of place where cooperative witnesses could be induced to relax and open up. Now they no longer treated him as a drug smuggler, Padilla was all smiles and hopes for the future. The pilot, Echeverria, was handed over as a sop to the DEA.

Padilla was amused to see the similarities between the Cuban and American interrogation sessions. The only real difference was that the Americans allowed him to sleep. In the cabana they paid close attention to his dignity and physical needs – a coffee, General Padilla, another cigarette, perhaps.

But as before there were so many questions and so many who wanted to talk to him or listen to his words – psychiatrists and military experts and analysts and all kinds of unnamed men and a few women who drifted in for their piece of what remained of his mind – that his head ached constantly and he felt ill.

The CIA team wanted him to go over and over again the details of his operation, the organisation of the Revolutionary Coordination Unit, who his contacts were, his chain of command, the state of morale within the defence ministry and as far as he could judge within the armed forces. They were in the business of lists. Lists of names: who was now in what position; how friendly was he with the next man? How supportive of the revolution were these people?

What, most especially, did he think of his former boss, General Juan Antonio Fernandez? How was he regarded? How powerful was he? How disillusioned? What were his motives in setting up the Revolutionary Coordination Unit? Might he be open to an approach? Over and over again, backwards, forwards, sideways then backwards again. Padilla had been warned that it would go on like this for months, years, that they would call him back again and again, that they would bleed him dry.

The lead CIA interrogator, a humourless man in his fifties who called himself Donald, spoke with a peculiar sibilance as pronounced in Spanish as in English. It was almost a lisp but not quite.

'Remember,' Donald said, 'that when you were in Cuba you were ssomething sspecial, at the highest levels of the Cuban military. Now you are here in Florida you are far less exciting, a defector, an emigré from Havana, and those we can buy for a few centss a dozen on any beach in ssouthern Florida. They wash up on our shoress daily like driftwood. Do we understand each other?'

Padilla nodded. They understood each other.

'Why have you brought me here?' Padilla joked, pointing round the country club. 'It is very nice, but I don't play golf.'

'I do,' Donald replied without a smile.

It had occurred to Padilla that one way of maintaining his value would be to hold as much back as possible, though he found it exhausting. In some ways this was more unpleasant than the interrogations in Cuba. There the stakes had been simple: they knew of his disaffection and little more. One mis-step and they would shoot him. But here in the United States there was neither a sense of imminent danger, nor of obvious reward. He felt all his abilities to rise to a crisis irrelevant in this dull and unrelenting atmosphere. Padilla was especially surprised that there was 'no question' as they put it, of allowing him to get in touch with his 'good friend' Phil Lewis who had promised him so much in Miami.

'Lewiss will probably end up in jail,' Donald said, matter of factly. Donald was balding at the front with badly cut blond hair. He spoke in fluent Spanish, though in English he had a pronounced Boston

333

accent. 'Lewiss iss not the sort of guy an immigrant like you wantss to be sseen associating with.'

'Will you tell him I'm here?'

'I guesss he probably knowss, though we're not ssure exactly where he iss. Whatever happenss, he hass enough to worry about trying to ssave his own sskin.'

They did contact Ileana, and she was allowed to speak to Padilla by telephone after a few days. It was a remarkable and difficult conversation for both of them, desperate to see each other again, knowing there were probably half a dozen others listening to their careless talk, speaking in the strange stilted way of friends who somehow think others will not notice they have become lovers. A decision was taken – Padilla never found out by whom, such was the formidable nature of this new north American bureaucracy into which he had entrusted himself – that the government was not going to announce his defection.

'At least for now,' they said.

Padilla shivered.

'Not for now,' he repeated.

A few days after his landing the Pentagon found itself in the position of 'neither confirming nor denying' rumours that a high ranking Cuban military officer had hijacked an aircraft to Florida, and that two Cuban airforce MiGs had been turned back as they approached US airspace. News leached out and was pursued by numerous journalists, who, without official confirmation or reliable leaks, got nowhere. In Havana the Ministry of the Exterior said they had 'no knowledge' of any such incident.

'What will happen to the pilot?' Padilla asked. 'He was just a dumb mule.'

'Not my businesss,' Donald replied. 'I jusst don't know. The DEA have him.'

For days Padilla eagerly awaited Ileana's visit. With Lewis clearly in trouble she represented his only friend in the United States and he became increasingly excited when Donald told him she was to be allowed to stay. When she arrived at the cabana Ileana told him that the aircraft had been impounded and the drugs destroyed, the pilot passed on by the DEA to the Immigration and Naturalisation Service to be thrown out of the country like any poor Hispanic wetback who had slipped into the United States illegally. A trial was not thought to be sensible, since no one favoured the appearance of General Oscar Padilla Sanchez as a witness.

Surrounded by this carefully false natural scene and imposingly designed holiday and leisure complex, Padilla felt more alone than at any time in his life, more desolate than in the Cuban jail. There was something which disgusted him about his dependence on Ileana, and it did not take any great sensitivity on his part to work out that she resented the role Donald expected her to play: companion, lover, guide. Keep Padilla happy so we can finish with him as soon as possible.

Padilla's unhappiness meant he began eating too much and exercising too little. For the first time in his life he was putting on weight round the belly. He ordered rum and limes and soda water and sugar and ice and had mint leaves specially brought to him so he could make *mojitos*. Donald would have one to be polite, and the others chose to follow Donald's superficially friendly but abstemious example.

Evening after evening Padilla anaesthetised himself from the pain of realisation that he had nothing whatsoever to bind him to the United States except Ileana's increasingly moody company and the knowledge that he would be worse off back home, arrested, jailed, shot.

'I have not escaped to America,' he told Donald. 'I have escaped from Cuba. There's a difference. And do not call me a defector. You know that has a barbarous meaning in Spanish.'

Donald nodded, poker faced. Like any immigrant Padilla thought he was without illusions about the difficulties ahead. Yet he had assumed he would be seen as a hero, not hidden away like some kind of family embarrassment, a deformed idiot child. In the evenings he became surly, drunk when he could, truculent when they tried to stop giving him rum because it made his interrogations impossible. He found them a peculiarly prudish lot, these Americans. When they made conversation with him it seemed one long nag about the dangers of smoking – none of them did; drinking alcohol – they swilled down something called 'light' beer which Padilla thought a waste of effort; and even sex, where one of the younger intelligence officers

335

spoke of AIDS like he had been indoctrinated in some lesson at school.

'You do not seem very happy,' Padilla had once yelled at them, drunkenly. 'You do not seem to take much pleasure from life. Tell me how you have fun?' Either from embarrassment at the question or his drunkenness none of them answered. 'Tell me what fun is in America? What is it, Ileana? Tell me what fun is? Do none of you know? Is there no fun here?'

Eventually they declared a truce. He could drink alcohol after six, but not before. They would withdraw and leave him in the evenings with Ileana to watch rented Spanish language movies or the local Hispanic television stations. So that was American fun.

From the moment of her arrival Padilla thought Ileana looked more beautiful than ever he had remembered, desirable like some fantasy of a new life which he hoped might still be possible.

She was wearing a pink dress and matching shoes, and he thought how striking the bright colours of her clothes looked after the washed-out dyes of Cuban material. She was smiling at him, asking how he was, her long black hair shining with life and health, filling him with happiness. At first they kissed like brother and sister, as Donald and two of the others stood by. After an hour of awkwardness, Donald suggested a game of golf and Padilla and Ileana were left alone. He leaned over and kissed her on the lips and then hugged her and kissed her again. But somehow she felt awkward in his arms as if for the first time she did not fit, kissing him back but with a twist of resistance which puzzled him. When they broke apart Padilla looked into her eyes and thought he saw something which cut him more than anything he had been forced to undergo during the interrogation sessions in Cuba or Florida.

Where once it had been desire, now it was pity. It was pity that caused her to make love when he suggested it, pity in her attempts at orgasm even though he knew she was faking, pity that kept her staying with him. Padilla was sure she would soon leave. She told him she felt suffocated, and he nodded, waiting for the inevitable conclusion.

In Cabana 9 there was now an established routine. There were four regular CIA minders. They shared two bedrooms in the cabana

336

allowing Ileana and Padilla a certain degree of privacy in the third, though the walls seemed paper thin, and neither of them could relax at the thought that everything was being recorded or spied upon by eavesdroppers.

'Did you not enjoy that,' he whispered in her ear, sweating and panting as he lay naked beside her, hoping he had misread it this time.

'No,' she murmured, then feeling she had hurt him, said it was not his fault. It was because she could not relax. 'I keep thinking they can hear everything, that they are watching everything. Even this. I can't relax. This is suffocation.'

That much at least was true. She was stiff and awkward with him. Where once she snuggled beside him like an interlocking piece of a puzzle, now they lay side by side silently in bed, parts of incompatible machines. Sometimes they whispered together, Padilla always talking about his future life, trying to keep his mind off the past, seeking clues to this very foreign land ninety miles from home.

'They will provide you with a new identity,' Ileana said. 'Under the FBI's federal witness protection programme. A house, some kind of income, credit cards, enough to protect you in case Havana decides to strike out at you, have you shot, maybe snatch you back.'

'Can't I just work?'

'Sure, Oscar,' she replied. 'They'll give you all the right papers, so in theory there is no problem. Except who would hire a man who speaks very little English, has no known work background in this country, and whose main skills are in money laundering and running the army of a communist country?' Then she spoke in English, a cry of exasperation, turning from him. 'For God's sake, Oscar. Get real.'

Padilla could make out her eyes glistening with tears in the few rays of moonlight which shone into the bedroom. He began to realise then what Ileana had known for days but not yet put into words. When they first met and slept together he was a grand romantic figure, a Cuban general engaged on a secret mission, a glimpse of the other side of the Cold War barricade. Now he had arrived in Florida he was just some broken down fifty-year-old with no job, no background and no friends.

He could hardly blame this bright, attractive girl if she was no longer interested in him, and he said so. She denied it but both of them knew it was true.

'Maybe my uncle might find you some work,' she said. 'Uncle Jorge has all kinds of business activities in south Florida and across the country.'

'Maybe,' he said. 'Though they are talking of moving me again, trying to give me a new identity, setting me up in some big Hispanic community in Texas or southern California. That's the way they're talking now. They say they may hold a press conference and ask me to perform, in a week or two. The plan is that in the news conference I stay hidden in a booth with a disguise. The translator beside me is the one who is filmed on television. I am supposed to talk of discontent in the Cuban military. No mention of drugs. They have it all scripted, like it was something out of Hollywood. I have to perform.' Padilla laughed. 'Like in a show trial.'

'Will you do it?'

'Sure. What have I to lose?'

Then he asked about Lewis. She explained what she knew, how the investment corporation had unravelled.

'He's more or less disappeared. Off the map. I tried to get in touch with him again through his lawyer to tell him you had escaped. The lawyer said he would pass on the message, but he did not think Phil would try to call. He hasn't.'

'Why?'

Ileana explained how Lewis thought his life was in danger and suspected that her uncle Jorge might have been involved in the Sheraton attack.

'And was he?'

She shrugged and turned her head away.

'Who knows? Who can tell what anyone is prepared to do any more?'

Later that night when she kissed Padilla Ileana noticed how much he smelled of tobacco. She wondered why such trivial things about him so disgusted her. She kissed his eyelids as he lay back trying to sleep, trying not to dream, then they slept in each other's arms for the last time.

During the following morning's interrogation session Ileana Del

338

Cid walked in the grounds of the golf course, watching the strange portly men in their check trousers hack and smash their way round the fairways, telling loud jokes, carrying their paunches in and out of golf carts. Ileana decided she really would ask her uncle if there might be anything for Padilla, a job, maybe speaking engagements to exile groups. But she doubted Jorge Lopez would be keen to help. He did not much care for recent arrivals from Cuba, the ones who had lived through so much of the revolution rather than abandon it thirty years before. People like Padilla, Ileana knew, and Lopez knew, had credibility in Havana, which might be important as the country fell apart. If there was a rebellion against Fidel it would push people like Padilla to the forefront of any new order. Uncle Jorge would not enjoy that. And he would not want to give someone he could not control an easy platform with the mainstream Cuban groups in the United States. Still, Ileana thought she would ask him anyway, seeking alms for the pitiful.

She wandered round the grounds and came to the central hotel with its five restaurants and small shopping mall marked 'Leisure Complex Stores'.

In the liquor store she made a purchase then walked back to the cabana where she knew Padilla's interrogation session would almost be at an end. He was irritable this morning, harassed.

'What is this you're asking me now,' Padilla was saying. 'Gossip or intelligence?'

'Ssame thing,' Donald replied.

'But why more about Fernandez?'

Donald sniffed.

'Because he's been arrested. Lookss like he's the sscapegoat for your esscape. What did you call him?'

'The Lion of Playa Giron.'

'Yeah, well lookss like thiss old lion's about to be put down. He's been sentenced to death. Execution maybe has already taken place.'

Padilla shook his head with sadness. There was nothing more he wished to say to these . . . these foreigners about Fernandez, or Cuba, or anything else at the moment. He stood up and walked to the window where he could see another bunch of golfers make ready to tee off on their absurd game. He suggested to Donald they take a break. After the morning interrogation they always rested for a few hours. Ileana might stroll with Padilla or they would swim together in one of the pools, or Donald would have the sense to pull his people out and leave them alone to talk freely and make love, if that was now the appropriate description. At Padilla's suggestion, Donald left quickly, eager to play nine holes though the sun was high and hot. As soon as he and the others had gone, Ileana produced her purchase from the hotel store.

'I have a present for you,' she said, holding out a carefully wrapped package.

Padilla tore open the paper. Inside was a bottle of Chivas Regal whisky. 'Welcome to America, Oscar. No more rum. No more *mojitos*. This is what American generals drink, if they drink at all. Scotch. On the rocks.'

He laughed uneasily and thanked her, then looked at her sad eyes.

'It's some kind of farewell present isn't it? I know.' He had played out scenes like this a hundred times before, but from another angle. She said nothing. A tear came, then another filling her eyes and overflowing silently down her cheeks. He put the whisky bottle to one side and held her. 'Listen,' he said. 'I'm Oscar, remember. Your friend. You can speak to me. Tell me what it is. What's happening.'

When she started the words fell out like a stream tumbling down a hillside, how she thought she loved him, but that was not right, she discovered she did not, that she had loved only the romantic idea of him, a false image. Or maybe she never had loved him, maybe she had always been mistaken, how she would always feel strongly for him, but she did not want to spend the rest of her life hiding with a man with no name in a string of safe houses watched over by the FBI, how she was too young for him, too young to settle.

'Chiquita,' he whispered. 'You don't have to go through all this. There is no guilt. No blame. When I was the elegant general I knew I was attractive to women. Now I'm going to have to make the best of whatever I have left, make my own way. Do not think I fault you. There was nothing for me in Cuba anyway, except perhaps a prison sentence or a bullet in the head. So go. Don't feel guilty about it, just go.'

She looked at him, relieved he was making it easy.

'Be brave,' he insisted. 'But do not worry about me. They can make me suffer no more now. I am dead to it all.'

He kissed her gently on the cheek and she stroked his arm until he broke away and stood up, gazing out of the window, his eyes unfocused.

'Today,' he said, trying to keep his voice calm, 'I heard from Donald that the man I most admire in Cuba, perhaps the only man I ever thought of as a hero, is to be shot. Or maybe has already been shot. He's the scapegoat for my escape, Donald said. Executed for me.'

'Who?'

'General Juan Antonio Fernandez, the most famous of our soldiers at Playa Giron, the Bay of Pigs. He was everything that was ever good about our struggle. Selfless. Without any personal ambition. Now they are claiming he's just an American spy, a traitor. It's absurd.'

Ileana saw his shoulders heave with sadness. She stood up and came behind him, slipping her arms round him with tenderness for what she knew would be the last time.

'Not absurd, Oscar,' she whispered. 'It's true. Fernandez was a spy. He was the one Lewis called Columbus. The one who would discover the New World.'

Padilla turned, aghast.

'At one time,' she continued, 'Lewis thought Fernandez might lead a coup against Castro, but in the end he realised it would be less risky just to keep him in place and watch the revolution fall apart. Or maybe Fernandez did not have the power to stage a coup. I don't know. He did not discuss the details with me. Just that he was hoping you would replace Fernandez when the time came . . .'

Padilla was not listening. He was thinking of the idea of Fernandez's treason, and what it meant compared to his own.

It meant there was nothing left. No honour, no comradeship, no future, not even a past. Nothing.

'But Donald kept asking me about Fernandez.'

'I guess he wondered if you had any suspicions. And you didn't.'

'But the drugs,' he blurted out. 'Whose idea?'

Ileana shrugged.

341

'I don't know. Lewis never said. It just happened.'

He grabbed her fiercely by the arm.

'But did Lewis insist on it? Or was it Fernandez? Or someone else in Cuba? Whose idea was the cocaine, Ileana? Who thought of it? Who brought us to that?'

She struggled and broke free, her arms bruised by his grasp.

'I told you I don't know, Oscar,' she shouted. 'Lewis did not tell me everything. He only told me about Fernandez after we started our affair. He knew then he could trust me without question. He knew Fernandez was due to retire, and that was why you were so important. I don't see why anybody needs to know who did what and when any more. You're safe, and Fernandez is dead. That's all there is.'

She ran from him and locked herself in the bathroom, hoping he would cool down. He stood in front of the window trying not to weep. He could not blame her for failing to understand. She was so young, for her all the sacrifices he had shared with Fernandez were like items from a history book, distant and vague.

He did not know which version he preferred: that Fernandez, like him, had become disillusioned with the revolution and tried to bring about its downfall, involving himself in the drugs trade at the insistence of the Americans; or that the cocaine shipments were truly the product of the diseased heart of the revolution, a symptom of the illness.

For a moment he wondered whether Fernandez and he himself could ever have become comrades again, standing together to outwit both the regime in Havana and the Americans. It was preposterous. They had believed in certain historical laws, in a grand process for which they were prepared to sacrifice. Now there was nothing except venality and personal ambition and betrayal. The idea of a purpose, a cause, had been the hoax which had corrupted a generation.

Thirty minutes later, her eyes puffy, Ileana Del Cid emerged from the bathroom.

'Will I see you again?' she wanted to know.

'If you choose. I will always want to see you, but maybe it will be best not to. You decide. I will make sure Donald gives you a number where I can be contacted. He said there is a Washington telephone exchange and postal address they use. They can forward calls. Wherever I'll be. You could use that.'

'I will,' she said, and sobbed again, though he knew she was lying.

He accompanied her outside and kissed and held her. She was still crying, and for the first time in years the sight of a woman crying almost cracked Padilla's mask. He breathed deeply until he regained control, staring into the warm brown Cuban eyes, eyes that made him think of the sunshine on the Playas del Este, of the sweetness of Cuban coffee, of the water splashing on the Malecon. Perhaps there was something left. Memories of pleasure. Ileana ran a hand gently down the side of his face, full of pity for the poor immigrant who stood before her, but determined to go. They kissed for the last time and Ileana Del Cid walked slowly across the grass to the hotel car park for the drive back to Miami. Padilla watched her every step, hoping she would turn at the last moment and wave, but she disappeared through the palm trees, never looking back.

32

The thing Lindy Bishop noticed was how they acted like honey-mooners. It was the way they looked at each other while she went about her business trying to check them in before they started making love in the middle of the lobby. She just knew it was an illicit affair. Both married, of course. But not to each other. They looked old enough to know better, smiles and giggles and stroking each other as she went through the formalities, filled out the forms, cut the keys, rapidly flashed her welcome smile on and off like a lighthouse lantern precisely as etiquette demanded, to send them on their way before they, well, did it, which she supposed would have brightened up her day but might have caused some of the older guests to have a coronary. As soon as they arrived at the fifteenth floor, Alex Newman opened the door of the hotel bed-room, picked up Helen DeVos and carried her over the threshold, worried that he might strain his back, but doing his best. Newman kissed her then threw her on the bed.

'Careful,' she giggled. 'Man of your age. Don't pull anything.'

Newman brought their bags in from the hall and closed the door.

He threw open the windows – very deliberately he had booked the most expensive floor with a balcony running round two sides of the room – and they stared over the lights of Miami. For the first time since he had been hit on the head Newman felt fine.

'The brain bone appears to be knitting rather well,' the neurologist had said with condescending informality on Newman's last visit to Georgetown Hospital. 'Just take it easy for a while. Absolutely no contact sports . . .'

344

Contact sports?

'No,' Newman interrupted. 'And I promise to wear a football helmet when making love.'

'And,' the doctor deadpanned, as if Newman had not spoken, 'I advise you to take things easy at work.'

'Oh, that's all taken care of,' Newman added ruefully. 'My damaged brain can remain in neutral for a month or two.'

In the hotel bedroom Newman pulled his new laptop computer towards him. He had replaced the stolen one with money from his insurance claim, and was now keeping a weekly diary of telephone calls on Deep Blue and their results, backing it up two or three times and sending copies to friends in England in case of another visit from the goons. Phil Lewis was not the only one who might need insurance.

'I had better write,' he said regretfully to Helen DeVos.

He was not sure who he was writing for any more, except himself. Holroyd had sucked his teeth and dodged when Newman mentioned the Cuban defector story, finally saying that if Newman sent something he 'would look at it', though they were really far more interested in the closing stages of the presidential election campaign. But the fact that some other top Cuban general called Juan Antonio Fernandez had been arrested in Havana tied in with the theme that Cuba was falling apart, and so the *Tribune* 'better have something, I suppose' Holroyd concluded. Newman opened his shorthand pad at notes from that afternoon's news conference by General Oscar Padilla Sanchez.

'You know,' he said to DeVos, 'I wondered whether you would object to staying in this hotel because of all the associations with Lewis and the attempt on his life. But I thought that if it had not been for what happened here I doubt if we would have ... you know, become such close friends. Funny, when you think of it.'

Helen laughed.

'You mean you still would have regarded me as a hard nosed sexless Yankee bitch.'

'Oh, come on. That's unfair. I never thought of you as sexless. Neurotic, yes. Manhattan weirdo, yes. Yankee bitch, no. Yankee bitches have more money.'

Newman settled into a chair at the desk, overlooking the skyline of Miami, twinkling in the darkness. The Cuban defector story did not amount to all that much, but he could play it up a bit. There was no obvious link with anything connected to Lewis, beyond the idea that Castro's government falling apart would be the final objective of Deep Blue. If it had not been for the arrest of General Fernandez in Havana you could argue that the whole story looked like a clumsy piece of US propaganda. Padilla's biography, or at least the one the Americans released, sounded like a Who's Who of the Cuban revolution: the Sierra Maestra, Bay of Pigs, Nicaragua, Angola, the whole bit. Newman would not have been surprised if the Americans had claimed Padilla had personally dug the silos for the Soviet missiles in the early 1960s. The missile crisis was the only event in three decades of Cuban history on which Padilla seemed to miss out. Anyway, Newman had his doubts about the story.

Defectors were pieces of meat. They said what was necessary rather than what was true, and so when Newman listed Padilla's supposed achievements he used the words 'claimed to be' or 'said to be' repeatedly. The Cuban government had finally released a statement saying Padilla had defected to escape 'revolutionary justice' because the Havana authorities were about to uncover his links with the Colombian drug cartel.

The discredited General Fernandez had been relieved of his command of the western military district 'pending further investigations'. Newman tried to work out which dose of bullshit was the more believable: the American version that General Padilla was a regretful Che Guevara who recognised the past thirty years of his life were wasted and now embraced the American way, like everyone else in the universe; or the equally impossible Cuban view that the prized US defector was really part of the drug smuggling scum of Latin America.

Helen watched as he hit the keys of the laptop computer. She was thinking how serious and determined he looked as he frowned and beat out the words, trying to make sense of the rambling series of facts he had been able to assemble. She worried about Lewis's warnings to guard against becoming obsessed with Deep Blue. There was something about Newman's latest scheme to talk to Lopez which frightened her, even though the *Miami Herald* reported Lopez was now likely to become a Congressional candidate in the mid-term elections, and consequently must be more respectable than she had assumed.

Newman sat back in his chair and stared out the hotel window, watching the lights of the skyscrapers in downtown Miami. He had finished his *Tribune* article, and was working out how best to tackle Lopez. On this warm night with DeVos sitting on his bed, Newman was also thinking that he might describe himself as happy, a fragile happiness, but one that was so real he could taste it. He telephoned London and sent over his story, for which the response was simply 'thank you', nothing more. He expected that if it accorded with what they read on the Reuters or Associated Press wire they might print his version anyway. It would be a simple indulgence, to keep him happy.

Newman stood up and walked to the television set, switching on the local news. The top story was, unsurprisingly, the Cuban defector. The translation of the news conference was as dull as Newman remembered, and the pictures showed nothing of Padilla's face, merely the grey screen behind which the shadow of his head could be seen moving in outline.

'Fearing an attack on his life by agents loyal to Fidel Castro's regime,' the reporter concluded, 'they are taking no chances with the life of a man who risked *his* life to fly to freedom and escape tyranny as so many have before. This is Mike Alpert, Channel Six Eyewitness News Investigation Team.'

Newman wondered why a news conference open to all could be described as an 'investigation', when all you had to do was turn up at the Federal Building and walk in. Maybe that was investigation enough. He looked over at Helen, stretched out on the bed, pillows behind her, half reading a book, half paying attention to this truly awful reporter on television. He smiled at the realisation that he liked this second adolescence in which he thought of her constantly and wanted to be with her like a sixteen-year-old enjoying a first affair.

'Hey,' Newman said. 'I've finished the work. What do we do now?'

DeVos put her book aside, sat up with her arms crossed. He switched off the television which had begun to irritate him.

'I forget,' she said. 'What is it we do now?'

'Come over here and I'll try to jog your memory.'

'Is that English slang for something beyond heavy petting?'

'It could be.'

'Then you'd better come here. I'm the one on the bed, in case you hadn't noticed.'

Newman came to her and kissed her, then began to unbutton her dress. After they finished, he looked at her body winding down the bed, stroking the rise of her thigh and her hip, gently running his fingers over the softness of her skin.

'I have something to tell you,' she said. 'Something you might like.'

'I'm listening.'

'I think I can move down to Washington.'

He blinked and smiled. She explained the Policy Studies Institute wanted researchers for a project called 'Defence 2000' on America's military needs for the next century.

'Are there any?'

She shrugged.

'I want to do it,' she said. 'To begin again.' She turned suddenly serious and frowned. Her next words did not come easily. 'But there's something you should know,' she said, looking at him carefully. 'I would have taken this job whether you were in Washington or not. I am doing this for me, not for you, Alex. You have to understand that.'

'I understand that.'

Then she brightened. 'But it also means I will be looking for a place to live in Washington and wondered if you have anywhere in mind?'

'Sure,' he said. 'For rent.'

She giggled, and he stretched out a hand to telephone for room service.

'Champagne. French champagne. Not American. What do you have? Veuve Clicquot will be fine. Two glasses.'

'What's this for?' she asked.

'To celebrate.'

'Well, I'm not drinking champagne on my own and you forgot to order your exceptionally flavourful water.'

'Ah,' Newman replied. 'I think I warned you before that you might drive me to drink. Well, it's finally happened.'

348

Helen decided nothing would surprise her any more, thinking of all the accidents and mistakes and wrong turnings that had somehow ended up on this bed, in this city, with this unlikely man.

'I wonder.' She hesitated. It was her last chance to warn him, and then she would shut up.

'What?'

'I wonder whether you should give up the idea of trying to find out more about Deep Blue. Of pursuing Lopez. There is no real point, and there might be danger, especially if he really did have something to do with the attack on Lewis. And on you the last time. Why look for trouble when we are so happy together, Alex? No book is worth that.'

Newman ran his hand up her naked body and cupped her breast gently, nibbling the soft skin at the side of her neck until he thought she had forgotten what she had said.

'I have to know,' he said, finally breaking the silence. 'I have to try to find out as much as I can. It's not the book. It's me. I have to make sense of this. I can't let go.'

And she could see there was a stubbornness in him she could not subvert. The champagne was such a long time coming he thought they might make love again, but a knock at the door finally interrupted.

Newman pulled on his towelling bathrobe to meet the waiter at the door. He signed the bill and carried the ice bucket inside by himself. Helen pulled on her own bathrobe as Newman again opened the doors that faced on to the ocean and the lights of Miami. He popped the champagne cork on the balcony, filling their glasses, watching the cork spin into the air and fall fifteen storeys into the shrubbery below. He wanted to give some pathetic little toast, then thought better of it. Their glasses touched, then their lips, then he drank the first alcohol he had tasted for two years.

'Better than Perrier,' he said, savouring the dry aftertaste on his tongue. 'Maybe nearly as good as Ramlosa.'

Newman felt the Veuve Clicquot bubble inside him, making him ever so slightly drunk after just one glass. It was a feeling both comfortably familiar and delightfully new, like falling in love again.

A warm wind was licking the palm trees, bending their tips as it came inland.

Tomorrow he would find Jorge Lopez and begin to finish all this. Tomorrow it would still be morning in America.

'You know what they say,' he murmured, a lilt in his voice.

'No, what do they say?' she replied.

'They say that news is what someone somewhere does not want you to find out. All the rest is public relations.'

'Well, that makes a change,' Helen laughed. 'You used to have, what shall we say, an even more cynical view of your profession.'

'That was in a previous life. Before I was brain damaged – by meeting you. Now I guess I just work for myself. And Alex Newman, formerly of the *London Tribune*, does not do PR. He does what he damn well likes. He's free. Re-born here.'

'Oh,' she teased. 'I never knew you were so big on the American dream.'

There was the distant sound of salsa music from the outside bar near the swimming pool, and the duller splashing of the waves on the shore. Newman thought of Phil Lewis for an instant, lying in his tub in some room nearby a few months before, bleeding like a stuck animal. Lewis who, if he had chosen a room with a balcony like this, might have been thrown over and spun to earth like the champagne cork and more conveniently killed, ending all this before it began. But an accident of history or some trivial change at the hotel check-in desk had pushed them all in a different direction. Newman looked at DeVos who was talking to him through the buzz of champagne, the air tinkling with the sound of her voice, cheerful, direct. For the first time in his life he realised he did not care what happened next, the next moves in a career or towards some uncertain but almost-planned future with her, whether the heat continued or there was a hurricane, whether there was champagne in his glass or the bottle ran dry, whether tomorrow he would be as happy as he was today or whether there would be tears and he would stand weeping under the Miami palm trees. Tomorrow he would wake and try to see Jorge Lopez. He would find out the truth to the best of his abilities. He would either adapt himself to the new world he was on the brink of discovering or he would adapt that world to himself. There would be change, progress. Whatever happened, Alex Newman felt relaxed, ready for the challenge, alive. For the first time in his life as he stood in the warm night air and swayed gently with the humid breeze, he thought how lucky he was to have no thoughts of before or after or above or below, lucky to be completely in love with the here and now.

33

Newman was beginning to enjoy being a pest, and he believed he was becoming good at it. He called *La Tortuga*'s main business office in downtown Miami yet again. The secretary took his messages, and responded stiffly that Mr Lopez 'did not speak to the press.'

'He spoke to them about his chances of running for Congress,' Newman replied, equally snottily. 'All I am asking is that you pass on that I would like to talk to him. Tell him that a mutual friend, Phil Lewis, was most insistent that we speak.'

'Who?'

'Phil Lewis. Tell him Phil Lewis called me only a day or so ago and suggested I contact Mr Lopez. He really should see me. It's very important.'

'To you or to him?' the secretary snapped back.

'Well,' Newman said with menace in his voice, 'I think it would be better for you to permit Mr Lopez to decide. After all, if you were to take it upon yourself NOT to tell him that Phil Lewis insists I should meet him, then Mr Lopez might come to the conclusion that you are a complete waste of space. Do I make myself clear?'

'I'll see Mr Lopez gets your message.'

In desperation Newman thought of repeating his stakeout procedure at the main building of Lopez's property company.

'Don't do it, Alex,' Helen said. 'Terrelli called the Secret Service. Lopez will call in his thugs.'

'I thought you'd formed the opinion he was respectable now he was likely to run for Congress.'

Helen snorted back contemptuously.

About an hour after Newman's latest try with Lopez's secretary, when he had all but given up, the telephone rang in the Sheraton hotel room. He thought it might be one of the *Miami Herald* reporters who was trying on Newman's behalf to track down the new home number for Lopez, and who advised most strongly against attempting a stake out. On the line there was a Hispanic accent and a gruff, commanding voice.

'Mr Newman,' the voice said.

'Yes, this is Alex Newman.'

'Well, this is Jorge Lopez. I want you to come and see me. I hear you have been talking with Phil Lewis. I hope he is well.'

'Seems to be,' Newman said. 'At least he was when we last spoke.'

'Well, come over and let's talk about him.'

Helen still did not want him to go.

'He's after something, Alex. I warned you all these guys are playing some angle.'

Yet when he persisted she seemed resigned.

'I will telephone you in three hours,' he said, trying not to sound melodramatic. 'If I haven't called in that time, maybe it would be as well for you to get the police to drop in on Jorge Lopez, maybe in through the windows of the Florida Oval Office.'

She did not find it funny.

'Be careful,' she whispered, kissing him hard.

'Sure,' he said. 'I'll be careful. No contact sports. Doctor's orders, remember. At least not with big Cuban guys. Bad for the skull.'

Newman drove his rented Chevy Beretta over Rickenbacker causeway to Key Biscayne thinking of the attack on Lewis, the anonymous call about Helen and the burglary at his own apartment. The fact that Lewis believed Lopez was behind all three incidents sent a chill down Newman's back. It was one thing to try to track Lopez down, quite another to stand face to face with the Turtle. It would be like pushing open the door to his apartment. It might give way easily, and yet what he found inside might not be to Newman's liking.

When he reached the gate at the end of Jorge Lopez's drive, Newman hit the microphone button next to the keypad. He identified himself and stared at the whirring closed circuit television cameras. After a few minutes the gate opened and he drove past the tall hedge towards the house. Nothing had prepared him for the sight of the reconstructed White House. None of the bemused contempt of the *Herald* reporters managed to do it justice, and he stepped from the car on the gravel path, gazing up at the white pillars and wondering whether Jorge Lopez would meet him in his own re-creation of the Oval Office, or the Rose Garden or the West Wing. This was in the King Ludwig of Bavaria looney tune league, yet it was uncanny how much it looked like the real thing. As Newman stood on the gravel marvelling at what he saw, the front door opened and a tall, heavily set Cuban with a touch of black blood strode out.

'I'm here to see Mr Lopez.'

'Yeah, I know.' Kiki Mendoza was thinking about the last time he had seen Newman, and figuring that the doctors had done a good job on the head, bearing in mind the force with which he had brought the Glock pistol down behind his right ear. Medical science really was something. 'Newman,' the Bear said. 'You're expected.'

He showed Newman in to the conservatory where behind the ferns and greenery there was a man with a reddened face and rough folds of skin on his neck. The man was drinking coffee and smoking a large cigar. By his side was a much older woman who spoke in shrill Spanish, which Newman could not understand. The Turtle took the cigar from his mouth, stood up and shook Newman by the hand.

'Jorge Lopez,' he introduced himself. 'And this is my mother.'

'Pleased to meet you,' Newman said, as the old woman muttered incomprehensibly.

'Coffee?'

'Please.'

Kiki Mendoza walked out from the conservatory and called in Spanish to the maid.

'Thank you for seeing me, Mr Lopez,' Newman began. Lopez swept his hand in the air in a grand gesture.

'I wanted to meet you, even though I neither like journalists nor normally agree to see them. But I have read your articles about Phil Lewis. And I hear you were beaten up in pursuit of the story. That's brave of you. I admire that. Courage and principles. What this country was founded on. I think you must be nearer to finding out the truth than anyone. I wish someone would explain it all to me.

354

Maybe you can. I am interested because I lost a lot of money, and also because you say you have seen Phil recently. We are old friends, even if he has a lot of explaining to do.'

'No,' Newman corrected. 'I have not seen Phil. But I have talked to him. Frequently. He calls me at least once a week, sometimes more often.'

'Oh,' the Turtle said, wrinkling his face into a smile. 'And how is he under all this strain? Well, I hope.'

Newman replied that Lewis was up and down, sometimes full of life and anxious to finish the whole affair, sometimes desperately depressed.

'I thought he was not supposed to speak to journalists,' Jorge Lopez said. 'That the CIA or the government had silenced him.'

Alex Newman laughed. 'Well, Phil does not think of me as much of a journalist any more. Not since my apartment was burgled and I was hit over the head. My editor believes it permanently affected me. Made me half crazy. Obsessed. He brought someone else over to cover the election and I am on sick leave. Meaning, they think I'm sick and would be delighted if I leave.' Newman chuckled at his bad joke. 'Maybe being cracked on the skull has affected me. It has made me see things more clearly than before.'

Lopez wondered what things he meant. Newman took a deep breath. He was pushing his luck and he knew it.

'Oh, you know, the way in which events seem to be inter-related. A pattern. The burglary of my apartment. The attack on Lewis, those kind of things. As if some person or organisation is behind all of this. Pulling the strings. I just want to find out who or what it is. Piece it all together.'

If Newman was hoping for a reaction he was to be disappointed. The Turtle shell slammed firmly shut.

'Well,' Lopez said carefully. 'These are all interesting matters. I look forward to reading about them in your newspaper. And no doubt if Phil Lewis tells you the whole story you could win a few Pulitzer prizes.' The Turtle laughed, a disconcerting cackle. Then he turned serious. 'Where is Phil now, or where was he when you last talked to him? I should like to see him again. It has been a long time since we last met. Maybe he thinks I bear grudges because the money

355

has gone. Sure I'm a little sore. But like you I want explanations. If he would meet with me for a while – maybe at his lawyer's office – I'd be grateful.'

'I wish I knew how to contact him,' Newman said truthfully. 'He moves around from hotel to hotel, using up what money he has left, though I suppose we'll see him at his trial. He tells me it will be all over in a few weeks, a formality, because the government case is so tied in knots they will have to give him the kind of plea bargain deal he wants. Especially if they want him to keep quiet. That's what he says anyway.' Now Newman laughed. 'The trouble, Mr Lopez,' he continued, 'is that the world is divided into two groups. There are those like me and the investors, who are desperate for Lewis to say what it is he knows so we can get to the bottom of all this. And then there's the other group. The guys who hit me over the head and slashed him, and who are desperate that he says nothing. What the knock on the head taught me is that the angels are always on the side of disclosure and letting in the fresh air. It's the same everywhere. Europe. America. Cuba, probably. You can tell the bad guys because they are always the ones who want to keep everything covered up.'

La Tortuga was disappointed. It was not that he expected Newman immediately to blurt out the whereabouts of Lewis, though that would be convenient. But at least he thought Newman would know where Lewis was, even if he was coy about revealing it. Now he realised, regrettably, that the journalist was probably telling the truth, that he did speak frequently to Lewis but did not know where he was located. The Turtle's mind raced through the possibilities, trying to decide whether there might yet be a way of using Newman. Lopez had an idea.

'What happened in all this, Mr Lopez?' Newman was asking. 'Do you believe that Lewis was a crook?'

The Turtle pulled on his cigar. Beyond the skin problem which was red and inflamed, Newman saw in the wattles on his neck and the hoods over his eyes something which began to make him afraid. He sensed that this was a man utterly without values. It was difficult to believe that someone like this could ever be elected to Congress. But Newman found the same thing equally difficult to believe of others who currently graced the House and Senate.

356

'It is impossible to say,' Lopez began, unenthusiastically, 'what lies behind this disaster. Of course Lewis seemed like myself: an immigrant who wished to make his way, who wanted to create wealth and who was prepared to help others. A patriot. Now . . . now I am not so sure. As I said, I lost a considerable sum in the collapse of Winston, Hamilton, and that makes me uneasy. Maybe he really was a swindler. It is hard for me to admit to anyone, even to myself, that I lost so much money, that I was duped. But maybe I was.'

'May I ask how much?' Newman said politely.

The Turtle smiled.

'A considerable sum. That's all I can say. A very considerable sum.'

Kiki Mendoza opened the conservatory door and allowed the maid to walk through carrying a tray of coffee. She picked up the small dirty cups beside Jorge Lopez and Dona Maria, gave them fresh coffee, and passed a cup to Newman. When she left, Kiki Mendoza closed the door behind her and stood beside it watching Alex Newman like a bouncer at an especially rough disco.

'I suppose if you want to quote me saying something, Mr Newman,' Jorge Lopez continued, 'then the best I can do is this. If there was some CIA involvement in Winston, Hamilton, Bellingham, Lewis and Lopez, then I was unaware of it. I was not consulted about it. Nor do I understand where the money has gone. It is a big mystery. I should be delighted if you would find out. Perhaps you might ask Phil Lewis to explain when you next talk to him. Do you expect your contact with him will continue?'

'Oh, I suppose so,' Newman replied. 'He likes to stay in touch. You know, one Englishman abroad seeks another. Something like that. We both feel we have been abused. We both have a sense of grievance.'

The Turtle nodded.

'Like Cubans,' he said. 'You stick together. I understand that. I like loyalty.'

Newman looked at the old wrinkled face of Dona Maria, nodding at the incomprehensible English chatter, proud of her son and scowling at the rest of the world. She was tapping her feet gently to an unheard rhythm. He wondered whether he dare frame the question he had come to ask. Kiki the Bear stood, blank faced, staring down at him, arms folded, muscles bulging through his shirt.

'Deliver us, O Lord,' Newman thought. He cleared his throat nervously. 'Mr Lopez, there is something in particular I should like to put to you, and I apologise in advance if it causes offence.' He paused waiting for a reaction, but there was none, just a cloud of smoke and the old lady tapping her shoe. 'It was Phil Lewis who suggested I talk to you, as I said earlier, because my apartment was broken into and I was beaten up.' Newman glanced at Kiki Mendoza but there was no reaction. Back to Lopez. Nothing. 'I was hit over the head and my computer files and documents relating to Phil were stolen.'

'Yes,' the Turtle said. 'I read about this, also. A sordid affair. Sordid.'

'I asked Phil whether he had any idea who might have done such a thing.' Newman paused again. His heart was beating hard, blood pounding in his chest making the words stick in his throat. 'He said it was probably the same people who tried to kill him. He sees a pattern. I'm trying to establish if he's right.' The bear at the door stood like a statue, dumb, uncomprehending, the old lady's feet continued their gentle rhythm, unbroken, the Turtle staring at him with hooded eyes. 'He said you would know the answer to the riddle, that you could see the pattern. He said you were the person to ask.'

The Turtle puffed on his cigar and Newman felt another wave of smoke push towards him.

'If by that,' Jorge Lopez said flatly, waving his cigar so the tip cut a rapid circle in the air, 'if by that you mean that I was somehow connected with these things, then you have wasted your journey, Mr Newman. I know nothing about them. I am a businessman who one day hopes to seek elected office in this country and when I do I shall be pressing for tougher penalties against criminals like those who attacked you in your own home. That was outrageous. I am not the sort of man who would be involved in something like this. Why would it benefit me? To return to the point you made a few minutes ago, I am with the angels. It is absolutely to my advantage that everything about Phil Lewis and his business dealings is published in the newspapers. It might not suit some people in our government to have these things known, but it suits me. I need to know where my

358

money has gone. Far from trying to silence you or obstruct you, I would wish you God speed in your efforts.'

Lopez puffed on his cigar as if he had just made his definitive statement. Newman watched the wattles shake with conviction, then he decided to win or lose it all.

'Look, Mr Lopez, Lewis believes you wanted to kill him because he lost your money. Simple as that. Whether you were involved in my break-in I don't know. Maybe that's all nonsense. But what about the attempt on Lewis? What can I tell him to convince him you had nothing to do with it?'

The Turtle appeared to laugh, a strangled sound came from somewhere between his throat and his chest.

'I can hardly tell you I am happy about losing money,' Lopez said. 'But there is plenty more where that came from. I am a man of some means. No . . .' He leaned forward and took a sip from his coffee cup. 'No, there are plenty of people in Miami who might wish Phil Lewis dead. I am not one of them. I feel sorry for him. I feel disappointed in him. To an extent I feel betrayed by him because we were such close friends and he has cost me, well, you asked for a figure and millions of dollars is all I will say. Millions of dollars. More than the cost of this house. Much more. I am angry and upset and I want my money back. But that is all. However angry I become it would not cause me to do as Lewis alleges. Besides, that would not bring my money back, would it?'

'So you had nothing to do with either the attack on him or the burglary in my apartment.'

'Nothing.'

'Or an attempt to implicate a colleague of mine, Helen DeVos, in drug smuggling?'

The Turtle shook his head.

'I have never even heard of anyone of that name. Or of what you say until now.'

'Do you know who might be behind these things?'

The Turtle looked as if the interrogation by questioning his own moral values caused him real physical pain.

'There are many criminals, Mr Newman. Many bad people here in Miami and elsewhere. But I have no knowledge of who might have done these things otherwise I would have contacted the police. But,' he leaned forward again and finished his Cuban coffee, 'but I do have one piece of advice for you. Since Phil Lewis is making these ridiculous charges against me, perhaps you should ask him some questions about his own dealings next time you speak. You might then be able to pull things together a little better. It could help you assess what kind of man Lewis really is. Especially if you are thinking of writing a book on this unhappy affair.'

'What kind of questions, Mr Lopez?'

Lopez looked straight at Newman, blinking his eyes in the smoke, thinking: curiosity killed the cat. And the journalist.

'Ask him to explain to you about the drugs, Mr Newman. Ask him to tell you who Columbus is. Or was. And the drugs.'

'Columbus?' Newman repeated.

'Columbus.'

'And drugs?'

'And drugs.'

The two men gazed at each other silently through the cigar smoke.

'Look,' Lopez added eventually. 'These are matters I know little about, and I said to you I was not aware of any CIA connection directly in the investment corporation. But Lewis knew of the company within the company that was at the heart of our operations. That is what I am so angry about. I hear that there was some connection with discontent inside Cuba being exploited by Lewis.'

Newman was utterly stunned.

'And drugs,' he repeated.

'And drugs.'

'So the Cuban accusations are true, that the recent defector General Padilla was a drug smuggler?'

Newman asked the question robotically, still trying to comprehend the enormity of what Lopez was saying. 'Yes,' Lopez said. 'According to my sources. And you can well imagine that this may be the first and only time in my life as a Cuban emigré that I would confirm that allegations made by the Castro regime are true. This is not just Communist propaganda, but it does show the corruption at the heart of Cuba.'

Newman was unsure what to do next. It was beginning to sound

360

like one of Chuck Lowell's lunatic conspiracies in *Combat*, except in this case, the conspiracy might just be true. Newman said he would, of course, ask Lewis about the allegations, but maybe Lopez himself could say a little more.

'Good try, Mr Newman,' Lopez chuckled. 'But I do not know the whole story. Maybe Lewis does not either. But he knows more than I do. All I can say is I was shocked when I heard about Lewis, the drugs and Columbus. Anyway, you must ask Lewis about it, face to face. And when you have learned something of this perhaps it will affect how you view him and the credibility you attach to the rest of his story. That is my advice.'

Newman tried to ask the Turtle more questions to put the jigsaw together, but Lopez made it clear he had better things to do. Newman stood up, his head spinning as if he had been hit on the skull again.

'I don't follow all this. Drugs, Columbus. What do you mean? What is this about, Mr Lopez?'

The Turtle laughed his strangled laugh.

'Ask Phil Lewis, not me. Just ask Phil Lewis. All will be clear. Now we must go, Mr Newman. Kiki will show you out.'

The large muscled statue by the door began to move, ushering Alex Newman into the hallway.

'Thank you, Mr Lopez. It was a pleasure to meet you. A real pleasure. I will let you know what Lewis has to say.'

The Turtle smiled widely until his teeth showed behind the redness of his skin. He was pleased he had seen Newman. He knew he had perfectly aroused the journalistic libido. Newman would pursue Lewis like a dog after a bitch on heat. Drugs. Columbus. Lewis. The dog's nose was twitching as he followed the rank scent. All Lopez had to do was to follow the dog.

'Oh,' Lopez said, bidding Newman farewell with a fine smile. 'I do not think keeping me informed will be necessary. But please give Phil my regards when you see him. Tell him I would like to meet with him some time. Tell him I hope it will all work out for the best. I'm sure it will. Goodbye, Mr Newman.'

34

On New York's East 52nd there was a street festival. They were selling Peruvian blankets and painted ornaments and Vietnamese food and Mexican burritos and Salvadoran pupusas and the other things which make New York New York. There were great grazing herds of locals and tourists moving from stall to stall eating spring rolls and soft pretzels with mustard and drinking Diet Pepsis and ordering low-cal yogurt from a Haitian lady who was complaining to the Koreans that they were burning the barbecued ribs and she was choking from smoke. There were a few panhandlers on street corners near Fifth Avenue at St Patrick's Cathedral shaking polystyrene cups on kinder, gentler festive streets, asking for loose change.

'Spare a quarter, ma'am.'

'Sir, help out a hungry man.'

'Sir! Sir!'

'Catch you next time, sir.'

There was a jackhammer pounding away on Fifth, and a siren on Madison where an ambulance was locked in traffic. A delivery truck was trying to drop off half a dozen beer kegs at O'Brien's but the traffic policeman said you couldn't deliver this time of day, buddy, forget it. And when the driver started to argue the cop said, what the fuck do I look like, and the driver said, a cop, what the fuck do you think you look like, a ball-ay fucking dancer? And then he drove off oh, fuck you, fuck you, fuck you, into the Manhattan streets. Fat Phil Lewis pushed his way through the noisy crowds from his hotel on the corner of East 52nd and Lexington. He had a few hours to kill before the flight from JFK airport out of the United States to

London Heathrow, to whatever awaited him in England.

Lewis found what he had been looking for further up East 52nd, a shoeshine stand, manned by two black guys from Harlem who looked as if they could have been basketball players but had fallen on hard times. Lewis climbed into the chair, watched carefully by one of the former basketball stars who wondered if this fat geek was gonna cause the chair to collapse or what. The chair stood up to the pressure and the basketball star carefully inserted pieces of cardboard between Lewis's socks and shoes so the polish did not spread everywhere. He started making conversation because after two years on the street he figured the one thing out-of-town white customers liked was the chance to talk to a real African American from Harlem.

'You ain't from around here by your accent,' the basketball star said, only Lewis was not in a mood to talk and said, 'You're right.' – which killed things from the start.

The basketball star knew from his attitude the fat man was a small tipper, so he brushed and shined and stayed surly and silent, which was just fine as far as Lewis was concerned. He had continued to lose weight, a further twelve pounds, but not enough to make him anything other than a fat man rolling through the New York crowds. Yet it was a kind of progress which cheered him, made him feel more in control. It was as if his whole life was changing direction again, and he liked the feeling that he was able to steer it this way or that, alter what he did, where he lived and what he looked like, as he had done twenty years before when he moved to the United States. Now he would change again by returning to England, which might confirm what he had begun to suspect, that the New World and the American Dream had nothing to do with geography or nationality.

The dream belonged to everybody, and fat Phil Lewis on his way out of the United States was taking it with him, the dream which he now recognised was possible anywhere optimism could thrive. Like England.

The deal with Boone and Terrelli turned out to be more painless than he thought. Instead of delaying everything until after the election, they speeded it up so most of the publicity the case might have received was drowned in the final stages of the political campaign. Holgate had screwed out of them an amazing plea bargain, proving

363

himself a mean son-of-a-bitch even for a Florida white powder lawyer.

Holgate scented blood like a barracuda. The agreed sentence was two years in jail, but Holgate made sure it was suspended for five years, and the government caved in. Completely. The judge processed it like some easy divorce and Lewis walked out of the Miami federal courthouse and through the electronic forest of television cameras with nothing much to say, three days before the presidential election, happy, and if not quite vindicated, something just as good. Free.

The reporter Alpert was there trying to ask the fat man what he felt for those he had swindled, and Lewis wanted to turn round and ask him what it was like being, you know, a perfect professional sphincter. But a deal not to talk to the media presumably included abuse, and Lewis was determined to keep it all according to the script until he made sure there was no chance of being re-arrested, no dirty tricks from Boone or Terrelli.

'My client has nothing to say for now,' Tom Holgate said, pushing the camera crews aside. 'Except that he is relieved justice has been done, and been seen to be done.'

Even though relations between lawyer and client had become strained, fat Phil had to admit that Holgate turned on a stunning bravura performance in court in his short public statement as the judge considered the plea bargain.

'The money has largely been repaid, thanks to my client Philip Lewis's help,' Holgate told the court. 'Mr Lewis has gone to extraordinary lengths in the face of crushing obstruction from the US government to uncover every last red cent of the assets of the company. And in so doing, I would submit to the court, Mr Lewis has also recovered his own honour and dignity, something the darker forces at work in our government and our society would have denied him. In fact I am pleased to tell the court that my client has been instrumental in aiding the recovery of a further $13.5 million dollars. This money was not traced by the FBI during their lengthy investigations. Mr Lewis was the man who was able to direct the government towards those funds. They are, I am told, sufficient to pay off most of the outstanding obligations of Winston, Hamilton, Bellingham, Lewis and Lopez. My understanding is that no one has

364

made any significant losses from the collapse of the company, thanks to Mr Lewis's actions. I am sure the prosecution can confirm that fact.'

'We can confirm that your honour.'

And so it went, as painless as Boone had promised, except for the predictable humiliation of being forced to plead guilty to something which Lewis still could not believe was a crime.

'My client also wishes to make clear,' Holgate continued, 'that his earlier allegations concerning CIA involvement in his company were true, but such involvement was peripheral, and played no part in his own errors of judgement or in this case. He wishes that to go on the record, fearing that otherwise he might malign a patriotic group of Americans who are doing the hard work of freedom, who helped this country triumph through the thankless struggles of the Cold War, and whose expertise is needed now more than ever.'

Holgate did his duty, though their friendship had died and he thought Lewis little better than the class of drug smuggling vermin he usually defended. At least regular druggies did not try to dress up their greed in patriotism. When the lead FBI agent, Leon Kramer, took Holgate aside and talked him through the way in which the financial organisation of the company had been set up, Holgate was disgusted.

'It's like he blew his nose on the flag,' Holgate said.

'Yeah,' Kramer replied. 'Only I guess the flag didn't mean so much to him. Seeing as how he's British and all.'

The basketball star with the shoe polish finished his work. Lewis paid up, and surprised him by handing over a dollar extra as a tip.

'Thank you, sir, y'all come back any time you care to, y'hear. I'll be waitin'.'

Lewis thought it might be a long wait. He was now hungry. He wanted to eat breakfast, his last breakfast in America. He pulled into a little Jewish deli on East 53rd and ordered a coffee and a toasted bagel. Lewis ate hungrily, chewing the bagel between his fleshy cheeks, stuffing it down and slurping the too-hot coffee until his lips smacked and the coffee was drained and he wiped the wetness from his mouth with a paper napkin. He felt good, happy, and intrigued by the news from Alex Newman who told him what Lopez had said.

365

'I am to ask you about someone called Columbus. And about drugs.'

'Oh,' Lewis replied, thinking maybe he had underestimated Newman. 'I'll call you again. We have many things to talk about. But not those subjects, okay?'

Lewis thought about it for days and decided to avoid any further contact with Newman until after the court case. He came to the Miami Federal Courthouse under FBI protection and they swept him away afterwards so no one could follow. Lewis knew enough about Lopez to assume he would try again to kill him. He was like a pit bull. Once he decided to fight, only his own death would stop him from bringing it to a finish. So Lewis made sure that the private eye Steve Ortiz was always with him in Miami as a personal bodyguard, as well as the FBI. He trusted no one. As soon as the plea bargain was accepted and the minimal sentence passed, Lewis was driven away by the FBI, changed cars twice and then set out on his own with Ortiz. They travelled to Tampa and from there he called Newman.

'I want to talk,' he said. 'Now it's over. I'm heading north to answer some of the questions you asked. We have to meet before I leave the country for good. I still don't trust the bastards, and I want as much insurance as I can get. I'll tell you most of it, but you can't publish until I say so, or until someone tries to get rid of me. Once that happens all bets are off.'

Now in the Jewish deli, fat Phil Lewis ordered a final refill of coffee then drained it quickly while it was still scalding hot, paid the check, and went back into the noise of the streets. He felt Manhattan's energy pump around him as if the city was one huge permanent party. In his remaining hours he wanted to drink in the best New York had to offer. It was a simple conceit: to leave the United States by way of Ellis Island, the place through which a quarter of the population could trace their arrival in the Americas, now a museum to immigrants. Today was his last chance to read for himself the exhortation on the Statue of Liberty to the tired, the poor, the huddled masses. And it was exactly what he needed to hear on the day of a presidential election on which so much depended.

He stood on Fifth and hailed a cab to take him down to Battery Park, where he picked up the ferry with the tourists. There were a dozen blond Scandinavian teenagers at the front of the boat speaking some gutteral language which he assumed must be Swedish. A middle aged and well dressed black couple, the man loaded down with video equipment, filmed everything that moved. Lewis stayed at the stern of the ferry watching it cast off from the pier, churning the brown and oily waters of the Hudson river as it turned to push across to the Statue of Liberty. He looked behind towards the skyscrapers of Wall Street and listened as the blaring sounds of the city seemed to be cast adrift too, receding in the distance as the ferry picked up speed. The smell of diesel fuel caught his nose and he stood back from the stern hoping there might be enough of a breeze to carry the fumes away. There was a small police launch heading uptown and overhead the clatter of sightseeing helicopters, spinning the tourists round the pillars of Manhattan.

Lewis remembered all those years ago when he had first come to the United States, the country he knew or thought he knew because of the Western films he watched in his childhood, the hardboiled Raymond Chandler heroes, the John Ford Westerns, the Americans he met in England, the friends of his father who had seemed such colourful figures compared to the shabbiness and gloom of Britain in the 1950s. He looked down at his own spreading belly and thought of the young man who had come to this country twenty years before, thinner but stuffed fat with illusions and optimism for a land which meant John F. Kennedy and Marilyn Monroe and Rawhide and Philip Marlowe and Damon Runyon and John Foster Dulles and John Glenn and John Wayne and skyscrapers and power and freedom.

Now the wind had changed and the diesel fumes were being carried away down the Hudson. The air had a strange smell, the dampness of the river and a touch of the sea, the vague far-off scents of the city. Lewis felt a chill shake his body. He turned to stare at the approaching green form of the Goddess of Liberty at the gateway for countless generations who arrived with empty bellies and full hearts.

As the ferry boat slowed on its final approach he looked up at the statue's enigmatic smile, and thought of the idea of freedom he had dedicated himself to, the ultimate abstraction. Then he thought of Boone in his office, his powerful hands like hams pounding on the desk as he made some point about the defence of the nation. He thought of the limousines gliding in and out of the White House, and the president sitting down to discuss the nation's most secret secrets with the inner circle of its defenders. And he thought of Padilla drinking rum with limes and ice and smoking constantly and joking with him about what he would like to do with Ileana Del Cid.

He thought of every trip he had taken, every hour he had worked, every reluctant client or contact he had pressed for an investment or to become part, witting or unwitting, of the great information machine upon which the foundations of security and liberty rested. And he knew he would finally tell Alexander Newman the whole story, the drugs, the corruption, the secret bank accounts, the insider trading, Columbus, every damn thing, because he wanted everyone to know about his part in history. He wanted to tell it because for him the war was over and he had played a glorious part in the victory. It was not some awful secret that dare not speak its name. It was raw patriotism and he wanted to yell it from the crest of the great green statue standing rock solid in front of him, bawl it out into the New York sky that he, Philip Andrew Lewis had done his part in the Great Dirty War for Liberty on this day when the American public took their decisions, and the world would soon know the result, that the president had been re-elected and the forces of darkness defeated once more.

The ferry docked and Lewis walked with the crowds of Americans and foreigners who had come to see the view of the United States from the Goddess of Liberty, the crowds who were planning to ascend and look back over the world's most famous skyline with its noise and its mean streets, its excitement and richness and culture and dirt and crime and poverty and despair. And he stood in the long line of those who wanted to see and be part of it, thinking of the new Europe more than three thousand miles away, of the old and most heavily militarised continent the world had ever seen trying to make sense of itself again like some new frontier on which there were dangers to be faced, opportunities to be seized and fortunes to be made. And Phil Lewis put a pudgy hand up to the cheeks which swelled out red on his face and began to rub away the wetness of his tears.

35

Alex Newman found the Manhattan air cold, autumnal. He decided to walk from where he was staying in the Beekman Towers hotel near the United Nations a dozen blocks across town to Fifth Avenue to check whether he was being followed, then pick up a cab for his arranged meeting with Phil Lewis. At the UN there were hundreds of uniformed police officers on the streets as the delegations came and went for a Security Council meeting on some further proposal about Israel and the West Bank. As Newman wrapped his coat around him in the hotel lobby he could see the front desk manager was watching television, listening to the cross country reports of voters streaming into election booths and being interviewed on their preferences for president.

'Straight Republican,' one said. 'All the way.'

'Sure, I think he deserves another term. Job ain't but half done.'

'Ya don't rewrite a hit.'

'Time for a change. Time to move on from empty rhetoric.'

'Get rid of the party of the rich. Don't forget the working man.'

'Doesn't matter, whoever we get. Goes from bad to worse.'

'Who does anything for the middle classes, that's what I want to know?'

'They all raise taxes, only some lie about it.'

Newman could not hide his anxiety about meeting Lewis again after all those months, compounded by nervousness that he should not be followed. As he walked block by block across town in the grey early afternoon light he checked and re-checked that no one was behind him, doing everything he could to ensure his security.

DeVos had first tried to persuade him not to go, and then switched tack, offering to come with him. He had firmly refused, though parting with her in Washington had not been easy. To his surprise, Newman found himself suddenly fascinated by the larger political drama of the presidential election. After months of wishing it would go away, he knew the country stood on the verge of writing its own history, of choosing the course for the next four years in a way which might set the tone of politics for a long time to come. He hoped he might be through with Lewis in time to watch the best of the election reports on television, computer projections, the declarations of victory and defeat. Newman was even beginning to feel twinges of disappointment that his replacement at the *Tribune* office would be having all the fun.

He passed a legless beggar sitting on a pile of cardboard boxes tunelessly blowing a mouth organ. The beggar had a cap with a few quarters in it and held up a badly written sign saying 'Homeless – Please Help.' Newman hurried by, and the cynicism returned as he thought of the day's great exercise in democracy as a twenty-four-hour wonder after which the rich would stay rich and the poor would stay hopeless. Then he thought about more important things – like Helen and what they were planning and it cheered him. She had moved to Washington, finished her life in New York and sloughed it off like an old skin, beginning work in the Defence Policy Institute with new energy and enthusiasm. *Combat* would stagger on for a while, but her links with it now were almost as tenuous as those with Chuck Lowell. Lowell, DeVos found out, had begun a new relationship with a twenty-four-year-old blonde who was a personal trainer in a slick gymnasium on the edges of Central Park. He was talking of marrying her and moving back to the west coast, perhaps establishing a New Age magazine in southern California. He asked Helen what she thought of the title *The Health Spirit*, and she said it sounded fine. Newman was impressed that Lowell had leaped from the 1970s to the year 2000 with one bound.

'We could get married too,' he said to DeVos, in what stopped slightly short of being a proposal.

'We could,' she replied. 'But there's no point unless we are to have children.'

370

And there it lay between them until Newman picked it up again.

'Sometimes I think we would be better to marry and move away to the West. To Colorado or Arizona or Wyoming, live in the mountains and do what we can. Get away from all this. Raise children. Have a big dog. A Jeep. Go where the real Americans are, not here.'

'You serious?'

'Maybe,' Newman replied. 'I don't know. All I do know is that ever since they cracked my skull open I've begun to think differently. Or maybe it was ever since I met you. I'm not sure. Either way, I have had time to think about what is important and what's not.'

'And what's the secret?'

'And . . . and I don't know. Of course I want to find out the thread that links Lewis and the things Lopez talked about. And maybe I can make a book out of it. It's important to try. But mostly it's difficult enough to make sense of our own lives without trying to pull together and understand conspiracies and scandals. Suddenly I feel that all the struggling is worth nothing compared to standing on a hotel balcony in Miami and drinking champagne and watching the city lights. Getting married or moving to the West and having children just seems so much more . . . valuable, I guess that's the word, more valuable than all of this. I suppose I would rather live life than understand it, that's what I'm trying to say.'

Helen DeVos laughed.

'I told you it worries me when you start talking like this,' she said, pointing to his head. 'Must be the cracked brain. Maybe we should get married. You need someone to look after you. And I need a lost cause now I've given up *Combat*.'

'Maybe,' he said.

The *Tribune* had delivered an ultimatum: he could stay in Washington until the Inauguration in January, but then he had to return to the newsdesk in London permanently. Immediately after the election he had to come back for a short period of 'consultations'. He told her he would not do it.

'I'm not going back to England. I want to stay here.'

'Doing what?'

'Writing the book. Looking for freelance work. If all else fails, I've always wanted to be a kept man. You could earn the money, and I could provide you with sexual services in exchange for room and board.'

He remembered how she giggled and they fell together for the last lovemaking before he caught the shuttle to New York. He was so happy he even thought for a moment of giving up the idea of pursuing Lewis, but it passed. How could he not meet him now? How could he let inertia take over and fail him on the last mile? Now in the Manhattan gloom Newman pulled his overcoat around him and walked briskly until he reached Fifth Avenue, crossed Rockefeller Plaza and looked up and down the streets. He checked again to see if he was being followed and saw nothing except the heaving, noisy crowd of the city, going about their business as if the presidential election was some not-quite-serious soap opera acted out for television. In the shop windows of the electronics stores hundreds of television sets showed the latest pictures from the news specials on all the main networks, interviews with politicians and pundits and psephologists, campaign managers and historians, piped out noisily on to the street to try to encourage customers. Newman hailed a yellow cab and told the driver Battery Park.

The ferry out to Liberty Island was even colder than the Manhattan streets and Newman wondered at Lewis's decision to meet him there.

It was such a tourist trap. But the fat man had been most insistent that despite all his years in the United States he had never seen the statue up close and Newman had to fit in with his sight-seeing itinerary. As he stepped on to the short dock Newman gazed around and from the crowds extending towards the statue's base Phil Lewis waddled into view, portly, cheerful. They shook hands. Lewis exchanged pleasantries like an old friend.

'Fancy meeting you here. Wonderful day for a stroll.'

'Bit too chilly for me, Phil. Couldn't you have picked somewhere warmer like the Empire State Building? Or tea at the Ritz. If there is a Ritz.'

Lewis asked about Helen. Newman told him of her move to Washington, and the prospects of marriage.

'And Nancy and the kids?'

'It's finished with Nancy,' Lewis replied firmly. 'Absolutely now. I thought after the court case there might be a chance, but there isn't.

372

I called her yesterday and she was friendly enough, but she regards me as having betrayed her. She said I would be like a spy in her bed. She's working now in an office in Phoenix. Kids are fine. Say they'll visit me in England when I get settled. Best thing really.'

They began strolling round the park at the base of the Statue of Liberty. Lewis seemed cheerful and relaxed. He said he was leaving for London the following night to attempt his new life.

'With a criminal record, I guess, but without being regarded as a bankrupt. Everybody got paid off in the end. It wasn't so bad.'

'What about money?'

'For me, you mean? I'll get by, Alex. Donations always welcome, but I'll survive. I've got the pioneer spirit. That's something you can't buy and they can't kill. I'll make it.'

They sat down on one of the park benches with the mass of the great green statue behind them. Newman turned to Lewis looking for the code that would translate all this jumble into sense.

'Phil, you know I want you to tell me as much as you can. Not just for the book. For me. The hints from Jorge Lopez about drugs and this Columbus thing have made it even worse. I need to know.'

Lewis pulled a packet of gum from his pocket and offered Newman some. He declined. Lewis took two pieces, unwrapped them carefully and put them both into his mouth.

'I told you about getting obsessed,' he said seriously. 'It'll turn you crazy. It nearly did with me. You want to know secrets. You want to be part of it. And when it all comes unglued you ask yourself whether there was ever anything there in the first place, anything substantial.' He chewed hard on the gum. 'I guess it must be like being one of those academics who taught Marxist Theory in the old Soviet universities. One day you wake up and discover no one believes this shit any more. It's over.'

Then Lewis began speaking slowly and quietly, telling Newman as much as he could in a long and detailed narrative. He sketched in the background of the kind of Cold War struggle they thought they were fighting, of the way in the 1970s there had been insurgencies in Argentina and across Latin America; of how they had turned back Marxism one way or another – Pinochet in Chile, the dirty war in Argentina, the blockade against Cuba, the struggle for Central

America. It was a history lesson Newman could have done without, but he listened politely while the fat man motioned to him that he wanted to walk again.

'What about the drugs?' Newman asked, as they started a slow circuit of Liberty Island. 'Lopez kept insisting about the drugs.'

Lewis explained how they monitored Padilla's operation, tracking the money, watching where the Cubans put it and what they spent it on.

'And I can't tell you how I felt when I heard he had defected,' Lewis said, his voice tinged with emotion. Newman thought he saw tears in the fat man's eyes. 'It was so wonderful that he got out of there.'

Newman laughed.

'So Columbus discovered America.'

Lewis looked puzzled.

'What do you mean.'

'Columbus finally got here.'

Lewis shook his jowls recognising Newman's mistake.

'Oh, God no,' he laughed. 'Padilla isn't Columbus if that's what you're thinking. Christ, no. We had Columbus in the bag for years. Padilla was just a bonus. We never quite got him completely. He was not really a traitor, you see. Not in the ordinary sense. He hated the bastards, of course, but he loved Cuba, and never much liked the United States. An old fashioned nationalist. That must have put him in a difficult position. But finally I guess he came to the point when he hated them more than us.'

Lewis started laughing again as if mistaking Padilla for Columbus was some huge, ludicrous joke. Now Newman was puzzled.

'But you suggested I might be interested in the Padilla news confer- ence. And when Lopez told me about drugs and Columbus, I . . .'

'You put two and two together and came up with five. God, no. Padilla's defection just shows that Cuba is rotten right through. He was maybe the last true believer, and even he had to jump ship.'

Newman caught hold of Lewis's lapel.

'Then if he is not Columbus, who is?'

Lewis moved away. The afternoon light was fading fast and he was anxious to return to the ferry. He had in mind a big steak dinner up in Smith and Wollensky's and there were a couple of bars he wanted to call on for old time's sake. He scratched his head in irritation.

'There is no Columbus,' he said. 'Not now at least. They shot him a week ago, just before my plea bargain came to court. His name was General Juan Antonio Fernandez. He was Padilla's boss, I guess you could say, but he was due to retire. We hoped to recruit Padilla to take his place, but no luck. Anyway, it hardly matters now. It's difficult to see how Cuba can be much of a threat when they don't have enough power to be able to make coffee. They are finished, and the beauty of it is, we don't need to care any more.'

With that Lewis said he had to get back to Manhattan, but Newman tugged at his sleeve again.

'This is my last chance, Phil, to put it all together. Please. Just a few more minutes.'

The fat man shrugged.

'What more do you need?'

'The drugs. Tell me about the drugs.'

Lewis explained in a matter of fact way as if it was as insignificant as the British Empire profiting from the Chinese opium trade.

'As long as there's demand,' he said, spitting out his chewing gum and taking two more fresh sticks from their wrappers, 'there will always be supply. We can't plug every hole. Closing down Padilla's operation would have had no effect on the supposed war on drugs. But it would have lost us contact with Padilla, and diminished the reputation of Columbus. And Columbus had to be a success. Anyway, what proves the moral degeneracy of the Communists more than the fact they were trying to poison American children with cocaine?'

He gave a few more details of how they monitored the drug money laundering, how they tracked the kinds of equipment the Cubans were trying to buy, and how they made sure anything especially sensitive was sabotaged before shipment. It was clear that Lewis found all this ancient history. He turned from Newman.

'So I guess it really is next year in Havana,' he said. 'Or this year. Or this month, who can tell. But soon. They are all finished. All of them. I'm proud to say I did my duty. So did Columbus, poor bastard.'

Lewis began waddling towards the waiting ferry, with Newman in his wake. Newman wondered whether Phil Lewis's ordeal had made him half crazy, capable of creating this fantasy. It sounded like one of Chuck Lowell's conspiracy theories from twenty years before, an intricate filigree of exploding cigars and secret meetings and shadow government operatives, drugs and spies.

'Good story, Phil,' Newman said at last catching up with the fat man. 'But is it true?'

Lewis blinked.

'Of course it is true. I was there. I was part of it. It was a means to an end, that's all. And we achieved that end. Believe it if you like. I don't care one way or the other now.'

On the short journey back to Battery Park Lewis explained without rancour how once the operation collapsed he became as useful as surplus military hardware.

'I don't hold grudges. Now all I've got to do is think of the future. See what I can make of it. I don't blame anybody. This is the land of personal responsibility, remember.'

Lewis laughed his heavy jowled laugh and slapped Newman on the back.

By the time the ferry docked they were swapping jokes about what he might find in England after all these years, how he might settle down.

'I'm a survivor, Alex. I'll make it. The word I hear from Washington is that when the president is re-elected tonight he will make Vince Terrelli the new Director of Central Intelligence. Rich Boone will get Army Secretary, though whether he'll want a job that requires Senate confirmation I doubt. Too many skeletons rattling around. Perhaps he'll stay at NSC. Either way, maybe I can do business with them in the future. Who knows. You see . . .'

They stepped off the ferry and Lewis signalled he wanted to walk towards where Steve Ortiz was sitting in his red Jeep Cherokee waiting to pick up the fat man and take him back to his hotel for his last night on American soil.

'You see, it comes and goes in waves. There was a time when Richard Nixon was the worst thing to happen to this country

376

since the Civil War. Well, the guy made more comebacks than Frank Sinatra. It will be the same with this. The kind of morality of everything we did isn't part of America any more. When I said if these were crimes, they were crimes of patriots, people scoffed. But in a few years time when things are not going so well, this country will need folk like me again. Maybe the enemy will be the Japs. Or the Chinese. Or the Europeans. Maybe I'll be on a different side then. Whichever. But those who try to sound moral – like that asshole Warren Cabot – will just come out of it as naive. And those like me who committed some terrible sin will be regarded as the right bunch of hard heads to get the job done again. That's all.'

They reached the Jeep where Ortiz was waiting. He leaned over to open the passenger door.

'Thanks,' Lewis said with an air of finality to Newman. He spat out the last of his chewing gum. 'It was good talking to you. You cheered me up and kept me sane when I was low. I won't forget that. I'll contact you when I get back to England.'

'Well, thank you,' Newman replied, 'for filling in the holes. I think I understand it all now. Even though I don't believe it.'

Lewis laughed.

'Then you should read St Augustine. He thought belief preceded understanding. Maybe you can move in the other direction.'

'Take care, Phil. Give my love to the Mother Country.'

'And you, Alex. Hope things work out with the job, and with Helen.'

'It'll be fine.'

As Lewis opened the Jeep door they could hear the sound of the radio news election programme that Ortiz had been listening to. The radio correspondent from the Democratic Campaign Headquarters was saying that the atmosphere there was very subdued.

'The final result is expected to be close, but with some projections indicating they could do even worse than expected, it is possible that the candidate . . .'

A Toyota van which had nosed into the street at the far end of the park passed the Jeep as Lewis and Newman said their last goodbyes, listening to the radio commentary. Suddenly the side and rear doors of the Toyota were thrown open. Miguelito Morales leaped from the back with an Uzi submachine gun under his arm and his lips drawn back in a twisted grin. As he hit the ground he began to fire burst after burst at Phil Lewis until the fat man's body spurted blood from a dozen openings.

From the side door of the Toyota Tony Montoya opened up with another Uzi at point blank range into Newman's stomach and chest, running round to the side of the Jeep and spraying Ortiz as he leaned on the steering wheel, hitting him full in the face. Lewis turned, clasping his fat gut, falling in a tortured pirouette dripping red in the grey light on the sidewalk. Ortiz leaned heavily on the Jeep steering wheel, sounding the horn, the blood dripping down the inside of the windshield. The gunmen climbed back inside the van, where big Kiki Mendoza put his foot to the floor, tyres squealing as they shot off into the Manhattan traffic. On the radio they were replaying the last defiant address from the Democratic candidate, not conceding the election but speaking of 'an uphill struggle' for 'new ideas', his voice battling to be heard above the deafening Jeep horn, compressed by Steve Ortiz's body.

Alex Newman lay in the gutter, his head resting against the rubber tyre of the Jeep, his blood draining quickly. He was numb and cold and he thought of DeVos and felt so sorry for what he had done to her, and how she would feel. The thought of her pain was worse than any wound, and Newman tried to yell out over the horn and the traffic noise for someone to tell her that he was sorry, but the words would not come. As the first of the gathering crowd turned him over to try to help, anxious hands unbuttoning his coat and loosening his tie, Newman summoned the last of his strength to whisper three words into the Manhattan gloom.

Deliver Us Lord.

36

The first snow had come, and the mountains were a string of white caps leading north from the ranch as far as the Canadian border. The upper trails were closed and so were the main roads through the mountain passes. Some of the ranch hands forecast a bitter winter, drawing on their experience of migrating birds and where the elk herds had gone to find pasture. Warren Cabot was not of a mind to pay attention to country wisdom about weather forecasting or anything else. The winter would come soon enough, whatever he thought about it. He would try to make the best of it, and had already checked his cross country skis and picked out a new pair of snow shoes he was thinking of buying. He wanted to see every corner of the ranch in winter, to take exercise and to think about whether to continue his retirement now his resignation had been made public or return to private legal practice, at least part time. There was no hurry. There never was in Montana. Deadlines were measured in seasons not minutes.

As soon as the election results were known Cabot sent the Director of Central Intelligence and the president copies of his resignation, detailing his disgust at the plea agreement reached with Lewis. The news of the New York murders of Lewis, Newman and Ortiz was not carried on the television stations in Montana, which preferred more local fare, and where it was assumed that murdering people was one of the things New York City was for. Cabot found out two days later. His delayed copy of the *New York Times* carried it as a page one story under the election result. Cabot tried to be surprised, but felt – like the onset of the Montana winter – that Lewis's death had a dreary inevitability.

He was shaken and very sorry that Newman had also been killed. He felt idle tears well in his eyes when he recalled their meeting in his Washington office, and his own warning about the dangers Newman faced. He could not make up his mind whether the journalist was courageous, stupid, or merely doing his job. Whichever it was, nothing like this should ever have happened.

Cabot wondered who might be responsible. Not who pulled the trigger, but who was responsible. It did not bear thinking about. There would, of course, be a short lived scandal, an inquiry, a report, but if Phil Lewis had not betrayed all his secrets in life, it was difficult imagining his ghost returning to haunt them all after death. In any case, the election was now won, the president assured another four years barring ill health or impeachment. Whatever damage extended beyond the grave of Phil Lewis would presumably be containable. Had he not himself admitted that CIA involvement in his company was 'peripheral'?

Since returning to the ranch Warren Cabot had tried to ride nearly every day, to fish and walk in the mountains. He felt ten years younger. His wife said he acted as if he had been given a reprieve from death row or a debilitating disease, no bags under the eyes, the greyness of the skin had gone, no snappish temper or irritability. Robyn Cabot had even talked him into buying a new horse to replace Cloudy, and he agreed they would choose one by the following spring.

Naturally, part of him still hankered after public service in Washington, but he had grown used to the rhythm of Montana. Like Cloudy, Cabot almost delighted in the idea of a time at pasture, a time for simpler values and pleasures.

The family's labrador dogs had been shipped out West and could not believe their luck at life on the ranch. It was as if they too were born again, scampering around the yard like puppies, living free after the confinement of the city. Cabot had tried to learn enough of ranch work to understand and help make decisions without overruling or offending the full time manager. He had ridden on the upper pastures bringing the sheep down as the first snows fell, and it was then he realised Cloudy needed to be pensioned off. The legs had gone, the joints weak, the strength failing. He patted the old appaloosa and whispered in his ear.

'A time to rest, Cloudy. A time for both of us to shed the burdens.'

With all this extra time together, Warren Cabot's relations with Robyn had never been better. It was like a second honeymoon, endless days without direct responsibility, free of worries and stress, and feelings of righteousness knowing he had been justified in deciding to quit. They sat by the fire, watching the election results as what – despite earlier reports – became a landslide for the president was added up.

'You did your duty, Warren,' she said, knowing how he must feel on a night such as this, on the sidelines of history. 'You made sure that nothing which could be used unjustly to damage an honest candidate came out during the campaign, and you resigned on a point of honour. I'm proud of you.'

Cabot sighed. The logs were burning brightly, allowing wisps of a delicious smoke to come from the fire. The dogs were sleeping in its warmth, he was with his wife, content in some pastoral idyll. And yet he felt the uneasiness of a man who has held power and influence and who knows others less capable are taking over. He was determined not to let it make him bitter.

He tried to see the world from a new perspective, not down one end of the Washington microscope but from the other end of the far Western telescope, the view from the frontier, the edge, where the wilderness was so close you did not take risks with civilisation and morality, you did not bend the rules. Along with his resignation Cabot went to his computer and drafted a personal note to the president expressing his deep regrets, and arguing that the president should ensure that there was a clean-out at the top of the intelligence establishment in keeping with the new times. He sat by the flickering green screen and then had a moment of inspiration. He walked over to his library shelves and hunted around until he found a copy of the 1947 essay by George Kennan, the architect of the policy of containing the Soviet Union during what became the Cold War.

'You will remember, Mr President, how much we admired the clarity of Kennan's thinking when we studied US-Soviet relations together in the 1950s. Let me offer my congratulations on your excellent and well-deserved victory and pray for the success of your second term. But in urging a clear-out of the dead wood, let me quote

Kennan to you: "To avoid destruction the United States need only measure up to its own best traditions and prove itself worthy of preservation as a great nation." That was the task we so successfully accomplished over the past decades. May I humbly suggest it is the task you also face in the future . . .'

Four, then five days passed with no response from the White House. Cabot sought to hear more about the deaths of Lewis, Newman and Ortiz and called friends in Washington for as much information as he could assemble.

He learned of the continuing purge in Cuba and the execution of General Juan Antonio Fernandez. For a moment the calm of Montana was broken by his former concerns. He became anxious, and then shrugged it off. Robyn quoted to him her favourite maiden aunt, who always used to insist she be patient as a child: 'What cannot be cured, must be endured, Robyn. Remember that. It will stand you in good stead for the rest of your life.'

The trouble was that Cabot suspected he was better at curing than enduring. It was a return of his old desire to set things right, and he fought against it. He rode Cloudy on the lower trails to the lake gritting his teeth in the cold northerlies and twisting his face in frustration at his inability to demonstrate that there was a substitute for victory, which was to act decently. Down at the lake, where small puddles on the edge had already frozen, he led the appaloosa by the reins under the ponderosa pines, watching a mule deer buck nibble at the last tufts of grass before the heavy snow became permanent even at this lower altitude. There were mallards on the chill water and Canada geese had passed through, paused then travelled further south. One of the ranch hands had reported seeing a bull moose at the north end of the lake, but Cabot was too noisy and Cloudy too awkward to stalk it. He pulled his hat tight on his head, his cheeks smarting in the cold from the wind's blast. It was not as if he even thought about the job of Director of Central Intelligence any more. The gossip said it would be offered to Vincent Terrelli. Cabot thought that the least bad choice of the old guard. He was sure Terrelli would proceed in his devious evolutionary way to set the tone for the new millenium without the air of crusade that Cabot would have employed.

382

And Terrelli would probably get there in the end.

When it was necessary to be dirty, Terrelli would be dirty. Now it was necessary to be clean, he would rinse himself off and oblige. Cabot allowed Cloudy to rest and then climbed back into the saddle, turning south on the lake trail with the bitter ice wind at his back. He pulled up the collar of his sheepskin jacket and trotted on the edge of what looked like a gathering storm. Heavy snow was forecast. They would have Thanksgiving with the family around them at the farm. They would live the lives of the retired public servant and his wife, and pursue happiness as best they could.

When he arrived back at the ranch house Cabot saw his black Jeep Cherokee parked in the yard covered in mud, signalling that Robyn had returned from town. He left Cloudy tied by the barn and told one of the wranglers to clean him down. Inside, Robyn smiled and handed him the newspapers and mail she had collected in Whitefish. He quickly ran through the bundle looking for a letter from Washington, the seal of the White House or something from Langley, but there was none.

Instead his hands found a thick manila envelope with a Miami postmark.

Cabot opened it and stared at the contents. They were sheets of paper and large black and white photographs, plus a letter addressed to him. The letter claimed that everything Phil Lewis did had the specific sanction of the Deputy National Security Adviser Richard Boone.

'Boone ran a series of bank accounts under the name David Appletree,' it said. 'Into which were paid profits from Deep Blue.'

Among the enclosures were photocopies of transactions from the Appletree account. Cabot studied them, then turned to the photographs. They showed Boone and Phil Lewis deep in conversation.

He turned them over and they were dated and marked. The location was a hotel in the Blue Ridge Mountains of Virginia, where Boone allegedly stayed under the 'Appletree' name. There was a photocopy of his registration form showing the same date as the photographs. Cabot looked back at the letter.

'The fact that you are reading this,' the concluding paragraph said, 'means that I am either dead or have disappeared in suspicious circumstances. Copies of these documents have been sent to the White House and numerous journalists and media organisations around the world.'

The letter was signed Phil Lewis. Cabot stared at his wife who was rocking gently by the fire, thinking what this might mean for the country and for his own repressed ambitions. He turned back to the letter, and read passages aloud to her, including the paragraphs alleging US complicity in drug shipments from Cuba, and giving details of Lewis's relationship with Padilla and the agent known as 'Columbus'.

'It was part of United States policy to encourage Columbus to use the Cuban military to facilitate drug shipments into the United States,' the letter read, 'in the hope of destabilising the Castro regime, corrupting its leading military officers and ultimately exposing the corruption. In these efforts we were largely successful.'

Cabot stopped again and sighed. He could sense that the fuse had now been lit. The only question was how long it would take to hit the explosive charge. An accompanying sheet showed the mailing list. It included all the main television networks in the United States, numerous Congressmen, the *New York Times, Washington Post, Miami Herald,* the BBC and a string of British newspapers including the *London Tribune.*

Cabot strode over to the window and looked out. The darkness had come quickly and the night was partly illuminated by the yellow glare of the yard lights. It had begun to snow, and the flakes were falling so heavily that for a time the airport at Kalispell would be closed. But the emergency would pass, the snow would clear and by late morning the airport and all the roads to it would be open again. Cabot looked at his wife, her eyes twinkling by the light of the fire, a smile on her lips.

'I think,' she said quietly, 'you should return to Washington, where you might be able to do something about this.'